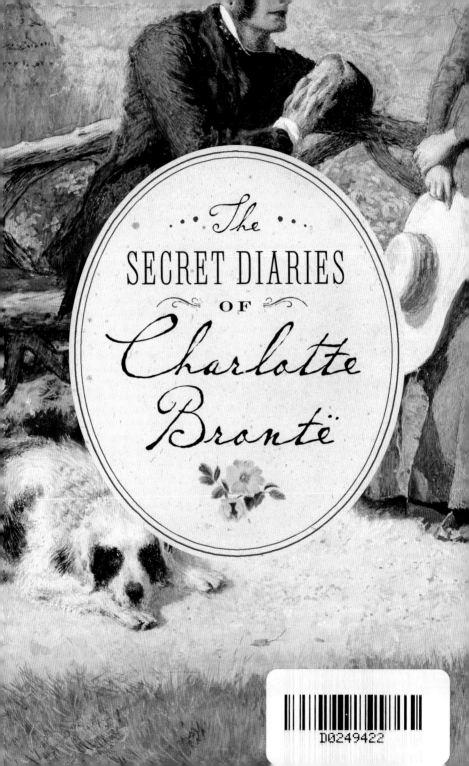

···The···

SECRET DIARIES

OF

Charlotte

Brontë

D0249422

Praise for

Syrie James

and

THE LOST MEMOIRS OF
Jane Austen

❧

"Tantalizing, tender, and true to the Austen mythos."

—*Library Journal*
(*Starred Review* Best First Novels 2008)

"Witty, deft, and impeccably researched, *The Lost Memoirs of Jane Austen* will pique the most jaded Austen palette. . . . So deftly done that it's hard to tell where the history ends and invention begins."

—Lauren Willig,
author of *The Seduction of the Crimson Rose*

"Utterly charming and remarkably authentic in creating Jane Austen's voice, Syrie James' *The Lost Memoirs of Jane Austen* made me want to pull out all my Jane Austen novels and read them again."

—Deborah Crombie,
author of *Where Memories Lie*

"James stays in perfect pitch as Jane Austen in this vivacious fiction. Fans of romance will love it."

—T. Jefferson Parker,
author of *The Renegades*

"If I hadn't seen the word novel on its cover, I would have sworn this enchanting 'memoir' was the real thing. At last, the designated spinster wins an earthmoving kiss and all Jane-ites everywhere (and who isn't?) get a delicious book."

—Mameve Medwed,
author of *Of Men and Their Mothers*

"Deserves front-runner status in the saturated field of Austen fan-fiction and film."

—*Kirkus Reviews*

"James doesn't disappoint—she is a fine story-teller, with a sensitive ear for the Austenian voice and a clear passion for research."

—Joceline Bury,
Jane Austen's Regency World Magazine

"A new and provocative look at one of the world's most beloved authors. This compelling novel should delight Austen fans far and wide."

—John Shors,
author of the bestselling *Beside a Burning Sea*

By Syrie James

THE SECRET DIARIES OF CHARLOTTE BRONTË
THE LOST MEMOIRS OF JANE AUSTEN

THE SECRET DIARIES OF

Charlotte Brontë

A NOVEL

SYRIE JAMES

AVON

An Imprint of HarperCollinsPublishers

HarperCollins books may be purchased for educational, business, or sales promotional use. For information please write: Special Markets Department, HarperCollins Publishers, 10 East 53rd Street, New York, NY 10022.

FIRST AVON PAPERBACK EDITION PUBLISHED 2009.

Interior text designed by Rhea Braunstein

The Library of Congress Cataloging-in-Publication Data
James, Syrie.
    The secret diaries of Charlotte Bronte : a novel / Syrie James.—1st ed.
        p. cm.
    ISBN 978-0-06-164837-3 (acid-free paper)   1. Brontë, Charlotte, 1816-1855—Fiction.   2. Diary fiction.   I. Title
    PS3610.A457S43   2009
    813'.6—dc22
                                                                    2009002487

09 10 11 12 13 WBC/RRD 10 9 8 7 6 5 4 3 2 1

For my husband Bill and our sons Ryan and Jeff,
for your never-ending love and support.

And in loving memory of my mother, Joann Astrahan—
a perceptive, wise, and generous woman—
who always said I should be writing books.

Acknowledgments

I would like to acknowledge the following people, whose contributions have proven invaluable to me in the writing of this novel. First and foremost, I am indebted to my husband Bill, for his daily support of my chosen profession, which keeps me locked away at my computer for days on end, and then still wrapped in a creative fog for many hours after I finally resurface. A grateful thank you to my sons Ryan and Jeff, who stayed up reading into the wee hours of the morning to give me their valuable feedback and insight. (Thank you, Ryan, for pointing out the significance of Emily's middle name!) Thanks to Yvonne Yao, for offering much-appreciated assistance at a time of need. Thanks to my agent Tamar Rydzinski, for her tireless support, and for always knowing exactly which paragraphs need to be cut. Thanks to my editor Lucia Macro, for her shared love of all things Brontë, and for reminding me to give the novel the focus it required; and to the entire staff at Avon, who always do such a great job with my books. Thanks to my eagle-eyed copyeditors, Sara and Bob Schwager, for their enthusiastic comments, and for meticulously double-checking every word of the text in their unequivocal quest to guarantee verisimilitude. Thanks to Ann Dinsdale, the Collections Manager at the Brontë Parsonage Museum, Haworth, for her kind welcome during my visit, and for allowing me a private viewing of original letters, manuscripts, and other documents written by Charlotte and all the members of the Brontë family; and thanks to Sarah Laycock, the museum's Library and Information Officer, for sharing all those wonderful details about Charlotte's wedding dress, veil, ring, night-shirt, honeymoon dress, and other clothing, as well as providing me with comprehensive descriptions of a variety of garments in the museum collection. I wish to thank Steven Hughes, Chief Executive of Hollybank Trust, for graciously giving my husband and me an unforgettable, attic-to-cellar tour one rainy afternoon of the Hollybank School in Mirfield, West Yorkshire—the former Roe Head School, whose setting and original structure still, remarkably, look very much as they did in Charlotte's day—and for sharing the stories of their resident ghost. I am greatly indebted to the works of many Brontë scholars, including Juliet Barker, Winifred Gérin, Christine Alexander, and Margaret Smith, and to both Smith and Clement Shorter for their edited editions of Charlotte Brontë's letters, without which this novel could never have been written. I owe a great debt to the novels and poetry of the Brontë sisters, for the window they opened onto their world. And finally, perhaps most importantly, I am grateful to Charlotte Brontë herself, to whose extraordinary spirit and talents I strove to remain true; I do hope that she would have approved.

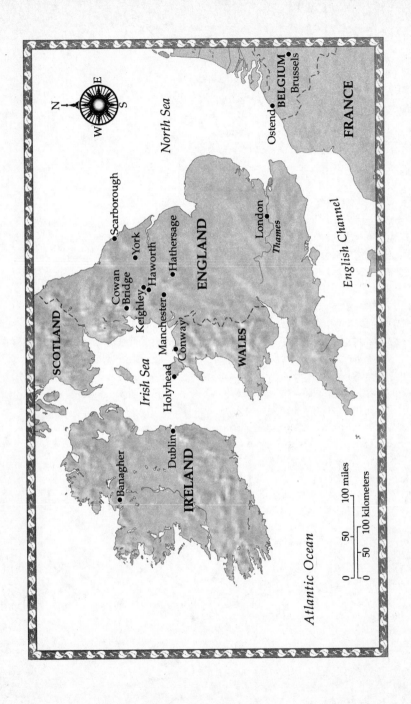

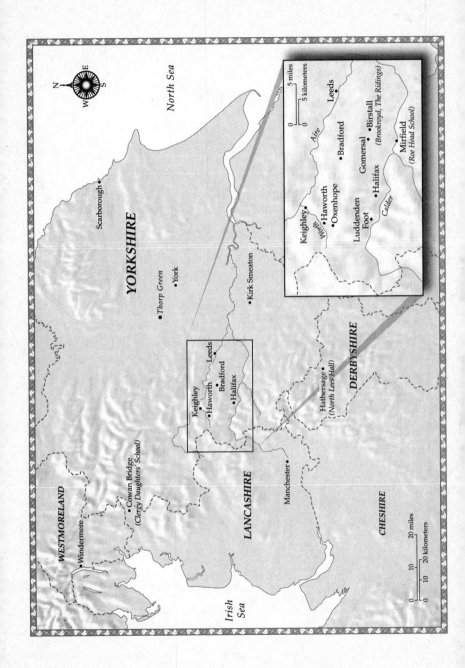

Author's Foreword

Dear Reader,

Imagine, if you will, that a great discovery has been made, which has sparked enormous excitement in the literary world: a series of journals, which have lain buried and forgotten for more than a century in the cellar of a remote farmhouse in the British Isles, have been officially authenticated as the private diaries of Charlotte Brontë. What would those diaries reveal?

Everyone keeps secrets. Charlotte Brontë—a passionate woman who wrote some of the most romantic and enduring fiction in the English language—was no exception. We can learn much about Charlotte through her biographies and surviving correspondence; but like all the members of the Brontë family, Charlotte had a deeply personal side that she did not share with even her closest friends and relations.

What intimate secrets did Charlotte Brontë harbor within her breast? What were her innermost thoughts and feelings, and her most private memories? What was her relationship with her brother and sisters, who were also talented and driven artists? How did an unknown parson's daughter, who lived nearly her entire life in the obscurity of a remote Yorkshire village, come to write *Jane Eyre,* one of the world's most beloved novels? And perhaps most importantly: did Charlotte ever find a true love of her own?

Seeking the answers to these questions, I began a meticulous study of Charlotte's life. I found myself particularly intrigued by a very important part of the Brontë story, which has rarely been explored: Charlotte's long and stormy relationship with her father's curate, Arthur Bell Nicholls. It is well-known that Charlotte Brontë received four marriage proposals, including—most famously—an offer from Mr. Nicholls. However, Arthur Bell Nicholls remains an obscure and shadowy figure in Brontë biographies, generally only referred to in passing until the latter part of the story, and even then in no great detail. Yet it is a fact that Mr. Nicholls lived next door to the Brontës for eight years, was in almost daily contact with them all that time, and was deeply and secretly in love with Charlotte long before he summoned the nerve to propose to her.

Did Charlotte ever return Mr. Nicholls's affections? Did she marry him? Ah—but as Charlotte herself might say—that is the crux of this story, and I like to think that the exploration of her feelings with regard to that very dilemma would have been the reason she wrote these volumes in the first place.

The story you are about to read is true. Charlotte's life story is so fascinating, that I was able to spin the tale based almost entirely on fact, conjecturing only where I deemed necessary to enhance dramatic conflict or to fill in gaps in the history, and adding selected comments and footnotes for clarification. Although some may consider the unfolding tale to more closely resemble one of Charlotte's beloved novels than a traditional diary, as she is looking back on past events, rather than recording them as they occurred, I believe that Charlotte would have written it this way, for this is a style and structure with which she felt most comfortable.

Here, then—with the greatest respect and admiration for the woman who inspired them—are *The Secret Diaries of Charlotte Brontë*.

Syrie James

THE SECRET DIARIES OF
Charlotte Brontë

VOLUME I

One

I have received a proposal of marriage.

Diary, this offer, which came some months past, has thrown my entire household—nay, the entire village—into an uproar. Who is this man who has dared to ask for my hand? Why is my father so dead set against him? Why are half the residents of Haworth determined to lynch him—or shoot him? Since the moment of his offer, I have lain awake night after night, pondering the multitude of events which have led up to this conflagration. How on earth, I wonder, did things get so out of hand?

I have written about the joys of love. I have, in my secret heart, long dreamt of an intimate connection with a man; every Jane, I believe, deserves her Rochester—does she not? Yet I had long since given up all hope of that experience in my own life. Instead, I sought a career; and having found it, shall I—*must I*—now abandon it? Is it possible for a woman to give herself fully both to an occupation and a husband? Can these two critical halves of a woman's mind and spirit peacefully coexist? It must be so; for true happiness, I believe, cannot be achieved any other way.

It has long been my practice, in times of great joy or emotional distress, to escape into the comfort of my imagination. There, in prose or poetry, I have given vent to my innermost thoughts and feelings behind the protective veil of fiction. In these pages, however, I wish to take a completely different tack. I wish herein to unburden my soul—to reveal certain truths which I have hitherto shared with only a few of my most intimate connections— and some which I have never dared breathe to a living soul. For I find myself to-day in a time of crisis, faced with a dilemma of the weightiest proportions.

Do I dare to defy papa, and incur the wrath of every one I know, by accepting this offer? Most importantly, do I wish to accept? Do I truly love this man, and wish to be his wife? I did not even like him when first we met; but a great deal has happened since then.

It seems to me that every experience I have ever had, everything I have ever thought or said or done, and every person I have ever loved, has contributed in some essential way to the human being I am to-day. Had one stroke of the brush touched the canvas in an altered manner, or splashed upon it a darker or lighter colour, I should be a very different person now. And so I turn to pen and paper in search of answers; perhaps in this way, I can endeavour to make some sense of what has led me to this moment, and come to understand how I feel—and what it is that Providence, in his goodness and wisdom, intends for me to do.

But hush! A story cannot commence in the middle, or at the end. No, to tell it properly, I must go back—back to where it all began: to that stormy day, nearly eight years past, when an unexpected visitor arrived at the parsonage door.

The 21st of April, 1845, was a gloomy, bone-chilling day.

I was awakened at daybreak by a great clap of thunder; moments later, the cloudy grey heavens opened up in a torrential downpour. All morning, rain spattered against the window-panes of the parsonage, pelted the roof and eaves, drenched the densely packed headstones in the nearby graveyard, and danced against the flagstones in the adjacent lane, merging into rivulets which flowed in a steady stream past the church, toward the steep, cobbled main street of the village.

Inside the parsonage kitchen, however, all was cosy, full of the fragrance of new bread and the warmth of a generous fire. It was a Monday—baking-day—which my sister Emily said was very convenient, for it was also my birthday. I had always preferred to observe such occasions with as little fuss as possible; but Emily insisted, as I was turning twenty-nine, that we should make time for a private celebration.

"It is your last year of an important decade," said Emily, as she expertly kneaded a mound of dough on the floured centre table. Already, two loaves were in the oven, another bowl of dough was rising beneath a cloth, and I was well under way with preparations for a pie and a tart. "At the very least, we must mark the occasion with a cake."

"I see no purpose in it," said I, as I measured out the flour for a pastry crust. "Without Anne and Branwell here, it will not feel like much of a party."

"We cannot put off our own pleasures in their absence, Charlotte," said Emily solemnly. "We are meant to prize life and enjoy it, so long as we retain it."

Emily was two years younger than I, and the tallest person in our family, other than papa. She was a complex personality with twin, diverse sides to her nature: brooding, melancholy introspection concerning the meaning of life and death; and sunny delight in contemplation of the world's many joys and natural beauties. As long as she could live at home, surrounded by her moors, Emily was happy and took life easily; unlike me, she was rarely distressed. She preferred being lost in thought, or in the pages of a book, to any other occupation in life—a preference with which I heartily agreed. Emily had no regard for public opinion, and no interest in fashion; although it had long been the style to wear neatly waisted, fitted frocks and full petticoats, Emily still preferred to wear the old-fashioned, shapeless dresses and thin petticoats which clung to her legs, and did not particularly suit her lean frame. As she rarely ventured out except to walk on the heath, it hardly mattered.

With her slender physique, pale complexion, and dark hair knotted up carelessly under a Spanish comb, Emily reminded me of a sturdy sapling: thin and graceful, yet unyielding; hardy in solitude; impervious to the effects of wind and rain. In the presence of strangers, Emily withdrew into herself, all gravity and silence; but in the company of family, her ebullient, sensitive nature found its full expression. I loved her as dearly as I loved life itself.

"How long has it been since we were all together for your birthday?" continued Emily.

"I cannot recall the last time," said I with regret.

It had, indeed, been a long while since all my siblings and I had been in one location at the same time, other than a few short weeks at Christmas and the summer holidays. For the past five years, our youngest sister Anne had been serving as a governess for the Robinson family at Thorp Green Hall, near York. Our brother Branwell, younger than I by fourteen months, had joined Anne there three years previously, as a tutor to the eldest son. In the years before that, I had been much away at school, first as a student, and then as a teacher, followed by a stint of my own as a governess. Then had come two years in Belgium: a sojourn which had proved to be the most powerful, exhilarating, life-altering—and heartbreaking—experience of my existence.

"I am making you a spice cake, and that is final," said Emily. "After supper, we shall sit by the fire and tell each other stories. Perhaps Tabby and papa will join us."

Tabby was our elderly servant, a good, faithful Yorkshire woman who had been with us since childhood. Over the years, when she chanced to be in good humour, Tabby had brought her ironing-table to the dining-room hearth and allowed us to sit about it. While she got up the sheets and chemises, or crimped her night-cap borders, she fed our eager attention with tales of love and adventure taken from old fairy tales and ballads—or, as I later discovered, from the pages of her favourite novels, such as *Pamela*.[1] On other occasions, our evenings by the fire had been enlivened by papa's thrilling renditions of ghost stories and ancient, local legends.

To-night, however, it was uncertain whether or not papa would choose to participate.

I glanced out the kitchen window at the moors beyond. A shower wept over the distant hilltops, hiding their crests with the low-hanging, dishevelled tresses of a cloud. "Wonderful weather for a birthday. At least the day matches my mood: dark and somber, with turbulent storms and no end in sight."

"You sound like me," rejoined Emily, as she mixed together the ingredients for her cake. "Do not lose hope. If we take one day at a time, everything may yet work itself out."

"How?" I sighed. "Papa's eyesight grows dimmer with each passing day."

My father was an Irish immigrant who, through perseverance and education, had risen far above his poor, illiterate family's station. When the registrar at St. John's College, Cambridge, could not understand the spelling of papa's surname due to his broad Irish accent, he wrote it down himself, changing it from Brunty to the more interesting Brontë, after the Greek word for thunder. A good, kind, lively, and highly intelligent man, papa was widely read, with interests in literature, art, music, and science which reached far beyond his province as the parson of a small Yorkshire parish. He enjoyed writing, and had had several poems and religious stories published, as well as numerous articles; he was greatly involved in the politics of the community; and he was a deeply committed clergyman. He was also greatly troubled: for to-day, at age sixty-eight, after a lifetime of faithful service to the church, our adored father was going blind.

"I must now do all of papa's reading and writing for him," said I. "Soon, I fear he will not be able to keep up with his most basic duties in the parish—and if he loses his sight entirely, what

---

[1] Samuel Richardson's novel *Pamela, or Virtue Rewarded* (1740) was the story of a servant girl who eventually married her master.

shall we do? Not only will papa forfeit all his scanty pleasures in life, and grow entirely dependent on us—a circumstance you know he greatly dreads—but he will no doubt be forced to forfeit his incumbency. We shall then lose not only his entire income, but our home as well."[2]

"In any other family, the son would come to the financial rescue," observed Emily, shaking her head, "but our brother has never been able to hold a job for long."

"Indeed, his stint as tutor at Thorp Green is the longest he has ever held a position," I added, as I rolled out my pastry crust. "He seems to be highly valued there; yet his income is barely enough to cover his own expenses. We must accept it, Emily: should papa's health fail, the entire burden of supporting the household will fall squarely upon our shoulders."

I believe I felt the weight of this responsibility even more keenly than did my siblings, perhaps because I was the eldest child—a position acquired by tragedy and default, and not by rank of birth. My mother, of whom I have only the vaguest of memories, gave birth to six children in nearly as many years, and died when I was five. My beloved older sisters Maria and Elizabeth died in childhood. My brother and younger sisters and I, schooled by our father and reared by a stern and orderly maternal aunt who came to live with us, retreated into a delightful world of books and fantasy; we roamed the moors; we drew and painted; we read and wrote obsessively; we all dreamt of becoming published authors one day. Although our dream of writing never faded, it had long ago been set aside by necessity: we were obliged to earn a living.

Only two professions were open to my sisters and me— teaching or governessing—both occupations of bonded servitude which I despised. I had, for some time, believed that our best option was to commence our own school. It was with that aim in

---

[2] When a clergyman retired, he was obliged to turn over his entire "living" to his successor, including both his income and the dwelling provided for his use during his incumbency.

mind—to gain attainments in French and German, to improve our chances of attracting pupils—that Emily and I had gone to Brussels three years ago, and I had stayed an extra year on my own. Upon my return, I had attempted to open a school at Haworth Parsonage; despite all my most concerted efforts, however, not a single parent was willing to send his child to such a desolate location.

I could not blame them. Haworth was but a small village in north Yorkshire, far from anywhere. In our entire moorland parish, there was not a single educated family other than ourselves. The region was blanketed in snow in winter and assailed by a cold and merciless wind three seasons of the year. There was no railway service; Keighley, the nearest town, lay four miles down the valley. Behind the parsonage, and surrounding it, lay the silent, sweeping, endless, windy slopes of the moors. Not every eye could discern the beauty which my siblings and I found in that vast, harsh, bleak landscape. To us, the moors had always been a kind of paradise, a place into which to escape, to allow our imaginations to run free and wild.

The parsonage, which lay atop the crest of a ruggedly steep hill, was a two-storeyed, symmetrical grey stone house built in the late eighteenth century. It overlooked a small square of crabbed lawn, which, on the other side of a low stone wall, adjoined the crowded, weedy graveyard, and beyond that the church. We were not enthusiastic gardeners; as the climate did not encourage growth other than the mosses which covered our damp stones and soil, we had but a few fruit bushes and some straggling thorns and lilacs along our semicircular gravel walk.

Although the garden may have been neglected, our house was not. Everything about it was kept lovingly, scrupulously clean, from the sparkling, Georgian sashed window-panes to the spotless sandstone floors, which extended beyond the kitchen to all the downstairs rooms. The unpapered walls were painted a pretty dove colour; because of papa's fear of fire (and the dangerous combination of children, candles, and curtains), we had always had internal shutters instead of curtains, and only small carpets in the dining-room and parlour (papa's study). All our rooms, upstairs and down, were compact but well-proportioned, our furnishings scant but sturdy: hair-seated chairs and sofa, mahogany tables, and a few bookshelves filled with the classics we had relished since childhood. The parsonage was not a grand house by any means, but it was the largest in Haworth, and as such held some distinction; we neither required nor desired more; we dearly loved its every nook and cranny.

"Here we are, seven months without a curate in Haworth to assist papa," said I, "if you do not count Reverend Joseph Grant of Oxenhope, who is too busy with his new school to be of any real help."

"Is not papa meeting with a prospective candidate for the curacy to-morrow?"

"Yes." Since I had been handling my father's correspondence for some months, I knew a little bit about the gentleman in question. "He is a Mr. Nicholls from Ireland. He responded to papa's advertisement in *The Ecclesiastical Gazette*."

"Perhaps he will suit."

"We can always hope. A good curate will buy papa a measure of time, and then we can all determine what we must do."

"There be no sich thing as a good curate ony more," grumbled Tabby, our white-haired servant, in her broad Yorkshire drawl, as she hobbled into the kitchen with a basket of apples from the larder. "Them young parsons to-day is so high an' so scornful, they set everybody beneath their fit. In this house, I'm a servant, an' so not worthy o' their civility; an' they're always speaking against Yorkshire ways an' Yorkshire folk. An' th' way they drop i' from th' sky for tea or supper at th' parson's house, why there be no excuse for 't. It's just for naught else but t' give women-folk trouble."

"I would not mind so much," I interjected, "if they would only seem satisfied with what we serve them; but they always complain."

"Th' old parsons is worth th' whole lump o' college lads," said Tabby with a sigh as she sank into a chair at the table and began to peel the apples. "They know what belongs t' good manners, an' is kind t' both high an' low."

"Tabby," said I suddenly, glancing at the clock on the mantel, "has the post come?"

"Aye, an' there be nothing for ye, bairn."[3]

"Are you sure?"

"I have two eyes, don't I? Who d'ye expect t' be writing? Didn't ye jist get a letter from your friend Ellen, not two days sin'?"

"I did."

Emily glanced sharply at me. "Do not tell me you are still hoping for a letter from Brussels?"

I felt a heat rise to my face, and perspiration break out on my brow; I told myself it was the warmth of the fire, and had nothing to do with Emily's remark, or the intensity of her penetrating gaze. "No, of course not," I lied. I wiped my forehead with the corner of my apron. In so doing, my spectacles became dotted with flour; I removed them briefly, and gave them a gentle polishing.

In truth, I had five precious letters from Brussels hidden in the bottom drawer of my dresser: letters from a certain man, which had been read and re-read so often that they threatened to crumble at the creases from wear. I longed for yet another missive, but it had been a full year since I received the last one, and the sought for letter never came. I felt Emily's eyes upon me; of all the people in the family, she knew me best—and she never missed a thing. Before she could say more, however, the wire of the door-bell began to vibrate; then the bell itself rang.

"Who could 'at be i' this awful weather?" asked Tabby.

At the sound of the bell, the two dogs who had been lying contentedly by the fire leapt to their feet. Flossy, our sweet-natured, silky-haired, black-and-white King Charles spaniel, just blinked with quiet interest. Emily's dog Keeper, a bulky, lion-like, black-headed mastiff, barked loudly and bolted for the kitchen door; in a flash, Emily grabbed his brass collar and held him back.

---

[3] Child; son or daughter (Scottish/ Northern English dialect).

"Keeper, hush!" exclaimed Emily. "I do hope it is not Mr. Grant or Mr. Bradley come for tea. I am in no mood to serve the local curates to-day."

"It is too early for tea," said I.

Keeper continued to yap furiously; it took all of Emily's might to restrain him. "I will lock him in my room," said Emily, as she hastened out of the kitchen and up the stairs.

I understood Emily's abhorrence of strangers well enough to know that she would not be returning with equal haste. As Tabby was old and lame, and Martha Brown, the servant-girl who generally handled the heaviest share of our house-work, had gone home for a week with a sore knee, it was my unspoken job to answer the door.

Hot and tired after a full morning in the kitchen, I had no time to consider my appearance, other than a passing glance in the entrance-hall looking-glass. I had never liked to look at my image; I was extremely small and short of stature, and I always found dissatisfaction in the plain, pale face reflected there. Now, to further my dismay, a brief glimpse reminded me that I was attired in my oldest and most unflattering dress; a kerchief covered my head; my apron was streaked with flour and spices from the pie in progress; and my hands and forehead were dusted with flour as well. I quickly dabbed at my forehead with my apron, which only made matters worse.

The bell rang again. With Flossy's toe-nails clicking against the stone floor at my heels, I hastened down the hall, went to the front door, and opened it.

Rain and wind blew in with a frigid blast. A young man who appeared to be in his late twenties stood on the steps before me, clad in a black coat and hat, beneath a beleaguered black umbrella, which, to his consternation, suddenly turned inside out in a gust of wind. With the partial protection of the umbrella now gone, he appeared, at first glance, like nothing so much as a very tall, drowned rat. His squinting, frantic efforts to right his umbrella and blink back the driving rain made it difficult to accurately perceive his features, a circumstance compounded when, upon catching sight of me, he immediately withdrew his hat, receiving in return an even more thorough dousing from the elements.

"Would your master be at home?" The Celtic lilt of his deep, rich voice, which at once announced his Irish origins, was further complicated by a hint of Scottish.

"My master?" I repeated indignantly—an emotion followed by mortification. He had mistaken me for a servant! "If you are referring to the Reverend Patrick Brontë, he is indeed at home, sir, and he is my father. Please excuse my appearance. I do not generally greet visitors covered in flour from head to toe. It is baking-day."

The young man did not appear in the least perturbed by his blunder (perhaps because he was being pelted by freezing rain), but only said, squinting, "I beg your pardon. I'm Arthur Bell Nicholls. I've been corresponding with your father regarding the position of curate. I wasn't expected until to-morrow, but as I arrived in Keighley a day earlier than anticipated, I thought I might drop by."

"Ah, yes, Mr. Nicholls. Please walk in," I urged politely, stepping back and allowing him to sweep past me into the entry way. When I had shut the door against the howling wind and rain, I smiled up at him and remarked, "It is truly a frightful storm, is it not? I keep expecting to see a parade of animals heading down the lane, two by two."

I waited for him to smile, or to respond in a similar light vein, but he stood staring at me like a statue, hat and umbrella in hand, dripping onto the stone floor. Now that he was in from the elements, I could perceive that he was a strongly built, dark-complexioned man with an attractive, broad-featured face, a prominent but handsome nose, a firmly set mouth, and thick, very black hair which, drenched as it was, lay plastered to his skull in streaming tendrils. He stood at least six feet tall—a full foot taller than I. I recalled from his letter that he was twenty-seven years old—nearly two years younger than I; he would look even younger, I thought, if not for the thicket of long, neatly trimmed black side whiskers which framed his otherwise whisker-free face. His eyes were reserved and intelligent; however, he now tore that gaze from mine and glanced shyly about the hall, as if determined to look anywhere but at me.

"I imagine," I tried again, "that you are accustomed to such downpours in Ireland?"

He nodded, staring at the floor, and made no reply; apparently, his declaration at the door was to be his only attempt at speech. Flossy stood at the newcomer's feet, looking up at him with curious, expectant eyes. Mr. Nicholls, although wet and clearly very cold, smiled at the dog, and bent down and gently patted his head.

Wiping my floury hands as best as I could on my apron, I said, "May I take your hat and coat, sir?"

He looked dubious, but silently handed me his dripping umbrella, then removed said garments and gave them to me. I saw that his shoes were soaked through and caked with mud residue. "Do not tell me that you walked all the way from Keighley in this weather, Mr. Nicholls?"

He nodded. "I'm sorry about your floor. I tried to scrape off as much mud as I could, before I rang the bell."

He had spoken! Two complete sentences, however brief! I considered this a minor victory. "This stone is quite accustomed to tracked-in mud, I assure you. Would you like to warm yourself by the kitchen fire, Mr. Nicholls, while I get you a towel?"

He looked alarmed. "The kitchen? No thank you."

I was taken aback by the surprised condescension in his tone when he spoke the word "kitchen." It implied, to my ears, an intrinsic repugnance to the very essence of the place: as if he considered a room so generally affiliated with women-folk too far beneath him to enter. My dander rose. "I am sorry there is no fire in the dining-room," I returned testily, "or I would offer you that. But it is very warm and cosy in the kitchen. You would be welcome to dry yourself there for a few minutes, with no one to disturb you but me and our servant, before I show you in to my father's study."

"I will see your father now, if I may," he replied quickly. "Surely he has a fire. I would appreciate a towel."

Well, I thought, as I moved off to obtain the requested item: here is a very proud, arrogant Irishman. Our former curate, the despised Reverend Smith, appeared to me a real prize in comparison. I returned a few moments later with a towel. Mr. Nicholls wordlessly wiped the excess moisture from his hair and face, then used it to clean off his shoes; finally, he handed the sodden and filthy article back to me.

Anxious to be rid of him, I crossed to the door to papa's study and said, "As I have been lately handling my father's correspondence, I believe I warned you: my father's vision is much impaired. He will be able to see you, but the image is hazy. The doctors say that eventually he will go completely blind."

Mr. Nicholls's only response was a grave nod, accompanied by: "Yes, I recall."

I knocked at the study door, waited for papa's response, then opened the door and announced Mr. Nicholls. Papa rose from his chair by the fire and greeted the newcomer with a surprised smile. Papa was a tall, thin but sturdy man, his formerly handsome face lined with age. He wore wire-rimmed spectacles similar to mine, sported his black parson's garb seven days a week, and his shock of white hair was the same colour as the snowy expanse of cravat which he always wound around his neck so abundantly (to ward off the possibility of catching cold), that his chin disappeared entirely inside it.

Mr. Nicholls crossed the room and shook papa's hand. I left them together and hurried upstairs to tidy myself, mortified that I had greeted a stranger in such disarray. I removed my kerchief and ensured that my brown hair was neatly arranged, swept up, and pinned in place. I then changed into a clean, silver-grey frock—silk, of course. (Since we came to Haworth, papa had read the burial service for so many children whose clothing had caught fire, resulting from a too-close proximity to the hearth, that he eschewed cotton and linen, insisting that we wear only wool or silk, which ignite less easily.) Newly arrayed in my Quaker trim, I felt more comfortable and at ease. I may, I thought, lack the advantages of personal beauty, but at least I would no longer embarrass myself before our visitor in my manner of dress.

Emily was back at work in the kitchen when I returned, and I re-enacted, for her and Tabby, the little scene that had occurred at the front door. "'The *kitchen?*'" said I, attempting to imitate Mr. Nicholls's voice and disdain. "'No *thank you.*' As if he would never deign to set foot in a room so generally inhabited by *women.*"

Emily laughed.

"He sounds like a right brute," observed Tabby.

"Let us hope it is a brief interview, and we will soon see the last of him," said I.

When I approached the study with the tea-tray, I could hear, through the partially open door, the deep tones of the two Irishmen conversing within. Mr. Nicholls's Irish accent was very pronounced, spiced by that intriguing hint of Scotch. Papa had tried to lose his own accent since the day he started college, but an Irish lilt always marked his speech, and it had rubbed off on all his offspring, myself included. The two men were going at it full tilt; there now came a sudden outburst of hearty laughter—a circumstance which surprised me, as I had been able to induce so few syllables out of Mr. Nicholls myself, and not a single smile.

I was just about to enter, when I overheard papa say, "I told them: stick to the needle. Learn shirt-making and gown-making and pie-crust-making, and you'll be clever women some day. Not that they listened to me."

To which Mr. Nicholls replied, "I agree. Women are at their best in the occupations God gave them, Mr. Brontë—when sewing or in the kitchen. You are indeed most fortunate to have two spinster daughters to run your household."

Sudden fury and indignation rose within me; I nearly dropped my tray. I was fully acquainted with papa's views where women were concerned; my sisters and I had spent a lifetime arguing with him on the subject, trying, without success, to convince him that women had as much intellectual prowess as men, and should be allowed to spread their wings beyond the kitchen door. He had relented in practice—by finally letting us study history and the classics along with our brother—but not in theory, firmly convinced that our learning Latin and Greek and reading Virgil and Homer was a complete waste of our time.

I could excuse such bigotry from papa, even if I could not condone it; he was sixty-eight years of age, a dear old man blinded not only in body but in mind, by the beliefs of the men of his generation. But from a young, college-educated man like Mr. Nicholls—who was being considered for a position which would require him to work closely with people of all genders and ages in our community—one would hope for a more open-minded, free-thinking perspective!

Seething, I leaned backwards against the door, pushing it the rest of the way open as I marched into the room. The two gentlemen were seated in close proximity by the hearth. The warmth of the fire had worked its wonders: Mr. Nicholls looked warm and dry, and his dark hair, now parted to one side over his wide forehead, was smooth and thick, with a healthy sheen. On his lap reclined our black tabby cat, Tom; Mr. Nicholls was smiling broadly and absently stroking the animal, who purred contentedly. The glowing look on the gentleman's countenance faded, however, as I approached; he sat up straighter, causing the cat to leap from his lap. Clearly, this man did not like me. I hardly cared, for with his last remark, I had just lost any respect I might have held for him.

"Papa, I have brought your tea." I set the tray on the small table beside Mr. Nicholls. "I do not wish to disturb you, so I will leave you in Mr. Nicholls's capable hands."

"Oh! Charlotte, do stay and pour out. How do you take your tea, Mr. Nicholls?"

"Any way it's served to me," replied Mr. Nicholls. Papa laughed. To me, Mr. Nicholls said abruptly, "Two lumps of sugar please, and a slice of bread with butter on it."

My feminine soul revolted from his manner of command; had I followed my inclinations, I would have cut the slice of bread and hurled it at his arrogant face. I restrained myself, however, and did as I was ordered. He had the decency to thank me upon receipt. I left the tea-tray and escaped back to the kitchen, where Emily, Tabby, and I spent the better part of the next hour exclaiming over the follies of narrow-minded men.

"To be called *spinster*—at age twenty-nine—by a man who considers himself too high and mighty to set foot in our kitchen!" I cried contemptuously. "And then, in the same breath, to expect me to wait on him, and butter his bread—it is too much to be borne!"

"He called *me* a spinster, too," said Emily with a shrug, "and he has never set eyes on me. I should not think you would mind. You always said you would never marry."

"Yes, but by *choice*. I have had two offers. I turned them down. The term *spinster* implies a decrepit old maid, unloved and unwanted by any one."

"*Now* who sounds high an' mighty?" interjected the widowed Tabby, clicking her tongue. "I wouldn'a think two offers *by post* are summat t' brag abaat."

"It shows I have standards. I will only marry where there is mutual affection, with a man who not only loves and respects me, but who respects womanhood in general." I sank into the rocking chair by the fire, greatly vexed. "Men are always quoting Solomon's virtuous woman, as the pattern of what 'our sex' ought to be. Well, *she* was a manufacturer: she made fine linen garments and belts, and sold them! She was an agriculturist and a manager: she bought estates and planted vineyards![4] Yet are women to-day allowed to be anything like her?"

"We are not," replied Emily.

"We are allowed no employment but household work and sewing, no earthly pleasures but an unprofitable 'visiting,' and no hope in all our lives to come of anything better. Men expect us to be content with this dull and unprofitable lot, regularly, uncomplainingly, day in and day out, as if we had no germs of

---

[4] Proverbs 31: 10–31.

faculties for anything else. I ask you: could men live so themselves? Would they not be very weary?"

"Men have got no conception o' th' hardships faced by th' women i' their lives," said Tabby with a weary shake of her head.

"Even if they did have," agreed Emily, "they would not do anything about it."

When, at last, I shut the front door behind Mr. Nicholls with a sigh of relief, I strode into papa's study and said, "I hope that is the last we will see of *that* gentleman."

"On the contrary," rejoined papa. "I have hired him."

"You have hired him? Papa! You cannot mean it."

"He's the finest candidate I've interviewed in years. He reminds me of William Weightman."

"How can you say so? He is nothing like William Weightman!" Mr. Weightman, papa's very first curate, had been loved by the entire community, and by my sister Anne in particular. Sadly, he had contracted cholera while visiting the sick and died three years before. "Mr. Weightman was bonny and charming and affable. He had a wonderful sense of humour."

"Mr. Nicholls has an excellent sense of humour."

"I saw no evidence of it—unless perhaps at the expense of women. He is narrow-minded, rude, and arrogant, papa, and far too reserved."

"Reserved? What, are you daft? Why, he talked my ear off. I cannot recall the last time I had such a pleasant and engaging conversation with a man."

"He barely spoke three sentences to me."

"Perhaps he's uncomfortable talking to a woman on short acquaintance."

"If so, how will he fare in the community?"

"I expect he will fare just fine. He comes highly recommended, as you know, and I can see why. He graduated last year from Trinity College. He's a good man, with a sensible head on his shoulders. We have much in common, Charlotte. Can you imagine it? He was born in County Antrim, in the north of Ireland, some forty-five miles from where I myself grew up. We both come from families of ten children; our fathers were both poor farmers; and we both were assisted by local clergymen to go on to university."

"All these similarities are very well, papa, but will they make him a good curate? He is so young."

"Young? Of course he's young! My girl, one can't expect to get a seasoned curate for £90 a year. He's not even ordained yet, so we shall have to wait another month or so for him to begin his duties."

"Another month? There is so much to be done. Can you afford to wait so long, papa?"

Papa smiled. "I trust Mr. Nicholls will be worth the wait."

Two

The last week of May, Mr. Nicholls became a tenant in the sexton's house, a low stone building adjoining the church school, only a stone's throw down the cobbled lane from the parsonage and its small, walled front garden. It was my duty to welcome him; and this I did, the day after his arrival, by preparing the usual basket of homemade items.

It was a fine spring morning. As I issued from the parsonage gate with my offering, I gave a friendly nod to the stone-cutter in the chipping shed, who was busily chip, chip, chipping away with his recording chisel, engraving the In Memoriams of the newly departed on one of the great slabs piled therein.

"Mr. Nicholls!" I called out, as I saw that gentleman leaving his lodgings. He turned up the lane to meet me; I presented him the basket with a smile. "My family and I wanted to welcome you to the neighbourhood, sir. I do hope you are settling in well."

"I am," answered he with a surprised bow. "Thank you, Miss Brontë. That is very kind."

"It is not much, sir, just a loaf of bread, a small cake, and a jar of gooseberry jam, but my sister and I made them all with our own hands. I might add that I also hemmed the linen servi-ette[5] myself. Since I know that you believe women are at their best in the occupations God gave them—when sewing or in the kitchen—I trust that you will find it a most suitable offering."

To my satisfaction, his face went scarlet, and he fell silent.

"I must run," I added. "I have much to do at home. I am deeply engrossed in reading Macaulay's *Lays of Ancient Rome* and Chateaubriand's *Études Historiques*,[6] and I am nearly finished trans-lating Homer's *Iliad* from the Greek. If you will excuse me."

I did not see Mr. Nicholls again until church on Sunday, when he took his first duty as curate. As he read the prayers aloud, the congregation appeared to greatly appreciate the hearty Celtic sentiment in his manner and tone. After the service, however, he only nodded and bowed solemnly to the congregants who came up to speak to him, uttering barely a word himself.

When I complained about this to Emily after we returned to the parsonage, Emily said, "Perhaps Mr. Nicholls is simply shy. He might share our own aversion to conversing with strangers; after all, he did only just arrive. And he *does* have a very nice voice."

"A nice voice hardly recommends a speaker," I replied, "if he is too reserved to speak, and when he *does* speak, his views are ar-rogant and narrow-minded. I am certain he will not improve upon acquaintance."

A few weeks after Mr. Nicholls's arrival in Haworth, I received a letter from Anne, announcing that she and Branwell would be coming home for their summer holiday from Thorp Green a week earlier than expected. Anne gave no reason for this sudden change of plan; but as her letter was delivered only a few hours before their train was due to arrive, Emily and I were obliged to set off almost immediately on the four-mile walk to Keighley to meet them.

---

[5] Napkin.

[6] Historical Studies.

It was a warm, sunny, blue-skied afternoon in June; we had not seen our sister and brother since Christmas, and we both looked forward to their visit with great anticipation.

"Here it comes," cried Emily, rising up from the hard wooden bench at the Keighley station, as a sharp whistle announced the approach of the four o'clock train. The locomotive roared up the tracks and pulled to a stop with a sharp squealing of brakes and a great outpouring of steam. Several passengers alighted; at last I spotted Anne, and we flew to her side.

"What a wonderful surprise," said Emily, embracing her, "to have you home early."

Anne was twenty-five years old, as short and slight as I, and blessed with a sweet, appealing face and a lovely, pale complexion. Her gentle spirit shone from her violet-blue eyes, and she wore her light brown hair pulled up and back, with ringlets that fell on her neck in graceful curls. As a child, Anne had been afflicted with a lisp, which she fortunately outgrew as she matured; the debility had, however, rendered her reserved and shy. At the same time, she was possessed of a calm disposition that rarely seemed to alter, buoyed up by her deep and abiding faith in a higher spirit, and her belief in the inherent goodness of mankind. How much her beliefs had recently changed with regard to this last notion, I was soon to discover.

When I studied Anne's countenance now, she looked more pale than usual; when I hugged her, she felt thin and bird-like in my embrace. "Are you all right?" I asked in concern.

"I am fine. I love your new summer dress, Charlotte. When did you make it?"

"I finished it last week." Although pleased with the garment, which I had constructed of pale blue silk shot through with a delicate pattern of white flowers, I was in no mood to discuss my clothing; it seemed to me that Anne had only mentioned it to distract me from the question I had posed. Before I could inquire further, however, my brother leapt down from the train car, barking orders to two porters, who brought down an old, familiar trunk onto the platform.

"Anne!" exclaimed I in surprise. "Is that your trunk?"

Anne nodded.

"Why have you brought it? Oh! Are you moving home?" cried Emily happily.

"I am. I have handed in my resignation. I will never again be returning to Thorp Green." A look of relief crossed Anne's countenance, but at the same time, her eyes seemed to be filled with some unspoken worry.

"I am so glad," said Emily, embracing Anne again. "I do not know how you stood it as long as you did."

I was astonished by this news. I knew Anne had been unhappy since the first day she began working as a governess for the Robinsons; she had been the most disappointed of us all when our plans to commence a school fell through, for that endeavour had promised her, as she expressed it, "a legitimate means of escape from Thorp Green." Anne had never confided in us as to the specific reasons for her discontent there, other than to admit to a general dissatisfaction with the position of governess, and I had not felt it right to pry.

It may seem strange to some, that sisters so close in age, so similar in education, tastes, and sentiments, and so closely bound by affection as we three were, could still keep a part of themselves entirely private; but such was the case. In childhood, when we suffered the devastating loss of our sisters Maria and Elizabeth, we became experts at hiding our pain—and as such, our innermost thoughts and feelings—behind brave and cheerful faces. When we split up years later and went our separate directions, the tendency persisted.

Indeed, despite all that I had suffered in my second year in Brussels, I had never breathed a word of it to either of my sisters. How could I expect Anne to be any more open with me than I had been with her? Now that she was home, however, and matters had come to a crux, I simply *had* to know what was going on.

"Anne," said I, "I applaud your courage in leaving Thorp Green, if you were unhappy; you know how much I despised the life of a governess. But to abandon such a secure position now, with our financial future so uncertain—it is most surprising. What has happened, to force this sudden and final departure? Why did you not mention it in your letter?"

Anne blushed, and unaccountably glanced at Branwell, who was busily arranging for her trunk and their bags to be loaded onto a waiting wagon, for later delivery to our house. "It is nothing of consequence. I have had my fill of being a governess, that is all."

Emily looked at her. "You *know* I can read your face like a book, Anne. Something is bothering you—something *new*. What is it? What are you not telling us?"

"It is nothing," insisted Anne. "Oh! How good it is to be home! Well—nearly home anyway. How I have looked forward to this day."

Branwell, his negotiations with the wagon driver now complete, turned to us with open arms and a wide smile. "Come, give us a hug! How are my favourite *older* sisters?"

Emily and I smiled and embraced him. "We are in the best of health, and even better spirits," said I, "now that you are here to keep us company."

My brother, at twenty-seven, was of middling height and handsome, with broad shoulders and a lean, athletic figure; a pair of spectacles balanced atop his Roman nose, and he wore a cap at a jaunty angle atop his bush of chin-length, carroty-red hair. Branwell was intelligent, passionate, and talented; he carried himself with an air of supreme confidence in his own male attractiveness. He also possessed an unfortunate penchant, developed over the past decade, for drink, and—to our everlasting horror and embarrassment—for the occasional dose of opium. To my relief, I saw that his eyes were now clear and sober and filled with good humour.

"Why did you never write?" I demanded, nudging him with affectionate annoyance. "I must have sent you half a dozen letters in the past six months, and you never replied."

"I have not the time nor the patience for correspondence lately. I have been occupied nearly every minute."

"It is good, then, that you have come home for a rest," said I.

"Papa is so looking forward to seeing you both," interjected Emily, taking Branwell's arm as we left the station. "If we walk briskly, we will be home just in time for tea."

"It is too hot to walk home now," complained Branwell. "Let us stop at the Devonshire Arms first, and wait until it cools down before we head back."

My sisters and I exchanged a glance. We knew full well that Branwell could never stop at an inn without taking a drink— and tea would not be his beverage of choice. One drink would invariably turn into three—or five; and the last thing we wanted was to see our brother drunk at his homecoming.

"I promised papa particularly that we would come straight home," said I.

"It is not too hot," added Anne quickly.

"It is a lovely day, just perfect for a walk," insisted Emily.

Branwell sighed and rolled his eyes. "Very well. I see a man's vote does not count in *this* company."

We proceeded down the main street of Keighley, a prosperous town, with its active, relatively new marketplace, and the row of handsome buildings surrounding it. The town's location was not especially appealing, lying as it did in a hollow between hills, its skies often darkened by the fumes from the many factories nearby; but we were frequent visitors none the less, as Keighley's many shops provided certain goods and services that were not available in our tiny village.

"How is papa?" asked Anne.

"He is never peevish, never impatient, only anxious and dejected," replied Emily.

"I worry about him so," said Anne. "What will become of him—and us—if he goes blind? Will he lose his incumbency, do you think?"

"Papa will *not* lose his incumbency," insisted Branwell. "He is very highly regarded in the parish—and did you not say in your last letter, Charlotte, that he has hired a new curate?"

"Yes: a Mr. Nicholls. I think him most disagreeable."

"Why?"

"He is very reserved and insular."

"But is he competent? Does he perform his job well?"

"It is too soon to tell. He started only a few weeks ago."

"This Mr. Nicholls must be a good man, if papa chose him," said Anne.

"Papa also chose James Smith," I replied, "and he was coarse, arrogant, and mercenary."

"Papa would never repeat *that* mistake," said Branwell. "If this Mr. Nicholls can handle even half of the parish duties on papa's behalf, he will be worth his weight in gold."

We had reached the outskirts of town now, and began the long, scrambling climb up the wave-like hills past the factories, which sprouted at the roadside between rows of grey stone cottages. "How long are you home for, Branwell?" asked I. "A good month, I hope?"

"I have to go back next week."

"Oh," said Emily, disappointed. "Why such a short stay?"

"I am needed at Thorp Green—but I will be home again in July. I will take the rest of my holiday when the Robinsons go off on theirs, to Scarborough."

"What is keeping you so fully occupied, that you cannot take a proper holiday?" I asked.

I saw Anne dart a silent, sidelong glance at Branwell; he unaccountably coloured, and said quickly: "Well, in addition to tutoring the young Master Robinson, I am now also giving art lessons to all the women in the household."

"Art lessons?" said Emily. "How did that come about?"

"Rather unexpectedly. When I mentioned one day to the lady of the house that I had studied drawing and painting as a youth, and had spent a year in Bradford trying to establish myself as a portrait painter, she insisted that I paint *her* portrait. Mrs. Robinson was so delighted with the result, that she asked me to teach her to paint—and her three daughters as well."

"What a fine outlet for your talent," observed Emily.

"As it turns out," Branwell went on with enthusiasm, "Mrs.

Robinson has quite an artistic bent herself. It is because she is so anxious to continue with her work in progress before they leave on holiday, that she has asked me to return within the week."

Diary: I admit I felt a tiny stab of envy at this delineation of Branwell's newest artistic endeavours. Forgive me for possessing these feelings, which I know to be less than gracious; I shall strive to overcome them; but how many long years did I share, in vain, my brother's ambition to become an artist? In our youth, my sisters and I all studied with the same drawing master as Branwell; for me, it became an all-consuming passion. I spent countless hours huddled over my drawing-paper and Bristol boards with chalks, pencils, crayons, and cakes of colour, creating pictures from my imagination, or meticulously copying mezzotints and engravings of famous works that had been reproduced in books and Annuals. When I was eighteen, two of my pencil drawings were even selected for showing at a prestigious art exhibition in Leeds—but because Branwell was a boy, papa decided that he should be the one to continue study. I did not begrudge my brother the opportunity; but oh! How dearly I had wished that I, too, could have learned to paint with oils! Instead, my lessons ceased, and in time I gave up the pursuit.[7]

"Have you written anything new, Charlotte?"

My brother's voice broke into my thoughts; I blinked and refocused my gaze, aware that I must have missed part of the conversation. We had progressed beyond the factories now, and were passing the treeless open fields, divided like a draught-board[8] into parcels by endless stone fences. Funny, I thought with a smile, that Branwell should ask about writing, when I had been musing about art; but the two endeavours did, in a way, go hand in hand.

---

[7] Nearly two hundred known drawings, sketches, and paintings by Charlotte Brontë are extant, all charming in their own right. They reflect the inherent promise of the artist, and the painstaking attention to detail that she was later to exhibit in her writing.

[8] Checkerboard.

Before I could reply, Emily said: "Charlotte has written not a word, as far as I can tell, in more than a year."

"Is that true?" asked Branwell in surprise.

I considered my response. In fact, ever since my return from Belgium eighteen months before, I had written both poetry and prose in secret, late at night, in an attempt to unburden the misery which continued to weigh down my heart. This practice, I realised, could no longer go on undetected, now that Anne had come home and would share my bed. "I have written nothing of late to speak of," said I, which was as close to the truth as I wished to go.

"Why not?" asked Branwell. "Writing is as deeply entrenched in your blood as it is in mine, Charlotte. You once told me that to live a single day without putting pen to paper in some capacity or another was pure torture to your soul. Admit it: you must at least be *thinking* about Angria and your Duke of Zamorna."

Angria was the imaginary kingdom that Branwell and I had invented as children: a balmy African landscape, first called the "Confederacy of Glass Town," which we had peopled with a roster of brilliant, wealthy characters who loved obsessively, waged wars, had great adventures, and were as real to us as life itself. My childhood hero had been the famous Duke of Wellington; when I outgrew him, I created an imaginary son for him, the Duke of Zamorna (alternately known as Arthur Augustus Adrian Wellesley, Marquis of Douro, and King of Angria). Zamorna was a poet, soldier, statesman, and passionate womanizer, who had captured my mind and heart over the course of countless stories—stories I was still writing with great pleasure in my mid-twenties, when I left for Belgium. I had not written a word about him or Angria since.

"I think our professor in Brussels said something to discourage her," said Emily.

A heat rose to my face. "That is not true. Monsieur Héger was very supportive of my writing. He said I had talent, and helped me to hone and perfect my craft. I learned more from him than any other teacher; but he also forced me to re-evaluate the type of writing I was doing and its place in the future course of my life."

"What future course is that?" asked Branwell.

"I am twenty-nine years old. There is no point in scribbling any more of those silly, romantic stories that we penned in our youth. At my age, the imagination should be pruned and trimmed, the judgment cultivated, and the countless illusions of youth should be cleared away."

Branwell laughed. "Good God, Charlotte! You sound like you are a hundred and twenty-nine, not twenty-nine."

"It is nothing to joke about. I must be serious now. I must focus on what is practical and prudent."

"We can be practical and prudent," interjected Anne, "without giving up writing."

"We?" I looked at her. "Have you been writing, Anne?"

Anne and Emily exchanged a glance. After some hesitation, Anne said, "Not really—at least nothing of consequence."

My curiosity was piqued; evidently, Anne *had* been writing, but was no more willing to talk about it than I. As to the subject matter of her work, I could venture a guess. In childhood, Emily and Anne had created an imaginary world of their own, which they called Gondal—a dark, dramatic, passionate Northern world ruled by females—and they had recorded the adventures of their beloved characters in verse and prose. Although it had been years since my sisters had shared the fruits of their labours with us, I knew they still drew great enjoyment from play-acting scenes about Gondal in private, whispered conversations to that day.

"I suppose writing is in our blood," said I, "and I will always love it; but I feel that I must find something more useful and worthwhile to do with my time. One day, we all may have to support ourselves, and writing does not bring in an income."

"But it *can*," said Branwell, with a sudden, mysterious smile, as he removed his cap and tilted his head back, allowing the hot sun to shine fully upon his face.

"What is that smile?" asked Emily. "Have you sold something, Branwell?"

"I have. I just had four sonnets published in the *Yorkshire Gazette*."

"Four sonnets!" I exclaimed, surprised and thrilled. "When was this?"

"Last month. They printed *Blackcomb* and *The Shepherd's Chief Mourner*, which I wrote years ago, and a new pair as well, called *The Emigrant*." Branwell immediately launched into a passionate recitation, delivering his new verses to the fields and sky. As I listened to his clear, strong voice, I could not help but feel a rush of pleasure and affection. Branwell's animated delivery style was a gift he had possessed since childhood; he could make even the most ordinary poem sound like a masterpiece. At the conclusion of the performance, my sisters and I applauded; Branwell thanked us with a bow.

We had reached the bottom of Haworth's one steep, narrow, winding street now. We plunged uphill with renewed vigour, our feet attacking the flagstones as we passed the closely-packed, slate-roofed, grey stone houses and shops on either side, deftly circumventing two horses and carts taking up the better part of the road. We soon reached the Haworth graveyard, on the hill before the church. It was wash day: a bevy of wives and washerwomen were gathered in the churchyard, chattering happily as they spread their wet sheets and laundry over the tombstones to dry. Since the majority of the tombstones were great stone slabs lying horizontally atop low pedestals like a table, they made a most convenient drying space.

"It is highly disrespectful," intoned a deep Irish voice, as we turned left into Church Lane. I saw Mr. Nicholls exiting the sexton's house with Mr. Grant, the curate of Oxenhope, a young man well-known to us, as he had assisted papa in the parish on many occasions over the preceding year. "A churchyard is a sacred place," Mr. Nicholls went on. "To see the headstones covered over in damp sheets, shirts, and chemises is a travesty."

"I don't disagree with you," replied Mr. Grant, a thin man with a red complexion and a high-pitched, nasal voice, "but a custom is a custom, and you don't want to go up against all the women of Haworth, I assure you."

Catching sight of us, the youthful Levites broke off their conversation. Mr. Nicholls and I had not spoken in the three weeks since I delivered his welcome basket, and he stiffened at the sight of me. Both men turned down the lane in our direction. Mr. Nicholls glanced curiously at Anne and Branwell, as the curates simultaneously tipped their clerical hats, and said, "Good-afternoon."

"Good-afternoon," I replied. "Mr. Nicholls: may I present my brother Branwell and my sister, Miss Anne Brontë. Branwell, Anne: this is the Reverend Arthur Bell Nicholls, the new curate of Haworth."

Mr. Nicholls shook hands with Branwell and bowed formally to Anne. "I thought I detected a family resemblance. It's a pleasure to meet you both."

"A pleasure to meet you, sir"—"And you, sir"—were Branwell's and Anne's replies. Emily, in typical fashion, said nothing.

"It is good to see you both again," said the livelier Mr. Grant, amidst more hand-shaking and bowing. I thought Mr. Grant a self-complacent and snobbish man, from his turned-up nose and elevated chin to his clerical black gaiters and square-toed shoes, but he did seem to be an active and devoted parish priest. "Are you home for the summer?"

"Sadly, I must return in short order," answered Branwell breezily, "but Anne is back for good. Had her fill of governessing, apparently."

"Well," said Mr. Grant, "that is totally understandable. To be locked away on a remote country estate, miles from anywhere, with no access to high society—it would indeed be deadly dull."

"I thought so myself, at first," remarked Branwell. "The first three months I was so bored, I thought I would tear my hair out; but the place grew on me."

Anne frowned and said suddenly, "If you will excuse me, I am most anxious to see papa."

"I will go with you," said Emily.

My sisters darted off. I was eager to join them, and was about to say good-bye, when Branwell said, "Would you gentlemen like to join us for tea? If I am not mistaken, Tabby and Martha will have a feast of some sort awaiting us."

Mr. Grant smiled heartily. "Thank you, we'd be delighted."

My heart sank. I had looked forward to an intimate family gathering, just the five of us, to celebrate Anne and Branwell's homecoming; I believed that papa had, too. Every time we had shared our table with the local curates, I had found them to be a self-seeking, vain, and empty race—and I did not wish to dine with Mr. Nicholls, in particular. My brother, however, had always been a gregarious, sociable being—and now the die was cast.

"I will see you gentlemen inside," said I, forcing a smile. I then hastened down the lane towards the parsonage, after my sisters.

As I entered the house through the yard door, the delectable aroma of roast beef and Yorkshire puddings assailed my nostrils. My sisters were both crouched down in the kitchen, happily receiving enthusiastic canine kisses from their respective animals. Our mastiff belonged to Emily; Flossy had been a gift from Anne's pupils, the Robinsons; to her distress, they had so mistreated the lovely spaniel that she had been obliged to bring him home, where he stayed under Emily's excellent care.

Tabby (bent over the stove, boiling potatoes) and Martha (removing puddings from the oven) both squealed with delight at the sight of Anne, and they were soon in each other's arms.

"How we've missed ye, lass!" said Tabby, wiping happy tears from her eyes with a corner of her apron.

"How good it is t' see ye, Miss Anne!" cried Martha. Just seventeen years old, Martha Brown was a cheerful, slender woman with soft, dark hair and a pleasant face. The second eldest daugh-ter of Mary and John Brown of Sexton House, just a few doors away, Martha had come to live with us at the tender age of thirteen, taking over the heavier share of the housework. "Roast beef an' puddings bein' a favourite o' your'n an' good Maister Branwell's," Martha told Anne, "we've took care t' mak' a proper Sunday dinner for your homecoming, although it be only a Tuesday."

"Thank you both," said Anne with a smile.

"I hope you have made enough for two more," said I, "be-cause your 'good Master Branwell' has just invited Mr. Nicholls and Mr. Grant to dine with us."

"There be food aplenty," said Tabby with a frown, "even if your guests do be sich lowly specimens as 'em young curates."

"Curates?" repeated Emily in dismay, as she broke from Keeper's hug. "What—are they coming now?" She leapt up like a spring and started for the kitchen door, as if to close it; but at that moment, I heard the sound of the men's arriving chatter as they entered through the front door. Both dogs' ears perked up and they instantly bolted past Emily into the passage.

"No!" cried Emily, dashing after them.

I heard some bustle; then the dogs erupted wildly in the hall, amidst whose hollow space their deep barks resounded formida-bly.

"Down, sir! Down!" exclaimed a high-toned, imperious voice, which I recognised as Mr. Grant's.

I raced into the entrance-hall with Anne at my heels. Keeper was bellowing ferociously and leaping on poor Mr. Grant. "Down, Keeper!" Emily and Branwell cried in unison. The dog paid no heed.

Mr. Grant, under attack, held up his arms to protect his face and wildly eyed the front door; but Branwell, Mr. Nicholls and papa (who had just joined the party from his study) stood be-hind him in the passage, blocking that avenue of escape. Instead, Mr. Grant turned and fled up the staircase two steps at a time. Keeper flung himself after the escaping gentleman. Emily threw herself bodily in front of the tawny beast, barring his access to the stairs as she struggled to grab hold of his large brass collar. The hound bayed and howled and hurled himself against her; Emily resolutely stood her ground, but she could not last long under such an onslaught.

I was about to rush to Emily's aid, when all at once there came an entreating whistle, of the dog-calling variety. Keeper froze; with curious eyes and twitching ears, he looked round. The whistle had issued forth from the lips of Mr. Nicholls, who stood calmly in the centre of the hall.

"Here, boy," said Mr. Nicholls, eyeing Keeper with close attention as he patted his thigh. "Come on, boy. Come here, now. There's a good dog."

Three

*D*iary, it was well-known to all the inhabitants of the village, that the mastiff at the parsonage was a singular animal. For the most part, Keeper was sullen, aloof, and indifferent to the rest of the world, shunning all attempts at affection except those of his mistress, whom he adored. On occasion, the beast took a fierce dislike to a particular individual; but I had never seen him tamed by any one other than Emily.

To my astonishment, the fire now instantly dissipated from Keeper's bull-dog eyes; he descended onto all fours; and, as if a child responding to the Piper of Hamelin's call, he trotted obediently back to the curate's feet and calmly settled on his haunches. Mr. Nicholls crouched down and affectionately caressed the animal behind both ears, under his muzzle, and atop his head, speaking soft words of encouragement, as all assembled looked on in wonder and amazement.

"Thank you, Mr. Nicholls," said I, as Emily, stunned and speechless, recovered and straightened her skirts.

"You are a genie, sir," observed Branwell. "That dog has never let me so much as pat his head before."

"Yet he is generally harmless," I added. "I do not know what set him off."

"Perhaps it was when Mr. Grant started kicking him," said Mr. Nicholls.

"Ah!" I replied. "*That* he will not take." Moving to the balustrade, I called upstairs, "Mr. Grant! You may come down now. The coast is clear!"

I heard the sound of a chamber door opening from above, followed by timid footsteps on the stairs. Mr. Grant's face appeared at the bend in the staircase as he peered cautiously over the rail. "Is the dog gone?"

Keeper, detecting the visitor's re-emergence, cocked his head in that direction and emitted a low growl, even more terrible and menacing than his bark.

"*No,*" said Mr. Nicholls quietly but firmly.

The growl stopped as quickly as it had begun; the dog held up his huge, blunt, stupid head to be patted, and soon was again panting and slobbering contentedly. I was beginning to wonder if I had misjudged Mr. Nicholls; a man who was so good and gentle with animals might have other hidden qualities, might he not?

"There is no reason to be frightened," said Emily, stifling a laugh as she glanced up at Mr. Grant. "Keeper will not hurt you. His uproars are all sound and fury, signifying nothing— and he is quite calm now."

"I will not come down until that dog is locked up, or put outside!" was Mr. Grant's reply.

"Emily, put him out," said papa, who had been standing silently beside Flossy through the hubbub.

"Yes, sir." Emily obediently retrieved the animal from Mr. Nicholls with a silent nod, and removed him to the yard.

Papa took advantage of the reprieve to embrace Branwell and Anne and heartily welcome them home. Mr. Nicholls, meanwhile, turned his attention to Flossy, who now basked in the same affectionate treatment Keeper had received. "What's this fellow's name?"

"Flossy," I replied.

"Aren't you a beauty?" said Mr. Nicholls. "One of the finest King Charles spaniels I have ever seen."

"That *other* dog is a menace!" cried Mr. Grant, as he descended the stairs and rejoined the party. "Did you see how he sprang at me? Why, he very nearly bit my head off! I was afraid for my life!"

"Next time," said Branwell, "you ought to let Mr. Nicholls go in the door before you. He clearly has the magic touch."

"There will be no next time," asserted Mr. Grant, as we all filtered into the dining-room, where Martha was adding two more place settings to the table. "I will not set foot in this house again, without an assurance that that animal is locked up and out of sight. I wonder, Reverend Brontë"—(with a stern glance at me and Emily, as she returned)—"that you allow your daughters to keep such a dangerous creature at the parsonage."

"Dangerous?" replied papa with a smile. "Why, Keeper wouldn't hurt a cat. He eats like a horse, and he costs me eight shillings a year for the dog tax, but I think he's worth every penny."

"We *keep* him, sir," added Emily, "because we are fond of him. It is how he earned his name."

"You cannot be serious," said Mr. Grant. He and Mr. Nicholls sat down across the table from my sisters and myself, while papa and Branwell took their customary positions at the head and foot. "I can't fancy a lady fond of an ugly brute like that. 'Tis a mere carter's[9] dog."

"A carter's dog?" I repeated in amusement. "I hardly think so." Martha began serving out the meal. Wine was conspicuously absent from the table; we never risked serving an alcoholic beverage when Branwell was home, and every one in the room knew why, except perhaps the newcomer, Mr. Nicholls—but either he did not notice, or he was too polite to mention it.

I felt Mr. Nicholls's eyes on me across the dining-table, and

---

[9] Someone whose work is driving carts.

returned the gaze. He immediately looked away. "Mr. Nicholls: you got on well with our *ugly brute*. Pray sir, defend our choice."

"A mastiff is a fine animal, and one of the noblest of his race," said Mr. Nicholls, glancing at me briefly. "However, they are bred as guard dogs and attack dogs. In truth, Miss Brontë, I think you'd be better off giving him to one of the farmers in the parish to protect his livestock, and purchasing in his stead a breed more appropriate to the fairer sex."

Emily gave a little gasp of annoyance at this statement; I found it only amusing. "Indeed?" said I. "What breed of dog might you consider more *appropriate* to a person of our gender, Mr. Nicholls?"

"Ladies as a rule typically prefer lap-dogs," replied Mr. Nicholls.

"Something small and sweet," agreed Mr. Grant with a nod, "like a pug or poodle."

I laughed out loud. "Well then, please consider my sisters and me as exceptions to the rule."

"My sisters are an exception to *every* rule," said Branwell with a chuckle.

Although Emily rarely spoke when we had visitors, she now said heatedly, "I am at a loss. Why do you gentlemen consider men and women to be so vastly different, that you would assign them a particular breed of dog?"

"I meant no offence," answered Mr. Nicholls. "I was only expressing an opinion, based on my own observations of dogs—and women."

"Your observations?" retorted Emily. "Yes; Charlotte has shared some of your *observations* with regard to women, Mr. Nicholls. As I recall, she said that you approve of only two occupations for womankind: cooking and needlework—both of which you claim to be assigned by God himself."

Mr. Nicholls seemed taken aback by this declaration. Branwell laughed again; but the other men all grew quite serious, as they busied themselves attacking their roast beef and puddings. For a long moment, the only sounds in the room were those of vigorous chewing, the tinkling of silverware against the plates, and the chirping of our canary, Little Dick, in his cage by the window. At length, Mr. Nicholls replied, "I only meant, Miss Emily, that women are at their finest when carrying out all those feminine duties which they were born to do, and at which they excel: when managing the home, and as supportive wife, dutiful daughter, and caring mother."

"Hear, hear," said Mr. Grant.

"A truer word was never spoken," said papa.

"You must be joking," said Emily.

I felt the sudden heat of indignation rise within my chest. (What brief, misguided notion had compelled me to think that Mr. Nicholls might be worthy of my better opinion?) "Do you mean to imply, sir," said I, "that women can only excel at these *feminine duties, which they were born to do?* That, in short, females should never aspire to anything more lofty than baking pies, washing dishes, knitting stockings, playing on the piano, and embroidering bags? Do you seriously believe that anything more is above a woman's comprehension—that women do not have the same mental capacity to learn as men?"

"Answer that at your peril!" warned Branwell.

"I did not say that," began Mr. Nicholls.

He was cut off by Mr. Grant, who said: "It is really not a question open for discussion, is it? It is a simple matter of science: of the physiological differences between the sexes. Alexander Walker said it best, I think, when he pointed out that man, possessing reasoning faculties, muscular power, and the courage to employ it, is qualified for being a protector; while the woman, being little capable of reasoning, feeble, and timid, requires protecting. Under such circumstances, the man naturally governs: the woman naturally obeys."[10]

"Oh! Oh!" exclaimed Emily and Anne together, appalled.

"I agree that man is naturally the protector," interjected Mr.

---

[10] From Scottish Physiologist Alexander Walker's trilogy on *Woman*, 1840.

Nicholls, "and that a woman's forte is softness, tenderness, and grace. But the question of men and women that so preoccupies our society to-day, has all been laid out for us quite clearly in the Bible—and nowhere better than the doctrines delivered in the second chapter of St. Paul's first Epistle to Timothy."

"What doctrines are those?" asked Branwell (who, to papa's regret and mortification, had not cracked open a Bible or attended church in years.)

"Let the woman learn in silence, with all subjection," quoted Mr. Nicholls. "I suffer not a woman to teach, nor to usurp authority over the man; but to be in silence. For Adam was first formed, then Eve."

Emily groaned aloud, and threw her napkin down upon the table. "Sir: where the Bible is concerned, do you allow the right of private judgment for both men and women?"

"I do," replied Mr. Nicholls.

"I disagree," said Mr. Grant. "Women should take their husband's opinions, both in politics and religion."

"Shame on you, sir, for such a stupid observation!" cried Emily.

"You might as well say that men should accept the opinions of their *priests* without examination!" said I.

"So they should," replied Mr. Nicholls.

"Of what value would a religion so adopted be?" I cried, aghast. "*Reason* must be allowed to inform theological interpretation and judgment; otherwise, it is mere blind, besotted superstition! Are you by any chance a Puseyite, Mr. Nicholls?"

"Yes, I am a strong advocate of the principles of the Reverend Dr. Edward Pusey and the founders of the Oxford Movement," answered Mr. Nicholls proudly.

"Well, I am a proponent of latitudinarianism,"[11] said I, struggling to contain my annoyance, "and I strongly object to

---

[11] A system of belief espoused by a group of Anglican Christians opposed to the dogmatic positions of the Church of England, allowing latitude in opinion and conduct.

Puseyism, and every word of the *Tracts for the Times*. I find its rigid principles dangerously close to Romanism, and most of its followers intolerant and abusive towards the dissenting Protestant sects. But, that aside: I have read the biblical passage you quoted, sir, in the original Greek, and I found that many of the words were wrongly translated."

"Wrongly translated?"

"Yes. With the tiniest alterations, the passage could be interpreted to mean something quite different: that a woman should and *must* speak out whenever she sees fit to make an objection; that she be freely permitted to teach and to exercise authority over man, and that man should hold his peace."

A guffaw erupted from all the men at the table. "You see, gentlemen," declared papa, "what I am obliged to deal with in my own household? Since childhood, Charlotte and Emily have challenged me over every similar point in the Bible. Only Anne, my good sweet Anne, accepts its precepts gracefully and without question. My daughters all cajoled me, however, into allowing them to study subjects that are better left to men. And here they sat, at this very table, all the years that they were growing up, pouring over the musty pages of Grecian and Roman literature, translating entire works from the Latin, plodding through the windings of difficult mathematical problems, until they educated themselves above the level of any man from here to York."

"I cannot for the life of me imagine what they think to do with all that knowledge," said Mr. Grant, "while they are baking bread or making up the beds."

The men all laughed again. Inwardly, I fumed. Martha now entered with a berry tart.

Emily stood and said: "I have no appetite for this conversation, or for dessert."

"If you will excuse us," added Anne, also rising. They both quickly left the room. I had half a mind to join them, but from the prevailing tone of the evening, I feared that womankind might suffer without a higher, feminine voice to defend her; and so I stayed. After Martha served out coffee and dessert and departed, Branwell thankfully changed the subject by proudly announcing the recent publication of his two poems. A debate ensued regarding the value of poetry, which Branwell, papa and I championed, and Mr. Nicholls and Mr. Grant opposed.

"Poetry is a rather useless affectation," asserted Mr. Nicholls, "just a lot of flowery words that are meant to impress, yet only serve to confuse and exasperate."

"How can you say so!" cried I, with rising passion. "There is enough of hard practicality and *useful* knowledge in this world forced on us by necessity. We require something beautiful and artistic to soften and refine our minds. Poetry is a means to that end. Poetry is more than *useful,* sir: it is a delight. It lifts us; it elevates us; it can take something coarse and make it god-like!"

Mr. Nicholls looked at me, as if surprised by my force of feeling; he then lowered his eyes and said, "I am glad you find it so, Miss Brontë. Perhaps I never really understood it. When I studied poetry, I always found it difficult."

"Speaking of poetry," interjected Mr. Grant through a mouthful of berry tart, "I received a note yesterday, Nicholls, filled with great gobs of rhyming nonsense, from one of the young ladies in my parish—a Miss Stokes."

"Do you like her?" asked Mr. Nicholls.

"I could not say." Mr. Grant held out his now-empty plate to me across the table, with a silent uplifting of eyebrows that implored a refill; I performed the duty and resumed my seat. "She is the *handsomest* of the girls in her family," continued Mr. Grant, "of which there are *five,* all unmarried—and all of whom have trained their eyes on me. I declare, since the first day I came to Oxenhope, every lady in the district has been after me. Rumours are constantly circulating that I am to be married to Miss So-and-so, or Miss Such-and-such. On what grounds this gossip rests, God knows. I seek female society about as assiduously as does Mr. Nicholls, here."

"You only look down your nose at love," said Branwell, as he sipped his coffee, "because you have never felt it."

I glanced at Branwell, wondering at this assertion. He had never been in love before either, as far as I knew.

"Even if I did feel it, I should not be *swayed* by it," said Mr. Grant.

"You are very wise, sir," observed papa. "It is decidedly the best plan to remain single. Millions of marriages are unhappy; if everybody confessed the truth, perhaps all are more or less so."

"You and mama were very happy, were you not, papa?" said I.

"There are exceptions to every rule," replied papa. "Your mother was a rare and special woman, and what we felt for each other was equally rare. Most people tire of each other in a month and become no more than yokefellows."

"Marriage can, I believe, be an advantageous connection," remarked Mr. Nicholls, "when formed in consonance with dignity of views and permanency of solid interests."

"Oh?" said Mr. Grant, as he picked berry seeds from his teeth with his fork. "Are you looking for a wife, Nicholls?"

Mr. Nicholls blushed. "Hardly. I could not afford to keep one. My thoughts are occupied with other things at present."

"Yet women do not seem to understand that," intoned Mr. Grant with annoyance. "All they can think or talk about is courtships and dowries."

Branwell laughed. "Money can, indeed, bring a great deal to the equation."

Listening to this, my heart beat thick, and my head grew hot; it was all I could do to keep silent. These self-satisfied gentlemen, by the simple accident of gender, had all the world at their disposal! What gave them the right to think, much less to speak, in such demeaning terms about women, love, and matrimony?

"The sole aim of most single women, I have observed, is to be married," said Mr. Grant. "They scheme, they plot, they dress, they put on airs, all to ensnare husbands, yet the majority will never get one."

"The matrimonial market in this district does seem to be overstocked!" laughed Mr. Nicholls.

I could contain myself no more. So hastily did I leap to my

feet, that my chair clattered to the floor. "What do you expect single women to do in this day and age, gentlemen, if not to seek a husband? Does society allow them any other occupation?"

A stunned look crossed all four male countenances. I continued heatedly, "Perhaps you think it unseemly to give voice to grievances that are unpopular, and which society cannot readily cure—but I will risk your scorn and your contempt, I will dare to trouble your ease, by pointing out a few well-measured truths. Look at the numerous families of girls in this neighbourhood: look at the Stokeses, whose daughters Mr. Grant has so happily maligned. Their brothers are all in business or in professions. Their sisters, on the other hand, have minds with equal prowess to theirs and to your own, yet they have nothing to do! This stagnant state of things makes them decline in health; it is no wonder that their minds and views shrink, likewise, to wondrous narrowness. With no way to earn a living, they know they are destined to become nothing but a burden to their fathers and their brothers, and to live out a meager, impecunious, solitary existence. If the great wish—the sole aim—of every one of them is to be married, a state which at least gives them *some* occupation as cherished wives and proud mothers, and the only state in which they can be regarded with any respect by society—how can you blame them?"

My pulse pounded, and my entire form trembled from the effort of releasing this tirade; the men stared at me in consternation, as if struck dumb. I quickly righted my chair and strode towards the door, thinking: I am *glad* I did it; it needed to be said.

As I reached the doorway, however, I heard Mr. Nicholls say, in his quiet, Irish lilt: "The words, gentlemen, of an ugly old maid."

This statement was met by an outburst of laughter. My cheeks flamed; I turned in utter disbelief to stare at my oppressor, unsure that I had heard correctly. Could any one with a heart and soul have truly uttered words so unfeeling? Mr. Nicholls caught my eye; his smile vanished; he blanched, and then his face went crimson.

I fled, determined not to give these men the satisfaction of seeing me burst into tears.

I rushed upstairs to find Emily helping Anne unpack her trunk in my bedroom, the chamber which Anne and I were now to share. Taking one look at my face, my sisters stopped what they were doing and asked me what was wrong.

I sank down upon the bed as I hastily wiped away some tears, the impotent evidence of my anguish. "Oh! It is too awful. The men were speaking so callously just now against unmarried women, that my temper lost its balance. I spoke my mind, and struck them all dumb."

"I wanted to speak out once or twice myself earlier," said Anne, sitting down beside me, "but I had not the nerve."

"I am sure they deserved it," added Emily. "It is nothing to cry about."

"I am not crying," I insisted, even though I was, "and I do not regret what I said. Only—as I was leaving the room, Mr. Nicholls said—oh! I can hardly bring myself to repeat it."

"What did he say?" asked Emily, sitting cross-legged on the floor before me, like a Turk.

"He called me—" I took a deep breath, struggling to calm myself. "He called me 'an ugly old maid.'"

"He never did!" said Anne in disbelief.

"Are you certain it was Mr. Nicholls who said it?" inquired Emily.

"There is no mistaking Mr. Nicholls's voice and accent."

"I cannot believe Mr. Nicholls would say something so cruel," insisted Anne. "He seems like a nice, polite young man, for all his narrow views, and he was so wonderful with the dogs. Surely you must have heard wrong—or heard some one else."

"I know what I heard," said I, wiping my eyes and nose with my handkerchief. "I do not mind so much that he called me an old maid. I may despise the term in general, but I know it is correct, and I already knew Mr. Nicholls regarded me as such: he referred to me as a spinster the day we met. But to be called *ugly!*"

Diary, I hope that I do not suffer from the sin of vanity; most true it is that "beauty is in the eye of the gazer." As such, I realise that one should not take to heart the opinions of a single individual; yet I could not delude myself. The world revered a perfect complexion, rosy cheeks, a straight nose, and a cherry mouth; it admired a woman who was tall and stately, with a finely developed figure. I was none of those things.

"I know I am small and plain," I said with a sigh, "but there is a world of difference between *plain* and *ugly*. A plain woman can endure, knowing that although others may not delight to look at her, at least her visage gives no offence. An ugly woman, on the other hand, is a blot on the face of creation: a poor, wretched, despicable thing, whose very presence creates discomfort, whispered tittering, and averted looks of silent pity. Ugly! I do believe it is the single most crushing word in the English language!"

"Charlotte: you are not ugly," said Anne gently. "You are very attractive. I have long told you so."

"You have a good, sweet, and pleasant face, which we love to look upon," said Emily.

"You only say that because you are my sisters."

"I say it because it is true," declared Emily. "We are none of us agonizingly beautiful in this family, but what of it?"

"Do you not wish, sometimes, that you *were* beautiful?" I asked.

"I am what God made me," said Emily with a shrug. "I do not desire to be different."

"When I have those thoughts," said Anne, "I push them away, and concentrate on my inner being: on becoming the best person I can be. God does not care what our exterior form looks like."

"*He* may not, but people do. They judge us by our looks; they form first opinions which rarely waver. When I caught Mr.

Nicholls's eye after he spoke, he looked ashamed of himself; but that does not excuse the saying of it. He is truly an obnoxious man, and Mr. Grant is no better."

"They are not so bad," observed Anne, as we all rose and set to work unpacking her trunk. "The views they expressed with regard to women—at least the ones I heard—are not really any different from papa's or the other men I have met, or those we read about in the daily papers. It is just what men are brought up to believe."

"Just because men are dolts in general does not excuse that pair for becoming part of the norm," I said.

"Perhaps not," said Anne, "but I still say, I think you heard wrong, Charlotte. I cannot imagine Mr. Nicholls saying something so unfeeling. I think he likes you."

"Likes me? Do not be ridiculous. Mr. Nicholls does not like me or any woman. He thinks our entire gender as lowly and devoid of intelligence as a gnat. I think he made that point very clear."

At half-past eight that evening, the household gathered in papa's study for prayers. The only person not present was Branwell, who had long since declined to participate in any such ecclesiastical pursuits. When papa concluded the service at nine o'clock (on the dot, as always), Anne matter-of-factly broke the news about her departure from Thorp Green.

"I don't understand," exclaimed papa in concern. "You had an excellent position with the Robinsons, and were well paid for a governess. Were you mistreated there?"

"No, papa," said Anne quietly.

"Then why did you leave?"

"I simply felt it was the right time for me to go," insisted Anne.

"Well, it seems a daft thing to do."

I could discern the blush that crept across Anne's countenance, although my father, with his clouded vision, could not. Papa bolted the door, wound the mahogany long case clock that stood halfway up the stairs (his nightly ritual), and went up to his chamber. As we all followed to prepare for bed, and Emily and the servants disappeared into their respective rooms, I became determined to broach the subject with Anne one more time.

Anne and I changed into our night-shirts; as we unpinned and unbraided our hair, which had grown very long of late, we agreed to brush each other's tresses instead of curling them. I sat down upon the bed behind Anne and set to work. Hair-brushing was a practice which Emily had no patience for, but which Anne and I had performed for each other with the greatest pleasure ever since childhood, and greatly missed when we were apart. After some time thus employed, I said, "I am so glad you are home, Anne. I have never seen Thorp Green, and you have shared very little of what your life was like there; yet I can completely understand your desire to leave it."

Anne started in surprise. "You can?"

"Yes. I was miserable myself, as you may recall, in both of my posts as governess, particularly the first one."

"Oh—I see," was her reply.

"To be a governess is akin to being a slave," said I, as I pulled the brush vigorously through her light brown locks. "Even the most enormous house, surrounded by the most beautiful woodlands, green lawns, and winding white paths, cannot make up for the lack of a free moment or a free thought to enjoy them in."

"True."

"I was twenty-three when I went to work for the Sidgwicks. Mrs. Sidgwick did not care to know me at all. Her entire purpose in life seemed to be to squeeze the greatest possible quantity of labour out of me. For a pauper's wage, I was expected to teach a dozen subjects to children who had no interest in learning. From the instant I awoke to the hour of their bedtime, the children were constantly with me; I was then expected to sew by candlelight until I dropped from exhaustion—not only the usual hemming of handkerchiefs and tablecloths, but an entire wardrobe of doll clothes."

"So was I," admitted Anne. "In addition to sewing and making doll clothes, I was obliged to do fancy-work and paint pictures and write musical compositions, and pretend that they were my pupils' own original work."

"Oh! That makes my blood boil."

"Were you ever allowed to join the adult company, Charlotte?"

"Join them? No. When the Sidgwicks entertained guests, it was my duty to keep the children out of their way. On rare occasions, I was obliged to present them arrayed in their best garments, to be paraded around the drawing-room in an ecstasy of vanity and excitement for the ladies to pet and admire—but I was instructed to sit in a corner—ignored and unwanted."

"Unwanted, but not *unnoticed*," added Anne, as she took the brush from me and we switched positions on the bed.

"Exactly. Did they ever talk about you as if you were not there, or were too ignorant to understand what they were saying?"

"All the time."

I sighed, trying to relax as the brush in Anne's hand tingled against my scalp and tugged pleasantly at my hair; but the memories we evoked brought back the sense of frustration and isolation I had felt six years earlier. "My employers did not consider me as a living and rational being, except as connected with the duties I had to perform. The servants would have nothing to do with me, either; as an educated woman, I suppose they considered me above them—so I did not fit in anywhere."

"Nor did I. Were you banished to a room at the top of the house?"

"Yes."

"What were your pupils like?"

"Incorrigible little beasts, most of the time."

"Were you allowed to exact discipline?"

"Never, not even when Benson Sidgwick threw a Bible at me, or hurled stones at my face and nearly broke my nose."

"Oh! Charlotte. I am so sorry; but I understand. That was such a trial for me. How the Robinsons expected me to maintain order without discipline, is beyond me. The youngest daughter was a rude, swearing hoyden, and the two oldest girls went out of their way to flirt with perfectly decent men for whom they would never care a fig, just so they could win their esteem and break their hearts—and then boast of their many conquests. Sadly, the adults were no better than the children! They—" Anne stopped herself, then added quickly: "I should not have spoken so. All that is past, and it is wrong to speak ill of others."

"Anne: you have left the Robinsons' employ. Surely, after all these years, you may feel free to speak of them *now* with impunity—if only to me. The sharing may do you good, and you know I will not tell any one."

"No." Anne set down the brush and climbed into bed. "The Robinsons loved me in their own way, and that is how I hope to remember them."

I closed the shutters and slipped into bed beside her. "At least tell me one thing," I said as I lay back on my pillow. "How is it that Branwell is so satisfied with his position at Thorp Green? Every time he comes home, he seems so anxious to go back there. Does he not suffer the same degradations as we did? Or is it different for him, because he is a man and a tutor, rather than a governess?"

Anne fell silent; even in the dim evening light, I could discern a blush rise in her cheeks. "He is very valued there," was all she said. She then closed her eyes, bade me an affectionate goodnight, and turned her back to me.

Clearly, I thought, she has not told all; but I could see that I would have to be content with that for the present.

That night, I dreamt that I was back in the garden at the Pensionnat in Brussels. It was a moonlit night in April; the air was heavy with the fragrance of pear blossoms, mingled with the smoky scent of a cigar; my master and I stood together, just as we had stood two years before. Even in dreaming, my heart pounded with ferocity, and I awoke trembling.

As I lay there in the early-morning darkness, I strove to calm myself so that Anne beside me would not stir. Why, I wondered, did I continue to dream of my former professor, night after night? Why could I not forget? Often, I had tormenting dreams, in which I saw him always severe, always saturnine and angry with me. In this dream, however, he had been kind, affectionate, and tender, as he had been on that fateful evening. Perhaps the dream was an omen, then: not a bad sign, but a good one. Perhaps it meant that to-day, my wish would be fulfilled: I would at last receive another letter from Brussels.

I could see the shape of that letter in my mind: the envelope of enameled white, with the Cyclops's eye of crimson wax in the centre. I could almost feel the hoped-for envelope itself: firm, substantial, and satisfying, with the promise of at least a single sheet of paper inside. A little thrill ran through me at the thought. It was earlier than I was accustomed to rising, but I left my warm bed with excitement and quietly got dressed.

Not long after, as I sat reading one of my French newspapers downstairs, the church bells tolled the early-morning hour; moments later, I heard the familiar, sharp report of papa's pistol discharging above. Ever since the days of the Luddite riots more than thirty years before, papa had gone to bed with a loaded pistol at his bedside, and his first duty on awakening was to fire it out his bedroom window, usually taking aim at the church tower. This rather eccentric daily habit had become the accepted signal to all the household—and no doubt all the neighbourhood—that it was time to rise. I heard the expected stirring from above; soon Martha appeared, expressing surprise to see me up before her.

After breakfast, I went about my household duties in a sort of fog, listening with fevered anticipation for the approaching footsteps of the postman. At last he came. I ran to meet him at the front door, where I secured his handful of deliveries and glanced through them. A surge of disappointment washed over me; the letter was not there.

"What are ye up to?" said Tabby, as she hobbled down the hall and snatched the mail from my grasp. "The letters be my job, an' well ye know it. Ye can read 'em t' your father later, after tea."

Tabby shuffled into papa's study; as the door opened, the sound of music trilled out into the hall. Emily was practising at the cottage piano; through the open doorway I glimpsed Anne sitting on the bench beside her, turning the pages. I knew I ought to return to the dining-room, where I had been polishing the fender; but my heart was too heavy; I had no will to move. The long-awaited letter would have been the answer to my prayers, my ransom from the devastation of months of deprivation; but it had not come.

As Tabby passed me on her way to the kitchen, I gave myself a mental shake. "Stop acting like an idiot. It is only a letter," an inner voice sternly cried. "He will write again one day; surely he must." Another voice, far sweeter and more cajoling than the first, quickly followed: "if you cannot have the satisfaction of a *new* letter, there *is* one recourse." My heart beat faster; I was fraught with indecision. "It is time," I silently scolded myself, "to give up your guilty pleasure." But I could not help myself.

A quick glance into the study convinced me that Emily and Anne would be engaged at the piano for a good half-hour, at least. Hastily, I stole upstairs to my chamber, took my keys from my pocket, and unlocked the bottom drawer of my bureau. From its depths, I removed a small rosewood case which had once belonged to my mother. I unlocked the case and took out a bundle shrouded in silver paper; this I unwrapped, to reveal a small packet of letters tied with a scarlet ribbon. Five letters only: these were the sum total of my treasure. I sat down on the bed, untied the precious bundle, and eyed the first letter in the stack: the one that had come just a few weeks after I returned from Belgium.

Oh! What delight I had felt upon its receipt, and on the arrival of its four successors. Each new letter had been as if an aliment divine: a godsend, sweet, pure, and life-sustaining. Even now, knowing every word of their contents so intimately that I could recite them in my sleep, a mere glimpse of each cover with its direction, "Miss Charlotte Brontë," in that clean, decided, and familiar hand—stamped on the reverse with the well-cut impress of three beloved initials—caused a thrill to run lively through all my veins and warmed me to my very core.

How many letters had I sent to Brussels, I wondered, in the past eighteen months? Too many to count; yet, in all that time, I had received only these five precious replies. Some I had read at the very moment of receipt; others—like a perfectly ripe peach, too good to be tasted at once—I had saved for a later devouring, when they could be enjoyed away from prying eyes and questioning tongues. Each one I had opened with the greatest of care, gently sliding a knife blade beneath the seal, to leave the molten circle intact in all its crimson beauty.

Now, I picked up the first envelope and slipped out the crisp, white pages just as cautiously, so as not to crease or despoil the edges; with rapidly beating heart, I unfolded them and gave myself over to my treat. The letters were, of course, written in French. I had, while in Belgium, developed a certain level of prowess in that language; since I left that country, I had committed myself to reading a half page of a French newspaper every day, to keep alive my skills. Now, I took my time, slowly savouring each and every word, one epistle at a time, until I had read all five. When I was through, I tied and wrapped them as before, replaced them in their box, and returned them to their hiding place.

Diary, you may ask: what did these letters contain, that caused me to await them with such fervent anticipation, and peruse them over and over again with such eagerness? Were they Shakespearean in their might and brilliance? Were they akin to Byron, the outpourings of a tortured, poetic soul? Hardly. They were simply good-natured letters, written in a benignant mood, sharing news of people we both knew and imparting sage counsel. And yet to me, they seemed the elixir of a divined vintage; a draught which Hebe might provide, and the very gods approve. They nourished my soul; they gave me vital comfort. When that comfort was withdrawn—as the months ticked by, and one season followed another, without a word from him—I was tormented exceedingly, locked like the letters in my drawer in a state of stasis from which there was no escape.

What had I done to deserve this silence? After that night in the garden—after all that he had said, and all that had happened—it seemed impossible that he had forgotten me; and yet it seemed that he wanted me to forget him.

People who have undergone bereavement often gather together and stash away mementos of their dearly departed; it is not supportable to be stabbed to the heart each moment by sharp revival of regret. As such, I had stowed his letters out of sight, and had tried to stop reading them. For months, I had forbidden myself the pleasure of speaking about him, even to Emily, the only person in my household who knew him.

Oh! The folly of the human heart! If only we could choose, through prudence and discernment, the recipient of our admiration. It was different with corporal afflictions, I thought, like the blindness from which papa suffered; in such cases, we were sadly compelled to make all those who surrounded us sharers in our anguish. The troubles of the *soul*, however, *should* and *must* be kept hidden; I could not speak of my secret to any one, not even my family. They must believe that I felt—and *had* felt—only friendship for my master; that I merely held him in the highest esteem as my teacher, and nothing more.

For Monsieur Héger was married, and had been married the entire time that I had known him in Brussels.

Four

For some time, I had been desirous of a change of scenery from Haworth, if only for a brief respite. My sisters convinced me that, with Anne's return, there were now two of them to assist papa; and so I ought to avail myself of a long-standing invitation to visit my oldest and dearest friend, Ellen Nussey.

I had known Ellen since I was fourteen years of age. We were faithful correspondents, exchanged frequent visits, and had taken several pleasant holidays together. Ellen currently lived with her mother and unmarried siblings at a house called Brookroyd in Birstall, about twenty miles distant. It was not, however, to Brookroyd that I was now directed, but to Hathersage: a small village in the Derbyshire Peak District near Sheffield, a place I had never seen. Ellen had been at Hathersage the past few months supervising alterations to the vicarage as a favour for her brother Henry, a serious-minded clergyman who had recently found himself a bride.

On the second of July, I corded up my trunk and sent it with the carrier to the train station. Early the next morning, my sisters walked with me to Keighley to see me off on the first leg of

my journey, to Leeds. With great excitement, I boarded the locomotive, wherein I was fortunate enough to secure a window
seat. My own place of residence being so remote, and every field,
hill, and valley so familiar, I always found great pleasure in looking out, as I travelled, at the many and varied scenes passing by:
in imagining who might live in that quaint farmhouse, or what
fascinating landscapes might lie on the other side of that pale,
distant mountain.

On this excursion, however, as I relaxed into my seat, jostled
and lulled by the movement of the train, instead of focusing on
the vistas spread out before me, I found myself staring at my
own countenance in the window, which was reflected back to
me against the shadowy backdrop of the misty day. I saw before
me a mouth too wide, a nose too large, and a forehead too high,
all set in a complexion that was too ruddy; the only redeeming
feature, if there was one, were the soft brown eyes. As I stared,
the stinging remark which Mr. Nicholls had recently made came
back to me:

The words, gentlemen, of an ugly old maid.

The statement haunted me. I had been called ugly only once
before, a long time ago; it had been, in fact, on the day I first met
Ellen Nussey—the very friend I was travelling to see. I could
laugh about the incident now; but then, it was no laughing matter. As I sat back in my seat, my thoughts drifted away to that
other time and place, some fourteen years earlier: when I was a
lonely new arrival at Roe Head boarding school—an establishment which was to for ever change my life in innumerable, unexpected ways.

It was a stark, grey day in early January, 1831, when I first
learned that I was to be sent away to Roe Head School. I was
adamantly opposed to the idea of going to school at all—and
no wonder. For years I had taken charge of my own studies,
and worked at my own pace at home; the prospect of giving
up that delicious freedom, and of being separated from my
loved ones, filled me with grief. Far more grievous, however,

were the harrowing memories of the last school I had attended, when I was eight years old—the Clergy Daughters' School at Cowan Bridge—a truly horrifying place, whose tenure had resulted in a tragedy of such enormous proportions, that it haunted my family to this day. My father, who I think never quite forgave himself for that catastrophe, insisted that this school would be different.

"Roe Head is a wonderful establishment," he assured me, as we sat by the hearth in his study with my aunt Elizabeth Branwell, who was busily knitting a sweater. "It's a brand-new school on the outskirts of Mirfield, not twenty miles from Haworth. They take only ten pupils, who all live in a fine old house which has just been acquired for that purpose. I can only afford to send one of you girls at a time; as the eldest, you'll be the first."

"But papa," said I, stunned by this unexpected news, and fighting back the sudden threat of tears, "I enjoy a wide-ranging education at home. Why must I leave?"

"You are nearly fifteen years old, Charlotte. I have kept you at home long enough," papa insisted.

"You must be equipped to earn your own living as a teacher or a governess, in case you do not marry," added Aunt Branwell. A very small, antiquated lady, my mother's sister had reluctantly but dutifully removed from Penzance to Haworth after my mother's death to care for us children. As always, she wore a false front of light auburn curls over her forehead, held in place by a white cap large enough for half a dozen of the caps in fashion at the time. Beneath her voluminous, dark silk skirts peeked the pattens[12] which she wore when downstairs to protect her feet from the cold stone floors of the parsonage. A practical and disciplined woman, Aunt Branwell had for years managed our household with skill and precision, if not great affection, overseeing

---

[12] Thick wooden clogs with metal straps, normally only worn outside; they slipped over a lady's delicate shoes to protect them from poor weather.

our lessons and household chores and teaching us to sew, while often wistfully recalling the warmer climate of her beloved Cornwall, and the social pleasures she had enjoyed there. My father enjoyed their frequent, lively intellectual discussions; my sisters and I respected and appreciated her; my brother loved her as the mother we longed for but did not have.

"There are accomplishments a young lady must possess, Charlotte," Aunt Branwell continued, "further studies in language, music, and deportment, for example—and other subjects which your father and I are not qualified to teach, which will be of importance to a future employer."

I burst into tears now, too miserable to speak.

"Don't look upon this as the end of the world, Charlotte," said Aunt Branwell. "You've spent nearly all your life in this one house. This school will be good for you."

"You'll see: you'll learn new things," said papa, leaning forward and squeezing my hand with affection. "You'll make new friends. You might even grow to like it."

I saw no prospect of my father's prediction coming true on that bitterly cold day two weeks later, the 17th of January, as I made the long and bumpy journey to Roe Head School. A hired gig being too dear, I was conveyed to my destination in the back of a slow-moving covered cart, of the kind used to deliver produce to the main centres on market days. When at last I arrived, stiff-legged, nauseous, and frozen, in the fading light of that wintry afternoon, I was prepared to dislike my new home on sight; to my surprise, I could not help but be impressed. The grand, three-storeyed house of grey stone had an attractive double-bowed frontage; it was situated atop a hill with wide, sloping lawns to the front, and surrounded on both sides by gardens which, I imagined, would be lovely in spring; and its high position offered commanding views of the woods, the river valley, and the distant village of Huddersfield.

As I was admitted into the oak-panelled entrance-hall, however, and gave my name and cloak to a waiting servant, I overheard three girls (each dressed *à la mode* and stylishly coiffed) whispering about me in a nearby doorway—and my doubts and fears instantly returned.

"She looks so old and shriveled, like a little old woman," said the first girl.

"Look at her hair, it is all a frizzle," whispered another.

"Her dress is so old-fashioned!" cried a third, to which they all laughed.

My face grew hot, and I wrapped my thin arms around me, as if that act could somehow shield from view the sight of my old, shabby, dark green stuff dress. I was far more mortified, however, by their comments about my appearance. I was, at the time, still as small as a child and exceedingly thin, with tiny hands and feet. I was too proud to wear spectacles (an affectation I did not overcome for several years), and so short-sighted that I squinted to perceive anything not placed directly under my nose. My hair was dry and screwed up in a mass of tight curls— the result, although I did not then understand it, of an overzealous practice of tying it up too tightly at night. Looking back, I realise that I was at a disadvantage from the other girls, having come from a motherless household where little or no attention was paid to outward appearances.

My heart pounding with embarrassment, I followed the servant—a neat-looking girl of perhaps eighteen years of age, with a sympathetic smile—who led me up a fine oak staircase to the galleried first floor. As we entered the room which I was to share with two other girls, I gasped with delight. It was three times the size of my own chamber at home, furnished with a mahogany dresser and wardrobe and two comfortable-looking beds, and the large windows, hung with floor-length drapes, overlooked a stretch of wintry garden. Papa was right about one thing, I thought: this was nothing at all like the vast, dismal dormitories at the Clergy Daughters' School; as to whether or not I would fit in with the students here, *that* was another question.

"There still be one more girl t' come, an' she'll be your bed-fellow," the servant explained, "but she's not expected till next week. Th' other bed belongs t' Miss Amelia Walker, whose family paid extry so she might have a bed all t' herself."

I knew of Amelia Walker, although I had never met her. She was the niece of Mrs. Atkinson, my Godmother, who had first suggested this establishment to papa. I thanked the servant, declined her offer of food and drink, and she withdrew. As I unpacked my trunk and hung my things in the wardrobe, I could not help but feel a discomfited pang when I compared my few, homely articles of clothing to the beautiful, brightly-coloured frocks and the rich, dark velvet cloak hanging within. With a sigh, I changed into my best Sunday frock—knowing full well that it would make no better impression on my critics than had the first, for it was just as plain, and equally as old—and then made my way downstairs to the schoolroom, where I had been told to present myself.

The schoolroom was large, high-ceilinged, and entirely panelled in oak, with bookcases lining one wall, and a bow-window on the opposite side overlooking the expansive front lawns. In the centre of the room stood a long table covered with a crimson cloth, where four teachers and eight pupils were engaged in study. As I entered, all heads swivelled in my direction, and I found myself the silent, uncomfortable object of their scrutiny.

At the head of the room, at an ornate writing-desk, sat a short, stout woman of perhaps forty years of age, clad in a cream-coloured, embroidered dress. I knew her at once from papa's description; this must be Miss Margaret Wooler, the owner and headmistress of the school.

"Good-afternoon and welcome, Miss Brontë," said she, rising gracefully from her chair and introducing herself. Miss Wooler was not what I would call handsome; but with her hair plaited like a coronet around her head, and long ringlets falling to her shoulders, she projected the quiet and imposing dignity of a lady abbess. There followed a brief introduction to the other teachers, all of whom were Miss Wooler's sisters, and to the girls, who looked to be my age or a year or two younger. As I struggled to assimilate all this new information, the girls went back to their lessons, and Miss Wooler bade me to sit down opposite her at her desk.

"It is my duty to determine your position in the school, Miss Brontë," said Miss Wooler in a low tone, "with an oral examination. Do not worry if you cannot answer every question. This will simply give me an idea of the breadth of your education."

She then proceeded to ask me a long series of intimidating and sometimes baffling questions, covering a wide variety of subjects. It seemed as if the quiz would never end; when it did, Miss Wooler said, "Well, Miss Brontë. You show remarkable awareness and comprehension of history and the works of literature, some knowledge of French, and an excellent aptitude in mathematics. However, you are deficient in several other subjects—on the theory of grammar in particular—and you appear to possess very little knowledge of geography. Although your age places you among the senior girls, I am afraid I will have to place you at the junior table until you catch up with your contemporaries."

This wound to my pride, coming on a day which had already been marked by so much heartache, was too much to bear; I immediately burst into tears. As I shook with sobs, Miss Wooler grew quiet; I sensed that she was observing me.

"Would it upset you so much, Miss Brontë, to sit with the lower class?"

"It would. Please, *please*, Miss Wooler, let me sit with girls my own age."

"All right. I will admit you to the senior class on one condition: that you complete some private reading and additional studies in your free time."

"Oh! Thank you, Miss Wooler! I am quite accustomed to private study. I will apply myself diligently, I promise."

"I am sure you will," replied Miss Wooler with a kind smile.

Later that evening, as I wearily entered my room to prepare for bed, I became acquainted with my roommate for the first time. Miss Amelia Walker was tall, beautiful, and fair-haired; she was also one of the three girls who had made fun of me upon my arrival; and she was wearing the loveliest, snowiest white night-shirt I had ever seen. I set down my candle beside hers on the dresser (each pupil was supplied with her very own candle and holder; quite a luxury) and undressed in silence. Amelia hung her exquisite pink silk frock in the wardrobe, and, with a decisive shove, moved all her garments as far down the rod as possible from mine. "Do not touch my things," warned she imperiously. "They are all new, and I do not wish to have them spoiled. Also: never sit on my bed. I am very particular about that."

"I do not see how any contact with me or my clothing could spoil your things," I replied, as I hung up my dress.

She glanced at me. "What a strange manner of speaking you have. Are you from Ireland?"

"No. My father was from Ireland. I am from Haworth. Your aunt Atkinson is my Godmother."

"Oh! Je comprends. Vous êtes *cette* Charlotte,"[13] declared she in an affected manner, as if speaking French was the world's loftiest accomplishment. She retrieved a box of curl papers from the dresser and sat down upon her bed; we each quickly tied up our hair. "My father is a squire. He says the Irish are a very lowly race. You must be very poor," she added, with a pitying glance at my night-shirt, which I had made myself, and mended any number of times. "Your *vêtements*[14] are so old."

"We are not nearly so poor as others in our parish. We have enough to eat, and fuel for the fire, and plenty of good books to read."

"Books!" Amelia scoffed. "Who cares how many books you have? You cannot *wear* books!" Presently, she climbed beneath her quilt, and said: "You may blow out the light."

Although the candles were much closer to her bed than mine, I dutifully extinguished them and felt my way through the inky

---

[13] I understand. You are *that* Charlotte.

[14] Clothing.

darkness back to my own bed. In spite of my exhaustion, however, I found no great refuge there. It was the first time I had ever occupied a bed all by myself; Emily had been my bed-fellow as far back as I could remember, and the empty expanse between the frigid sheets felt strange and frightening. In consequence, I lay wide awake into the wee hours, trying not to think about how many long months it would be before I saw my beloved family again, and pondering what the next day would bring.

To my surprise, the Roe Head School regime turned out to be very agreeable. The teaching methods catered to the individual talents and abilities of each pupil. When we were ready with our lessons, we came to Miss Wooler to recite them. She had a remarkable knack for making us interested in whatever we had to learn; she taught us to think and analyse and appreciate; and she awakened in me an even greater thirst for knowledge than I had yet possessed. Unlike my previous school—where the food had been scant or inedible—the meals at Roe Head were well prepared and in plentiful supply. Miss Wooler demonstrated a high regard for our physical well-being in general, allowing sufficient time for rest and play, and insisting that daily walks and outdoor games were essential to our health.

Unfortunately, I had no experience with outdoor games. On a frosty afternoon the day after my arrival, while the other girls were engaged in a game called "French and English,"[15] I retreated to the safety of a great, leafless tree on the frozen lawn, where I stood perusing Lindley Murray's *English Grammar*. After some time thus employed, I heard a voice at my elbow.

"Why do you hold that book so close to your nose? Do you need spectacles?"

"No," I said indignantly, turning to face the girl addressing me. "I can see just fine."

---

[15] "French and English" was a popular nineteenth-century tug-of-war game without a rope, in which two lines of children, holding each other around the waist, pulled in opposite directions.

"I did not mean to offend you. Your name is Charlotte, is it not?"

"Yes. You are Mary Taylor, and you have a younger sister here called Martha."

"You have a good memory." Mary, who I discovered was ten months younger than I, was astonishingly pretty, with intelligent eyes, a perfect complexion, and dark, silky hair. I could not help but notice, however—although her clothing was nicer than anything I owned—she was not as well dressed as the other pupils (a result, I later learned, of her father's bankruptcy over an army contract.) Mary's red frock had short sleeves and a low neck, a style then worn only by younger girls; her gloves had been stitched all over for longer wear; and her dark blue cloth coat was outgrown and far too short. The ensemble gave her a rather childish appearance; but it did not appear to bother her in the least, and it only served to put *me* at greater ease.

"Come join us, we are going to play ball," said Mary.

"Thank you, but I do not play ball."

"What do you mean? Every one plays ball."

"Not I. I would much prefer to read."

Before I could elaborate further, the other girls called urgently for us to join in their new game. "Come on," urged Mary, holding out her gloved hand to me. "Hannah stayed in with a cold, and we need another girl on our side."

It seemed that I had no recourse but to comply. Setting down my book, I took Mary's hand, and we raced across the lawn to where the other six girls were waiting. They named their game of preference; I admitted that I had never played; a hurried explanation ensued; suddenly the action began. I ran along with the others and struggled to take part. When the ball was thrown in my direction, however, my clumsy attempts to catch it were all in vain.

"What*ever* is the matter with you, Irish?" exclaimed a plump, dark-haired girl called Leah Brooke, whose velvet cloak and black beaver bonnet proclaimed her the daughter of a wealthy family. "Are you blind, or just an idiot?"

"I told you, I do not know how to play."

"Don't they play ball in Ireland?" teased Amelia.

"I am not from Ireland!" I cried.

"She needs spectacles," ventured Mary. "That is the problem. She cannot see the ball."

"Stand out then, Irish!" cried Leah. "We will do better without you."

Mortified by my own inadequacy, yet relieved at my escape, I fled the field and retreated to my quiet spot by the tree, where I read my book for the remainder of the hour.

No one asked me to join in games again. The rest of the week, I applied myself to my studies. The teachers were attentive and patient, but a group of girls, led by Leah and Amelia, took advantage of every opportunity to make fun of me, my accent, my appearance, and my ignorance in class. When I was unable to distinguish between an article and a substantive, or to name some obscure river in Africa, a chorus of snickers went around the room. Oh! How I longed to tell them that, although I might not be well versed in a study of grammar or the globe, I had created my very own kingdom in deepest darkest Africa, and had written scores of stories, essays, and poems; but I did not dare reveal this, for fear they would scorn me even more.

One afternoon, eight days after my arrival, matters came to a head. The girls were gathered in the entry way, chattering gaily as they donned their cloaks and bonnets for the play hour. I passed by, en route to the schoolroom with a book, when Amelia announced with a prideful smile, "Have you heard, Charlotte? You are *last* on the list!"

"What list?" I asked.

"We have taken a vote as to who is the prettiest girl in the school. Mary is first. *I* am second. And *you* are last."

I froze in stunned dismay at this newest evidence of their cruelty. Mary added matter-of-factly: "Do not be upset, Charlotte. Some one has to be last. It is not your fault that you are so very ugly."

Ugly? Was I truly *ugly*? It was the first time in my life that any one had described me thus; I was so mortified, I wanted to die. I saw Mary's eyes widen, as if surprised by my reaction, as I fled from the room.

The laughter of the other girls followed me as I darted into the schoolroom, where I threw myself onto the floor before the bow window and wept. Never had I felt so utterly alone, so deeply ashamed, and so thoroughly inadequate. My desolation in that strange place was now complete; I believe I lay there, weeping from the depths of my soul, for a good half-hour.

At length, I realised that some one had entered the room. I dried my eyes and rose, shrinking back against the window, hoping to avoid detection. From the corner of my vision, I observed a girl of medium height in a pale green dress standing by the bookcase—a new-comer. I wondered if she was the pupil who was to share my bed.

"What is the matter?" the girl asked gently, as she joined me by the window.

I turned away in silence, embarrassed to have been discovered at such a private moment.

"Why were you crying?" the girl persisted.

Clearly she was not going away. "I am just homesick," I answered begrudgingly.

"Oh! Well, *I* have only just arrived. Next week it will be your turn to comfort *me,* for I shall surely be quite homesick by then."

The sweetness and sympathy in her voice had an immediate effect; I turned and looked at her fully for the first time. She was very pretty, with a pale complexion, docile brown eyes, and dark brown hair that fell in soft curls to just below her chin. As she sat down on the cushioned window-seat and motioned for me to join her, she said, "My name is Ellen Nussey."

I introduced myself. I learned in short order that Ellen was the youngest of twelve children; that she was almost exactly a year younger than I; and that she lived just a few miles away. "Last year, I attended the Moravian Ladies' Academy a mile from home, but that school has not been the same since the Reverend Grimes departed, so mama sent me here."

"You have a mother?" I said with envy.

"Of course. Don't you?" When I shook my head, Ellen took my hands in hers, and said softly, "I am so sorry. I cannot imagine having no mother, but I know what it is like to lose a parent. My papa died five years ago. I miss him dearly." We shared a silent, quivering smile, Ellen's gaze reflecting a deep and genuine empathy. I did not know it then, but one of the greatest and most enduring friendships of my life had just begun.

At first, I was not sure I would love Ellen, as we were different in many essential ways. Ellen was a strict Calvinist, devoted to the rigid religious doctrines I had learned to abhor at the Clergy Daughters' School, and unquestioning in her conformity to social and moral codes of behaviour. I, on the other hand, found myself questioning everything on a daily basis and struggling to behave within the limits that seemed to be expected of a clergyman's daughter. Moreover, although Ellen was intelligent and conscientious, she was not intellectual; she read, but admitted that she did not comprehend or seek any deeper meaning in a work, which was so important to me. She was calm by nature, whereas I was passionate and romantic. On several occasions, I was obliged to deprive her of her book when she attempted, without any sense of the dramatic, to haltingly read aloud passages by Shakespeare or Wordsworth.

Ellen was, however, a good, true, and faithful friend, and a sympathetic listener. She soon became a welcome presence in my bedroom, serving as a buffer between myself and the uncertain temper and affected mannerisms of Amelia. Affection, which began as a germ, became a sapling, then a strong tree; sharing beds with Ellen—my dearest "Nell," as I came to call her—I was able to enjoy a calm sleep every night.

A few weeks later, another friendship began in an unexpected quarter. It was twilight; while my school-mates chatted merrily around the fire in the schoolroom, I knelt close to the window with a book, making use of every last ray of daylight to continue my studies.

"I thought, when first we met, that you could not see well," observed Mary Taylor, as she took a seat on the floor beside me, "but I was wrong. Not only can you *see,* Charlotte Brontë, it appears that you can see in the dark."

Mary had been avoiding me ever since the day of Ellen's arrival; perhaps, I thought, she felt remorse for the brusque manner in which she had called me ugly. Now, I turned to find her gazing at me with twinkling eyes. "There is still enough light to read by—but only just," I admitted. We both laughed.

"We have been studying all day, and will continue after supper. Can't you take a little while to rest, as we do?"

"I would rather not. Every day that I am here, I am an object of expense to those at home. I feel a responsibility to learn, to use every opportunity to attain the knowledge which will fit me to one day find employment."

"It *is* important, my father says, that all women find a way to earn their own living," Mary agreed. She glanced over my shoulder at the book I was reading. "Is that the poem we are to memorize? Oh! How I dislike that poem! I do not understand a word of it."

The poem was *The Rime of the Ancient Mariner.* "I have known this entire piece by heart since I was a child. We have only been given a small part to learn. Would you like me to explain it to you?"

"I would."

I spent the remainder of the hour explaining the poem to Mary, and reciting its most dramatic and eloquent stanzas. When I had finished, Mary nodded with satisfaction, and said, "It does sound far more interesting when you explain it. You are a most intriguing person, Charlotte Brontë. There is more to you than meets the eye."

"I would *hope* that to be true, particularly since that which meets the eye is so *displeasing.*"

Mary blushed and fell silent for a moment. "I am very sorry, Charlotte, for what I said all those weeks ago. I often speak without thinking; my sister Martha is just the same. We have been taught to say what is on our minds—but I did not mean to be unkind. Will you forgive me?"

She did not, I noticed, imply that her remark had been untruthful, or that she had only been teasing; but her sincerely apologetic tone and manner did much to appease my injured pride. "I forgive you."

Mary smiled. "I am glad. Now we will be friends."

That night, an event of some magnitude occurred, which dramatically and permanently altered my fortunes. A storm began to brew at sundown; by bedtime, the snow was swirling outside our windows in great flurried gusts, and the howling wind made the very house groan. Amelia, Ellen, and I had just changed into our night-shirts and completed our *toilettes,* when an even eerier sound rent the air: a high-pitched wail, which we determined to be of human origin.

"Some one is crying," said I, listening at the wall, "and it seems to be issuing from the chamber next door."

The weeping continued, and was soon accompanied by an exchange of dialogue that we could not decipher. Ellen and I decided to investigate. I grabbed a candle; Amelia, protesting that she did not wish to be left alone, quickly joined us. We padded softly into the corridor and knocked at the door of the adjacent room. Presently, a girl called Hannah opened the door and glanced out, holding her own candle aloft. "Yes?" Hannah was a serious, thin girl who had been ill for the past fortnight, and was only recently recovered.

"We heard some one crying," said Ellen. "Is everything all right?"

"It is Susan. I think she is afraid of the snowstorm."

"Perhaps we can comfort her," I offered.

"Do as you wish," said Hannah, leaving the door ajar as she turned back into the room. "We have tried everything."

The three of us entered. The chamber, which was similar to ours, housed four girls. Leah Brooke and her sister Maria occupied the bed on one side of the room. Amelia, Ellen, and I crossed to the other bed, where, in the flickering candlelight, I perceived a lump of human size beneath the quilt. "Susan," I intoned softly.

"Who is that?" came a small, muffled voice.

"It is Charlotte Brontë. We heard you crying. You need not be afraid of the storm. It is only the snow and the eaves and the wind talking to each other."

The quilt was suddenly thrown back, and its sturdy, red-haired, thirteen-year-old occupant sat up, a look of great distress on her tear-stained face. "I am not *afraid*. Mama says that a snowstorm is a gift from God, for it carpets the world afresh in sparkling white." With this statement, Susan's face crumpled anew, and she burst into fresh tears.

"If you are not afraid, then what is wrong?" inquired Ellen.

"Whenever it snowed," explained Susan tearfully, "mama and I always watched it together at the window. Or if it was late at night, and the storm was very fierce, she would sit on my bed and tell me a story. Oh! How far I am from home! How I miss mama!"

"We all miss our mothers," replied Leah Brooke crossly from her bed, "but there is no point in carrying on so."

"I offered to borrow a book from the schoolroom and read to her," said Hannah with an offended sniff, "but she was not keen on *that* notion."

"I would rather listen to nails on a slate," wailed Susan, "than to hear your pathetic attempt to read a story."

I had heard Hannah read aloud in class, and could not disagree with Susan's assessment of her abilities. Without stopping to think, I blurted, "I could tell you a story." No sooner had I uttered the words, than I wished I could retract them. Every one turned to me with sudden interest; my cheeks grew warm. Quickly, I added, "My brother and sisters and I made up stories all the time, to entertain each other."

"Did you?" asked Susan, as she wiped the tears from her face. "Are they good stories?"

"You must be the judge of that."

"Well, go on then." Susan moved back up against the head-board and smoothed the quilt, making room for me on her bed. "Tell me one."

My stomach fluttered as I sat down. I glanced at the others. "Shall I really?"

"I do not mind, if it will get her to stop whining," replied Leah, with a corroborating nod from her sister.

"This is stupid!" sneered Amelia. "We are too old for a bed-time story."

"You may leave if you do not wish to listen," said Ellen, curling up beside Maria Brooke.

Amelia hesitated, then sank down reluctantly on a nearby chair. All at once, our three other school-mates strode into the room. "What is going on?" asked Mary Taylor, who was wrapped in a quilt, her dark hair (as with most of us) tied up for the night in curls.

"Charlotte is going to tell us a story," answered Hannah.

"Oh! How lovely!" Mary spread her quilt on the floor and sat down. She was joined by Cecilia Allison and Mary's boisterous, twelve-year-old sister Martha, who cried, "I love stories!"

My heart began to hammer with distress. What ever had compelled me to speak so rashly? The tales that my siblings and I had invented while traipsing across the moors, or gathered around the fire of an evening, were private stories, concocted for our own amusement; we had never shared them with any one. The girls were looking at me expectantly, however; if I did not follow through with a tale of some interest, I knew I should never live it down. It would be best, I decided, to invent a brand-new story, tailored to the tastes of this audience. Taking a deep breath to still my nerves, I began, in a low, dramatic tone:

"Long, long ago, in a distant kingdom, a widowed Duke lived with his only daughter in a great, turreted castle, built on a towering cliff high above the sea. The young lady's name was

Emily. She was eighteen years of age, and no wild rose bloom-
ing in solitude ever equalled in loveliness this gentle flower of
the forest."

A stillness descended on the room. Every one was listening
with interest; every one, I noticed, except Amelia. I went on:
"Emily was not only beautiful, but accomplished. She could play
the harp; she could read and speak three languages; she was a
skilled artist and wrote delightful poetry; and she was known to
walk many miles through any kind of weather to help a family in
need."

"She sounds too perfect to live," said Amelia scornfully.

"*Do* be quiet," cried Susan. To me she said: "Please go on."

"Emily's goodness, intelligence, and beauty caught the attention of a handsome young gentleman from a neighbouring county,
the Marquis of Belvedere, whose name was William. They met;
they fell in love; and their wedding date was set. The night before the wedding, Emily fell asleep in a state of blissful anticipation, dreaming of the event the next day, and of a lifetime with
her beloved William. The rest of the castle and all the members
of the wedding party were also fast asleep, tucked into their respective beds. It seemed that nothing could disturb Emily's rest
or safety, or the happy couple's impending nuptials. But this was
not the case. For the truth—the terrible truth—was that Emily
was a somnambulist."

"A what?" asked Leah.

"A somnambulist," I repeated, to which Mary added, with a
thrilled edge to her voice:

"A sleep-walker!"

"Oh no!" exclaimed Susan, enthralled.

I had thoroughly warmed, by now, to the telling of my tale,
and found I was enjoying myself immensely. "Emily's father,
aware of this dangerous proclivity, had for many years posted a
nurse outside Emily's door, to ensure that she could never wander out at night. To-night, however, when Emily arose barefoot
from her bed and issued sound asleep from her chamber door,
her nurse—who had imbibed far too much wine at the dinner

party that evening—was sound asleep in her chair. Emily slipped past her down the long corridor, then climbed the stairs to the top of the castle's tallest tower, which was situated at the edge of a high cliff overlooking the sea. She reached a door leading to the tower roof, and opened it."

"The tower roof!" cried Hannah in alarm, the blood draining from her already pale face.

"As Emily ventured out," said I, "she was met by a blast of cold ocean wind; but even this did not wake her. She thought herself walking along a path in her favourite meadow, and smiled at the wind in her face as if it were but a refreshing gust of spring. Emily crossed to the low, crenellated wall which encircled the tower roof, and placed her hands upon it. The stone felt rough against her finger-tips, no different from the rocky crags she was accustomed to clambering over in the meadow with such ease. But Emily stood not in a meadow; she stood atop a battlement at cloud height, overlooking the surging sea. Beyond the wall was nothingness; just starry night, and a sheer drop to the waves which crashed against the rocks many hundreds of feet below."

I paused; my audience, I noted to my delight, were all wide-eyed and sitting forward in breathless anticipation, awaiting my next words.

"What did she do?" asked Amelia eagerly.

"As if in a trance," I went on, "Emily climbed up onto the narrow edge of the stone wall."

A chorus of alarmed gasps arose from the assembled girls.

"Emily stood still for a long moment atop the parapet, the wind whipping through her thin night-shirt and her long golden hair. In her mind's eye, she saw her beloved William standing ten yards distant, waiting for her with outstretched arms. 'William!' she whispered softly. 'I will come to you!'"

I rose and acted out the scene: "Emily then began to walk, one measured step at a time, each footfall landing with miraculous precision atop the notches of the battlement, unaware that one false movement, one slight waver, could lead to certain death."

"Oh!" cried Hannah in terror, her hand at her mouth.

"At the very moment that Emily was making this perilous journey, William, who was sleeping in a chamber far across the castle courtyard, awakened with a start, certain he had heard Emily calling to him. Whence had her voice issued? Following some impulse he could not explain, William went to the window. The sight that awaited his eyes made him gasp with terror. Emily, dressed like a wraith in flowing white, was traipsing along the circular parapet of the highest tower. Worse yet, he saw that dead ahead of her, the stone ledge—damaged by harsh sea-winds—was broken and crumbling."

Another chorus of alarmed cries from my listeners met this pronouncement.

"Emily's foot touched down," I continued ominously. "Suddenly the wall trembled; the mortar gave way. 'Emily!' cried William. The young lady wavered, teetering back and forth on the edge of nothingness, her arms reaching out to grab for some support, but none was there!"

A piercing shriek suddenly split the air; I smiled, pleased that my story could produce so stimulating an effect. But when I glanced in the direction of the sound, my smile vanished: for my listeners were all staring at Hannah, who lay gasping and trembling violently on the bed, her eyes rolled back into her head, her hands at her heart.

"She is having a fit!" exclaimed Mary.

"Call Miss Wooler!" said I, in great distress.

Miss Wooler was immediately summoned; a doctor was called in; Hannah was deemed to be suffering from violent palpitations and given a sedative of some kind; our entire party was sternly lectured about talking after hours and summarily dispatched to bed.

So filled with remorse was I at having been the cause of Hannah's seizure, that I barely slept that night. I could not help imagining the horrifying consequences that might have ensued, had her attack proved fatal, and I fully expected to receive a round of distressing reprimands from my school-mates and teachers at breakfast. However, as I wearily took my seat at the dining-table the next morning (Hannah was still confined to bed, and the teachers had yet to join us), to my surprise, I encountered the opposite reaction.

"That was *quite* a performance last night," smiled Mary, as she sat down beside me.

"I have never heard such a thrilling story!" exclaimed Susan, beaming. "I forgot all about being homesick."

"I thought I was going to die of fright, just listening to it!" cried Martha Taylor with enthusiasm.

"Hannah nearly *did* die of fright," Amelia pointed out acerbically.

"That was not Charlotte's fault," said Ellen.

"Next time," said Leah, smiling at me (the first time Leah had ever smiled in my direction, and this was quite an approving and appreciative smile), "we will meet in *Charlotte's* room, and Hannah can stay behind."

"There will not be a next time," I insisted. "Miss Wooler was quite put out. We do not want to be fined for late-night talking."

"Then we will just have to do our talking *earlier*," said Martha.

"Or be careful not to get caught," added Mary—a statement met by laughter and a lively chorus of agreement.

Susan glanced cautiously towards the doorway; there was, as yet, no sign of the teaching staff. In a conspiratorial tone, she said, "Tell us how the story ends."

"Charlotte," gasped Ellen, worried, "you *dare not* answer."

"Miss Wooler did not say anything against talking at *breakfast*," insisted Martha.

"Yes, yes!" cried Leah. "How does it end?"

Such a round of eager questions followed—"Did Emily fall?" "Did William save her?" "Did she marry?"—that I could not help but smile. I deemed it safe to reply.

"What happened is this: When William saw Emily atop the tower, he called out her name. Although it was far too great a distance for his voice to reach her, particularly over the howling wind, somehow Emily clearly heard his voice, and awoke with a start. Upon seeing where she was, Emily regained her footing, safely descended from the wall, and fled back to William, who raced to join her. They were wed the next day, and lived a long, happy life together, bearing five children, who were all perfect, beautiful, and extremely intelligent."

Susan sighed happily. "That is the perfect ending."[16]

From that day forward, my standing amongst the girls at Roe Head School was immeasurably and permanently improved. I was never again teased about my looks, my clothing, or my accent. I became accepted for who I was, even by Amelia. Ellen and Mary became my closest friends, and those girls who had once regarded me with disdain, now seemed to view me with new-found respect, and often came to me for help and advice with their studies.

As the term continued, I was persuaded on many occasions—despite the danger to our fortunes and reputations—to tell stories after hours. In an effort to avoid detection, we gathered in a far corner of my room by the light of a single candle, and spoke in hushed tones. Hannah conquered her timidity and joined us. Sometimes I spun tales aloud; other times, we exchanged secrets, shared treasured memories, or expressed our hopes and dreams for the future. On the one occasion that we were assessed a fine for "talking after hours," my conspirators and I privately admitted that we did not mind being caught. It had been worth it; and it was a thrill to have done something, for once in our lives, that was against the rules.

I applied myself with such devotion to my studies at Roe Head, that I completed the course of instruction in only eighteen months. There was only one subject in which, although I

---

[16] This mystical "call and answer" theme between lovers appeared frequently in Charlotte's juvenilia, and was famously employed in a crucial scene between Jane and Mr. Rochester in *Jane Eyre*.

loved it, I could not excel: music. I had such small fingers that I could not span the keys of the piano, and I was so short-sighted that I had great difficulty reading the music; I was therefore permanently excused from that study. In all other subjects, however, I rose to the head of the class, competing with Mary and Ellen for the scholarship awards. By the time my tenure ended in late May 1832, I had been awarded the top honour—the Silver Medal for achievement—at the end of every term. I left Roe Head with pride in my accomplishments, a renewed faith in my own creative abilities, and friendships with three people which would last a lifetime: Mary Taylor, Margaret Wooler, and Ellen Nussey.

As the omnibus from Leeds pulled up at Sheffield on a July afternoon many years later, I caught sight of Ellen Nussey waiting at the roadside. Glimpsing her well-loved, familiar face and form, I felt a rush of affection. Although Ellen had grown a few inches taller since our school-days, and her figure was more fully developed, she was still just as pale and pretty as she had been the day we met; and as I stepped down from the conveyance into her embrace, she regarded me with the same affection in her docile brown eyes.

"My dearest Charlotte!"

"Nell! How good it is to see you."

"I prayed all morning that nothing would prevent your coming. How was your journey?"

"Uneventful—although the passing country-side was so magnificent, I was filled with longing to leap from the train and then the carriage, and to dash out into the undulating green meadows on foot."

"I am relieved that you restrained yourself; but Derbyshire *is* lovely country, is it not?" Ellen wore a becoming dress of yellow silk, modestly cut in the latest fashion; a matching ribbon adorned her bonnet, beneath which her soft brown hair was tidily arranged.

"I have missed you so, Nell, and longed for some excellent

gossip," I cried, as we climbed into the coach Ellen had hired, and I clasped her hands in mine.

"As have I. What news is there from Haworth? How is Anne?"

"Fine, I think, and happy to be home."

"What do you think of your new curate?"

"Oh! Let us not spoil the day by talking of Mr. Nicholls."

"Why? You do not like him?"

"I do not, and never shall. I wish papa had never hired him."

"What has Mr. Nicholls done, to earn such a violent dislike?"

I knew, were I to inform Ellen about the unflattering remark Mr. Nicholls had made about me, I would be met with the same reprimand regarding the importance of inner versus outer beauty which my sisters had intoned. Being in no mood for this lecture, I simply said, "Mr. Nicholls is a Puseyite, and too narrow-minded for my taste. But enough about him! Tell me about you, Nell. I wish to know everything that has happened since you got here!"

Five

*C*hattering like magpies, we drove the few miles to Ellen's brother's new home. Hathersage turned out to be a tiny village surrounded by farms and inhabited by workers in local needle factories. Like Haworth, it consisted of a cluster of stone cottages that lined a steep road rising up to the church and vicarage: a pleasant, two-storeyed stone house not unlike our own, similarly situated atop an eminence.

"Please excuse the dust and disarray," said Ellen, as she showed me through the house, which was undergoing a major extension, with the addition of a large, bay-windowed drawing-room and a new bedroom above. "Every day there has been some new complication, the plasterers have a great deal more work to do, and the new furniture has yet to arrive; but Henry says that he and his wife will come in four weeks' time, whether or not we are ready for them."

"It all looks very grand. I am certain the newly-weds will be delighted with the place, and grateful to you for taking on this burden."

After tea, Ellen suggested a rest, but I admitted that after a long day of sitting, I was anxious to explore the beauties of the region. We donned our bonnets and gloves once more and left forthwith to take a stroll in the cool of early evening. Leaving the house, we ambled down a path which led through a wide, green field; I caught my breath in wonder and delight at the surrounding landscape, which was far more magnificent than that of Haworth, comprised of poetically undulating low hills and valleys covered with pasture and woodland, which formed a dramatic contrast to the higher, distant slopes of the moors.

"How beautiful it is here!" I cried. "I am glad Henry gave up the idea of being a missionary. He would never have lasted two months in the Indian climate. He has done well for himself, in choosing this location."

"He has. I only hope he has done as well with his choice of bride."

"From your letters, this Miss Prescott—that is, *Mrs. Nussey*—" (for they had been married some weeks past) "sounds like a fine woman. She must be, if she fitted Henry's criteria, for we know he was very exacting in his search for a wife."

Ellen looked at me, perceived that I was teasing, and we both laughed. In fact, Henry—a dull, earnest young man—had made offers to a great many women over the past six years, and each time had been summarily rejected; I was the first person he had approached.

"You know," said Ellen with sudden wistfulness, "I often think about what might have been, had you accepted Henry's proposal all those years ago. We would be sisters now. I would see you on a regular basis; we might have even shared a house together."

"You would have soon tired of me, Nell, had we lived in such close proximity."

"I could never tire of you."

"Nor I of you," I declared truthfully, as I squeezed Ellen's hand, "but Henry and I did not suit. I barely knew him. I could not love him. And to propose by post! His letter simply informed me, without a word of flattery or cant, that the rectory where he resided was too large for one person, and would I consider looking after it as his wife?[17] This is not, you must admit, the manner in which a woman dreams of receiving an offer of marriage. To think it has happened to me twice!"

"That is right! Did you not once receive an offer from a total stranger?"

"I did: a young visiting Irish clergyman named Mr. Pryce. He came to tea one afternoon, spent perhaps two hours in my company, and wrote the next day to propose. I have heard of love at first sight, but that did beat all! Coming as it did, just five months after your brother's offer, it occasioned much teasing from my brother and sisters."

We laughed, and walked on in silence for some moments, taking in the breathtaking view of the Derbyshire country-side. Insects buzzed; sheep baaahed; birds twittered; wildflowers bloomed in abundant glory; and all about us was fragrant, green, and lush, bathed in the golden glow of the setting summer sun, in a pink and amber sky.

When I glanced again at Ellen, to my surprise, she looked downcast. "Is something wrong, Nell?"

"No. Yes." Ellen sighed. "I was thinking about Mr. Vincent."

"Oh." Mr. Vincent was the young man who had once loved Ellen deeply, and whose proposal *she* had refused. "You do not regret your choice in that affair, do you?"

"Sometimes I do. My family thought him entirely suitable."

"So they informed me, in numerous communications. As Mr. Vincent was a clergyman, and the eldest son of an eminent and wealthy surgeon, he did sound like your ideal counterpart."

"Perhaps in theory; but it took him *for ever* to get around to actually making me an offer. Oh! Charlotte, if only you could have seen him. He was so eccentric, and so shy and awkward; he

---

[17] Charlotte gave many of Henry Nussey's characteristics to the zealous, brooding minister St. John Rivers in *Jane Eyre*, including a most unromantic proposal.

could barely manage a coherent syllable in my presence. When I tried to imagine spending the rest of my life with him—and sharing my *bed* with him—it made me sick and anxious."

"Well then, you made the right decision," said I. "If I ever do marry, I must passionately adore my husband. I must be able to look up to him, to revere both his character and his intellect. He must have the soul of a poet, and the sense of a judge; he must be kind and considerate, esteemed by all who know him; a man who admires women and sees them as his equal; and he must be older than I."

"How old? Do you wish for some white-haired or bald-headed swain?"

"No thank you; but he must be at least thirty-five, with the sense of forty."

"The gentleman you just described is a tall order. Have you conjured him out of thin air, or is he based on any one in real life?"

I felt a blush cross my countenance; I had, I just realised, unwittingly described my Belgian master—a man Ellen knew very little about, and a relationship of which I had never spoken. "He is entirely a product of my imagination," said I quickly.

"Perhaps we will both be lucky, and find a suitable parson or curate among our acquaintances who fills the bill."

"Oh! I am convinced I could never be a *clergyman's* wife. My heart is too hot, and my thoughts too wild, romantic, and wandering, to suit a man of the cloth."

"Most of the eligible men we meet *are* clergymen. Whom else are you to marry, Charlotte, if not a member of the clergy?"

"No one, perhaps. To be honest, at our age, I think it highly unlikely that some model of male perfection is going to show up and offer us his hand. Even if such a man did exist, and even if he *did* appear, I probably should not want him. We will just be old maids together, Nell—and live very happily on our own."

"But if you do not marry, what will you do? If I remain single, I have my brothers to support me; whereas you—" Ellen broke off.

"Whereas my brother is perfectly useless," I finished for her. "Do not be afraid to say it, Nell; it is no secret. Branwell is a charming fellow, when he is sober; but he is unreliable, and he is no bread-winner. How he has managed to keep his position at Thorp Green for such a long time is a mystery to me." I sighed. "Papa, God bless him, will not live for ever. When I look to the future, I must look to myself. Mary Taylor told me years ago that every woman should and must be able to earn her own money, and she was right."

We were both a little in awe of Mary Taylor. Still the vibrant and independent soul she had been in our school days, Mary had studied in Belgium at the same time as I, although at a different school, and had travelled a great deal on the Continent. When it became clear to her that she would not marry, she decided to join her brother Waring in New Zealand, to help run his general store. She had set sail only a few months before.

"Have you heard any more from Mary?" asked Ellen.

"Not since her last letter. Imagine, writing from four degrees north of the equator, and living on board ship for so many months, with all the heat, sickness, hardships, and dangers that entails! Yet Mary's spirits seemed excellent."

"New Zealand. Can you imagine it? To go off to a new country—"

"—to a new *hemisphere*! What a grand adventure! To attempt something brand-new and unheard of—would it not be thrilling?"

Ellen shook her head. "No. I think Mary is very brave; but to leave England permanently—to choose to live one's entire life amongst foreigners, in a strange land—I would never wish it."

"Perhaps you are right," observed I, more soberly. "But—oh! I do so long for the *possibility* of change, Nell. I am twenty-nine years old, and I have done nothing yet with my life. I need to find an occupation, to become something better than I am. There must be some way for a proper Englishwoman to earn a living, without leaving home—or the country! I intend to find it some day, or perish in the attempt."

During my stay at Hathersage, Ellen—always a gregarious individual—filled our days with various and sundry adventures and many social calls, including tea with all the prominent families in the area. One of these calls, which made a deep and lasting impression on me, was a visit to North Lees Hall—an ancient, fifteenth-century gentleman's manor-house at Outseats, inhabited by the Eyre family.

North Lees Hall was an immense grey stone house standing three storeys high, with battlements and turrets round the roof-top that gave it a picturesque look. Farther off were quiet and lonely hills, which created such an illusion of seclusion that it seemed impossible to believe the village of Hathersage lay so nearby. The house was situated on spacious grounds, with a wide green lawn in front and a rookery behind, whose cawing tenants circled in the sky above as we drove up.

"Is it not a wonderful old house?" declared Ellen.

"It reminds me of Rydings," I replied.

The Rydings was Ellen's childhood home: a large, old Georgian house that belonged to her uncle, with a similarly battlemented roof and rookery; it also lay in a vast, landscaped parkland of centenarian trees, including chestnuts and some double-thorns. I had greatly admired the house and grounds during my many visits there.

Now, as we alighted from the carriage outside North Lees Hall, I was struck by the grand, foreboding aspect of the place, which seemed to hint at some great secret hidden within its walls. The interior was even more impressive than its hoary front. From the moment we were welcomed inside, I caught my breath in wonder, exclaiming over the gleaming oak panelling, the sumptuous velvet draperies, the splendid antique furnishings, and the massive oak staircase that rose to the galleries above.

The drawing-room was particularly elegant, ceiled with snowy mouldings of white grapes and vine leaves, the marble floors blanketed with white Turkey carpets brilliantly woven with garlands of flowers. It was in this room that the formidable Mrs. Mary Eyre, a white-haired widow splendidly attired in black satin, graciously received us for tea and cakes, with her three grown, unmarried daughters at her side. We sat on an assortment of crimson couches and ottomans, our images reflected back to us by large mirrors between the windows, which made the immense room appear doubly wide in size.

"The Eyres are a very old family," explained Mrs. Eyre as she sipped her tea. "In St. Michael's church, you will find brasses decorating the tombs of many an Eyre dating back to the fifteenth century. Some of the furniture in this house is very old as well."

I was particularly taken by a large black cabinet, which was painted with the heads of the apostles. When I asked about it, Mrs. Eyre said with pride, "We call that the Apostles Cupboard. It has been in the family for nigh on four hundred years."[18]

After tea, Mrs. Eyre's son George, a curly-haired lad of perhaps nineteen years of age, took us on a comprehensive tour of the house, ending with an ascent up a narrow flight of stairs to the battlemented rooftop, from which we enjoyed a sweeping vista of the hills and valleys beyond. So delighted was I by the view, that it was some time before I could be persuaded to descend. On our way down, we passed a heavy wooden door, which our guide explained led to the top floor's servants' quarters. "It is said that the first mistress of North Lees Hall, an Agnes Ashurst by name, was locked up on that floor in a padded room."

"Why was she locked up?" I asked.

"Because she went stark raving mad. It is said the mad wife died in a fire."

"A fire?" I repeated, greatly interested. "Did she set the fire herself?"

---

[18] The Eyres' unique Apostles Cupboard, which Charlotte described in *Jane Eyre,* is now in the Brontë Parsonage Museum.

"No one knows, it happened so long ago. But they say her husband escaped, and that much of the house burnt down and had to be rebuilt."

"What a terrifying tale," remarked Ellen with a shudder.

What a *fantastic tale,* I thought. It was not the first time I had heard a story about a madwoman confined to an attic; the practice was not uncommon in Yorkshire, for in truth, what other recourse did a family have, when a loved one succumbed to a debilitating mental disorder?

Roe Head School had also come with its own legend about an occupant of the uninhabited upper storey of the house. In that case, it had been a female spirit—the first wife of the landholder who built the house—who tragically fell down the stairs on her wedding night and broke her neck. My fellow students and I had spent many an evening exchanging whispered theories about the mysterious Ghost of Roe Head, whose silk dresses could be heard rustling against the attic floors above late at night.

As legend had it, the last surviving occupant of Roe Head, before it was relinquished to Miss Wooler, was an old gentleman of generally sanguine disposition, who heard a piercing laugh, then saw the departed spirit floating above the first-floor gallery. He was so frightened out of his wits that he left the house and vowed never to return. Although I had never seen evidence of the Ghost of Roe Head myself, I had not been able to get that story out of my mind; and this new tale—set against the spooky environs of ancient North Lees Hall, with its legend about a fire—particularly captured my imagination.

Some day, I vowed, I would write about it.

In the second week of my stay at Hathersage, I awoke in the middle of the night shivering in terror from a vivid, foreboding dream.

I have long believed in dreams, signs, and presentiments. When I was young, Tabby often told us that to dream of little children was a sure sign of trouble, either to one's self or one's kin. She had offered up several personal experiences as proof of this belief, which she had reported with such grave solemnity, that I could not forget them. Over the years, I noticed that I remembered my dreams with far more frequency than any one else, except perhaps Emily. At age eight, on the eve of my departure for the Clergy Daughters' School, I had had a horrifying vision in which I found myself standing over the bed of a sickly little girl. When I told papa, he had only tousled my hair and said that, as I was a little child myself, it was only natural that I should dream of children, and I should not worry myself over superstitious nonsense. I had again dreamt about a small child before I sailed to Belgium for the second time; I ignored the warning; later, I fervently wished that I had taken heed of it.

Now, I had another such vision, and it filled me with a dire presentiment. Diary: it was the 17th of July, 1845, a Thursday; I mention the date, because it proved to have significance. Ellen and I had retired early that night. According to custom, we slept in the same bed during our many visits, even when necessity did not so dictate. We enjoyed this time together now equally as much as we had as school-mates; normally, we talked for a little while, and then drifted into a peaceful slumber.

This night was different. For some time after we went to bed, I could not sleep. As it was a summer evening, it did not grow dark for some time; when it did, the wind rose and began to blow with a low, sullen sound, more eerie than any gale. Shadows played on the wall, occasioned by the rattling, moonlit branches of the trees against the window. This effect, accompanied by the mournful moan of the wind, seemed to be the manifestation of some great, unearthly, and unholy power. I felt overwhelmed by a sudden, inexplicable sense of impending doom.

When at last I fell asleep, I dreamt. I found myself anxiously following, on foot, the windings of the road towards Haworth on a dark and gusty night. I sensed I was needed desperately at home and must reach that place without delay. As I trudged up hill, I carried an infant wrapped up in a shawl; the tiny creature squirmed in my arms and wailed piteously in my ear; I tried to whisper to it—to hum a lullaby—to offer solace and comfort—but so deep was its sufferings that my words failed to reach it. My arms were tired, and the child's weight impeded my progress. It seemed to want any one but me, but I could not lay it down anywhere; I must do my best to keep it safe and warm.

With great effort, I reached the summit of the hill. To my dismay, the parsonage was not there. My home instead was a foreign place, more akin in aspect, size, and scope to North Lees Hall; and yet, it was North Lees Hall no longer: it was a dreary ruin. All that remained of the stately front was a roofless, fragile-looking, shell-like wall, with a gaping hole where the massive front door had once stood. Where was my family? I wondered in horror. What had happened?

The wind continued to wail; all at once, I realised the sound was not the wind at all; it was my father's voice, and Anne's, and Emily's, and Branwell's, all in one great cacophony of anguish; and it came from within the ruined structure.

"Where are you?" I cried, trembling. "I am coming to you! I am coming!"

Still carrying the child, I rushed inside. The interior walls still stood, but the hall was littered with the crumbling remains of roofing, plaster, and cornices. I waded frantically through the wreckage from room to room, until at last I found them: all the members of my family were there assembled in a forlorn tableau, weeping—all except Branwell, but I knew that he was suffering, too. His wailing, from somewhere unknown, was the loudest of all—and in perfect tune with the cries of the piteous infant in my arms.

I felt a sudden wrenching of my heart, as if that organ was tied to Branwell's by some invisible, living thread; and by that connection, I was able to feel the paroxysms of pain that engulfed him.

"What has happened?" I tried to cry, but no words came from my mouth. All at once, the walls around us began to crumble; they gave way; loose stones and plaster rained down in a great storm upon me and my loved ones. I covered the child to protect it from the onslaught, and lost my balance; I felt myself falling; I awoke with a great gasp.

"Charlotte, what is it?" said Ellen, stirring beside me.

I clutched the covers to my chin and shivered, trying to still the frantic beating of my heart. "Oh, Ellen! I have had such a terrible dream."

When I finished telling Ellen the particulars, she grasped my hand reassuringly in the dark and said, "It was only a dream, Charlotte dear. Do not distress yourself so."

"It was a dream about a *child*," I insisted, still filled with anxiety. "You know what that means. Some great calamity is going to befall me, or one of my loved ones."

"That is just an old wives' tale. I am sure your house and family are fine."

"I am not worried about the house. It is just a symbol for something else: some ruinous event which is about to occur, or has occurred in my absence. Branwell will be home by now from Thorp Green, for his summer holiday. Oh! I am filled with such dread, Ellen. I must go home at first light."

"Go home? But your two weeks are not finished, and you said you might stay yet another week."

"I have changed my mind. My family needs me. I do not know why, I only know that they do."

"I feared you might make some such protest, Charlotte, on account of your annual Sunday School services coming up—so I wrote to Emily to seek permission for you to stay. At least wait to hear from her before you make your decision."

Emily's reply arrived the next morning:

16 July, 1845–Haworth

Dear Miss Ellen,

If you have set your heart on Charlotte staying another week she has our united consent; I for one will take every-thing easy on Sunday—I'm glad she is enjoying herself:

let her make the most of the next seven days & return
stout and hearty—Love to her and you from Anne &
myself and tell her all are well at home.

Yours affecty—
EJ Brontë

"You see?" said Ellen, after we read Emily's letter. "All are well at home. I told you so. You may stop fretting now about your dream, and do as she says: make the most of the next week."

I was sceptical; I still felt, to the very marrow of my bones, that something was amiss at home; but Emily's cheerful, reassuring tone could not be denied.

I wrote to my sister in reply, announcing my intention to remain at Hathersage through the 28th of July. Ellen and I amused ourselves, receiving a variety of visitors, overseeing the installation of Henry's new furniture, and undertaking one last trip to North Lees Hall, where I was relieved to see that it was still standing and not a refuge for bats and owls.

At length, however, I could not ignore my inner misgivings; on Saturday, the 26th of July, I determined that I must go home without delay.

As I decided to leave Hathersage at the last minute, and earlier than anticipated, I was unable to give word to my family of my arrival, and knew that no one could meet my train.

On board the railroad carriage from Sheffield to Leeds, I forgot my worries for a moment when my eye was caught by the gentlemen seated opposite me. I was overcome by a little shock of recognition: for in facial features, bodily proportions and mode of dress (the cut and tailoring of a suit coat fashioned by a French seamstress is unparalleled, in my experience), he resembled in many respects my Belgian professor, Monsieur Héger.

So sure was I that the gentleman must be a Frenchman, that I ventured to say to him, "Monsieur est français, n'est-ce pas?"

The man gave a start of surprise and answered immediately in his native tongue, "Oui, mademoiselle. Parlez-vous français?"[19]

A thrill went up my spine. Although I tried to read a little French every day, I had not heard that language spoken aloud even once since my return from Brussels; hearing it now reminded me of how dearly I had missed it. The gentleman and I engaged in a pleasant conversation for a few minutes, at which point I inquired—much to his surprise and puzzlement—if he had not passed the greater part of his life in Germany. He said that my surmise was correct, and wondered how I had arrived at such a conclusion. When I told him I had detected a trace of a German accent in his French, he smiled and remarked, "Vous êtes un magicien avec des langues, mademoiselle."[20]

I enjoyed our repartee, and was sorry to be obliged to bid him au revoir when I left the train at Leeds. For the duration of my journey, I was immersed in memories of Brussels.

Upon my arrival at Keighley, however, my agony of anticipation about the fate of my family returned full force. So late was the hour, and so determined was I to reach home with haste, that I paid for a coach to drive me thither.

It was a clear summer night. Normally, I would have relaxed in my seat and observed the final declension of the sun from a painterly perspective, and felt a rush of pleasure in viewing its golden glow upon the familiar expanse of heath and meadow; for no matter how much I delighted in seeing new sights, it was always a welcome relief to return home. This evening, however, I could barely sit still, so beset was I by thoughts and feelings of foreboding, and an inexplicable presentiment that I was coming home to sorrow.

It was nearly dark when the coach turned up Church Lane, passed the sexton's house and schoolhouse, and stopped beside the low wall leading to the front garden of the parsonage. I paid

---

[19] "Monsieur is French, isn't that right?" "Yes, Mademoiselle. Do you speak French?"

[20] "You are a wizard with languages, mademoiselle."

the driver, who set down my trunk on the flag-stones and left. I was about to head to the gate when I noticed a figure approaching in the shadows: it was Mr. Nicholls—the last person I wished to see!—apparently taking an evening stroll. He stopped a few feet away and regarded me, his expression very grave and worried.

"Miss Brontë."

"Mr. Nicholls. Is anything wrong?"

He did not immediately reply. All at once a cold wind rose up, so fierce that it would have blown off my bonnet, had it not been securely tied. I was infused with an eerie chill, which had nothing to do with the temperature of the gust.

"Have you not heard?" asked he.

"Heard what?" said I, with growing alarm. I glanced at the house. Dim lights flickered in the downstairs windows, indicating that some one was still awake. Now I heard shouts from within the parsonage. My heart began to pound with alarm and dread, for I recognised the voice: it was Branwell's, but not the Branwell I knew and loved; this was the Branwell who had had far too much to drink. "Oh no."

"He has been like that for more than a week." Picking up my trunk, Mr. Nicholls said, "Let me help you with this." Before I could utter a protest, he started for the house.

I hurried ahead of him to the front door. Finding it locked, I knocked; a few tense moments passed as I stood on the doorstep, uncomfortably aware of Mr. Nicholls's presence, while bursts of insensible rage issued from within. At last, the door opened, and my eyes met Anne's; her visage was stricken; our brief, wordless exchange confirmed our mutual anguish.

I darted inside; Mr. Nicholls followed and set my trunk down in the entrance-hall.

"Tell that stupid ass of a mongrel to keep away from me!" I heard my brother shout in an angry slur, from the dining-room beyond. My cheeks burned, to think that Mr. Nicholls should be such an intimate witness to my brother's dissolute behaviour.

"May I be of any further help, Miss Brontë? Would you like me to speak to him?"

"No! No thank you, Mr. Nicholls. I am sure we can manage. Thank you again. Good-night, sir."

With a reluctant frown, Mr. Nicholls left. Anne locked the door. I glimpsed papa in his night-shirt, warily descending the stairs at the end of the hall. Anne and I rushed at once into the dining-room. There were only a few glowing embers in the hearth, but the glow of a single candle, along with the last fading rays of daylight, revealed the scene to my horrified eyes.

Branwell stood unsteadily beside the black horsehair sofa, his back to the door. His red hair and clothes were disheveled, and he was waving a fist at an uncertain and distraught Emily, behind whose skirts Flossy was cowering. "A man can't even take a damned nap around here," shouted Branwell in an intoxicated tone, "without that God-forsaken, mangy cur jumping up on top of him and slobbering all over his damn face!"

"Branwell, calm down," said Emily quietly, her eyes darting briefly to mine and acknowledging her alarm. "Flossy did not mean any harm. He was only being affectionate."

"Affection be damned!" snarled Branwell, as he snatched up a book from the dining-table and hurled it at the dog's head. Flossy flinched in time to deflect the blow to his side, but he set up a piteous outcry on impact, and scampered past me out the door into the hall.

"Branwell!" Anne and I cried in unified horror. At the same moment, papa entered; I knew his near blindness would be further hampered by the dimness of the room.

"That's enough!" said papa sternly. "Get hold of yourself, son."

"Shut your mouth, old man!" Branwell took a tottering step towards Emily, grabbing hold of the table to keep his balance. "This is between me and my sister, and that damned stupid dog!"

"Branwell, please stop this," said I, as I advanced cautiously towards him, my heart pounding. I was uncertain precisely what to do, for he was both taller and stronger than I; and I knew from previous experience that his strength only increased when he was inebriated.

Branwell turned, regarding me with blinking surprise in his bloodshot eyes. "Charlotte. Where've you been?"

"At Hathersage, visiting Ellen." I hoped, by talking calmly, to distract him and calm him down.

"For a minute, I thought you'd gone back to Belgium," slurred he, his anger dissipating as a stupid look lit his feverish countenance. "Funny—I was just talking to Anne about that the other day. What was it? Oh, yes. I said, 'Have you noticed how sad Charlotte has been ever since she came back from Belgium?' Anne said I was imagining it. But I said, 'No, no, our Charlotte is sad all right. Mark my words: she is hiding something behind that staid, placid countenance of hers.'"

"I am not sad, and I am not hiding anything," I insisted, but my cheeks grew warm, and I felt Emily's questioning eyes on me.

"You *are* sad," said he drunkenly. "I've seen it in your eyes. I should know. I know all about sad." To my consternation, Branwell's face suddenly crumpled, and he burst into tears. "Oh God! What am I to do? The misery—the anguish—the despair!" He dropped to the floor on his knees, and cried out, "How can I live without my life? How shall I bear it?"

So stunned was I by my brother's erratic behaviour, that I could only stand in a state of paralysed dismay. Emily went to him; she soon coaxed him, weeping, to his feet, and led him from the room. I knew she would take him upstairs and settle him in bed, as she had done on many such occasions in the past. In the deadly quiet that followed, papa let out a small sob. He stood just inside the doorway, his gaunt countenance ravaged with grief and disappointment. I wrapped his thin frame in my embrace and held him tight, at a loss for words. "I am here now, papa," was all I could think of to say.

"I am glad of it, child," was his broken reply.

"Let me help you back to bed," I offered, but he waved me off with a firm hand and shuffled out of the room.

The moment papa was gone, Anne burst into tears. My own anguish, which had been suppressed for nearly a week, now welled up like a white heat within my chest and spilled forth in a torrent from my eyes.

On previous occasions when Branwell was drunk, my sisters and I had tried to maintain a strong, united front, pretending that all was well once the worst was over, even when it clearly was not. This time, however, I was too distraught to be brave; I saw, in Anne's answering gaze, that she was equally incapable of the task. In unison, we moved into each other's arms, where we held each other tightly and indulged our tears for some minutes. At last, we dried our eyes and sank down on the sofa, where I regained my composure.

"What on earth has happened?" I asked, as I took off my gloves and bonnet. "Why is Branwell so distraught?"

"He has been dismissed from his post."

"Dismissed? But why? You said Mrs. Robinson thinks so highly of him!"

"She did. Oh, Charlotte! I feel so naive—so stupid. From almost the first day Branwell arrived at Thorp Green Hall, I saw that he was the favourite of all the household. I was proud of him, and delighted. Mrs. Robinson was always commenting on what a remarkable young man he is. I thought she admired and appreciated him for his skills as a tutor and an artist. Until last month, I never thought—I never imagined that *she,* that *he* could do something so—so—" Anne's voice quivered, as fresh tears spilled onto her cheeks.

"What? What has Branwell done?"

"He has been having a love affair these three years past with Mrs. Robinson!"

I stared at Anne in shock and consternation. "A love affair? You cannot mean it. She is a married woman, and so much his senior. Surely they did not—"

"They *did*. Imagine the very worst and most sordid possible behaviour, Charlotte, and that is what they are guilty of. A week ago Thursday, Branwell received a letter from the Reverend Edmund Robinson, expressing his outrage and sternly intimating that he had discovered Branwell's proceedings. He charged Branwell, on pain of exposure, to break off instantly and for ever all communication with every member of his family!"

"Did you say a week ago Thursday—the 17th?"

"Yes."

Diary: it was that same Thursday night that I had had my terrible dream. A great numbness washed over me; for some moments, I was too stunned to think or speak. "Is it possible that Mr. Robinson is mistaken? Are you certain there is truth to the charge?"

"If only there was not. It is all true, Charlotte. Branwell has admitted everything. He claims that Mrs. Robinson has been at the helm of the affair from the beginning."

"Do you believe him?"

"Yes. We both know Branwell too well, with all his Northanger-land fantasies, to think that he would lie about being seduced."

Northangerland was the central character in Branwell's fiction—an amalgam of Buonaparte, Satan, and the quintessential Byronic hero—a rakish figure my brother so closely identified with, that he had used the name as his pseudonym for most of his published poetry.

"I suppose you are right. In his eyes, if he could have boasted that he swept the lady of the house off her feet and into his bed, he would have seen it as a far bigger feather in his cap."

"He said Mrs. Robinson sought him out just a few months after he arrived at Thorp Green. Branwell admired her, and was grieved by her husband's callous treatment of her on several occasions. You know our brother has never been one to hide his emotions."

"No; he is not."

"When he openly and rashly expressed his feelings for her one day, to his surprise she declared feelings of her own. By the end of that first summer, she had encouraged him to—to—to go on to extremities. They met in secret at the house, or when Mr. Robinson was away. He says he is deeply in love with her. The way he talks—it is as if she has become all that matters to him in life."

"Oh! This is too horrible. But this explains Branwell's strange, irritable conduct over the past few years. He seemed to hate coming home for holidays, and when he *was* here, he exhibited such a wild range of feelings, from the highest spirits to the blackest of depressions—I could not understand it. On more than one occasion, I thought I detected an expression of hidden guilt in his eyes, but he always denied it."

"I thought the same."

"He is passed out in bed," announced Emily, entering the room and sinking heavily into the easy chair beside us. "If we are very lucky, we will not hear a peep from him till morning."

"Anne," said I, "how and when did you learn the truth about all this?"

"I was taking a walk one afternoon last month through the woods behind Thorp Green, when I came upon Branwell sitting beneath a tree, writing in a note-book. When I asked what he was writing, he blushed. I was not going to press the matter, but he thrust the note-book at me and told me to read it. It was filled with poems of his own composition—most of them impassioned love poems about Mrs. Robinson. I was shocked and horrified. He only laughed and said, 'Do not be such a prude.' He then told me the whole story. I wanted to die of shame. I knew I could not stay in that house a moment longer."

"I do not blame you for leaving," said I. "I would have done the same."

"Oh, Charlotte! You speak of blame. In some ways, I cannot help but blame myself for what has occurred."

"What do you mean?"

Anne hesitated. Already, in the past few minutes, she had talked longer and expressed more emotion than in any conversation we had held in the past five years; I was afraid she might again withdraw into her quiet shell; but she did not.

"I have been unhappy at Thorp Green Hall for a long time, but not only with regard to my dissatisfaction with my duties as governess. I have had many other, unpleasant and undreamt of experiences of human nature, which—which have troubled me greatly. Knowing—even suspecting—what I did, I should never have recommended Branwell for a post at that house."

Emily sat up straight in her chair and stared at Anne. "What experiences, Anne? What are you not telling us?"

Anne averted her gaze, and a blush crept over her cheeks. "I am loath to even speak of it, but since you both know nearly all already—" She took a breath, and went on, "I have seen Mrs. Robinson flirt openly with other gentlemen—guests and visitors to the house. I suspect that she was *overly friendly* with many of them—and it was not just my mistress who behaved so. In the years since Branwell's arrival, I have observed numerous examples of base immorality between adults who are married, but not married to each other; all the while, their own spouses were in the house or on the grounds; at times, they were in the very next room. It grieved and sickened me to witness such immoral behaviour, and to be powerless to stop it—for how could I come forward with my suspicions? Surely I would have been dismissed on the spot. I blush with shame when I reflect that, simply by remaining silent, I became an unwilling accomplice to their indiscretions. And even more when I recall that, on one occasion a year past, one of their male guests, after imbibing too much liquor, attempted to become overly familiar with me."

"Oh Anne!" cried Emily. "What did you do?"

"I fended him off. He never spoke of it again; I believe he was too drunk to recall what had happened."

"Anne, I am so sorry." Tears stung my eyes as I took her hands in mine. I realised, of a sudden, that my own experiences as a governess, which I had once thought so oppressive, were in fact quite tame and inconsequential in comparison with Anne's. "All this time, I had no idea of what you were suffering. If only you had told me, I would have insisted that you leave Thorp Green years ago."

"That is precisely why I did not mention it. It would only have caused you needless pain. How could I be certain, if I did leave, that circumstances would be different anywhere else?" Anne gave a deep sigh. "It mortifies me now, to think that while all this was occurring, Mrs. Robinson was on intimate terms with *Branwell*—and I had no inkling! It must have fed her vanity that, at forty-three years of age, she could seduce a good-looking young man, seventeen years her junior—particularly with three beautiful daughters in the house."

"How did they get away with it so long, I wonder?" I asked.

"Apparently, Mrs. Robinson's lady's maid and the family doctor were both in collusion with her," replied Emily.

"I must admit," added Anne, "Mrs. Robinson was very adept at deception. To her husband's face, she always appeared entirely proper. Behind his back, she constantly complained that he was old and sick, and could not—could not sufficiently attend to her needs."

"Was it true, do you think?" I inquired.

"I do not know. He did not become sickly until recently, and he is not so very old; Mr. and Mrs. Robinson are the same exact age, in fact. He is a stern and intractable man, but for all his faults, I think him a far better and more respectable person than his wife."

"How did *he* discover his wife's infidelity?"

"We found that out only yesterday," replied Emily, "when Branwell received a letter from the Robinsons' doctor, whom he had befriended. As if Branwell's previous actions had not been depraved enough, he did another incredibly stupid thing. Unable to be parted from that woman even for the few weeks of their holiday, he secretly followed them to Scarborough."

"No!"

"The Robinsons' gardener accompanied them on their journey, to assist the groom with the horses and luggage," continued Emily. "He observed Branwell and Mrs. Robinson together in a boat-house, just below their lodgings at The Cliff. Apparently, said gardener felt a greater loyalty to his master than his mistress, for he wrote to Mr. Robinson upon his return home, revealing all."

"And now Mr. Robinson has written, threatening to shoot Branwell if he dares to set foot again at Thorp Green Hall!" exclaimed Anne. "Branwell is utterly destroyed. Since Thursday he has done nothing but drink and storm and rage about the house in a frenzy of grief. We have not had a moment's peace, except when he is at the tavern, or passed out cold."

"I have never heard such ravings," said Emily. "He is like a soul in hell."

"Oh," said I, "to think that I was whiling away my time at Hathersage for more than a week, and you were all suffering so. I wanted to come home a week ago Thursday; I *knew* I should have."

"I am glad you stayed a little longer, if you enjoyed yourself," said Emily. "God knows, it is not going to be any fun around *here* for a long while."

"Charlotte, what are we to do?" said Anne.

"I do not know."

On one point, I felt compassion for Branwell, and great sympathy for his plight: the fact that he had been attracted to, and had great love for, some one who was already married. It was a hopeless situation, beset with agonies, heartaches, and torments which (I acknowledged only in the deepest, most private recesses of my mind and heart) I had some past, mortifying experience.

"I am utterly heart-sick," I said at last, taking careful measure of my words. "We cannot choose the objects of our affections, any more than we can choose our parents. If, however, by some misfortune, our feelings lead us in a direction that is not condoned by God or by society, we can—*we must*—*exert self-control*; we must *not act* on those unlawful desires. The fact that Branwell did—that he succumbed to temptation with Mrs. Robinson—is truly wicked."

Emily glanced sharply at me at this pronouncement; the shrewd expression in her eyes told me she perceived that a personal truth lay behind it. However, she only said, "I agree with you. Branwell has tried to blame all this on Mrs. Robinson; but no matter how blatantly that woman threw herself at him, he was an equal player in all of this. He cannot justify his actions."

Branwell held every one in our household a hostage of his torment for the next ten days, alternately drowning his distress of mind with alcohol or stunning it with opiates. He had only to cross the street from Haworth church to buy a sixpence-worth of opium, readily available at Betty Hardacre's drug-shop; and to our great despair, nothing we said or did could dissuade him from the practice. When we could bear it no longer, my sisters and I sent him away to Liverpool for a week in the company of his friend John Brown, where they took a pleasure steamer along the coast of North Wales. I believe the brief respite did him good.

"I know what you think of me, Charlotte," said Branwell one warm, August evening, not long after his return. "I know I have brought all my miseries upon my own head, but I am determined to fix myself."

I was seated on a stile in a meadow behind the parsonage, overlooking the moors, which were lushly carpeted in the brilliant purple hue of summer. I had ventured out alone to find a bit of cool breeze to read by in the fading light of day, when Branwell appeared. Closing my book now, I said, "I applaud your determination. I look forward to meeting the new and improved Branwell."

"You can wipe that sceptical look right off your face. Look at the progress I have made: I am standing here, cheerfully speaking to you, without the stimulus of six glasses of whisky!"

"An admirable achievement—but occasioned, as we both know, only by the absolute want of means—as papa has steadfastly refused to give you any money."

"I tell you, Charlotte, I am going to change." He perched on the stile beside me and gazed out pensively across the moor. "Nothing will ever again bring me so low as the nightmare of my old days, years ago, at Luddenden Foot. I would rather cut off my own hand, than to undergo again the groveling carelessness and malignant debauchery which too often marked my conduct when I was there."

"Why, Branwell? Why did you act thus? You always said that you liked that job."

"I did. The railroad is an exciting new venture, and it allowed me to earn my keep. But you *must* know, having been raised on Virgil and Byron, I aspired to greater things than 'clerk-in-charge' of a tiny, out-of-the-way rail station, housed in a rude little hut. There was nothing to do! My only friends were in Halifax, and I could not go there as often as I liked. What other recourse did I have, besides drink?"

"Surely you do not expect me to dignify that with an answer?"

"At least I was not entirely lost to *everything* while I was there. I did write—or rewrite—a lot of poetry."

"I remember." I sighed. "I am a little envious of you, you know."

"Envious of *me*? Why?"

"Because your poetry has been published. I have long dreamt of being published myself."

"Well, *dreaming* of it will not make it happen, sister dear. You have talent, and you know it—but as they say: nothing ventured, nothing gained. To be published, you must first write something worthy of *being* published, and then you must be bold enough to submit it."

"True." I met his gaze. The affection in his eyes was so genuine, and he looked so bonny and fine, sitting there with the rays of the setting sun burnishing his carroty hair to gold, that for a moment he seemed like the Branwell of old. As children, we had been soulmates, inseparable, in perfect tune with each other; we had been able to complete each other's sentences, and anticipate each other's every thought and move; and we had both delighted in a continuous rivalry of creativity and composition that lasted nearly two decades. Was it possible that we might get a measure of our friendship back? Would Branwell truly try to "fix" himself? I said: "I have greatly missed you of late."

"You will have no cause to miss me now. I am here—and will remain here, until the day Lydia Robinson is free. Then she will marry me, I will be lord of her estate, and live in genteel splendour with her for the rest of my life."

My heart sank. "Branwell, please tell me you are not serious."

"About what?"

"You cannot truly expect to *marry* Mrs. Robinson!"

"Of course I do. Her husband is very sickly. It will not be long now until he dies."

"What a sick and morbid thing to say, even sicker to say it with hope in your eyes."

"I am not the only person who hopes and longs for it. Lydia does not love her husband. She loves me."

"Oh, Branwell. Even if that is true—do you truly think a woman of her rank and fortune would marry a man seventeen years her junior, with whom she had a scandalous affair?"

"I know she will. She told me we would be together for ever. I have only to wait. And while I am waiting, I will not sit idle. I intend to find some occupation, and—I promise you—I will remain sober as a judge."

Keeping that promise proved to be beyond Branwell's power. The very next afternoon, while my father was out on church business with Anne as his aide, and Emily was up in her room doing I knew not what, I was reading in the dining-room, when I heard shouts from outside, followed by a rap at the front door.

To my mortification, I encountered my brother on the doorstep, hurling drunken obscenities and being physically restrained and supported by Mr. Nicholls.

Since my return from my trip to Hathersage, every time I had seen Mr. Nicholls come up the walk on his way to meet with papa, I had gone upstairs, or sequestered myself in the dining-room behind a closed door. Now, there was no avoiding him.

"I was passing by the Black Bull," announced Mr. Nicholls, as he strained to control my struggling brother, "when he and another gentleman burst out the door, cursing and throwing punches at one another. I sensed an outright brawl was likely, and thought it best to bring him home."

"Unhand me, you God-damned, miserable lout!" thundered Branwell with savage vehemence, as he vigorously and fruitlessly attempted to break free, "or I'll set the dogs on you, I swear to God I will!" Although my brother had engaged in boxing with the town toughs for some years in his youth, he was long out of practice; and despite his drink-fueled anger, he was in size and frame no match for the much taller, much-sturdier-built Mr. Nicholls.

"I have no fear of dogs," retorted that gentleman, "in fact, I particularly like them." To me, he added somewhat apologeti-cally, "Where would you like me to put him?"

"In the dining-room," said I, my cheeks warm with embar-rassment, as I stepped back to admit him. Every one in the vil-lage, I knew, had been apprised of my brother's dismissal from his post within a day of its occurrence. As a result of Branwell's repeated, drunken outpourings of heart and soul at the pub, they were now equally well acquainted with every sordid detail of his humiliating conduct there, and his absurd expectations for his future. I cringed when I saw the pity in the eyes of the shopkeepers on Main Street; my heart smote me when I ob-served the averted gazes of the congregation on Sunday, when papa took his place at the pulpit; but I felt even greater shame to think that our new curate should be such a close observer of Branwell's decline.

I already knew that Mr. Nicholls regarded me as a dried-up, bitter old maid, too unattractive to look upon. My father was a nearly-blind old man; add to that a drunken sot of a brother, who started brawls in the middle of the afternoon; how he must pity me, and my whole household! How he must laugh at us be-hind our backs! Still, I thought, I must not let my wounded pride get the better of me. As the curate dragged a still-squirming and swearing Branwell into the dining-room, I squared my shoulders and followed, determined that Mr. Nicholls would never know how much his cruel comment that night at tea had hurt me; indeed, if I could help it, he would never perceive a moment of weakness from me.

Mr. Nicholls deposited my brother in an easy chair, where, maintaining a firm grip, he insisted upon a verbal promise from his captive to sit still and quietly, before he would set him free. Branwell uttered another oath, and then reluctantly agreed.

"Villain!" Branwell spat out, as Mr. Nicholls let him go. "How *dare* you! I am the parson's son, by God! I warn you, Nicholls: if you ever touch me like that again, I'll have you shot, or sent back to Ireland!"

"Let us pray, then, that a similar occasion does not ever

arise," was the curate's rejoinder, as he straightened his black coat and adjusted his collar.

"Branwell, please do not address Mr. Nicholls in such an insolent manner," said I.

"I'll address him any way I like," snarled Branwell. "Now get out, Nicholls! You have done your Christian duty. You have played the Good Samaritan, and brought the prodigal son home. Now go back to church where you belong."

Emily suddenly entered the room, a concerned look on her countenance. Martha, close at her heels, stopped just inside the doorway, where she crossed her arms and shook her head. "La, la, an' what have we here, Maister Branwell? Two o'clock i' th' afternoon, an' already three sheets t' th' wind?"

"Martha," urged Branwell, with a sudden smile, and a voice diffused with charm, "be a good girl and bring me some of that wine I know you keep in the locked cupboard."

"I will not, sir," said Martha.

"Emily? Surely you would not deny your brother a drop, in his hour of need?"

"I believe you have had quite enough already," observed Emily quietly.

Branwell sank farther down into his chair in a sullen pout. "You are parasites, the lot of you! Determined to suck the life out of me."

Turning to Mr. Nicholls, I said with cool formality, "I am very grateful to you, sir, for bringing my brother home." When I raised my eyes to his, to my surprise, I did not encounter the pity and derision I had anticipated; instead, I found compassion and concern, tempered by humility—and nerves.

"Will you be all right, Miss Brontë?" asked Mr. Nicholls quietly.

In some confusion, I replied: "I will, thank you. Martha and Emily are here."

He nodded and glanced at the door. I hoped he would leave then, but he did not; he stood for some moments in the centre of the room, deep in thought, as if trying to drum up the courage to ask something. I was perplexed and a little annoyed; why was this tall, strong man, who had, only moments before, single-handedly tamed and dragged home my wayward brother, now standing before me like a timid statue?

The sudden sound of snoring filled the room; I saw with relief that Branwell was fast asleep in his chair. The noise seemed a humorous but fitting end to so much drama; and alternating as it did from brief, nasal snuffles to harsh, vibrating snorts, it was so comical in nature, that I struggled to hold back a smile. The sound seemed to breathe life back into Mr. Nicholls, for he smiled, too; then he let out a laugh. Emily and Martha were equally infected; soon I could not help but join in the laughter. For some moments we all indulged, straining to laugh as quietly as possible, so as not to wake the errant sleeper.

Emily now turned and bumped into the table, accidentally knocking a candlestick to the floor with a clatter. She caught her breath in alarm; all eyes flew to the easy chair; but its occupant continued snoring unabated, causing a renewed outburst of laughter.

Martha left the room, still chuckling. Mr. Nicholls cleared his throat. He looked down at me, then at Emily, and said, "Miss Brontë, Miss Emily: there is something I have been wanting to ask you. I wonder: would you consider allowing me to take one or both of your dogs for a walk on the moors now and again? I enjoy a daily stroll and would be grateful for the company."

The request took me by surprise. "It is not my place to say, sir," I replied, with a glance at Emily.

After some hesitation, Emily said, "I am certain Flossy would be delighted to accompany you, sir, but I must ask Anne, first. I am only his care-taker; he is her dog, in point of fact. As for Keeper: you have my blessing, but I will leave the final decision up to him."

"I will stop by in the morning, then," rejoined Mr. Nicholls, looking pleased. He bowed, and with a parting glance at Branwell, added, "Should you require any further assistance, Miss

Brontë, to-day or at any other time, please do not hesitate to call on me."

"Thank you again, Mr. Nicholls," said I.

With a nod, he departed.

The summer passed. Papa and my sisters and I watched in helpless dismay as Branwell became a steadily weaker and more nervous wreck. Mrs. Robinson sent Branwell money, and, I believe, even met with him secretly once or twice at an inn in Harrogate; he kept apprised of her news via letters from her lady's maid and doctor, and never attempted to break the ties that bound him to her.

When money arrived from "his darling Lydia," or whenever Branwell managed to wheedle a few shillings out of papa or his friend John Brown, he either went straight down to Betty Hardacre's to buy a dose of oblivion, or he crept off to the Black Bull. After several hours of hard drinking, he would stumble home singing or laughing like a lunatic, or (on more occasions than I wish to remember) he was brought home, angry and irascible, by the ever-patient Mr. Nicholls.

When Branwell had no money to support his habits, he lay about the parsonage day and night in a frustrated rage, screaming at us over nothing and reducing us to tears. When I reminded him that he had promised to seek employment, he wrote to his friend Francis Grundy, badgering him for a position on the railway, but he received no encouragement. He refused to go to church; he refused to assist with any household duties; he refused to do anything, except to make us all wretched.

"I am a soul in torment. I am in hell!" Branwell would cry with stricken countenance, as he paced up and down before the hearth like a caged beast, while my sisters and I engaged in our nightly sewing, knitting, or ironing. "Lydia! Lydia! Oh! My heart's darling! I'll have her in my arms again! I cannot live without my soul!"

"If this truly be love," observed Emily with a frown, "then I hope and pray *I* never experience it."

Our despair over Branwell's decline, however, was soon eclipsed by an astonishing—and fateful—event, which was to move our fortunes in an entirely new and promising direction.

It was the 9th of October, 1845. That morning, I went into Emily's room at the top of the stairs, intending to make up her bed with a fresh set of sheets, when I chanced to find Emily's portable writing-desk lying open on the bed. This was most unusual. Emily always kept her desk closed and locked. I had, a few times in the past (on those rare occasions when Emily had left her door open) observed her writing in her room, with Keeper at her feet and her desk upon her lap. I knew that Emily rarely wrote letters; she had no friends with whom to correspond; but she was such a fiercely private person, I did not dare ask her what she was working on.

To-day, not only was the desk unfolded upon the bed, but a note-book lay open upon the sloped writing surface. Emily's pen lay beside it, and her ink bottle, in the little compartment at the top, was uncapped, as if she had been interrupted in the very act of composition. The bed stood directly in front of the open window; the sky beyond was a cloudy grey, which threatened rain; and a breeze blew in, ruffling the pages of the note-book. I instantly worried that some harm might come to it.

I quickly set down the folded bed-sheets and capped the ink bottle. I was about to close and put away the note-book in the little desk drawer, when the poetic lines atop the page—for a poem it was (and, as it turned out, a long one; this was from the final page)—grabbed my attention:

Thus ruth and selfish love together striving tore
The heart all newly taught to pit and adore;
If I should break the chain, I felt my bird would go;
Yet I must break the chain or seal the prisoner's woe.

Short strife, what rest could soothe—what peace could
    visit me

While she lay pining there for Death to set her free?
"Rochelle, the dungeons teem with foes to gorge our
   hate—
Thou are too young to die by such a bitter fate!"

My heart, inexplicably, began to pound; I knew I should stop
reading; Emily would not like me to continue. But those two
short stanzas sparked my interest. They contained such a wonderful vibrancy and musicality; I could not help but wonder
what the poem was about. Who was Rochelle? Why and where
was she a prisoner? Who was the speaker? Was the rest of the
poem as good as those few lines?

I picked up the note-book. It was a limp-backed, wine-
coloured volume, similar to one or two of my own, resembling
nothing more elegant than a laundry book; the cover was inscribed "Emily Jane Brontë. GONDAL POEMS." I leafed
through it. The faintly-lined pages were filled, in Emily's minute,
cramped hand, with a great quantity of poems—poems that she
had apparently drafted elsewhere, and transcribed here in their
final form for safe-keeping. Although Emily's minuscule handwriting was difficult for some to decipher, I was familiar with it.
Many of the poems had composition dates; most were untitled,
but at the head of some appeared a person's name or two, or
simply initials, which (I reasoned) must represent the *dramatis
personae* portrayed in the poems.

So *this* is what Emily had been up to every time she locked
herself away in her room! She had been writing poetry about her
fictional world of Gondal!

I was not entirely surprised by this discovery; I had always
known that Emily could and did write verse. As children, we
used to share everything we wrote, and seek each other's advice
and counsel. Of late years, due to prolonged periods of separation, and a growing desire for privacy, this habit had been dis-
continued. I realised, now, that I was entirely ignorant of the
progress Emily had made.

I knew for a fact that Emily and Anne had just gone out with the dogs for a long walk. Branwell was still in bed, after a very late return from the tavern; Tabby was also asleep; papa was downstairs in his study; Martha was in the kitchen. Conscience told me that I should go about my business, make Emily's bed, and leave; but Conscience fought a brief, silent war with Curiosity.

Curiosity won out.

I closed the window, sat down on the bed, and began to read. I started with the last poem in the book—the one that had initially caught my attention. It was dated that very day; apparently, Emily had fair-copied it into the book that morning, upon arising. Entitled simply "Julian M. and A. G. Rochelle," it was a dramatic ballad about a young woman in prison, during a war (Gondal's great, fierce Republican-Royalist War, I would later come to learn), and a man torn between love and duty, as to whether or not to set her free. The effort was both lyrical and thrilling; it took my breath away.[21]

I leafed back to the beginning of the note-book, and consumed its contents. My excitement mounted as I read on. These were not common effusions, nor at all like the poetry women generally wrote. Emily's verse was vigorous and genuine; a sense of urgency existed in her lyric voice and narrative ballads that I had never before encountered. Her subject matter, too, was unusual. Her invented characters and situations (in this note-book, all inspired by inhabitants of Gondal) had enabled her to repeatedly examine the themes that preoccupied her: the cyclic continuity and changeableness of nature, the uncertainty of time, and the extremes of isolation, exile, and death.

My blood rushed through my veins; I knew I had discovered

---

[21] The long ballad is one of Emily's most famous; it has a complex narrative structure, in which the speaker's present situation frames an earlier dramatic event, a technique Emily was to hone later in *Wuthering Heights*. Its subject presages that work, as well, in that the beautiful prisoner has repeated visionary experiences, offering her a foretaste of death and the liberation of the afterlife: "a messenger of Hope comes every night to me/ And offers, for short life, eternal liberty."

something of immense value. So engrossed was I, as I pored through the volume, that I did not hear the approaching foot-steps upon the stairs; I could only leap to my feet, red-faced, note-book in hand, when Emily strode into the room.

She froze and stared at me in shock; then she said, "How did you get that?"

"I am sorry. I—"

Emily darted forward and grabbed the note-book from my grasp. "This is mine. Nobody was to see this but me. You knew that." Emily, by nature, was not garrulous; when deeply moved by serious fears or joys, she seldom allowed that emotion more than a furtive and fitful conquest of either eye or tongue. At this moment, however, her countenance was suffused with fury, and her voice rose in pitch, harsh and strident. "What did you do? Steal the key to my desk? Or force it open?"

"No! Your desk was lying open on the bed. Your note-book and ink bottle too, everything was open." I saw Emily's eyes briefly narrow, as if registering this unintentional neglect. I went on quickly, "I noticed it when I came in to change the sheets. The window was open. The wind was blowing. I only meant to recap the ink and close the note-book to—"

"Then why didn't you?" Emily's eyes flashed as she stared down at me; I had never seen her so angry. "Did you read this?"

"I—yes, I—"

"You had no right! How *much* of it did you read?"

"Nearly all."

"Nearly *all*? How dare you!" With a forceful swing of her hand, she slapped me full upon the cheek.

The shocking blow brought tears to my eyes and sent me staggering back a step, onto the bed. I had never, in all my life, seen Emily slap any one, other than her own beloved Keeper, when he had misbehaved. I had rarely seen her angry, and when I had, that anger had never been trained on me; yet I knew that I deserved it. I righted myself, sitting on the bed, my hand to my burning cheek, which was now wet with tears.

"I am so sorry, Emily. I feared you would be angry, but oh,

how I hope you will forgive me! Your writing is beautiful—wonderful—incredible! In reading it, I feel that I have been given a gift."

I glanced up, hoping to see a hint of forgiveness in Emily's eyes, but I saw only fury. Through the open door, I glimpsed Anne standing in the hall, staring at us in silent consternation.

"*Get out of my room*," exclaimed Emily, in a tone so fierce and deliberate, that it sent a chill up my spine.

I did not move; I knew, if I fled, she would shut the door and not come out or speak to me for the rest of the day; the rest of the week, perhaps. I would stay my ground; I would risk her wrath, and even her violence if it came again, to earn a chance to say what was on my mind. "Please, Emily: listen to me. I only intended to move the note-book out of harm's way—nothing more. But a line or two caught my eye, and—once I had begun reading, I could not stop."

"Liar! You could have stopped. You chose not to!"

"It was beyond my power to stop. Your poetry is so good, so original—it is like condensed energy, full of pathos, with a wild and peculiar music—melancholy, elevating—"

"I do not care for your flattery; you are trying to cover your shame. You *knew* how I felt, and yet you violated my privacy. You are a traitor; and I want you out of this room, now."

Seven

*E*mily slammed the door on my heels and did not reappear for two hours, until she was obliged to come downstairs to help prepare dinner.

I attempted to plead my case further as we worked side by side in the kitchen, but Emily silenced me with one stern reproval: "It was bad enough that you read one poem, Charlotte. But to read all—*all*! That was unforgiveable."

Emily did not speak one word to me at the table—a tense and awkward meal, in which papa remarked: "You are very silent today, girls," and, "Please don't slam the platter down; the sound is quite harsh and grating."

Immediately following that ordeal, I noticed Emily sitting on the front steps, absently stroking Keeper, who lay at her feet. I grabbed my shawl and joined her.

The sun had just set, taking with it what little warmth it had given to the day, and the wind still could not rest; a shiver ran through me as I sat down beside my sister on the cold stone steps. Light was fading fast; there was only one cloud in the autumn evening sky, and it curtained from pole to pole, shrouding the church before us in a grey mist. We sat in silence for some time, as I gathered my thoughts. At last I said:

"We live in the same house, Emily. We work in the same kitchen. We eat at the same table. My bedroom door is but a few feet away from yours. You cannot stay angry with me for ever."

"Watch me."

Her clipped words stung like arrows. I flinched, but refused to be wounded. "Allow me to present a scenario for your consideration."

"Do not bother."

"Pretend, for a moment, that I have a portfolio of pictures I have drawn in secret, pictures which I consider my private property, and which I have made plain that I do not wish to share with any one."

"Please abandon this ridiculous discourse."

"Pretend you walked into my room and saw the window open, my portfolio open upon the bed, and the pictures scattered across the floor. Would you leave them there and walk away, or would you pick them up?"

Emily rolled her eyes. At last, she said begrudgingly: "Is the wind blowing?"

"It is."

"Is there a threat of rain?"

"This is Yorkshire."

"Are Flossy and Keeper in the house?"

"They could bound in at any moment."

"Then I *suppose* I should pick them up."

"Even though I had *expressly forbidden* any one from touching them?"

"Even so. I would worry that they might be spoiled. But knowing they were *private* pictures, I should be *very careful not to look at them.*"

"An admirable plan. But is it not possible that—despite your best intentions—your glance might inadvertently fall upon one of them?"

"A glance, nothing more."

"What if, in that brief glance, you chanced to glimpse a picture of such splendour, and such exquisite beauty, as you had never before beheld? Would you avert your gaze? Would you squeeze shut your eyes? Or would you feel compelled to look upon it in full; in short, to feast your eyes upon it, and all the rest, for the pleasure they afforded, grateful for the opportunity of admiring the genius behind them?"

Emily sighed and threw her hands up in the air. "Fine! Fine! You would have made an admirable solicitor, Charlotte! *I forgive you.* There! Do you feel better now?"

I heaved an answering sigh. "I do." A gust of wind rushed up with renewed force. I closed the distance between us on the step, put my arm around her, and wrapped my shawl around us both, drawing her close. "What were you thinking, coming out without your shawl?"

She laid her head against mine. "I am sorry I slapped you."

"I am sorry I read your poems without asking permission."

We sat some minutes thus, shivering in each other's arms, as we watched the muffled, moonless, starless sky darken from grey to black. Harmony now restored, I allowed my mind to wander to another subject which had hovered at the edges of my consciousness all day, ever since the discovery of those pages. Was it too soon, I wondered? Did I dare to mention it?

I dared: "They should be published."

"What?"

"Your poems. They merit publication."

Emily pushed me aside and stood up in disgust. "You are a despicable and infuriating human being, Charlotte Brontë. If I felt my rhymes too private for *your* eyes, why on *earth* would I want them to be seen by others?"

"Surely you must have some spark of ambition," I said, as I leapt to my feet and followed her and Keeper into the house, "to see your work in print."

"I do not."

"Why else did you copy them out so carefully into your notebook?"

"To preserve them for my own review, not for any one else's!"

"They deserve—they cry out—to be published!"

"Never!" cried Emily as she fled up the stairs, Keeper at her heels. Seconds later, I heard her door slam.

The next morning, I was awakened by the sound of a drawer sliding open. I opened my eyes to the hazy sight of a slight female form, shrouded in white, removing something from the dresser. I sat up in bed, retrieved my spectacles and brought the hovering figure into focus, proving that it was indeed Anne. On seeing me awake, Anne came to the bed and sat down uncertainly beside me, cradling something to her chest.

"What is it, Anne?"

"Since Emily's verse gave you so much pleasure," said she quietly, "I thought perhaps you might like to look at these." She held out two note-books, similar in size and make-up to Emily's.

I took the proffered treasure with surprise, and looked inside. "How long have you been writing poetry?"

"For years and years: the whole time I was at Thorp Green, and for a long while before that. I have filled three other copybooks."

"Why did you never say?"

"I used to feel as Emily does—that they were my private musings, for my eyes alone. But when I heard you say that hers ought to be published, I could not help but wonder—I suppose I have always wondered—if my poems had any merit at all. Would you be willing to read them, and tell me?"

Touched by her modesty, and delighted by her willingness to share, I read her poems at once. I spent all day at it, and was surprised and impressed by what I found. Loving Anne as dearly as I did, I could not be but a partial judge; yet I thought that her verses, too, had a sweet, sincere pathos of their own. If not quite as brilliant as Emily's, they were equally worthy of publication.

As I contemplated what my sisters had been doing—that they had been writing secret poetry of such excellence—I felt a sudden surge of excitement, mingled with a hint of shame. I had written poetry, too, once upon a time; it resided, along with countless stories and novelettes, in a series of tattered boxes buried in my bureau. Almost all my life, writing had been my greatest joy and comfort: a place to express my happiest feelings, and my solace in times of pain. Although I had long burned to see my work in print, I had had no idea how to make that dream a reality; and since Anne came home in June, I had not written a single creative word.

Now, a sudden, renewed ambition burned within me: a desperate longing which I could not ignore. I waited until that evening, when my sisters and I were alone together in the dining-room, to bring up the subject. I was knitting a pair of stockings; Anne was sewing her grey-figured silk frock, newly dyed at Keighley; Emily was ironing.

"Anne showed me some poems she has written," I said casually, my eyes intent upon my knitting. "They are quite good."

"I know," replied Emily, as she expertly worked the hot iron over a night-shirt.

"I wrote poetry myself, a few years past," I added.

"I read Charlotte's poems," interjected Anne. "They are lovely."

"I do not pretend that my work compares in any way to either of yours," I continued, "but it occurred to me that we might, the three of us, publish a small collection."

Emily blew out a contemptuous breath. "Are we *never* to hear the end of this?"

"Have we not, since early childhood, all cherished the dream of one day becoming published authors?"

"I have," admitted Anne.

A blush crept across Emily's countenance, betraying what she could not hide, but she pressed her lips in a tight line. "No."

"We relinquished the dream years ago, when the necessity of

earning a living intervened. Now that we are all back home together, perhaps it is possible—if we put our minds to it—for dream and necessity to be combined. If we were to each choose our very best efforts, I believe they would make up a substantial volume of poetry, which we could sell for a good price."

"A ludicrous idea," retorted Emily. "My best poems are about Gondal. They would mean nothing to the public."

"I disagree. They are universal works in theme and execution. You would have only to title them, and amend the text a very little—perhaps change a few names here and there—to make them wholly accessible to any one."

"That is true," said Anne; for she had persuaded Emily to allow her to read the Gondal note-book, and had been equally moved.

"I doubt we could make any money from a book of poetry," argued Emily. "It would simply be an exercise to feed your vanity. Why cannot you both be content, as we have always been, to write to please ourselves? Why this sudden avidity for renown?"

"I do not seek renown," I replied. "In truth, I do not care if I ever see my *name* in print. It is the *work itself* I wish to share—not just mine, but all of ours."

"Why?" demanded Emily.

I realised I had never asked myself that question. "I suppose, after reading and admiring the works of others all my life, and feeling compelled for so many years to produce efforts of my own, I would like to discover—as Anne said, this morning—if they have any merit at all."

"So you wish to receive validation of some sort," retorted Emily, "from the world at large? You want to know if others—*strangers*—think our writing is any good?"

"Yes."

Anne admitted that she shared the same desire.

"It would be thrilling," I added, "to think that people we have never met were reading works that sprang from our imagination; that via tiny ink marks on a page, the thoughts and images of our invention were conveyed from our minds to theirs.

If, in reading, they felt some small measure of the pleasure I had in writing, it would prove a great reward."

I saw a flicker of concurrence in Emily's eyes; I knew that, deep down, she felt exactly as I did, although she could not admit it. If only, I thought, I could fan that spark to flame!

"What if others do not care for your work? Have you considered that?" asked Emily. "What if they despise your best efforts and call you a fool? How will you feel then?"

"If I agree with their assessment," replied Anne, "I shall feel chastened and educated, and I will endeavour to improve. If I disagree, I'll know they did not understand what I wrote, and I will disregard what they said."

"That is easier said than done," responded Emily with a frown. "Critics can be both harsh and cruel. More than one author of merit, I believe, has sunk under the mortification of bad notices. It is particularly hard, it seems to me, for women; from what I have read, authoresses are looked upon with great prejudice."

"I have noticed that," said I. "Critics sometimes do, in their reviews, use the weapon of sex or personality for their chastisement—or for their reward, a flattery which is not true praise."

"Well, I refuse to subject myself to that scrutiny," declared Emily.

"If Emily does not wish to participate, you and I might still publish a book of poems, Charlotte. We do not have to put our names on it."

My pulse quickened at this notion. "Good idea. I should be most thankful for the sheltering shadow of an incognito."

"We do not even have to reveal our gender," added Anne. "We could each adopt a *nom de plume*. That is, if you do not think our writing is too decidedly feminine."

"I do not see how any one could tell our sex from either the style or content of our work. Men do often write as women, and vice versa."

"What name would you choose?" inquired Anne.

"I have no idea," said I, with rising excitement, "but—"

"Are you picking *pen names,* now?" interrupted Emily, exasperated. "What do you two know about publishing a book? Not a thing! How would we even go about it?"

My mind seized on the word *we* in Emily's last sentence, and I smiled. "I do not know. I shall seek advice, I suppose."

Although Emily would not openly reconcile herself to our poetry book project for several more days, she listened in keenly on my conversations with Anne on the subject, and injected a comment or two. At last, one cold and wet October evening, after all the household was in bed, as Anne and I sat reading our poems at the dining-room table, Emily marched into the room.

"All right," said she, pulling up a chair and plunking two note-books onto the table, "I will participate in this folly—on one condition."

"Oh, Emily!" exclaimed Anne, her eyes bright. "I am so glad."

"What condition?" I asked warily.

"That we keep the entire enterprise a secret. Papa is beset by so many difficulties, I do not wish to worry him further, nor do I wish to raise his hopes, lest the venture should prove to be a failure. In the event the book is a success, secrecy will be crucial to preserving our anonymity."

"I agree," I replied.

"What about Branwell?" said Anne. "May we tell him, at least? He has written some wonderful poetry over the years. He might like to make a contribution."

"Do you really imagine that our brother could keep silent about something like this?" responded I, bristling. "And when would we tell him about it? When he is storming about the house, enraged because no one will give him a shilling? When he is lying bleary-eyed on the sofa, too ill to speak? Or when he is on his knees, sobbing like a three-year-old about his darling Mrs. Robinson?"

"He is despicable of late, no question," agreed Anne with a sigh, "but he is the only one of us who *has* been published."

"Yes," said I, "but this book will require hard work. After we revise and copy out our poems, we shall have a great many letters to write; if we are fortunate enough to secure a publisher, there will be decisions to make, and proofs to read. I doubt Branwell could stay sober long enough to be of any use in the process."

"Even if he did," added Emily, "knowing Branwell, he might try to take the project away from us, insisting that—as he is the *man*—he knows how to do everything best."

"Which, in his present state of mind, would prove disastrous," said I. "For once, I would like to do something that is just *ours*; to prove that three women, working together, can accomplish something worthwhile and wonderful, with no men involved. What do you say?"

"I say yes," exclaimed Anne and Emily together.

With great excitement, we began to prepare our little volume. We chose nineteen poems of mine, and twenty-one each by Emily and Anne. We agreed from the outset that we should submit the manuscript as the work of three pseudonymous authors, and gave great consideration to the choice of pen names.

"If we cannot be Brontës, do let us have a name that at least *begins* with a *B,*" said Anne.

We considered and rejected "Baker" as too provincial, "Byron" as too grand, "Bennett" as too Welsh, "Buchanan" as too Scottish, and "Brown" as too dull. Anne suggested "Bewley," but Emily thought that sounded too much like the bleat of a wounded animal, and the names "Bolster," "Bigler," and "Blenkinsop" only reduced us to tears of laughter.

We gave serious thought to our choice of Christian names, as well. We did not want to declare ourselves women, but at the same time, we did not wish to assume names too positively masculine, as that would be an outright lie.

"There are many names that are unspecific as to gender," said I.

"I intend to choose a name that begins with the same first letter as my Christian name," declared Anne.

"Let us all do that," said I. "Let us be perfectly, cleverly alliterative."

We offered up for scrutiny every ambiguous-sounding Christian name we could think of that began with *C, E,* and *A.* At any given point in time, we might have become "Cameron, Elliot, and Aubrey Brook," "Cassidy, Eustace, and Ashton Beech," or "Chase, Emery, and Adrian Bristol."

At length, we settled on Currer, Ellis, and Acton for our Christian names. At the end of October, we were still engaged in heavy debate about our surname, when all the most prominent members of our community gathered to celebrate the installation of our new peal of bells.

The original bells in our church tower had been old and comparatively small, the first dating from 1664, the other two added in the 1740s. Papa, wishing to improve their sound and status, and to make it possible for Haworth's team of ringers to engage in the new fashion of change-ringing competitions, had, that spring, organised a committee to raise a subscription to replace the three old bells with a peal of six. In two months, the money had been raised, enabling him to place an order for the casting of the bells with Mr. Mears of London. The new bells had only just been installed in the tower, and all those who contributed had been invited to an early dinner at the Black Bull Inn, which was to be followed by a bell-ringing ceremony.

My brother, thankfully, arrived sober to the dinner, and remained so for a good hour at least before he had to be carried home. Papa gave a brief welcoming speech to the assembled crowd, and thanked them for their support. John Brown, the sexton, a stout man in his early forties, followed with a litany of testaments in praise of papa's contributions to the community, with special appreciation for this latest achievement. As my sisters and I enjoyed the hearty meal of cold ham, parsley potatoes, and various vegetables, we listened with pride to the enthusiastic comments from our neighbours.

"You've done a wonderful thing, Mr. Brontë," declared Mr. Malone, the Irishman who ran one of the four beer-houses in the village, as he came over from the next table to shake papa's hand. "We can hold our heads up now against the folk in Keighley and Bradford, for truly we have got one of the best sets of bells in all of Yorkshire."

"So we have, Mr. Malone," replied papa proudly.

Mrs. Malone leaned towards me and murmured, "A wonder it is, that even with his infirmity, your father continues to work so tirelessly on behalf of the community."

"My father is a remarkable man," I agreed.

"Our new curate is a good man, too," said their daughter Sylvia, a plump, cheerful twenty-five-year-old with auburn curls and a freckled complexion. I had attempted over the years to strike up a conversation with Sylvia at the annual church teas, but as she had never been to school, had no interest in reading, and mainly liked to discuss her interest in and dissatisfaction with all the eligible bachelors in the community, I had never found much common ground between us. Her eyes now darted to a table on the other side of the room, where Mr. Nicholls sat engrossed in lively conversation with his friends Mr. Grant and Mr. Bradley, the curate of nearby Oakworth. "I see Mr. Nicholls every now and then, walking your dogs across the moor," continued Sylvia with a wide smile. "He is so tall and good-looking."

"Mr. Nicholls gives a fine reading in church," observed Mrs. Malone.

"The children at the Day school and Sunday school seem to like him very much," said Mr. Malone.

"It seems that Mr. Nicholls has taken over the parson's duties in the parish most capably," added Mrs. Malone. "Is it true that he handles almost everything now, except the giving of the Sunday sermon?"

"Yes," I replied coolly. Every morning, I knew, Mr. Nicholls taught religious instruction at the National School; every afternoon, he visited the poor and the sick. He now performed the majority of the marriages, baptisms, and burials in the community; enrollment at the Sunday school had greatly increased under his sway; he led all three Sunday services; and he assisted papa up the stairs to the high pulpit to deliver the weekly sermon—one of the few obligations not impeded by papa's near blindness, since papa had always made a practice of speaking extemporaneously, with an uncanny sense of timing that enabled him to finish after precisely thirty minutes. "Mr. Nicholls discharges his duties well," I added.

"It must be a great relief to Mr. Brontë, to have some one on whom he can rely so completely," said Sylvia.

"Indeed," said I. As the Malones turned back to their meal, I sighed and said to my sisters in a low tone, "I do wish people would not go on and on so about the virtues of Mr. Nicholls."

"All they said is true," insisted Anne. "With Branwell's indisposition and papa's disability, I do not know how we should get on without Mr. Nicholls. We are fortunate to have him."

"I know; and I admit, I am beginning to think a little better of him than I did previously. He has been helpful to us in times of need; for that I am very grateful—but at the same time, it is upsetting to be *obliged* to be grateful to a man like that."

"A man like what?" asked Anne. "He is always very polite to me."

"Did you not see the way Mr. Nicholls lost his temper last Sunday, just because that poor Quaker wore his hat in the church? Mr. Nicholls gave that parishioner such a black, dark look, and spoke to him so harshly, I believe the man may never attend services again."

"After services," interjected Emily, "I overheard Mr. Nicholls talking about Dissenters in the most insulting manner. He has no patience or respect for any one who does not follow his High Church views."

"Mr. Nicholls *is* rather unreasonable on that subject," admitted Anne, "and he can be rather harsh and insensitive at times—but I still like him—and I feel certain he likes you, Charlotte."

"Why do you keep saying so? He made very plain what he thinks of me, that night at tea."

"That was months ago, Charlotte," said Anne softly. "You

must find it in your heart to forgive him. Have you not noticed the look in Mr. Nicholls's eyes, every time he has brought Branwell home? And the way he has been staring at you all through dinner?"

I glanced across the room; to my dismay, Mr. Nicholls *was* looking in my direction. Unaccountably, I blushed, and averted my eyes. "He is not looking at me; he is looking at all of us."

After the cakes and pies had been served, and a great quantity of tea and coffee had been consumed, papa announced that we should gather in the churchyard for the ringing of the bells. Chattering excitedly, the crowd all donned their hats, coats, shawls, and gloves, then filtered outside the inn and surrounded the adjacent church. In the brisk chill of late afternoon, we all stood with eyes focused on the tower, waiting in a fervour of anticipation as the hour drew near.

Then it came: the sudden and joyous clash of the six new bells, ringing out from high above. A hush fell on the crowd as the bells pealed four times in quick succession; then, as the day's special treat, the bellringers launched into the program they had been practising all week: a rousing musical performance that lasted a full quarter of an hour, its mighty and varied notes resounding through the air with a pleasing musicality. At its conclusion, the crowd erupted into cheers and applause.

"Are they not magnificent!" I exclaimed.

"They are so much more sonorous than the previous bells," said Emily with a smile.

"What a comfort and delight it will be to hear their regular report, marking the passing hours," said Anne.

People began to drift away now. As the crowd thinned, I noticed Mr. Nicholls standing some distance away across the yard. Our eyes met; he tipped his hat. I nodded in response; he hesitated, as if contemplating coming over; then he apparently changed his mind, and headed towards his lodging.

My sisters and I were halfway to the door of the parsonage when Emily said suddenly: "What about Bell?"

"What *about* bell?" said I.

"For our literary surname," explained Emily. "It is Mr. Nicholls's middle name—his mother's maiden name, I think. Seeing him just now, and having heard the bells, made me think of it. We could be the anonymous 'Bell brothers.'"

"Oh!" replied Anne. "I like that. It is a nice, simple name, and it is easy to remember, pronounce, and spell."

"I would rather not use any name associated with Mr. Nicholls," said I dubiously.

"Why not?" asked Emily.

"If he finds out we stole his name, he might see it as some kind of personal tribute, which could not be further from the truth."

"If we *do* publish, we are to be anonymous," insisted Emily. "Mr. Nicholls will never know a thing about it."

A brief silence fell. "Well," said I quietly, as we entered the house, "I suppose 'Bell' does have a nice *ring* to it." We all burst out laughing.

Before we could proceed further on our tenuous first step into publishing, we required a great deal more ink and writing paper, both for copying our poetry, and for the correspondence involved. Writing paper was costly, but we each had a small legacy of £300 from Aunt Branwell—(she had left nothing to our brother, believing that, as a man, he could take care of himself)—and the income from those investments gave us the financial means to pursue a few interests of our own. Having already purchased the last bottle of ink and the last packet of paper in stock at our local stationer and bookseller's, we were obliged to go to Keighley to buy more.

A few days after the bell-ringing ceremony, leaving Emily to assist papa, and Branwell languishing in typical fashion in bed, Anne and I set out for Keighley. After a brisk walk, we arrived in town just in time to hear the bells in the Keighley church tower strike one o'clock.

"How much lovelier our own church bells sound," said I with a happy smile, as we opened the door to the stationer's shop, to the accompanying tinkle of yet *another* set of tiny bells hanging thereupon. The shop was devoid of customers. The proprietor, a diminutive, bespectacled, and bewhiskered man with rosy cheeks was known to us, as we had applied to him for writing supplies on several occasions over the past twenty years.

"Well, if it isn't the Misses Brontë!" cried he, looking up from behind the counter. I noted apprehension behind his smile, and wondered if it was occasioned by some news he might have heard regarding Branwell's indisposition; this, I soon discovered, was not the case. "It has been a great long while since you two ladies crossed our threshold! Why, I almost did not recognise you! How have you been keeping yourselves?"

"Very well, thank you, sir," I replied.

"Well! What a delight to see you both. Why, Miss Anne, I remember when you were no bigger than a grasshopper. How is your sister—what is her name again?"

"Emily."

"Yes, Emily. I cannot even recall the last time I saw Emily. She is a shy one, is she not?"

"Emily is quite the homebody," said I, "but she keeps as busy as a bee, and is very content."

"For many years, I used to put by a packet of paper on a special shelf in back, just in case a member of the Brontë family should make a sudden, unexpected appearance. My wife used to say to me: 'Who can those young people be writing to, that they require all that ink and all that paper? They must have a great many friends indeed!'" The bells on the shop door tinkled, and the proprietor briefly glanced in that direction with a laugh before continuing: "Well! How can I help you to-day?"

"In precisely the same manner, sir," I replied. "We require two bottles of your best India ink, half-a-dozen new steel nibs, and three large packets of writing paper."

"Ah! I was afraid of that. I can readily supply you with ink and nibs, ladies, but I am sorry to inform you that I am completely out of writing paper at this juncture."

"Out of writing paper?" said Anne in dismay.

"I am so sorry; but I do expect another shipment next week."

"This is distressing indeed," said I, knowing that there was no other outlet within many miles where we might obtain the necessary article. "We shall simply have to find a way to survive without it a little longer. I suppose we might as well purchase the ink and nibs, and return for the paper when it comes in."

"Very well." As the shopkeeper gathered the aforementioned items and wrote up a bill of sale, a deep, familiar voice with an Irish lilt spoke from behind me:

"Miss Brontë, Miss Anne?"

I turned and, to my surprise, encountered Mr. Nicholls standing behind us.

"How nice to see you, Mr. Nicholls," said Anne, as we curtseyed to meet his bow.

"What brings you to Keighley, sir?" I asked.

"Church business, on behalf of your father. I just finished meeting with the vicar of Keighley. I saw you two ladies entering this establishment, and thought I might come in and say hello."

"I am glad you did, sir," said I politely.

"I do not mean to intrude," said Mr. Nicholls, "but I could not help overhearing your predicament. Three packets is a great deal of writing paper. May I ask what is it for?"

My cheeks grew warm; my eyes flew to Anne's; she appeared equally uncomfortable. "It is a private matter, Mr. Nicholls," said I, "about which I have been vowed to secrecy. I know you would not wish me to break my word by imparting even the merest hint about it to you."

"I see. Forgive me, Miss Brontë. I will inquire no further."

Anne and I completed our transaction and left the shop. As Mr. Nicholls accompanied us out to the street, he said, "Do you have further business in Keighley?"

"We are walking home directly, sir," said I.

"May I have the honour of accompanying you?"

I could think of no graceful manner in which to refuse his offer; before I could reply, however, the decision was removed from my power by the events which immediately followed.

Anne touched me on the arm and said, "Is not that Miss Malone?"

Following her gaze, I caught sight of two young women crossing the street towards us, arm-in-arm. The first, I recognised: it was Sylvia Malone, the young woman who had been so keen in her praise of Mr. Nicholls at the bell-ringing dinner a few nights before. Her companion was a pleasant-faced, auburn-haired girl in her early twenties, who resembled Sylvia both in form and feature, although she quite outshone her in terms of apparel. Whereas Sylvia was dressed in a drab merino pelisse and cottage bonnet, the other young lady wore a well-made wool cloak and a lovely silk frock, with a matching ribbon in her stylish bonnet.

"Miss Brontë! Miss Anne!" cried Sylvia, hurrying towards us with her companion on her arm. Demurely, she added: "Hello, Mr. Nicholls."

As the young ladies stopped before us, the newcomer and Mr. Nicholls both started in shocked recognition, coloured, and averted their gazes.

"May I present my cousin, Miss Bridget Malone, who is visiting from Dublin for a few weeks," said Sylvia with a smile, unaware of that young lady's discomfort, or the fact (obvious to me) that she was previously acquainted, and clearly in no happy manner, with the gentleman in our presence. "Bridget: this is Charlotte and Anne Brontë, the daughters of our parson, and here is our own curate of Haworth, Mr. Nicholls."

We all exchanged greetings, and curtseyed or bowed. Bridget alone remained mute.

"What a surprise to find you all here in Keighley!" exclaimed Sylvia.

"Indeed, it is a most unexpected occurrence," murmured Mr. Nicholls, adding abruptly: "I am sorry to say, I must take my leave. I am expected back in Haworth shortly. Good day to you, ladies. Have a pleasant afternoon." Tipping his hat, he turned and moved off up the street.

"He was certainly in a great hurry," said Sylvia with a frown, watching Mr. Nicholls's retreating figure. "I was hoping for a chance to speak to him. He is a fine-looking man, is he not? He is so tall and strongly built, and has such lovely eyes."

"His eyes may be fine," declared Bridget with a hard edge to her strong Irish voice, "but don't let them fool you. That man has a heart of granite."

"Why do you say that, Bridget?" asked Sylvia in surprise.

"Are you acquainted with Mr. Nicholls?" I inquired.

"I am," replied Bridget. "We met in Dublin, a few years back. He—oh! It is a long story." Bridget's face suddenly crumpled, and she burst into tears.

"Bridget! Good God!" cried Sylvia in alarm. "I had no idea you knew him. You must tell me everything, and all." To us, she added, "There's the Devonshire Arms, just up the road. Will you join us for a beer or a cup of tea?"

Anne and I exchanged a look; I saw from her expression that she was as keenly interested in this turn of events as I. "We would be delighted to join you for tea," said I; and to the Devonshire Arms we quickly adjourned.

VOLUME II

Eight

The Devonshire Arms was a busy coaching inn with an old-fashioned charm, which we had frequented on many occasions. When we were comfortably situated at a table near the fire, with a steaming pot of tea and a plate of scones and jam, Miss Malone told us her story.

"I was born in Dublin," said Bridget in her strong Irish brogue, as she sipped her tea. "I have lived there all my life. My father is a businessman. He owns several shops, and we live in a very nice house."

"I have never seen it," put in Sylvia, "but my father has, and he says it is very nice indeed."

"From the day I turned sixteen," Bridget went on, "I had many suitors, all very wealthy and eligible men that my mam and da were keen on me to marry, but I said no, I won't marry for money. I'll wait to find my One True Love. Then one day, my brother brought a young man to the house: your very own Arthur Bell Nicholls. He and my brother were school-mates, you see, at Trinity College. For nigh on to six months, Mr. Nicholls came to the house nearly every week-end. In my eyes, the moon rose and set on that gentleman, and he fell equally in love with me; but we had to keep our love a secret, for Mr. Nicholls, you know, comes from a very poor family—he's one of ten children, I think."

"I have heard that," I said.

Bridget paused to spread a dab of butter and jam on a scone, and took a dainty bite. "Well, at length, Mr. Nicholls proposed. He said he didn't have a penny, and it must be a long engagement, for he still had years of college to finish before he could be graduated and ordained; but would I wait for him? I said yes, I would! I thought I'd like to die of happiness! But when Mr. Nicholls went to my father for permission, my da laughed him out of the room. He said I was free to marry whomsoever I liked, but he wouldn't give a farthing for a dowry to a daughter who married the son of a poor farmer, who was destined to be no more than a poor curate."

"How cold and unfeeling of him!" I cried, my heart going out to her.

"What did you do?" asked Anne.

"Surely, if you loved each other," said Sylvia, "you could have married, even without your father's money or permission."

"I told Mr. Nicholls so," said Bridget. "I was perfectly ready to give up everything and all, and wait for him. But the next day, he didn't come to call; nor the next week; and I never heard from him again."

"Oh!" I exclaimed, my hand jerking with such dismay that I spilled half the contents of my tea-cup into my saucer. "To abandon you like that—to withdraw his affection so coldly, without a word—it is inexcusable."

"It liked to break my heart," said Bridget, as tears started in her eyes. "I was so ashamed to think I could have loved him. It wasn't until years later that my brother told me Mr. Nicholls had gone to England. He is the worst kind of degenerate, to my way of thinking, for he was clearly only after me for my money."

A volley of similar censures issued from Sylvia's lips, while Anne sat in silent consternation. We soon finished our tea and left the establishment, continuing our conversation as we walked back to Haworth. For the first three miles, Sylvia confided in us as to her own previous and numerous disappointments of the heart; for the last mile, Bridget told us how she had been coping in the years since Mr. Nicholls's betrayal, and about the many suitors who had tried in vain to win her hand.

"I think my heart is broken," declared Bridget with a sigh. "I try to like a man, but no matter how kind and decent he may appear, I'm too full of fear. I now see only treachery and deceit."

When we reached the Malones' beer house at the edge of Haworth village, Anne and I hugged our companions good-bye, and I invited them to stop by the parsonage any afternoon for tea. Bridget graciously declined, insisting that she would stay close to home, as she did not want to take a chance, during her visit, of running into *that gentleman* again.

"Oh!" said I, as Anne and I began the steep climb up Main Street. "I disliked Mr. Nicholls before, but my regard for him has plummeted to new depths."

"I would not be so quick to judge Mr. Nicholls," replied Anne. "There may be some other explanation for all this—some misunderstanding that exists between him and Miss Malone."

"What kind of misunderstanding?"

"I do not know—but I find it hard to believe that Mr. Nicholls would knowingly behave in such a cold and callous manner. He is, at heart, a good man."

"I fail to see the germs of goodness in Mr. Nicholls that you imagine he possesses, Anne. If Mr. Nicholls saw a young woman and a common hound lying bleeding in the street, I believe he would go first to the aid of the dog, before he would even think to help the human being. For *my* part, I would be happy if I never set eyes on him again."

Two nights later, Emily, Anne, and I were assembled in the dining-room behind a closed door, with our entire collection of assorted poetry spread out on the table before us, when the door-bell rang. Knowing that Martha would answer, I paid little attention.

"I think your best poem is *Cold in the earth, and the deep snow piled above thee,*" I told Emily, quoting that piece's first line. "It breaks my heart to think the speaker has had to live fifteen years without his beloved. But it still needs a title."

"I have decided to call it 'Remembrance,'" replied Emily. "I have titles for all of them, and I have finished my editing, but I cannot progress further without more paper."

A sudden knock sounded at the door to our apartment. I opened it a crack and peeked into the passage, where Martha stood waiting. "Yes?"

"Mr. Nicholls is here, ma'am." (Martha had, for many years now, called me *ma'am* instead of *miss*; I supposed it was a sign of respect, as I was the eldest daughter in the house.)

"Please show Mr. Nicholls into papa's study," I replied abruptly. I was about to shut the door, when Martha interjected:

"He says he's here t' see *ye,* ma'am."

"To see me? Well, I have no wish to see him. Tell him I am not at home."

"I already bade him enter, ma'am," whispered Martha with quiet urgency, her eyes darting towards the vestibule. "I said ye be here. He claims he has summat for ye."

"What could he have to give me?"

"I dunnut, but he insists he must give it ye hisself. He's waiting just there, in th' hall."

"Oh—all right. Tell him to wait. I will be out in a moment." I shut the door and took a deep breath, steeling myself for the encounter, determined to remain composed.

"Who is it?" asked Anne, looking up from her work at the dining-table.

"Mr. Nicholls. Apparently he has brought me something."

"How nice," said Anne.

"You think every one and everything in the world is *nice,*" observed Emily. To me, she added, "Must we put everything away?"

"No. I will get rid of him."

I issued forth into the hall, firmly shutting the door behind me. Mr. Nicholls stood in the entry way holding a parcel, wrapped and tied with string, that was about the size and shape of a rather large book. He met my gaze as I marched up and stopped before him.

"Miss Brontë. I sensed your distress the other day, when the stationer at Keighley was out of paper. I went into Bradford yesterday and took the liberty of securing some. I hope you and your sisters can make some use of it." He offered me the package.

I gave a startled gasp. So that was the mysterious "something" in question: writing paper! The paper that we so dearly needed! For a brief, confused instant, my resolve left me. Mr. Nicholls was offering me a gift—a gift which he had clearly gone to great effort to procure, for Bradford was twelve miles away. Perhaps this was some kind of peace offering, for the comment he had made all those months ago? But then I thought: no! *No!* This man had once cruelly insulted me behind my back, and made no apology. Far worse, some years ago, he had mistreated an innocent young Irish lass in the most callous and heartless manner. I wanted no part of any peace offering from him.

"I am sorry, but I cannot accept it."

Mr. Nicholls's complexion paled; his eyes were all confusion. "I beg your pardon?"

"I cannot accept the paper."

"But why?"

"I think you know why."

"Mr. Nicholls!" came Anne's voice from behind, as she hurried up the passage and stopped beside me. "Do my ears deceive me? Does that package contain writing paper?"

"It does," said he, his face now bright red.

"Wherever did you find it, sir?"

"In Bradford."

"How kind of you to think of us, sir. I apologise for my sister; she is too proud, and can never bring herself to accept help from any one. Emily and I will be honoured to accept the paper on her behalf, and of course we will pay you for it."

"It is a gift," said Mr. Nicholls, still looking mortified, as he gave the parcel into Anne's keeping.

"Thank you sir," said Anne, "for your thoughtfulness and generosity. We are very grateful."

Mr. Nicholls darted a brief, uncertain look at me—and, finding no welcome there—bowed and quickly departed.

"Whatever were you thinking?" cried Anne, when he had gone. "I suspect he went all the way to Bradford entirely on our behalf, and we need this paper desperately!"

"To accept it would make me beholden to him; and the very notion of being in debt to Mr. Nicholls in any way, is entirely despicable to me."

"Oh! You are impossible!" Anne strode back into the dining-room with the package, which was met with great enthusiasm by Emily.

I staunchly refused to use a single sheet of Mr. Nicholls's paper, waiting until a new shipment arrived at our local stationer's before copying out my own poems, and writing letters of inquiry to prospective publishers.

Branwell made one rallying effort that autumn to fix himself; an effort which, as it turned out, had valuable and far-reaching consequences which he could not have foreseen. One stormy afternoon in late November, as I sat by the dining-room fire sewing a garment for the poor, Branwell strode in and made an unexpected announcement.

"You will be happy to hear I have begun a new project," he announced, as he pitched himself down onto the sofa.

"Have you? What project is that?"

"I am writing a novel."

"A novel?" I replied dubiously.

"Yes, and this novel is going to be different from and better than anything I have written before. This one, I mean for the world to see. I intend to be published."

"Published?" Now I looked up from my sewing with interest.

Branwell's eyes were bright with enthusiasm. "I once be-

lieved that getting a book published—a real, full-length novel—
was an unattainable goal, for such as I; that my only hope of
ever seeing my work in print rested on the poems I placed in
the newspapers and journals. But now, I know differently. I
have done some research. It seems that in the present state of
the publishing and reading world, a novel is the most saleable
article."

"Is it, indeed?"

"Yes! Were I to write a great scholarly work, which would
take years and years and years, and require the utmost stretch
of a brilliant man's intellect, I might be lucky to be offered ten
pounds for it. But for a novel—three light volumes whose composition would require the mere smoking of a cigar and the
humming of a tune—for a *novel,* two hundred pounds could be
offered, and just as easily refused!"

My heart began to beat faster. "Are novels really so popular,
and so sought after?"

"They are. Would you like to read what I have written so
far?"

I said I would. Branwell darted from the room and quickly
returned, bringing me the first forty or so pages of his novel in
progress, a work entitled *And The Weary Are at Rest.* I immediately perused it. It was the story of a virtuous young woman
named Maria Thurston, a neglected wife who longs for love,
and is driven, despite herself, into the arms of her lover, Alexander Percy, the Earl of Northangerland.

"It is compelling and dramatic," I told Branwell, when I returned the manuscript that evening. "I always liked that old
Angrian tale you wrote ages ago. I see that you have revised it to
be about you and Mrs. Robinson, with a slightly different outcome."

His countenance reddened as he seized the pages from me.
"So what if I have?"

"I meant it as a compliment. The story will be all the better
now, I think, for a little life experience. Did not Chateaubriand
say that 'great writers are only telling their *own* stories in their

works'—that 'one only truly describes one's own heart by attributing it to another'?"

Branwell nodded. "He said: 'the greater part of genius is composed of memories.'"

"Exactly. I did not understand that when we wrote as children; neither did you. We wrote wherever our fancies took us. I am wiser now. I have come to believe, in any work of art—be it poem, prose, painting, or sculpture—it is always best to draw off of real life."

"Perhaps you are right."

"If you can finish it, Branwell—if you can translate your heartache into your fiction, I believe you can write something truly worthy of publication."

It was a hope that was never to materialise. Although Branwell did manage to have two more poems published in the *Halifax Guardian,* he abandoned his book after the first volume.

His attempt, however, along with his assertions, lit a fire under me.

For the past two months, all my spare time had been occupied by the poetry book my sisters and I were compiling, a work which was now complete and ready for submission, should I find any interest from a publisher. However, as I lay wide-awake in bed the night after my conversation with Branwell, I was overcome by a sudden, startling realisation that set all my nerves tingling. The poetry book had been just an exercise: a means to an end. It was an attempt to be published, in any way I could. But what I *really* wanted—what I *had* wanted, more than anything in the world, for as long as I could remember—was not merely to be published; it was to be a published *author*.

I longed to write a novel.

Could it be that Branwell was right? I wondered with rising excitement. Could a novel, even from a new and unknown author, be a sought-after commodity? If so, perhaps I—a clergyman's daughter, living in a remote hilltop village, with no connections to the literary world—might have a chance at some modicum of success, however modest. I did not sleep all night, for thinking about the possibilities before me. I was anxious to look over my previous literary attempts, to see if any of them had merit. I had never completed a full-length novel before. My longest works to date were my Angrian stories; but I also had a new work in progress, which I had never shown to any one. Perhaps, I thought, I could take one of those works, as Branwell had done, and revise and extend it.

The next morning dawned grey and cold, but blessedly clear. After breakfast, when Anne and Emily left to take our customary walk, I said I thought I would stay in to write a letter. No sooner had they quit the premises, than I raced back upstairs to my chamber and unlocked the bottom drawer of my bureau: the same drawer that contained my rosewood box of letters from Monsieur Héger. Therein also resided a series of boxes of different sizes and shapes, which had begun their intentionally brief and disposable life with no other purpose than the delivery of various and sundry products; they now served as the sturdy repositories of my past creative works.

I removed one box and opened it. Within, lay a mountain of tiny, hand-sewn booklets, some no bigger than an inch across and two inches high, proportionate in size to the battalion of toy soldiers with which we had played as children. A wave of nostalgia washed over me as I gently examined them. Paper had been so scarce in our household, that Branwell and I had constructed the miniature books from scraps of drawing paper, advertisements, sugar bags and the like. In order to fit the maximum number of words on each page, we had perfected an infinitesimally small hand, designed to look like book print. Posing as fictitious historians, poets, and politicians—all of the masculine gender, in imitation of those we had read (I was usually Lord Charles Wellesley)—we had written plays, short stories, magazines, and newspapers, along with scurrilous reviews of each other's work. As I leafed through the pages, I was amazed that I could still read the microscopic print—if only when placed directly in front of my spectacles.

I replaced that box and rummaged through another. It

contained innumerable bundles of larger, loose sheets of paper, tied with ribbon or string: some were diary papers; others were the "novelettes" of my later teens and early twenties, all written in the same miniature hand. As I glanced through them now, I smiled fondly at such titles as *The Duke of Zamorna, Henry Hastings, Caroline Vernon, Mina Laury, Albion and Marina, Stancliffe's Hotel, The Secret, The Rivals, The Spell.*

Some stories I recalled as clearly as if I had written them only yesterday; others were enigmas to me. I read over bits and pieces of each of them, eager to determine if they might be worthy of another look. To my dismay, I found them to be for the most part silly, ornamented, and redundant. Oh! How lurid were the topics I had indulged in! How awash were they in spelling errors and non-existent punctuation! Why had I focused so often on the sensational, on rash, illicit love affairs, and on illegitimate children? Yet I could not forget how many hours of undiluted pleasure these stories had afforded me in their composition. I replaced them cosily in their box with a smile, determined that there they should remain—relics of my past—the passionate, imaginative expressions of my younger self.

I hesitated before a third box, my pulse beating a sudden frenzy. Therein lay the exercise books from my two-year education in Brussels: the countless essays I had written in French, with Monsieur's copious, emphatic, and instructive notes written in the margins. On how many occasions in the past two years had my eyes welled up with tears while perusing these documents, unable to forget that my Master's hands had once been in contact with every page?

No, I thought: this was no time for such reflections; they would only bring me pain.

I put the box away without opening it, and moved instead to the last receptacle. It contained a neat stack of pencil-written pages that comprised my most recent literary effort: twelve chapters of a work I had tentatively called *The Master.* I had sketched out a scheme for the tale while still in Brussels, but had not begun to write it until the previous autumn, after I returned. I had worked on the story in fits and starts until Anne and Branwell moved home, when I had locked it away.

At that moment, I heard the bark of the dogs and the slam of the kitchen door; my sisters had returned from their walk. I quickly returned my pages to their hiding-place and issued downstairs. I passed the remainder of the day in a state of such distraction, that I dropped a perfectly good dusting rag into the fire, and added coffee to the teapot instead of tea. Emily accused me of becoming prematurely senile; Anne suggested that I might need new spectacles; but all I could think about was my story.

The chapters that took place in Brussels—the few that I had completed—had proved particularly satisfying to write, and I had been sorry to set the work aside. The act of committing my memories to the page, of describing the people and places I knew and loved—or hated—even under the thin veil of fiction, had been both invigorating and comforting. It had made me feel closer to the person I could not banish from my thoughts; it had helped to pass the long, lonely evenings after my household had retired, and sleep would not come for me.

At the time, I had considered the project as one of countless stories destined for the storage box; I now viewed the composition in a new light. To finish it, even to the length of a single volume, would require a great deal of work; but if I *did* finish—would it make an interesting and saleable novel? The thought filled me with both excitement and trepidation. If I was to work on that story again, Anne and Emily would no doubt become aware of it; in fact, I would welcome their advice and counsel. The setting, however, was my school in Belgium; the hero, however idealised, was patterned after Monsieur Héger. Surely my sisters would recognise that. With that recognition, would they also see through my words, to the longing that lay behind them? In sharing this tale, would I not also be sharing the secrets of my heart that I had struggled so carefully to hide, and had so consistently denied?

That night, when every one else was asleep, I stole down into the dining-room and read over the manuscript that I had so far written. It was very rough; yet, I thought with mounting enthusiasm, the work seemed to have *some* merit. More importantly, I had revealed no overt expressions of feeling with regards to my hero. My heart pounding, I crept silently back upstairs, stowed my pages in my bureau, and crawled into bed beside Anne. My secret was safe, I decided, as I stared into the darkness; I *could* work on this book, even with my sisters' knowledge. Thus decided, I could hardly wait to inform them of my intentions.

It rained all morning. By early afternoon, the storm broke, and we three set out to traverse—at great risk to our shoes—the damp, solitary sweep of the moors, with Flossy and Keeper bounding happily beside us. A thick, grey canopy of clouds yet hung overhead, although the sun peeked out hopefully in spots, and a white gleam of sky hung at the very edges of the misty horizon.

"Branwell told me something very interesting yesterday," said I as we rambled along.

"Branwell?" remarked Emily, in mock surprise. "He actually said something lucid?"

"He did." I stopped and breathed deeply of the brisk, moisture-laden November air, delighting in the feel of the crisp breeze on my cheeks, and admiring the view: mile upon mile of grey-green heath, dissected here and there by low stone fences, with no other living creatures in sight except wild sheep, and no sounds but their frequent bleating, the whoosh of the wind and the cries of wild birds.

"Well?" said Emily, looking back, for she and Anne were already ten steps ahead of me, "are you going to tell us, or must we guess?"

I laughed and hurried to join them. "Branwell maintains that, in the present state of the publishing and reading world, a novel is the most saleable article."

"A novel?" Anne replied, an odd look on her face.

"He said an author might be offered two hundred pounds for such a work."

"Who can trust *anything* Branwell says," commented Emily sceptically. "He lies so often now. Every word that comes out of his mouth, I fear, is an invention to hide a transgression, or to puff up his vanity."

"He may be right about this," said I. "I admit, I know nothing about the business of publishing, but the reading of novels *does* seem to be increasing in both esteem and popularity. I was particularly glad to hear that, because—" I hesitated, then plunged ahead: "Now that our poetry book is ready for submission, I thought I might try to write a novel."

"Oh?" said Emily. "I thought you had given up that sort of writing to focus on what is *practical* and *prudent*. 'The imagination should be pruned and trimmed,' you said. 'The countless illusions of early youth should be cleared away'—I believe those were your words."

"I did say that, and I meant it. Instead of a romance or adventure, I want to write something that is real, plain, true, and homely. My hero would be no Duke of Zamorna, but a schoolteacher: a man who works his way through life, as I have seen real men work through theirs."

"That sounds promising," said Anne.

"It sounds *boring*," rejoined Emily, "incredibly so. Yet if that is what you wish to write, Charlotte, do not think about it or talk about it; *do it*."

"I have been!" I blurted. "I started working on the story last autumn. With applied effort, I believe I can turn it into a one-volume novel."

"Good," said Emily. A small silence fell, as we tramped along.

Then Anne murmured quietly and simply: "I am writing a novel, too."

"Are you? Since when?" I asked.

Anne's courage seemed to fail her; her cheeks turned crimson as she averted her gaze and said softly, "I began it a few years ago, at Thorp Green. I have been working at it, now and again, whenever I find the time. I wanted to tell you, but I was afraid you would laugh at me; you said such writing was frivolous."

"I am sure you would never write anything frivolous, Anne. What is your book about?"

"I call it *Passages in the Life of an Individual.* It is about a young woman's trials and tribulations as a governess, and the young curate she loves from afar."

I had barely a second to process this information, when Emily said:

"I have been writing a novel, too."

I stared at my sisters in great surprise: Anne, with her blushing modesty and quiet grace; and Emily, who had matter-of-factly mentioned her endeavour as if it were the most ordinary of accomplishments. "You have *both* been writing novels?"

"It began as a reworking of several of my Gondal stories," explained Emily, "but it seems to have taken the shape of a novel."

"How far along are you?" I asked.

"It is hard to say; perhaps two-thirds of the way through. I have written twenty chapters so far."

"Twenty chapters!" I cried, flabbergasted. "Emily, that is wonderful! What about you, Anne?"

"I have a first attempt completed," Anne admitted, "but I am not at all satisfied. I intend to rework the manuscript extensively."

I laughed out loud. The discovery that my sisters, whose only literary ambition I had thought to be poetry, had so outdistanced me in this regard, was a source of some mortification; at the same time, I was filled with pure, electrified delight. It was as if a gauntlet had been dropped before me, laying out an irresistible challenge.

We stopped on the crest of a ridge, overlooking the vast waste of heath and the distant hills beyond, which seemed rolled in a sullen mist. A sudden peal of thunder sounded, followed by a flash of lightning; fitting portents, I thought, for the uncertain future ahead of us; for it seemed at that moment as if we stood on the very brink of an adventure as wild, stormy, and unpredictable as the threatening tempest.

"Perhaps we can all be published authors together," I said, brimming with excitement and determination. "But before that can happen, I see I have a great deal of work to do, if I am to catch up with the two of you."

Now that the truth was out, my sisters and I were no longer required to write by stealth, at least with regard to each other. We continued the routine we had employed in the production of our poetry book: we sped through our chores and limited our daily walks; when an hour or two of quiet presented themselves of a morning or an afternoon, we locked ourselves in the dining-room or in our bedrooms, and applied our energies diligently to the writing of our respective tales. Every evening, immediately after prayers, when every one else was asleep, we reconvened in the dining-room to continue our work until midnight.

We did not worry that our activity would attract undue attention in the household. Tabby and Martha already considered us rather eccentric; and papa and Branwell thought nothing of it, since we had been scribbling stories in a similar manner ever since we were children. Emily and Anne had already made great progress on the pencil drafts of their books; I had far more work to do; but we all chose to go back and edit from the beginning, so that we could become equally acquainted with each other's work.

Once or twice a week, as certain points in our respective narratives were reached, we took time out from writing to read parts aloud—an activity of great and stirring interest to us all. A discussion followed; or rather, I should say, an argument: we shared our thoughts, and challenged and appraised our works in progress, in a spirit of absolute equality and frankness—all the while unsparing in our criticisms, and often erupting into heated discussions regarding style and content. Tired of sitting, we often conducted this verbal battle on our feet, striding single file round and round the dining-table—a habit I had learned from my days at Roe Head School, when Miss Wooler used to lead us girls on similar indoor strolls, which she claimed "improved the circulation and heightened the mental faculties."

"I adore your Mr. Weston," I told Anne one night, after a reading from her quiet and honest tale of a governess, which she had, at my suggestion, re-titled *Agnes Grey*. "He is such a sensible, sincere man, so affable and kind to the poor; a truly dedicated curate—far different from most of the young men we have known in that capacity."

"He is very much like William Weightman," observed Emily, referring to our much-loved curate who had died young and tragically from cholera a few years before.

"I did think of Mr. Weightman when I first wrote it," admitted Anne, as we walked around the table, "but now the character reminds me more of Mr. Nicholls."

"Mr. Nicholls?" said I. "Do not be absurd. Mr. Nicholls has none of the admirable qualities of your Mr. Weston."

"Yes he does," replied Anne.

"Martha said her mother is very beholden to Mr. Nicholls," said Emily. "He is a good and thoughtful tenant, and was a great help to her in the house when Mr. Brown was ill."

"Every one in the village likes Mr. Nicholls," said Anne.

"Every one in the village *except* the Malones," I argued, "and if they were not so discreet, and had shared that gentleman's *history* with others, the whole village might well feel very differently about him."

"I still believe there is more to Miss Malone's tale than we have yet heard," said Anne.

"And *I* have heard all I care to hear about Mr. Nicholls!" I cried, exasperated. "We are *supposed* to be talking about our books."

"I was going to say, Anne," said Emily, getting us back on track, "that although I find Mr. Weston too much of a goody-good for my taste, I do love your other characters. Agnes's pupils and employers are all so wonderfully self-involved, and they exhibit such interesting streaks of cruelty."

"Those are precisely the parts I *dislike*," said I. "I think readers might be put off by the incident where the little boy tortures and kills the birds. It is disturbing. I cannot imagine that a six-year-old would do such a thing."

"But he *did*," insisted Anne. "Cuncliffe Ingham, who was in my charge, committed those very acts. Indeed, every incident I wrote about is taken from first-hand experience, except—" (here she blushed) "except the ending, which you have not heard yet."

The next evening, we discussed Emily's complex novel, which was set in our own Yorkshire moors. She called it *Wuthering Heights,* after the house that figures prominently in the story—its name derived from the atmospheric tumult to which its station was exposed in stormy weather.

"I was not sure I liked your structure at first," I said, after Emily finished reading a particularly dark but fascinating chapter. "The way you move back and forth in time, and employ different narrators, neither of whom is very reliable—but now I think it quite brilliant."

"I agree," said Anne. "Shifting the viewpoint gives us an entirely new perspective. I think I will try it in my next book."

"Were you thinking of *Rob Roy* when you wrote this, Emily?" I asked. "Your book reminds me in some ways of Scott's themes and characters."

"Perhaps I was, a bit," mused Emily. "That has always been one of my favourite novels."

"Cathy *is* similar in many ways to Diana Vernon," commented Anne. "Both are misfits in a boorish family."

"And Heathcliff, with his diabolical determination to undermine the Earnshaws and Lintons by seizing their inheritances, reminds me of Scott's Rashleigh Osbaldistone," I said. "But Emily: your story is so much fiercer and darker. I truly *despise* Heathcliff. He is so savage, tortured, and relentless. I find him entirely unredeemable."

"Is he?" responded Emily, her eyebrows lifting quizzically.

"Or does his all-consuming passion for Catherine serve as his redemption?"

"His passion cannot excuse the systematic manner of his revenge on Hindley Earnshaw and the Lintons," I insisted, "or the way he degrades and brutalises Isabella Linton and Hareton. He is hateful!"

"I do not mind that he is hateful," said Anne. "Every story needs a villain."

"But *is* he the villain?" argued Emily. "Or is he more akin to Byron's Manfred, Mary Shelley's Castruccio, or Milton's Satan—a Gothic hero, a character who operates as a principle of evil?"

I shook my head. "He is a ghoul; a demon; an Afreet. I am not certain it is right or advisable to create beings like Heathcliff."

"I hear Branwell's voice in every one of Heathcliff's tortured ravings," said Anne.

"Yes!" exclaimed I. "The way he goes on and on about his precious Cathy—'Oh! My heart's darling! I cannot live without my soul!'—and how he wants to follow her to the grave—it is Branwell, through and through. But Branwell has made us all wretched, Emily. Who will want to read this? Why have you chosen to write a book that is so relentlessly grim?"

"It is the story I wished to tell," said Emily simply.

"The chapters you read last week were so violent and so fearful, that I did not sleep a wink," I added with a shudder. "The images they conjured up in my mind disrupted my mental peace all the next day."

"That is ridiculous," scoffed Emily. "I do not believe you."

"Can you not give *some* of your characters a few moments of happiness?" said Anne.

"I intend to," insisted Emily. "You will just have to wait until the end."

Emily was as unequivocal in her assessment of my novel, as I had been of hers. She disliked the title (*"The Master* sounds like a story about a landlord and his servant!"); I changed it therewith to *The Professor.* She then insisted that my story was slow in starting, that it lacked excitement in general, and that my male protagonist was particularly flat. I disagreed. I liked my story and characters as they were (I have since learned better); but at the time, I could not see its flaws; I was just thrilled to be writing again—and to be involved, on a daily basis, in a free and lively communion with two other vibrant, interested, intelligent, kindred spirits with whom I could share the innermost workings of my mind.

I met each new day filled with excited anticipation, eager to pick up my pencil and get to work, to discover what my characters would say and do next. I was happy; I felt newly alive; it was as if I had been asleep for half a decade, and had only just awakened; as if I had been existing on the brink of starvation for years, and had finally sat down before a feast.

As we wrote, the months sped by. Christmas came and went; 1846 dawned; the country-side was buried in snow. At the end of January, we had still not received a single reply to my letters of inquiry on behalf of our book of poems. I did, however, gain some very sensible advice from William and Robert Chambers, publishers of one of my favourite periodicals, *Chambers's Edinburgh Journal.* They explained that a book of poetry by an unknown author or authors would most likely not appeal to a wide readership; therefore, it would be rare indeed for any publishing house to take on any such effort—unless said author was willing to pay for the publication himself.

My sisters and I despaired at first; but on further consideration, we rallied. "We could use a small portion of our legacies from Aunt Branwell," I suggested, "if it is not too dear."

"I do not mind paying," said Emily, "but let us hope the book receives good reviews, so that we might see *some* return on our investment."

"If it paves the way for the publication of our novels, it will be worth it," agreed Anne.

I embarked on another round of letters, which I sent to a variety of publishers:

January 28th, 1846

Gentlemen

May I request to be informed whether you would undertake the publication of a Collection of short poems in 1 vol. octavo—

If you object to publishing the work at your own risk—would you undertake it on the Author's account?

> *I am Gentlemen*
> *Your obdt. hmble. Servt.*
> *C Brontë*

To our delight, the firm of Aylott & Jones, a small publishing house in London, soon agreed to undertake the printing of the book "at the author's expense." With great excitement, we bundled up our finished manuscript in two parcels and posted it to them. I explained that the authors were the "Bells," adding only that they were "three persons—relatives," and that all future correspondence should be written in care of their representative, "Miss C. Brontë."

After a brief and business-like exchange, we learned that—to our astonishment—the cost required to print our book of poems would be much higher than anticipated.

"Thirty-one pounds!" I cried, when I received the news. "It is twice what I earned in a year in Brussels."

"It is more than three quarters of my annual salary at Thorp Green," said Anne.

"Perhaps we should reconsider," said Emily.

I sat down heavily in my chair, and shook my head. "No. We have all worked too hard on this project to give up now. For months, I have been imagining that book in my mind. I long to see it in print—and to hold it in my hands. We cannot let a mere sum of money stand in our way. I will send Aylott and Jones a banker's draft for the named sum."

★   ★   ★

While we waited for our book of poems to reach the press, and my sisters and I worked diligently on our novels, papa's disability weighed heavily on my heart and mind. Unsatisfied with our local physician's prognosis of papa's condition, I decided to undertake a brief excursion to Brookroyd to visit Ellen, where I consulted with her cousin's husband, a surgeon who practised in Gomersal. The visit proved to be most illuminating.

"There is indeed an operation for cataracts," explained Mr. Carr, a pragmatic physician with a kind face.

"Would you recommend the operation for a man who is nearly sixty-nine years of age?"

"I would. Although there is some risk involved—a small percentage of patients are rendered blind following the procedure—if your father is going blind in any case, the risk is negligible. Most patients have an excellent outcome: their sight is restored in full."

"Where would we go for such a procedure, Mr. Carr?"

"There is an institution in Manchester that specialises in curing diseases of the eye. I am certain you could find your man there. You may have to wait a while, however. They cannot operate until the cataract is sufficiently hardened, and from your description, I do not know if your father's eyes are ready or not."

I returned to Haworth on the 2nd of March with newfound hope. Perhaps papa's blindness could be cured! My sisters had written that they would meet me at the train station, but I walked all the way home without seeing any sign of them.

"They must have taken the new road to Keighley," said papa, who I found in his study with Mr. Nicholls. "No doubt you just missed each other."

Mr. Nicholls and I exchanged cool but civil hellos. Although he came to the parsonage on a daily basis to go over the activities in the parish with papa, and I regularly encountered him at church and at the Sunday school where I taught under his direction, I had managed to avoid any undue conversation with him for the past three months, ever since the day he delivered that packet of writing paper. I was about to withdraw, but papa was anxious to hear what I had learned from Mr. Carr, so I plunged ahead with a brief overview.

"That's encouraging news," said Mr. Nicholls with enthusiasm. "If you can find a surgeon in Manchester who knows what he's doing, Mr. Brontë, I'd say it's worth a try."

Papa agreed, and seemed greatly cheered. I went looking for my brother, eager to tell him what I had learned. To my dismay, I found Branwell lying on the dining-room floor by the sofa, his hair and clothes in extreme disarray, his eyes closed as he muttered nonsensically to himself.

"Branwell!" I exclaimed forcefully, shaking him by the shoulders as I bent over him. "Wake up! I have something to tell you!" He took no notice. "Branwell! Can you hear me? I have spoken to a surgeon. I have learned something most encouraging about papa's condition."

I might as well have spared myself the trouble. Branwell just giggled, unaware that I was even in the room. How, I wondered, had he obtained the money for spirits? Papa had been denying him any funds for months.

I heard the front door open, and with it, Emily's and Anne's laughter and conversation as they hurried in, suffering from the effects of a sudden rainstorm. We embraced in the passage, lamenting the fact that we had missed each other on the road. I told them of Branwell's current condition, and asked what had happened.

"Branwell screwed a sovereign out of papa this morning, under pretence of paying a pressing debt," said Emily in disgust, as she and Anne removed their drenched cloaks and bonnets. "He immediately went and changed it at a public-house, and has employed it as was to be expected."

I sighed. "I was afraid something like this might happen, if I went away."

"You could hardly have prevented it, Charlotte," said Anne. Emily concurred. "Papa keeps hoping his 'boy' will improve—

but Branwell is deceitful and conniving. He struck at papa's weakest point; you know how he feels about leaving a debt unpaid."

"It is too, too awful," I said.

Emily shook her head sadly. "Branwell has truly become a hopeless being."

At that moment, I heard a noise behind me; I turned with a start, to find Branwell standing in the doorway to the dining-room, as if risen from the dead, regarding me with blinking surprise in his bloodshot eyes. "Well, well, look who's home," said he in a slurred tone. "If it isn't Charlotte the harlot."

I froze, taken aback by this unexpected and mortifying appellation. Branwell was wont to say and do terrible things when he was drunk, but he had never before addressed me in such a manner.

"I heard the most interesting piece of news while you were away," he went on. "It seems that I am not the only person in this house who is pining for an absent love."

This pronouncement rendered me entirely speechless. Anne gasped in dismay.

"Branwell, don't," said Emily.

"Don't what? Don't talk about Charlotte's big secret?" To me, he said, "Emily told me all about it. You've been writing letters to your professor in Brussels, and crying into your tea."

"Branwell," said Emily, darting me an apologetic look, "you misunderstood what I was trying to say."

"Oh, I understood just fine," drawled he. "What I don't understand, *Charlotte dear,* is why you judged me so severely for my relationship with the married Lydia Robinson, when you were carrying on in the very same manner with a *married man,* all the while that you were in Belgium!"

My cheeks grew hot; my pulse pounded in my ears. "That is a complete lie."

"That's not what Emily Jane tells me," intoned he, as he pushed past me and threw open the front door, admitting a blast of wind and rain. "Charlotte the harlot!" he called back with a strident laugh, as he stepped out, coatless, into the downpour. "You know what they say: if the shoe fits!" With that, he slammed the door and was gone.

A shattering silence filled the passage. My sisters and I stood in shock, as I tried to gather my senses. My voice shaking, I said: "What did you tell him, Emily?"

"I never said that you were *carrying on* with any one," replied Emily, shaking her head in annoyance. "I only said that you had developed *feelings* for our professor, and that—well, that things might have got a little out of hand."

"'Out of hand'?" I cried. "What exactly is that supposed to mean?"

"Do not look so high and mighty, Charlotte! I only told him what I believe to be true. I was trying to comfort him—he was so depressed, crying and going on about how much he misses Mrs. Robinson—I said he should follow your example, and learn to bear up under his misery with more fortitude."

"How dare you even *think* of comparing my situation to his?" I shot back with rising fury. "Branwell carried on a love affair for *three years*! He violated every rule of morality and decency! I did nothing of the sort!"

"Perhaps not," said Emily, "but you were smitten—besotted—infatuated. I know it!"

I stared at her. "How can you know what I felt, or what occurred? You went home after the first year in Brussels, Emily! You were not there!"

"Charlotte, do you think I am blind and stupid? Or are you so completely ignorant of your own heart? I have read your poetry: '*Unloved—I love; unwept—I weep.*' And *Gilbert's Garden*! Your yearning is plain to see on the page! You talked of nothing else but Monsieur Héger for a *full year* after you came home. Even now, you check the post every day, desperate for a letter from him that never comes!"

Hot tears sprang into my eyes; I could listen no more. I turned and—to my abject horror—saw that the door to papa's study, not three feet away, was standing ajar. Within, sat Mr.

Nicholls; I caught his eye; from his expression, it was clear that he had heard every word of the conflict that had just ensued.

Gasping with mortification, I fled upstairs. Emily, relentless, followed quick at my heels. As I dashed into my chamber and threw myself on my bed, she slipped in after me and slammed the door.

"I just realised," cried Emily as she advanced on me, her voice diffused with newfound surprise, "*that* is why your book is so passionless—so soulless. That is why the characters you now write are like sticks of wood!"

"What?" I wailed indignantly, looking up at her through my tears. "What has my *book* to do with any of this?"

"It has everything to do with it. You have been writing about your time in Brussels, but it is only a surface image, with none of its depths. You invested more emotion in your description of the scenery upon William's arrival in Belgium, than you did in a single scene between him and Frances. We feel nothing for your professor and his dull little lady, because you are *afraid to let us feel*. Admit it, Charlotte: something happened in Belgium—something you have not told us! You are still too affected by it, to write about *it*, or anything else, with any force of feeling. You will not even allow *yourself* to feel! You have walled up your heart!"

I burst into fresh tears. Burying my head in my arms, I cried, "Get out! Leave me alone!"

Emily went. I wept. I unleashed, in a great torrent, all the fury and humiliation that infused my soul. Branwell had called me a harlot. *A harlot!* He had accused me of carrying on with a married man, and Emily had corroborated it—all in earshot of papa and Mr. Nicholls! Oh, misery! Oh, anguish! What would they think of me, after hearing such sordid and base accusations as to my character? As I wept, I tortured myself with the recollection of every terrible thing that my brother and sister had uttered:

It seems that I am not the only person in this house who is pining for an absent love.

Things might have got a little out of hand.

Something happened in Belgium—something you have not told us.

You developed feelings. You were smitten—besotted—infatuated.

The accusations were true—every word of them. As darkness descended on the room, the memories came flooding back: memories I had tried to banish from my mind, of a journey which had begun with so much promise four years earlier, to a country far away from home: to Belgium.

Nine

~~~

elgium! What a complex myriad of emotions are raised within my breast, at the sound of that single word. Belgium! The name has become synonymous in my mind with a person, and a place, both of which—or of whom—combined to exert such a profound influence on me, as to irrevocably change my life.

It was a cold, wet morning on the 13th of February, 1842, when Emily and I gained our first glimpse of the Belgian country-side, determined—at ages twenty-three and twenty-five respectively—to become school-girls again for six months, to acquire enough proficiency in French and German to run our own school. At that time, Anne was in her second year at Thorp Green; Branwell was still working on the railroad; and Aunt Branwell, who had generously provided the funds for our educational venture, was alive and efficiently running the household at the parsonage.

We were chaperoned on our journey by papa, and piloted by my friend Mary Taylor and her brother Joe, who had both made the crossing from London several times before. As the new railway line between the port of Ostend and Brussels had not yet fully opened, we were obliged to take the diligence,[22] a journey of nearly seventy miles, which took an entire day.

"What a dreary landscape!" complained Joe Taylor (a practical and well-travelled young man who helped run his family's woollen manufacturing business) as we rode along. "Just a dull, flat nothingness."

"It is not dull at all," I countered, gazing out the window of the coach with a smile. "It is lovely in its wintry aspect." In truth, not a single picturesque object met our eyes along the whole route, yet to me—so happy was I to be in a foreign land—that all was beautiful, all was more than picturesque. As the sun set, it began to rain in earnest; and it was through the streaming and starless darkness that my eye caught the first gleam of the lights of Brussels.

We spent the night at a comfortable hotel. The next morning, Mary and Joe Taylor took their leave of us, for she was to join her sister Martha at the Château de Koekleberg, an exclusive German school.

The Pensionnat Héger, a "Maison d'education pour les Jeunes Demoiselles,"[23] was situated in the city's ancient quarter, in the rue d'Isabelle, a narrow street dating from the period of the Spanish Occupation. The street lay at the foot of a flight of steps leading up to the entrance to the central park, in close proximity to the Churches of Saint Michael and Saint Gudule, whose towers appeared to fill the sky, and whose great, melodious bells solemnly and comfortingly punctuated the hours.

"The rue d'Isabelle," explained Mr. Jenkins (the English chaplain to the British Embassy at Brussels, who, in the company of his wife, kindly escorted papa, Emily, and me in his carriage from the hotel to the school) "constitutes a halfway point between the lower, medieval part of town, and the fashionable eighteenth-century quarter above."

---

[22] Public stagecoach.

[23] School for Young Ladies.

"We have a lovely park and palace here," added Mrs. Jenkins, "and many splendid, aristocratic houses and hotels."

It was some time, however, before Emily and I found time to explore the fascinating city in which we had come to live. When I first beheld the Pensionnat on that grey February morning, I thought it a stark and unappealing edifice. Just forty years old, the building, which, at two storeys high, was much larger and a storey taller than those around it, had a row of large, barred, rectangular windows looking out upon the street. The bleakness of the exterior, however, belied the charms of the interior.

We were admitted by a portress, who led our little party of five through an entry passage paved with black-and-white marble. The long hall was painted in imitation marble as well, and lined with wooden pegs on which cloaks, bonnets, and cabas[24] were suspended.

"Look!" cried Emily, with surprise and a hint of a smile. "A garden!" She pointed to a glass door at the far end of the corridor, through which I caught a glimpse of trailing ivy and other wintry shrubs; but I had not much time to study it, for we were ushered into a room to the left, and bidden to wait.

We found ourselves in a glittering salon with a highly polished floor, colourfully upholstered chairs and sofas, gilt-framed pictures and gilded ornaments, a handsome centre table and a green porcelain stove. This type of stove, with which I was to become very familiar, was the Belgian equivalent of a fire-place; although it lacked the beauty of a flaming hearth, it served up heat very efficiently and effectively.

"Monsieur Brontë, n'est-ce pas?"[25] intoned a voice behind us, in an accent of the broadest Bruxellois.

I almost jumped, for I had not heard or seen any one enter. I turned and encountered, with some surprise, our Directrice. I say surprise, because I had unconsciously expected some one older and more spinsterish—some one more akin to my former

---

[24] Baskets; satchels.

[25] Mr. Brontë, is it not?

headmistress, Miss Wooler. Instead, the woman before me looked to be no more than thirty years of age (she was, in fact, thirty-eight). She was short and somewhat stout, but carried herself with grace. Her features were irregular—not beautiful, but neither was she plain; there was a serenity in her blue eyes, a freshness in her pure white complexion, and a shine to her abundant, nut-brown hair (formally dressed in curls) that was pleasing to behold. Her dark silk dress fitted her with a precision bearing testament to the skills of the French sempstress who created it, presenting her best features to advantage, in a sweet and motherly aspect—for she was then in her seventh month of pregnancy.

"Je m'appelle Madame Héger," said she, with a brief smile and a tone of formal welcome, as she held out her hand first to papa, then to Mr. Jenkins, Mrs. Jenkins, Emily, and me. She was the epitome of the well-dressed Continental woman. Light-weight slippers peeked out from beneath the hem of her gown—slippers which had allowed her, I realised, to enter silently by a little door behind us—a soundless method of perambulation which, I later discovered, proved an invaluable asset in the management of her establishment.

When papa conveyed that he spoke virtually no French, and she admitted, "My *Engliss* is no good," a rapid conversation followed between her and the Jenkinses, of which I understood very little. I realised, with a dash of panic, that my command of French, which I had presumed at least tolerably proficient before coming over, was in fact negligible; speaking a foreign language in an English schoolroom bore very little resemblance to the living, breathing experience of conversing with foreigners in their native tongue.

The Jenkinses served as translators, giving us to know that we would be allowed to settle in, and would meet Monsieur Héger that evening—for he was at present teaching at the Athénée Royal, the premier boys' school in Brussels, which stood next door. We would thankfully not be expected to begin instruction until the next day.

The main building was comprised of two distinct halves: the Hégers' private quarters on the left, and the school premises on the right. We were taken on a brief tour of the school, and allowed to peek into two large and pleasant schoolrooms, filled with young ladies at their devoirs,[26] and the long réfectoire, where, Madame Héger explained, we would dine, and also prepare our evening lessons.

"Well," said papa with a pleased expression when the tour was completed, "I am satisfied with the arrangements. I think you will get on well here, girls."

We thanked the Jenkinses for their guidance and assistance, hugged papa good-bye, and tearfully watched as the coach drove away, knowing we would not see papa for at least half a year, and concerned for his health and safety on his voyage. We were relieved to receive the letter he posted a week later, telling us how much he had enjoyed touring the sights of Brussels, Lille, and Dunkirk, before his return home by steamer from Calais.

No sooner had our elders departed, than a clanging bell rang out in the yard. At the same time, a clock somewhere rang out the noon hour. The corridor was suddenly filled with a horde of pupils—nearly a hundred in total—emerging from the schoolrooms in a tumult. The girls, who ranged in age from twelve to eighteen, were well dressed and chattering gaily; more than half retrieved their cloaks, bonnets, and satchels and poured out into the back garden; these, I thought, must be the day pupils, who had brought their own refreshment. Two maitresses [27] appeared, their shrill voices vainly endeavouring to enforce some sort of order upon the remaining pensionnaires, or boarders, but all their remonstrances and commands had no effect. Discipline seemed to be an impossibility, though this was considered one of the best-conducted schools in Brussels.

I had not long to wait, to discover the source of that well-earned reputation.

---

[26] Duties, tasks, exercises.

[27] Female teachers, as opposed to "masters" (male teachers).

Madame Héger (who had been standing in the shadow of the doorway to her salon) strode deliberately into the hall and, her brow smooth, her manner tranquil, pronounced one word, calmly and forcibly:

"*Silence!*"

Instantly, the assemblage quieted; order ensued; the young ladies began to pour en masse into the salle-a-manger.[28] Madame Héger observed their behaviour with a self-satisfied but critical expression, as a general might observe the movement of his troops. It was clear from the reactions of those around her, that both pupils and teachers regarded her with deference, if not affection.

Madame Héger quickly exchanged words with one of the teachers (a dried-up-looking, middle-aged woman, who I would come to learn was called Mademoiselle Blanche) and then took her leave. Mademoiselle Blanche showed Emily and me in to dinner, a delicious meal which consisted of some kind of meat, nature unknown, served in an odd but pleasant sauce; some chopped potatoes made savoury with I know not what; a "tartine," or slice of bread and butter; and a baked pear. The other girls nattered away, taking no notice of us.

Once the other pupils returned to the schoolrooms, Emily and I were shown to the dormitory above, a long room lit by five massive casement windows as large as doors. Ten narrow beds stood on each side of the apartment, each bed shrouded in a white curtain draping from the ceiling. Beneath each bed was a long drawer, which, Mademoiselle Blanche explained, served for a wardrobe; between each bed stood a small chest with additional drawers, upon which rested a personal basin, ewer, and looking-glass. Everything was neat, clean, and orderly, I noticed with approval.

"Madame Héger has reserved the corner for you," said Mademoiselle Blanche in French, as she showed us to the beds at the extreme end of the room, which were curtained off from the

---

[28] Dining hall.

rest. "She had these curtains hung especially, in deference to your age, believing you would wish a bit of privacy."

"How thoughtful of her," replied I in her language, as I glanced about our quarters with a smile. I sensed that we would be very happy here. It might be strange at first, to find myself a school-girl again at nearly twenty-six years of age, and to be obliged, after years of governessing and teaching, to obey orders instead of give them; but I believed that I would like that state of things. It had always been far more natural to me to submit, where the attainment of knowledge was concerned, than to command.

Emily and I spent the remainder of the afternoon unpacking and settling in. That evening, we received an invitation to join the Hégers in their family sitting-room.

I knew that Madame and Monsieur Héger had been married six years, and that they had, at the time of our arrival, three daughters, ranging in age from one to four years old. Nevertheless, I was unprepared for the scene which Emily and I encountered upon entering: Madame lay half-reclining on the sofa by the porcelain stove, one stout arm cradling to her chest her youngest girl; she held in her other hand a book, from which she was reading a story aloud; her oldest daughter sat listening attentively beside her, and her middle child played quietly on the carpet at her feet. It was a picture of such casual and complete maternal bliss as I had never encountered in all my time as a governess.

It was then that I understood what made this school feel so unusual: being run by a married couple, whose family lived on the premises, it was infused with a domestic atmosphere—and thus strikingly different from any educational establishment I had previously known. This difference was very shortly to become even more markedly pronounced.

Madame Héger smiled as we entered, and nodded towards the sofa on the other side of the room. "Bon soir. Asseyez-vous, s'il vous plaît. Monsieur approche dans un instant."[29]

---

[29] Good evening. Sit down, please. Monsieur will be here in a moment.

We sat. As promised, an approaching footstep was soon heard in the corridor, but—far from a gentle sound—it resembled the rapid, echoing boom of thunder, a portent of some coming fury. My heart began to pound with alarm even before, with a vehement burst of latch and panel, the door flew open. Like a harsh apparition, a dark little man stormed in, trailing a billow of cigar smoke. He was clad in a shapeless, soot-black paletôt, with a tasseled bonnet-grec balanced at a haphazard angle on his closely shorn black head.[30] In a terrible rage, he marched up to the woman on the sofa, wrathfully wagging his cigar and spewing forth a tirade in French, of which I caught very little substance, although from the frequent occurrence of the words "*étudiant*" and "*Athénée*," I assumed it had to do with a student at the boys' school next door.

Who *is* this horrible little man? I wondered, as Emily and I shared an alarmed glance, hoping against all hope that it was *not* Monsieur Héger. Madame listened calmly, silently, and patiently; the children barely blinked a collective eyelash.

"Mon cher," said the Madame, when her husband (for it was, indeed, Monsieur Héger) paused for an instant in his diatribe to inhale deeply from his cigar, "les pupilles Anglaises sont arrivées."[31] She nodded in our direction.

The little man turned and glanced at us. In the gentle flicker of candlelight which illuminated the room, I was able to ascertain his form and features. He was of less than average height; although still youthful (he was thirty-three years old—five years younger than his wife, just seven years my senior), he was a man of no great beauty. His complexion was as dark as the expression which (although slowly fading) had first ravaged his countenance, and the ring of thick, black whiskers which encircled his face and chin curled like those of a wrathful cat.

---

[30] A *paletôt* (French; *pal*-toh) was a long jacket or loose-fitting overcoat. A *bonnet-grec* was a peasant's cap.

[31] My dear, the English students have arrived.

"Ainsi je vois," mused he, studying us through his lunettes.[32]

As if by magic, his angry manner dissolved; in those three words, spoken in gentle, melodious, and purest French, were embodied surprise, warmth, hospitality, and friendliness. This new tone was so completely opposite to that which we had witnessed only moments before, as to seem to issue from a completely different person. He turned back to his wife and gave her an affectionate kiss, followed by a warm embrace for each of his children. Only then did he cross the room and hold out his hand to Emily and me. He spoke in French; indeed, *all* conversation that took place during our stay at the Pensionnat was in French; but for the sake of this diary, and for ease of transcription, I will record the preponderance in English.

"Welcome to Brussels, and our humble establishment," said he, his blue eyes twinkling as we stood and shook his hand in turn. "Sit! Sit! It is Mademoiselle Charlotte and Mademoiselle Emily, yes? I hope that you had an agreeable voyage?"

Emily nodded silently as we resumed our seats. I replied: "Oui, monsieur," pleased that I had understood him—but there the pleasure ended.

Monsieur Héger flung himself down into the wide, comfortable chair beside us, and proceeded to speak rapidly in his native tongue. His meaning, at that juncture, was scarcely intelligible to either my sister or to me, and not fully perceived until he translated it in retrospect, some months later:

"When you wrote to us, Mademoiselle Charlotte, my wife and I were so struck by the simple, earnest tone of your letter, in which you explained your ambitions, as well as your financial limitations, that we said: here are the daughters of an English pastor, of moderate means, anxious to learn, with a view of instructing others. Let us accept them at once, and give them advantageous conditions." He smiled as he paused, apparently waiting for a grateful reply. Receiving none, his dark brows bristled. "I assume you found our financial terms acceptable, as you are here?"

---

[32] So I see. . . . Eyeglasses.

When Emily and I remained mute and uncertain, he said, in an exasperated tone, "You wrote to me in French. I assumed you possessed at least a moderate command of the language. How else do you expect to get on? Do either of you even have the faintest idea of what I am saying?"

His verbal barrage so stunned me, that even had I understood his full meaning, I would not have been able to drum up an intelligent reply. As he glared at us, I had one more fleeting thought: how much worse this must seem to Emily! For, other than the six months of French lessons she had had during her brief tenure at Roe Head School, during part of the time I had served as a teacher there, Emily's only experience with that language was comprised of what I had taught her at home, and what she had learned herself from her reading.

"Monsieur," I faltered, my cheeks burning, "je suis désolé, mais vous parlez trop rapidement."

"Nous ne comprenons pas," added Emily in a simple, firm tone.[33]

He visibly winced; I perceived that our North Yorkshire attempts at a French accent sounded execrable to his ears. "Bah!" cried he, springing out of his chair with a scowl and striding lightning-wise back to his wife. "These girls are completely ignorant of our language! They will sink in classes with the general population. If they are to have any chance at all, I will have to tutor them privately myself!" With a great shake of his dark head, he threw open the door and barrelled out of the room.

That night, as Emily and I prepared for bed in our private corner, we wondered aloud what we had got ourselves into. Indeed, for the first few weeks of instruction we were lost much of the time. There were three resident women teachers and seven visiting masters who taught the different branches of education—French, Drawing, Music, Singing, Writing, Arithmetic, and

---

[33] Monsieur, I am sorry, but you speak too quickly . . . We do not understand.

German—as well as scripture, and "all the needlework that a well-brought-up lady should know." We were, as anticipated, compelled to speak, read, and write French all day, every day; all lessons (except German, of course) were taught exclusively in that language, and no concessions were sought or given on our behalf. Although I had eagerly looked forward to that circumstance, as the means by which my language skills would improve (and indeed, there is no better improver than immersion), the effort required in following our lessons in general subjects was far more difficult than I had anticipated. How dearly I wished that I had been better prepared before sailing to Belgium!

We applied ourselves diligently to our studies, however, and soon improved, thanks in large part to Monsieur Héger, that personification of both calm and tempest, who gave us weekly private French lessons, sandwiching them in between his classes next door at the Athénée. Emily and I would often sit in tense anticipation in his library, awaiting the sound of his approach, which would signal what his mood would be.

If his footfall was light and steady, it meant he would be in excellent spirits, would praise our progress with good humour, and find much to admire. If, on the other hand, we heard a thundering report of footsteps in the corridor, we shuddered, for it meant he had suffered a bad day. Emily and I would then serve as the whipping boys for his frustration, in a lesson that proved both taxing and brutal. He harangued us on the way we used our tongues when we spoke French, accusing us of mincing words between our teeth as if we were afraid to open our mouths. He often reduced me to tears; Emily, never; but to his credit, if tears would flow, he always quickly followed with an apology and a softening of tone.

Emily and I were not a perfect fit at the Pensionnat Héger. We were much older than our classmates, and all in the house were French-speaking Catholics except ourselves, one other pupil, and the gouvernante of Madame's children, an Englishwoman who served as both lady's maid and nurserymaid. This difference in age, country, language, and religion created a broad line of demarcation between us and the rest, a gulf widened by the private lessons Monsieur Héger gave us, which excited spite and jealousy among the other pupils. We felt ourselves completely isolated in the midst of numbers.

Emily, ever quiet and withdrawn in the presence of any one outside our immediate family, seemed to sink at first under all these difficulties; but then she rallied. "I will conquer these doubts and fears," she said resolutely one night. "I am determined not to fail." As the months drew on, Emily never spoke to any one except me, unless spoken to; she drew strength from our private society; and she did her work; she worked like a dog.

In contrast to my sister, I was happy from the start. I found my new life delightful, and much more congenial to my nature, than that which I had endured as a governess. I returned to learning with the same avidity as a cow, that has long been kept on dry hay, returns to fresh grass. My time, constantly occupied, passed rapidly.

We paid a few Sunday visits to the Jenkinses, but they grew visibly frustrated by their unsuccessful attempts to engage us in small-talk, an activity for which Emily and I had little talent, and these engagements were quickly dispensed with. We did greatly enjoy the lively, cheerful days we spent with our friends Mary and Martha Taylor at the Château de Koekelberg, an expensive boarding-school for girls, which lay in the country-side north-west of Brussels. Living amongst strangers, it warmed our blood and our hearts to be with friends for a time.

"I came here to learn French, just as you two did," said Mary, during our first visit to the Château de Koekelberg that March, as we strolled the impressive school grounds, "but most of the pupils here are English and German, and what little French is spoken is very bad."

"Do not be such a cry-baby!" retorted Martha, playfully pulling her older sister's dark, curly hair. Martha, the delightfully arch child who had so amused us all at Roe Head School, had bloomed into an equally vivacious and fun-loving young woman. "Our new French mistress is coming the day after to-morrow, and we will soon make all the progress you want."

"We have noticed something strange on our walks through the city," said I. "Is it our imagination, or do some of the gentle-men here paint themselves?"[34]

"They do!" cried Mary, with a laugh.

"It is all the fashion!" added Martha. "Is it not funny? I have half a mind to send some paint to Ellen, for her brother George. Oh! And something else is all the fashion nowadays: to send shoals[35] of blank paper to friends in a foreign land, instead of letters! Shall we send such a thing to Ellen, as a joke?"

Mary and I laughed at the idea, but Emily frowned and said, "That would be a great waste of both paper and postage," to which we all ultimately agreed. In high spirits, we repaired to the library, to add our comments to a letter Mary was already writing to Ellen.

In Brussels, I learned how to adapt my clothing to suit my small figure. Aunt Branwell had generously provided Emily and me with a small sum each for incidentals, and, having witnessed the precise skills of Belgian dressmakers, and being apprised of their reasonable rates, I spent a portion of my pocket money on a new dress. I was thrilled when it arrived! I chose a pale grey silk, and had it neatly waisted in a simple, fitted style, with a full skirt, narrow sleeves, and a white-embroidered collar. I also or-dered a new, fuller petticoat. It was only one dress, and I was obliged to wear it continuously, except for laundry day, mending it as needed; but thus attired, I felt that I no longer stood out quite so conspicuously.

Emily, on the other hand, insisted on wearing the same old-fashioned dresses and thin petticoats which she had preferred

---

[34] Use facial cosmetics.

[35] An antiquated word, originally referring to a school of fish; meaning any large number of persons or things.

since childhood. When the other girls made sport of Emily's odd style of dress, she would stonily reply, "I wish to be as God made me"—a response which was met with disbelieving stares, and only served to keep them at a further distance.

Six weeks after our arrival, Madame Héger gave birth to her first son, Prospère. As such, we saw little of her during our first few months at the Pensionnat; she was generally resting or taken up with nursery duties. Later that semester, as I had more contact with her, I found her to be a woman of dignity and a capable directrice. Within the bosom of this well-structured household, a hundred healthy, lively, well-dressed girls flourished, gaining knowledge without painful exertion or useless waste of spirits. The lessons were well distributed and simple to understand, there was a liberty of amusement and a provision of healthy exercise, and the food was abundant and very good. Many an austere English schoolmistress, I thought, would do well to imitate Madame Héger's methods.

At least, these were my initial impressions of her—and they did not waver until a great while later.

Emily and I saw Monsieur Héger, by contrast, every day from the beginning, in our Writing class, and once a week for our private lesson. He was an exacting but excellent teacher, and in temper and temperament, the direct opposite of his wife: irritable, tempestuous, volatile, and often unreasonable. Occasionally, however, he revealed a surprisingly different side to his personality: a far lighter, more playful side. It was Monsieur Héger's custom, on occasion, to burst in unannounced on the evening study hour, which was always held in the refectory, and turn that silent, nun-like encampment into an ebullient *affaire dramatique.*

"Mademoiselles!" he would cry, clapping his hands, and taking command of the room like a little Napoleon, "put away your books, your pens and your papers, and take out your work-bags. It is time for a little entertainment."

Teachers and pupils alike, all seated at two long study tables beneath central lamps, would respond with enthusiasm. Standing at the front of the room, Monsieur Héger would pull out a handsome volume or a series of pamphlets, and regale us with passages from some enchanting tale or witty serial story. He performed with zest and skill, taking care to omit any passages which might be deemed unsuitable for young ladies, often replacing them with hilarious, improvised prose and dialogue. These too-infrequent evenings left all assembled in high spirits, and I came to look forward to them with great anticipation.

The little man continued to be a paradox, however, wavering between light and dark, in patterns impossible to predict. I believe he liked to watch the emotions he could produce, with his ever-changing facial expressions and amazing turns of thought and temper. He could wither a pupil with a slight movement of lip and nostril, or exalt her with a faint flicker of an eyelid. We had been at the Pensionnat a little over two months, when, at one of our private lessons, Monsieur Héger flung my note-book at me, in disgust at my recent translation of an English composition into French.

"You write French like a little automaton!" he snarled. "Every word appears to be the production of an overanxious study of the dictionary and grammatical rules, but with no resemblance to the real pattern of speech! Your younger sister, the one who has less experience, she writes far better and more concise translations!"

"I am sorry, Monsieur," said I, deeply mortified.

"From now on, Mademoiselle, I forbid you to use either a dictionary or grammar in your translations."

"But Monsieur! How can I translate without a dictionary or a grammar?"

"Use your brain!" he cried, tapping himself on the head, and glaring at me like thunder through his lunettes. "Listen to what goes on around you! Hear the way French is spoken! And what you hear, let that come through your finger-tips when you write!"

"I will try, Monsieur." There was something in that man's anger—a vehement passion of emotion—that tended to draw tears. I was not unhappy, nor much afraid, yet I could not help myself: I wept.

Emily said sternly: "Monsieur, you go too far. My sister and I both work very hard. It is unkind to make her cry."

Monsieur Héger looked at me, apparently saw the sharp pain inflicted, and let out a long sigh. "Allons, allons," said he presently, his voice now softly humbled. "Decidedly I am a monster and a ruffian. Please, accept my apologies, and take my pocket-handkerchief." He withdrew the article from the pocket of his paletôt and extended it towards me; I received it with decorum, and wiped therewith my eyes.

"I have a solution to this conundrum, I think," mused he. He scanned the titles in his bookcase, a massive collection which filled his library shelves from floor to ceiling. "You are both capable of more than these dull translations and word studies. Let us try some more advanced work." He chose a volume. "I will read aloud to you, each week, a selected passage from the best of French literature. We will analyse each piece together; you will then be required to produce an original essay of your own, in a similar writing style."

Emily frowned. "Where is the benefit in that, Monsieur? If we copy from others, we will lose all originality of thought and expression."

"I did not say 'copy'!" countered Monsieur Héger heatedly. "I said you must write in a similar style, but on an entirely different subject, and of a sufficiently different character, so as to render unintelligent imitation impossible. In so doing you will, at length, develop a style of your own. I have tried this method before, I assure you, with my most advanced and able pupils, and always it produces an excellent result."

"On what subject would we write, Monsieur?" I asked.

"On a topic of your own choosing. It is necessary, before sitting down to write on a subject, to have thoughts and feelings about it. I cannot tell on what subject your hearts and minds have been excited. I must leave that to you."

★　★　★

I spent a great deal of time on that first composition, and turned it in with pride, believing that my true skill lay in prose, and hoping that such an effort—even if expressed in imperfect French—would, at last, earn praise from Monsieur Héger. To my dismay, my work produced the opposite effect.

"What is this vapid piece of nonsense you call an essay?" growled Monsieur Héger one afternoon after Writing class, as he dropped the offending article on my desk. "Such a river of sentiment! Such a barrage of unnecessary metaphors and adjectives! You have allowed your imagination to run away with you, Mademoiselle, as if the goal in writing was the accumulation of the greatest number of words."

My cheeks flamed at his harsh critique, my humiliation all the more complete by the amused tittering it had occasioned in the few other girls who had yet to vacate the room. "I am sorry you find my work so tedious and offensive, Monsieur. I only try my best."

"This is not your best." He faced me over my desk, the tassel of his bonnet-grec sternly shadowing his left temple. "I see that you have a great imagination, Mademoiselle Charlotte. You have vision! You have talent! But you also have a total disregard for style. This, we will have to work on, and most assiduously."

"I am eager to improve, Monsieur. Only tell me: what do you wish me to do?"

"Read my comments, Mademoiselle. Take them to heart." With that, he left the room.

I opened my note-book to my most recent effort, to see what comments Monsieur Héger had written in the margin. My poor little essay looked as if it had been attacked! Monsieur had offered more than mere comments, and corrected more than technical errors. Improper words were ferociously underlined, with the critique, "Ne soyez pas paresseux! Trouvez le mot juste!"[36] Sentences were ruthlessly tightened. "You are babbling!" he wrote here, and, "Why this expression?" there. Where I had

---

[36] Do not be lazy! Find the right word!

strayed from my topic to indulge in an elaborate metaphor, he cut the passage and wrote: "you are into the subject, go straight to the end."

At first I was mortified; but when I stopped to consider how much time he had taken over my little exercise, my heart swelled with gratitude. No one had ever critiqued my writing in this manner before. Under Monsieur Héger's tutelage, I realised, I would be subjected to an entirely new and harsh—but not unwelcome—discipline.

On the compositions of others, I came to notice, he might only make a comment here or a correction there, and perhaps add a sage remark or two; but from me, he would suffer no omission or defect. "As you unfold your subject, you must sacrifice without pity everything that does not contribute to clarity and verisimilitude," he said. "This is what gives style to prose—just as it gives to painting unity, perspective, and effect." His words were, to me, like priceless pearls of wisdom, and equally profound; I drank them in, always craving more.

One evening in mid-July, I was reading on a bench in the back garden. This delightful retreat was a long strip of cultured ground, immediately behind the school building, and completely enclosed. There was a sort of lawn, a parterre of well-trimmed rose trees and flower-borders in full bloom, and an alley bordered by enormous old fruit-trees down the middle. It was bordered on one side by a thickly planted copse of lilacs, laburnums, and acacias; on the other side, a wall and shrubbery divided the establishment from the Royal Athénée. Because a solitary window high up in the Athénée's dormitory overlooked the garden, the tree-shaded walkway beneath it was declared "out of bounds" for the female pupils: "l'allée défendue."[37]

The garden—perhaps rare for a school in the centre of a

---

[37] "Forbidden alley." From that solitary window, William Crimsworth spied into Mademoiselle Reuter's garden in *The Professor,* and an admirer tossed down love letters to Ginevra Fanshawe in *Villette.*

city—proved to be a haven from the noisy flurry of school life. It was a pleasant spot to spend an hour or two, particularly on a summer evening as lovely as this one. I was engrossed in a book, when I detected the aroma of a cigar, and a deep voice intoned over my shoulder: "What do you read, Mademoiselle?"

I showed Monsieur Héger my book: it was one of my French school texts.

"An excellent work, but not terribly riveting. Perhaps you would like to borrow this?" From beneath the folds of his paletôt, he produced a book and handed it to me. It was a handsome volume, mellow and sweet with age: *Génie du Christianisme*, by Chateaubriand.

"Monsieur! Thank you so much."

"The young Victor Hugo once said, 'To be Chateaubriand, or nothing.' Have you read any of his works?"

"Never, Monsieur. But I saw this book in your library. The title intrigued me."

"I think you will find the work intriguing, as well. Chateaubriand wrote it in an attempt to understand the causes of the French Revolution, and as a defence of the wisdom and beauty of the Christian religion."

"I shall look forward to reading it."

"When you are finished, we will discuss it, yes?"

"Yes."

He sat down beside me on the bench. His very nearness caused my heart to flutter; I moved aside to make room for him. "Do you recoil from me, Mademoiselle?" said he, offended.

"No, Monsieur. I merely wished to give you space."

"Space? I do not call this space. You have left between us a gulf, an ocean. You treat me like a pariah."

"I do no such thing, Monsieur. I moved aside but a foot or two. I thought my previous position too central. I feared you might think I occupied more than my fair share of the bench."

"Ah. You argue, then, that your motive was my comfort, rather than some aversion you have to sharing the bench with me?"

"Precisely, Monsieur."

"Well, then, I accept this motive, although I do not sanction it. I was quite comfortable before. I am a small man, you are a small woman, and it is a large bench. In the future, there is no need for you to move."

"I shall try to remember that, Monsieur."

He fell silent, puffing on his cigar, his attention fixed on a bird hopping about on the branch of a nearby pear tree. He then said: "I find I must congratulate you, Mademoiselle."

"Congratulate me? For what, Monsieur?"

"Your writing shows great improvement. You have, I think, some potential after all."

His tone was sincere, but the twinkle in his blue eyes intended to humble; its effect was felt. Joy spread through me; I bowed my head to hide my smile. "Thank you, Monsieur."

"You have, I think, great ambition for your writing, no? You wish some day to be known? To be published?"

"Oh, no, Monsieur! What ever gave you such an impression?"

"I see it in your words, on the page. I see it in your eyes, when we discuss the works of others: a passionate fire, which burns with felicity, or ire, or envy, depending on the quality of the work, and your mood."

I felt a heat rise to my face; I felt naked; as if he had seen emotions that I had never meant to display. "I do love to write, Monsieur. I always have, since I was a child. But I intend to commence a school. That is why I am here: to educate myself, in order that I might become a better and more-highly-valued teacher."

"A worthy goal. But teaching does not preclude writing."

"Any ambitions I may have had for a writing career, I hold no longer."

"And why is that?"

"I have been counselled on the subject by gentlemen whose opinion I admire."

"Who are these gentlemen that you so admire, and whose counsel you so trust?"

"The first is my father."

"Well, of course, you must accept the word of your father. Fathers *always* know what is best for their offspring, do they not?" The twitch of his lips, as he regarded me, belied his words.

"My father is a very good and wise man, and the others— they are great English writers and poets: Robert Southey and Hartley Coleridge."

"I have heard of them. Do you know these gentlemen?"

"No. But I wrote to them. I sent them samples of my work. They both made the same reply: that although my work showed some skill and merit, they felt it was not worthy of publication; and in the case of Southey, to whom I revealed my gender, that writing was not a proper occupation for a woman, and I ought to give it up."

He laughed. "I do not blame these gentlemen, if the work you sent them was written in a style as overblown, as execrable as that which you displayed in your first French compositions."

Now I was annoyed. "You wound me, Monsieur. If you think my work so horrendous, why did you bother to congratulate me?"

"I congratulate you because you have improved! I saw, at the outset, that you had talent—great talent—which only needed direction and training. You have responded exactly as I hoped. You have grown. You write with more confidence. You have learned to impose discipline on your pen. Now, I am satisfied that you are on the proper path: the path to more spare and elegant prose."

How quickly, I thought, he could veer from vicious critique, to restoring words of praise! My injured pride recovered just as quickly. "Have I truly improved so much, Monsieur?"

"You have. As for your Mr. Southey and Mr. Coleridge, I will tell you what I think. I think you should be very careful, where your writing is concerned, of taking advice from others, particularly men whom you have never even met. How can these strangers know what passions burn within you? What right do they have to quench that fire, with their advice from afar? Pay no heed to them, Mademoiselle—nor to me, for that matter, if you strongly disagree with anything I say. I am only your professor; I can only instruct you in what I know. In the end, you must listen to the voice within you. That voice will be your strongest guide. It will help you grow far beyond anything I can teach."

As July came to a close, the end of our projected six-month stay in Brussels was fast approaching. While Emily and I prepared for bed one evening, I said, "It would be a shame to leave this place, do not you think, when there is so much to learn?"

Emily glanced at me in surprise. "How could we afford to stay? Aunt Branwell's loan has been used up. I would not like to ask for more."

"Neither would I, but we might be able to *earn* our keep. We could teach English classes, and continue our studies in our spare time."

"Teaching is not my strong suit," replied Emily. Indeed, she had despised her brief, six-month tenure as a teacher at Law Hill school in Halifax. "But I admit, I would like to make more progress in French and German—and I suppose this chance might never come again."

Excitement mounted in my breast. "Shall I ask the Hégers if we might stay until Christmas? If they say yes, would you be willing?"

"I suppose. But what would we do over 'les grandes vacances?' "[38]

"I will think of something." I smiled and hugged her.

I applied to Madame Héger, who spoke to her husband. I assured them that I had taught before for several years—although in truth, a schoolroom of forty girls was far more than I had ever been obliged to handle. At length, they agreed to my proposal. Madame dismissed her English master to the First Division, who had lately become unreliable, and took me in his stead. It was decided that Emily, who had been studying with the best

---

[38] The five-to-eight-week-long "grand vacation," or summer holidays.

music teacher in Belgium, would teach piano to a certain number of pupils. For these services, we would be allowed to continue our devoirs in French and German, and to have free board. No salaries were offered; but we thought the arrangements were fair, and we accepted with alacrity.

On August 15th, the school closed for the summer vacation. The Hégers left for their annual sea-side retreat at Blankenberg, and all the teachers quitted the city. Nearly a dozen boarders, in addition to Emily and I, stayed at the Pensionnat. Over those glorious August and September days, we experienced, for the first time, how Asiatically hot a summer could be; and we had free time, at last, to explore Brussels in depth. I loved the pretty park, the vast, impressive Place Royale, and the clean, spacious streets. We toured the city's art galleries, churches, and museums with delight.

In no time the summer was gone, the house full again, and school in session. My experiences as an English teacher confirmed all my best and worst expectations. I had once thought British school-girls were difficult to manage, but England's worst would be as church mice here. The Belgian girls were truly robust, insolent rebels, bred with a sense of entitlement, with little respect for their elders. The First Division recognised me for what I was: an older student who had turned teacher to earn her keep, and whom they were now obliged to address as "Mademoiselle Charlotte." In the first months of my tenure, they put me to the test many times; but I rose to the challenge, determined to prove to them—and to the Hégers—that I could hold my own. I found the environment stimulating, electrifying, and I continued to thrive.

Diary: I have heretofore recorded many fond remembrances, as sweet as the honey drawn from flowers; but I must now turn from these pleasant musings. It so happened, that while life wagged on at a steady, graceful pace in Belgium, things were not so rosy back in Haworth. We learned in a letter from papa in

September that cholera had descended on the village. Many people had fallen victim to the disease. Among these was the charming young curate William Weightman; following a visit to the poor and sick, he had taken ill and died.

Bad news, I have found, often comes in threes, and that autumn was no exception. In late October, Martha Taylor died—also from cholera. That Martha could die at an educational establishment as superlative as the Château de Koekelberg in Belgium was unthinkable! I had never known a more care-free friend than Martha; she had been the darling of her family, and a treasured companion to her sister Mary; now, to my grief and astonishment, she had been snatched away at twenty-three, before her life had even truly begun.

The third blow fell just a few days later. Papa wrote to say that Aunt Branwell had died, after suffering from a bowel obstruction. Stunned by this rapid succession of mournful events, Emily and I quickly packed up our belongings. Although it was too late to reach home in time for the funeral, we knew we must return to England at once. Branwell and papa were alone; they could not manage without a woman to run the household.

The evening before we were to depart, I was alone in the dormitory, packing my trunk. As I worked, I was blinded by tears—grieving not only for the passing of my aunt, and Martha, and William Weightman—but for the brutal suddenness of our departure, which was tearing me from a life I had come to love. I heard the door open at the far end of the dormitory. Footsteps approached; male footsteps, instantly recognizable, which halted outside the white curtain, and were followed by Monsieur Héger's voice: "Mademoiselle Charlotte? May I enter?"

I tearfully replied in the affirmative.

He pulled the curtain aside and crossed to where I stood. "I am so sorry for your loss," said he, in a tone of the utmost gentleness and sincerity.

I thanked him. He came a step closer, and placed a book in my hands. Through my tears, I saw that it was a beautifully bound German text. "What is this?"

He produced his pocket-handkerchief—a ritual which had been performed countless times in countless schoolroom altercations between us over the past nine months—and as always, I used it to dry my tears. "The book is a gift. I hope it will enable you to continue your studies, in a language of which, I think, you are only just beginning to gain a true appreciation."

"Thank you," said I again, touched that he would think of this. I gave him back his handkerchief. As he took it, he squeezed my hand briefly and tenderly; the warmth of this precious human contact made me tremble.

"I understand what it is to lose some one you love very much."

I nodded silently, my throat too filled with emotion to speak; I assumed he referred to the memory of his father, or his mother. But he did not. He continued softly:

"I was married once before. Did you know?"

Surprise found my voice. "I did not, Monsieur."

"Her name was Marie-Josephine Noyer." He pronounced the name with reverence; his blue eyes flickered with moisture, which he blinked away. "We were barely married, when the revolution broke out in 1830. I joined the Nationalists at the barricades. My wife's young brother was killed at my side, one of the many martyrs who fell in the cause of Belgian liberty. Three years later, on the same morning, my wife and child fell ill. They both died of cholera."

Fresh tears spilled from my eyes. "I am so sorry, Monsieur." This, I thought, explained why he so often bore such a grim exterior, and fumed like a bottled storm. No one could emerge from such suffering unaltered.

"It was a long time ago. I only tell you so that you will understand: you are not alone. I sympathise."

"I would not compare my loss with yours, Monsieur. I have lost two friends, and a beloved aunt; but not a wife and a child."

"Still, your loss is great. Everything you feel, you feel deeply, Mademoiselle; but rest assured: the pain will fade in time. One day you will look back, and instead of sadness, your heart will be warmed by fond memories." At my tearful nod, he again extended his handkerchief. "Keep it, Mademoiselle. You have more need of it than I." He added: "Please know that you and your sister are always welcome here. Madame and I are both grieved by this parting. We feel as if you are part of our own family. Once things are settled at home, and you have paid your final respects to your aunt, you may come back if you wish."

"May we?" Events had occurred at such lightning speed, that I had not stopped to consider the future. "Will you not have to hire another English teacher in my absence?"

"We can bring on some one temporarily until Christmas. Your post, if you want it, will be here if you return. Would you like to come back to Brussels, and to us, Mademoiselle?"

I met his gaze, my eyes brimming, this time with tears of gratitude. "Oui, monsieur. I would like that very much."

From the moment my feet touched the soil of home, I longed to be back in Belgium. I had carried home a precious letter to my father from Monsieur Héger, containing a glowing account of our progress at the Pensionnat, and an eloquent appeal to allow Emily and me to return for a final year's study—this time with a salary, in exchange for teaching services. Two weighty matters needed to be resolved, however, before papa would sanction our return: who would run the household, now that Aunt Branwell was gone? And what was to be done about my brother? Branwell, who had been dismissed from his post at the railroad earlier that year after a dispute over missing funds, was still unemployed, and hanging about the Black Bull Tavern. The deaths of our aunt and William Weightman had greatly affected him.

"Willie had no thought for himself," said Branwell, his eyes moist and dull from drink, as we sat by the parsonage fire one stormy November afternoon. "His only concern was for the poor and sick and feeble. 'Who will look after them?' he wondered. 'Who shall take my place?' A better man never lived, I tell you! And aunt—my God! I sat at her bedside, day and night. I witnessed such agonising suffering as I would not wish my worst enemy to endure. For twenty years, she was my mother, the guide and director of all the happy days of my childhood—and now I have lost her. How shall I get on? What shall we do?"

I placed my hand on his affectionately. "The only thing we can do. We must honour her memory, in our hearts, our minds, and in the way we choose to live our lives. We must endeavour to make her proud of us." He stared at me blankly, unable to grasp my meaning. "You must not drink so much, Branwell. It has to stop!"

"What else am I to do with myself? There is no occupation in this God-forsaken village."

It was that December that Anne wrote from Thorp Green with her solution to the problem: the Robinsons had offered to hire Branwell as the tutor to their son, Edmund Junior. The answer to our domestic issue was also resolved, when Emily declared her intention to stay home and keep house for papa. It did not surprise me; I knew how much she missed our moors. A few days later I received a letter from Madame Héger, reiterating the offer in her husband's letter.

"Are you very certain you want to go back to Brussels?" Emily asked me, after papa had given his consent.

"I can think of nothing else. I feel idle and useless here."

"We need not be idle. We have achieved the attainments we sought in Brussels. Our French is now equal to or surpassing that of most English school-teachers, I should think. We can take steps now to open our school, as planned."

"I am not ready to start a school yet. I wish to be better prepared."

Emily looked at me. "Are those your real reasons for going back?"

"What do you mean?" I felt my face go hot. "Yes, those are my reasons! But not my *only* reasons. I liked Brussels. It was thrilling to live in a great city, away from this quiet corner of the world—and the Hégers both earnestly wish for my return. I do not wish to disappoint them."

There was another reason, too, but it was a reason I could, at the time, neither understand nor explain: some irresistible force was drawing me back to Brussels. Although a tiny voice flashed warnings at the corners of my conscience, I ignored it, concentrating all my thoughts on one thing: *I must go back. I must.*

Ten

ad Aunt Branwell been alive to know that I travelled alone from England to Belgium in January 1843, she would have seriously disapproved; but finding no escort, I was obliged to make the voyage on my own. My train was so delayed, that I did not reach London until ten at night. Having already visited the city on my previous journey, I went straight to the wharf, where the coachman dropped me unceremoniously in the midst of a throng of swearing watermen, who struggled for me and my trunk. The packet refused, at first, to let me board at that late hour; at last, some one took pity on me. We sailed the next morning. This time, after reaching the Continent, I was able to take the next day's midday train to Brussels.

With joy and relief, I arrived at the Pensionnat that evening. It was the dead of winter: the trees were bare and the evening very cold; but how good it felt to be ushered through that familiar, arched stone doorway, into that quaint, black-and-white-marbled entry hall! How wonderful to return to surroundings so beloved to me! I was no sooner in the door, my luggage at my feet, and removing my cloak, than Monsieur Héger emerged from the salon, shrugging into his own surtout.[39] He caught sight of me and his face lit up.

"Mademoiselle Charlotte! You are back!"

"I am, Monsieur." I flushed with pleasure at the sight of him. The sound of his voice was like music to my ears; I did not realise how much I had missed it while I was away.

"Where are your companions? Surely you did not travel alone?"

"I did, Monsieur. My father, having no curate, has taken all the duties of the parish upon himself. He could not leave, and there was no one else to ask."

"Well! Thankfully, you have arrived safe and sound." He stepped back briefly into the salon, called out for Madame, then turned back to me. "I must go; I am giving a lecture next door. Good-night, Mademoiselle, and welcome home." With a bow, he issued from the door.

Madame received me with kindness. "Le maître Anglais qui nous avons employé pendant votre absence était absolument incompetent, et les jeunes filles ne cessent pas de demander de vos nouvelles. J'espère que vous resterez longtemps."[40]

I assured her that I intended to stay a long while—as long as they would have me.

"You are like our own daughter," added Madame, with an uncharacteristic smile. "Please consider our sitting-room as your own, and feel free to join us at any hour, or to relax there whenever your schoolroom duties are completed."

I operated in a new schoolroom, on the playground adjoining the house. In addition to teaching English and continuing my studies in Writing and French, I now served as surveillante[41]

---

[39] Overcoat.

[40] The English master we hired in your absence was absolutely incompetent, and the young ladies will not stop asking about you. I hope you will stay for a very long time.

[41] Supervisor.

over the First Class at all hours. My salary, at £16 per annum, was modest and did not go far; yet a new duty was soon added to my programme. Monsieur Héger asked if I would consider giving English lessons to him and to Monsieur Chapelle, the brother-in-law of his late wife. I was only too pleased to oblige.

We met in my schoolroom two evenings a week. Monsieur Chapelle was well-mannered and intelligent, and both men showed a sincere desire to learn. These sessions, which brought about a reversal of roles between myself and Monsieur Héger, also brought out his natural ebullience; he could cast off the stern mask he wore all day, and make himself charming.

These lessons became one of my favourite duties. I found myself looking forward, all through the week, to that day and moment after hours, when Monsieur Héger (generally a few minutes behind Monsieur Chapelle) strode into my schoolroom and dropped into a vacant desk, booming out, "I have arrived! Let us commence the speaking of English." Having learned, in recent months, the art of managing a roomful of difficult students, I was able to bring an exacting energy, imagination, and confidence to the enterprise.

"It is eight hours," Monsieur Héger would say, as he stared at the clock in my hands.

"Eight *o'clock*," was my correction.

"How many years have you?" he would inquire.

"How *old* are you?" I would instruct.

"My parents were all the two from Brussels," Monsieur Chappelle would intone.

"Say *both* instead of 'all the two,' Monsieur."

We started with the basics, but Monsieur Héger—who proved to have a natural aptitude for languages—got on with wonderful rapidity. In a month's time, he began to speak English very decently. I soon structured our lessons to fit within his more sophisticated tastes and aptitudes. Their earnest attempts to imitate me, however, as I tried to teach them to pronounce like Englishmen, were an amusing spectacle for all concerned. Monsieur Héger's enunciation of a brief passage by

"Weelleeams Shackspire" ("le faux dieu de ces païens ridicule, les Anglais,"[42] he teased) brought tears of laughter to my eyes.

At times, when Monsieur Héger's written work needed immediate correction, I playfully motioned to him to rise from his desk, and I installed myself in his place, as he had so often done to me in his schoolroom.

"A pencil, please," I would say, with an imperious smile, holding out my hand to him—mimicking the request he had so often made of me. He gave me the pencil; but while I underlined the errors in his exercise, he was not content to stand deferentially at my side, as I had been expected to do. Instead, he hovered over and behind me, his arm stretched over my shoulder, his hand leaning on the desk, his head close to mine, as he watched my progress and read aloud my written notations, as if determined to memorise every word.

As I felt the warmth of his breath against my cheek with every utterance, my heart would race, and it became difficult to think. I told myself these physical reactions on my part were only due to the lateness of the hour, and the heat in the room, from an overactive stove; but in my heart, I believe I knew the truth: they were brought on by his nearness, and the sight of his hand so close to mine.

Early one morning, in the first week of my return, I received a shock. When I opened my desk in the still-deserted schoolroom, an unexpected odour assailed my nostrils: it was the pale blue breath of Monsieur Héger's Indian darlings—the smell of a cigar. Along with this olfactory surprise, came a visual one: some one had rearranged the contents of my desk. Not disarranged—everything was neatly in place—but in a different place than before, as if some unseen, Godlike hand had descended to do a little gentle ransacking.

Moreover, there were two new additions. An unfinished composition I had left, still full of faults, lay atop my papers,

---

[42] The false God of those ridiculous pagans, the English.

now carefully annotated and corrected. Better still, on top of my worn grammar and sallow dictionary lay a brand-new book, by a French author which I had earlier professed myself keen to read. An accompanying note read simply: "A loan. Enjoy."

My heart smote me. To think that, with all the many responsibilities which occupied his days and evenings, Monsieur should take a moment to think of me! And more: to think that, while I slept, he stole into this room and made his way to my desk; his gentle, olive hand raised the lid; and there he sat, with his nose buried among my books and papers, examining every item and then carefully putting it back, without even attempting to disguise his machinations. Some people, I thought, might view this act as an invasion of privacy; but I discerned his intent. He wished only to show he cared, and to do me good.

No good, however, could come from that smell. I raised the lid of my desk, opened the nearest window, and carefully waved the book outside in an attempt to purify it in the early-morning breeze. Alas! The schoolroom door burst open and Monsieur himself appeared; catching sight of my activity, and interpreting the inference, his face contorted in a scowl. He bounded towards me across the room. "My offering offends you, I see."

I quickly brought the book in from the window. "No, Monsieur—"

Before I could say more, he snatched the tome from my startled grasp. "You will be troubled with it no more." He strode directly to the glowing stove and unlatched the door; to my horror, I realised that he meant to thrust it inside.

"No!" I cried. Racing forward, I grabbed hold of the book; a struggle ensued; had he truly wished to win, there would have been no contest, for my strength, even when roused to fury, could not hope to compare with his. At last he gave way, and I wrestled the spoils from his hands. With relief and a pounding heart, I said, "It is a beautiful new book! How can you even think of destroying it?"

"It is too dirty, it has too much the smell, for your delicate sensibilities. What do you want with it?"

"I wish to read it! And," I added, with a half-concealed smile, "I am grateful to the genie who loaned it to me, along with my corrected school-work."

I detected an answering smile in Monsieur's eyes. "You are not offended, then, by the smell of smoke?"

"I do not like the smell, I admit. The book is no better for it, and neither are you. But I will take the good with the bad, Monsieur, and be grateful."

He did smile, then; or rather, he laughed, as he turned and strode from the room.

I continued to find such treasures in the ensuing weeks. Watch as I could, however, I never caught the cigar-loving phantom in the act. Most often, it was a classic work that appeared like magic atop my papers; once or twice I discovered a romance, offered for light reading. In time, I held the volumes to my nostrils upon discovery, and inhaled their pungent aroma. It pleased me immensely to think that Monsieur Héger was on intimate terms with my desk.

I was content that first month, although the weather continued bitterly cold through February and into March. I shivered beneath my cloak as I walked alone, every Sunday, to one of the Protestant chapels across the city. I had no friends in Brussels, as Mary Taylor had left after her sister's death, and I did not like the other teachers, all insincere, bitter old maids who did nothing but complain of their cruel lot in life. I had tried to take up Madame on her kind offer to share their sitting-room in the evening, but found it impractical. Madame and Monsieur were always busy with their children, or engaged in conversation which seemed too private for my ears. As such, I found myself alone most of the time, out of school-hours. I dearly missed Emily's presence, and came to realise that her companionship had played a great part in making my first year in Brussels so enjoyable.

March 11th was Monsieur Héger's patronal day: the feast of Saint Constantin.[43] It was the custom, on such a fête day, for pupils to bring their masters flowers. I gave him no bouquet, however; instead, I had planned a more personal and lasting gift. After our English lesson that evening, when Monsieur Chapelle had quit the schoolroom, I felt the time had come to present my little surprise. Before I could do so, however, Monsieur—sitting at his desk—let out a little sigh, and said: "You brought me no flowers to-day, Mademoiselle."

"No, Monsieur."

"Neither do you have a bouquet hidden in that desk of yours; if you did, I would have detected its fragrance long ago."

I hid a smile. "You are correct, Monsieur. I have no flowers."

"Why is that? It is my fête day. Are you not still my pupil?"

"Surely you cannot bemoan the loss of a bouquet from me, Monsieur, when you received so many others to-day."

"It is not the quantity which has meaning, but the identity of the bearer, and the thought behind it. But wait, I think I remember—you made me no gift of flowers last year, either!"

"I did not."

"You do not think highly enough of me, is that it? I am not worthy of such a gift?"

Now I wanted to laugh; I had half a mind to keep what I had made for him. "You are very worthy, Monsieur, and well you know it. But last year, on your fête day, my sister and I had only been in Belgium a few short weeks. We were not acquainted with the custom. Even if we had been, I still could not have bought you flowers."

"Ah!" He nodded, with eyebrows raised. "I see—because of the expense. Flowers *are* quite dear, and few are to be found in the garden this time of year."

"It is not the expense, Monsieur. It is something else entirely.

---

[43] A day, according to the Catholic faith, honoring a patron saint, and celebrated by M. Héger on March 11 because Constantin was his first name.

Although I love to see flowers growing, I find no pleasure in them when they are torn from the earth. They appear to me then as far too perishable; their similarity to life, and this assault on their brief mortality, makes me feel sad. I never offer flowers to those I love, and I have no wish to receive them."

"A curious philosophy. I wonder: do you feel the same way about food? A carrot or potato is also torn, roots and all, from the ground. Every vegetable and fruit is ripped from its stem or branch. And what of the lamb who gives his very life for your nourishment? Do you tremble to eat, Mademoiselle?"

"I do not. I enjoy a pear, a potato, and a green leaf as much as any one. Sometimes, I admit, I feel remorse for the lamb or cow. But it is the way of nature, Monsieur: we must eat or die. We do not, however, require flowers to decorate our tables, to exist."

He chuckled and shook his head. "An excellent argument; and delivered with the same clarity of thought and firmness of conviction as you present in your compositions. I concede. You have won me over."

"Good. As it happens, Monsieur, I do have a gift for you—just not of the variety that grows in the ground."

"Do you?" He had begun to rise from his desk, but he quickly sat back down. The expression on his countenance was almost childlike in its anticipation and delight.

"But perhaps you would prefer to continue our discussion about flowers?"

With downcast eyes, endearing in their humility, he said: "That subject is closed. I will issue no further recriminations."

I quickly retrieved a small box from my desk, and handed it to him. "For you, Monsieur." I had purchased the box especially; it was made of some tropic shell, and decked with a little circlet of sparkling blue stones.

"It is beautiful." He opened it. Inside the lid, I had carefully engraved, with my scissors' point, the letters C.G.R.H., to stand for his full name: Constantin Georges Romain Héger. A smile lit his face. "How did you know all of my initials?"

"I know a great many things, Monsieur."

A length of plaited chain lay coiled within the box, which I had wrought of brightly-coloured silk and decorated with glimmering beads; for the clasp, I had removed the gold fastening from my sole necklace, and attached it thereupon. "I saw you working at this the last few nights, at study-hour. I had no inkling that it was for me. Is it—a watch-guard, I presume?"

"It is, Monsieur."

"Well! I like it very much. Thank you." Beaming, he stood, opened his paletôt and attached the watch-guard, taking special care to arrange it across his chest. "Do I display it to optimum effect? I have no wish to conceal something so decorative."

The friendly affection on his face set my heart aglow. "It looks very handsome, Monsieur."

"The box will be a superb bonbonnière," pronounced he, which greatly pleased me, for I knew he was fond of sweets, and liked to share them with others. "I thank you again. Your gift, mon amie, has proved the perfect end to a most enjoyable day."

I smiled. So often, in the past, he had presented me with a bland expression, an angry glare, or a disdainful look. Now, he had called me *mon amie,* a phrase which, I had come to understand, carried a greater sense of intimate affection than the English word *friend.* I felt in that moment entirely happy, and as light as a balloon that might soar up into the sky.

A few weeks later, I received a summons to Monsieur's library. He was sitting behind his desk correcting papers when I entered.

"Ah! Mademoiselle Charlotte. There you are. Please shut the door, and sit down."

I did as I was bidden, taking the chair opposite his desk. I spied the watch-guard that I had made him, peeking from beneath his black paletôt, and smiled.

"I have something for you. I had a chance to read these." From a drawer, he removed three small, bound manuscripts and set them on his desk. I recognised them, and panic seized my throat. They were my manuscripts: a few samples of my early writings which I had brought from home, and had given to Monsieur Héger the week before. Now that his English had improved enough to make some sense of them, I wanted to share these spontaneous creations of my youth. With one look at the expression on his face, however, I wished that I had not.

"You did not like them, did you? You thought them moronic and stupid."

"Far from it. My English is not too advanced as yet, so I did not understand everything. But they seem to me quite charming, youthful, lively. *The Spell* is particularly fearless and fantastical—yet at the same time, infuriatingly inaccessible—and most amusing."[44]

"Inaccessible? Amusing?" My heart sank; that story was meant to be thrilling and dramatic, not humorous. "And—youthful?"

"Yes. But it is to be expected. You were young when you wrote them, eh? You had no direction, no guidance. You had only the impulse to write, and a love of words. You wrote what was then in your mind, and your heart." Here ensued a pause, in which he produced a cigar from a box in his desk. "You do not mind if I smoke, Mademoiselle?"

I shook my head, steeped in misery.

He lit the cigar, placed it to his lips and inhaled, then breathed out a trail of smoky incense into the room. "Enlighten me: what is in your mind and your heart now, Mademoiselle? Other than the compositions you write for me, what other subjects do you wish to explore in poetry and prose? What stories do you burn to tell?"

---

[44] Unknown to Charlotte, Monsieur Héger preserved these samples of her juvenilia (*The Spell, High Life in Verdopolis*, and *The Scrap Book*, written under the *nom de plume* of Lord Charles Florian Wellesley), and later had them bound in a volume entitled "Manuscrits de Miss Charlotte Brontë (Currer Bell)." They were found in a secondhand bookshop in Brussels after his death, by a university professor who sold them to the British Museum.

"None, Monsieur."

"I do not believe it. Such a passion for writing in one's youth, does not dry up and go away by itself."

"It was a hobby, Monsieur; a hobby which I have put behind me."

"Then why did you show these to me?"

"I do not know."

He made an impatient noise. "You are not being honest with me or with yourself, Mademoiselle. You sought my opinion, and now that I have given it, and you do not like the essence of it, your face turns crimson, and you shrink back shyly from your intent, as a mouse would shrink into its hole."

He spoke the truth; but I could not admit it. "My intent is to run a school. It is the best, and only, occupation open to me."

"From what I hear, you are a fine teacher; but as I have said, teaching does not preclude writing, nor should it. A well-organised person can do both." He leaned back in his chair and looked at me. "Do you know what I wished to be, in my youth, Mademoiselle?"

"No, Monsieur."

"I wished to be a barrister."

"A barrister? Truly?" I was astonished.

"I grew up in wealth and prosperity, with very rosy prospects, knowing that I could attend any university I liked, and become anything I wished to be. Then one day, my father—he was a jeweler, and a most caring and generous man—he lent a large sum of money to a friend in distress, and lost it all."

"*All*, monsieur?"

"All. Overnight, my prospects were reversed. I found myself in my teens without a profession, and ill equipped for life. My father sent me to Paris to seek my fortune. My first post was as a secretary to a solicitor, an initiation into the legal world, which greatly attracted me. But now, I had neither the time nor the money to consider such a profession. So I began to teach. The only pleasure I could allow myself at the time was to go to the Comédie Française as a hired applauder. My love of the court-room and the stage, I was obliged to consign to the schoolroom and the study-hall."

I believed a sympathetic response was in order, but I blurted out: "Perhaps it is selfish of me, Monsieur—but I cannot regret your loss, for it has been my gain."

He laughed. "So this is your response, to my tale of woe?"

"I am sorry. I do feel badly for you. Do you regret it, Monsieur? The giving up of your dream?"

"No. I am very happy with all I have. Of what use is it to look back, and wonder what might have been? But what is true for me, is not necessarily true for you, Mademoiselle. You have not yet begun your career. Is this what you truly wish for yourself? A life of teaching?"

"I—I do not know, Monsieur."

He rose and walked around to the front of his desk, where he stopped immediately before me, half-leaning back upon the desk, his shoes nearly touching my shoes, the dark folds of his long paletôt brushing up against, and blending with, the skirts of my black dress. There he stood, smoking and brooding, just inches from me. For a while, the only sound in the room was the steady tick-tock of the clock on the mantel, which could not keep pace with the rapid beating of my heart. At length, he said: "I have read your early writing. I am well acquainted with your work of to-day. May I be honest with you, Mademoiselle? May I share with you, my true impressions?"

"Please, Monsieur."

"I find your work remarkable. I think you have elements of the genius in you."

My breath caught in my throat. "Genius, Monsieur?"

"Yes; and I believe, with further exercise, this genius can be trained into something very worthy."

My mind feasted on that single word: *genius*. All my life, I had believed that I possessed a gift of some kind, a gift shared by other members of my family, but so far unacknowledged and unrecognised. The strong pulse of ambition returned full force, and beat in every vein I owned; yet something rankled, too. "If I truly have genius, Monsieur—*if* I do—then is all this training and exercise really necessary? Why all these endless compositions, where I have been obliged to imitate the form of other writers? Why can I not simply write what I wish to write?"

"It is imperative to study form. Without form, you are no poet; with it, your work will be more powerful."

"But poetry—is it not the faithful expression of something which happens, or has happened, in the soul?"

"One could say that, yes."

"And is not genius something innate, a gift given to us by God?"

"Man receives this gift from heaven, indisputably."

"Then I believe that genius, by its very nature, must be rash and daring," said I, "and should operate like that of instinct—without study or pause for reflection."

"Genius without study is like force without a lever, Mademoiselle. It is the soul which cannot express its interior song, save in a rough and raucous voice. It is the musician with an out of tune piano, who cannot offer the world the sweet melodies he hears within. It is like these works of your youth, Mademoiselle." He leaned forward, bent his face down towards me, and gazed directly into my eyes. "Nature gave you a voice, Mademoiselle; but only now are you learning how to employ that voice—to turn it into art. An artist you shall become. Study, persevere, and you will be truly great. Your works will live."

My heart pounded, in part from his nearness, but even more, I think, from the impact of his words; it was as if a whole new world had been opened up to me. I felt a joyful warmth spread through me, permeating my chest, and rising, like the heat of the sun, to my face.

At that moment, the library door opened, and Madame Héger walked into the room. Her glance fell upon her husband and me, situated thus, and she froze.

Monsieur Héger straightened and puffed casually on his cigar. "Madame?"

Their gazes met. "I did not realise you were holding a lesson," said she coldly.

"I was only giving Mademoiselle Charlotte some sage advice about her future, and her writing." To me, he added, "We are finished, Mademoiselle. You may go."

I issued immediately from the room, my heart still pounding. Madame averted her eyes and stood back to let me pass.

I left Monsieur Héger's library, trembling with excitement. I needed to get away, to feast my mind on all that he had said. I dashed upstairs, grabbed my cloak, and darted out into the garden.

Darkness had long since fallen; all was cool and still. I stood upon the lawn and inhaled the crisp night air; it smelt fresh and clean from a recent April rain. A canopy of stars twinkled above, beside an incandescent moon, whose reflection glowed upon the tiny, white, emerging blossoms speckling the dark branches of the orchard trees. As I wandered down the central path, my heart was gladdened by the cheerful, chirruping cadence of the crickets and the many-mingled sounds of the surrounding city, which rose like the gentle hum of a distant ocean.

I heard the raising of a latch, and saw the rear door to the Pensionnat swing open on its silent hinges. A figure emerged, paused, and then approached. I knew it was he. I waited. He caught up and fell in step with me. "A beautiful evening, is it not?"

"It is, Monsieur." We strolled. A smoky essence emanated from his clothing. "Where is your cigar, Monsieur?"

"I put it out. I did not wish for anything to interfere with the fragrance of the spring blossoms." He inhaled deeply, and smiled. "Now that I see that you are to be my walking companion, I am even more glad of the omission, for I know you do not like it."

"I have grown accustomed to your cigar, Monsieur. I have even grown to appreciate its aroma, for it reminds me of you."

"Then you no longer wave the books I loan you out the window?"

"I would not dare to, Monsieur, for fear that you would swoop down on me like an avenging angel, and try to snatch away my prize."

"Your prize? I am pleased to hear that you consider my little loans in that way."

"The books that you have shared—they mean the world to me. To think that you would take the time, to think of me, merely a student at your school, and a teacher in your employ— it honours me, Monsieur."

"Merely a student at my school, and a teacher in my employ?" he cried, shaking his head in bemusement. He then turned to face me, compelling me to stop before him as he gazed at me fondly. "We have been both pupil and teacher to each other, Mademoiselle. But you must know that you are far more to me than that. You are my friend, Mademoiselle; a friend for life."

My heart swelled with such pleasure as I had never before felt; his words resounded in my ears. *A friend for life*. He had proclaimed it with unfettered affection in his eyes. With a sudden, all-consuming rush, I knew that I had profound feelings for this man. Once, I had feared him; in time, I honoured and respected him; later, I valued him as a friend. Now, I realised, my feelings had grown and changed into something much deeper: I loved him. *I loved him*.

Oh! I thought, as I averted my gaze and froze, confusion washing over me. How could this be? How could I love Monsieur Héger? He had a *wife*; a family to whom he was devoted, as he should be; a domestic life of which I could never be a part. To love Monsieur Héger was wrong—*wrong*—a violation of all that was proper, moral, and decent! How could I have allowed my feelings to so carry me away?

With pounding heart, I frantically tried to understand this profound revelation. If I loved Monsieur Héger, there was only one way to justify it: I loved him *not* as a bride loves a bridegroom, or as wife loves a husband; *no!* I loved Monsieur only as a pupil loves her master. Of him I had made an idol; and as a lower being worships an idol, I had no need for my love to be returned in kind. I was—*I must be*—entirely content with what he could give: this pure and simple friendship that he was so freely offering me. This silent assessment reassured me and assuaged my conscience, until another realisation, just as sudden, followed; with it came a weight of sorrow so great, it brought tears to my eyes.

"Why do you cry, Mademoiselle? I have just said you are my friend for life."

"As I am yours, Monsieur," said I softly, brokenly.

"And this makes you sad?"

"No, Monsieur. It is something else which makes me grieve."

"What is that?"

"It is the knowledge that one day I must leave Brussels, Monsieur."

"But England is your home. Your family is there. Surely you will be happy to return to them."

"Yes. But Brussels—this Pensionnat—it has been my home for more than a year now. I have lived here a delightful life. Here, I have talked, face to face, with what I reverence, and with what I delight in—with an original, a vigorous, an expanded mind. I have come to know *you,* Monsieur; and it fills me with sadness to contemplate that one day I must leave you—that we will no longer be able to talk in this way."

"Even if we are parted, Mademoiselle, we can still communicate with each other."

"How, Monsieur? A letter can be a most precious thing; I often re-read the letters from my friends and family, and they mean everything to me. Yet even if I wrote to you every single day, and you replied as often, it would not afford one thousandth the pleasure of a face-to-face conversation."

"It is fortunate, then, that we are not obliged to rely on letters and the post to stay in frequent touch, is it not?"

The open affection in his eyes disarmed me. "What do you mean, Monsieur?"

"Another form of contact can exist between two people who

are separated, but who are really fond of one another—an in- stantaneous means of communication between distant hearts." He touched his chest, then reached out and gently placed his fingers against my own chest. "It is a form of communion that does not require paper, or pen, or spoken words, or messenger."

His intimate touch exhilarated me. I could barely think. "What is this magical means of communication, Monsieur?" asked I, my voice now but a whisper.

He took his hand away. "It is not extraordinary. You yourself have experienced it a hundred times, but perhaps you did not realise. You have only to take a private, quiet moment, and sit down and close your eyes; then think of that other person. He will appear in your mind, just as you know him to be. You will hear his voice, and you may talk with him, to your heart's content."

"Such silent musings may have to do, Monsieur; but they will never be sufficient to content my heart."

"Remembrance can be a fine thing. It can make those dis- tant seem even better than they are." He raised his hand to my cheek now, where it wiped away my tears, and then came to rest with the gentle softness of a caress. "If the sea should come be- tween us, this is what I shall do: at the end of the day, when my duties are over, when the light fades, I shall sit down in my li- brary and close my eyes. I shall evoke your image, and you will come to me—even if you do not wish it so. It will be as if you are here before me; and we shall meet again, in thought."

The deep timbre of his voice seemed to ring through me; my pulse hammered in my ears; I could not speak. The moon was full, and he was not blind; surely he could read in full the depth of feeling that my countenance could not hide.

And then it happened: his hand tilted my face up to his, he bent his head to mine, and he tenderly kissed first one cheek, and then the other, in the custom of the French. Then I felt the soft brush of his lips against my own. His kiss was brief and gentle, yet its touch sent a jolt racing through my body, electri- fying me to the innermost core of my being.

He drew back slightly, his hand still at my chin, his face mere inches away, his eyes boring into mine. I was suffused with heat; I felt as if I might melt into the earth itself; I could not breathe; I tore my gaze away. My eye was caught by a tiny, distant gleam emanating from the glass door of the Pensionnat. A candle shone in the window. Monsieur Héger, who had his back to the building, could not see it. Was some one watching us? If so, who? Now I felt a sudden chill, and trembled.

"You are cold, Mademoiselle. You have been too long in the night air. You must go in."

Unable to speak, I nodded my assent and fled back to the building, my cheeks still burning. When I pushed open the door and entered the back hall, there was no person, no candle to be seen.

Till morning dawned, I lay awake, tossed on a buoyant but unquiet sea. I replayed the scene in the garden over and over in my mind, recalling every word that Monsieur had spoken, the way he had looked at me, and the way his lips had felt against mine. I struggled to reassure myself that I had done nothing wrong, and neither had he. Monsieur was a man of spotless fame, of great integrity and principle. He was also a boisterous, affectionate man; I had seen him kiss other friends and pupils in a similar manner, and had thought nothing of it; it was the French way. His kiss had only been a sign of his regard: benign and insignificant. By now, he would have forgotten it—and so must I. Everything would go on as before; we would be friends, as before; as if it had never happened.

The next morning, however, a note was delivered to me from Madame:

April 10th, 1843

Mademoiselle Charlotte:

My husband and Monsieur Chapelle have requested me to inform you that, with regret, their increasingly busy

*schedules will no longer permit them to avail themselves
of your services as an English teacher. They thank you
for your past efforts, from which they have both benefited.
In addition, my husband finds that he no longer has time
to teach you French individually, although you may of
course continue with your writing class, and all your
teaching duties.*

I remain,
Mme. Claire Zoë Héger

I was shocked and upset. Was this really to be—this abrupt
cessation of the English lessons which had proved so delightful
and satisfactory on both sides? I could not believe this was Monsieur's wish; after all he had said and done last night, why would
he choose this hour to abandon our private study? Surely it was
Madame's doing; she must have been at the window, observing
us. Perhaps she had sensed, even before I did, the truth of my
feelings for her husband; perhaps she was jealous. Jealous, of *me*!
It was ridiculous!

From that day on, I rarely, if ever, encountered Monsieur
Héger alone again. If, at the end of class, I heard his approaching footstep in the corridor, and would hurry out to greet him,
he would have magically disappeared, as if in a puff of cigar
smoke; while strolling in the garden, if I caught a whiff of that
pungent perfume, and tried to find its source, it would again
vanish into thin air; if he strode into the dining-room at study
hour, and I glanced up in expectation, *she* would always appear,
two steps behind him, and spirit him away.

Banished from his society, any glimpse of him became all
the more precious to me. Yet my only contact now with Monsieur Héger were the corrected essays I found in my desk, and
the books he still kindly left for me in the night—but now with
nary a note attached. These books provided the only pleasure or
amusement I had. I never again saw the watch-guard, which I
had taken such pains to make. The shell-box I gave him was

gone, too; when he passed out candies amongst his pupils, they were in his bonbonnière of old.

Once, when Monsieur Héger did chance upon me in the schoolroom alone, he frowned and said, in great annoyance beneath his bristling dark brows, "I see you keep very much to yourself, Mademoiselle. Madame thinks you ought to make friends with the other teachers. A little universal benevolence and goodwill on your part could be of great benefit, I think." With that, he left.

I had no wish to befriend the other teachers. I had tried, and failed. Monsieur's irritable behaviour did nothing to shed light on my situation. When he kissed me in the garden, he had been expressing affection for me—I felt it! I saw it!—even if it was only meant in a friendly way. Where then had that affection fled? Was Monsieur angry—and avoiding me—out of guilt, because he had kissed me? Did he fear that, with one brief kiss, he had overstepped his bounds, or had given me the wrong impression as to his feelings? Did he perceive *my* feelings, and fear they would only be fanned into greater flame by the slightest contact with him? Or was he merely obeying some command of his wife's to have nothing more to do with me?

Madame doubled my assignments, giving me charge of all the English classes at the school, for which I was given a small increase in salary; it also left me little time for anything else. I was condemned to breathe the stifling air of the schoolroom all day long, where I spent myself drilling into the minds of Belgian girls the precepts of the English language; in the evening, I was buried beneath the weight of papers to read and correct.

Was this increase in responsibility a "reward," as Madame claimed—or a punishment? By report, I knew that Madame highly praised my work to others. She continued to be civil to me, but I often caught her staring at me in the corridor, or across the table in the refectory, with an expression in her shaded blue eyes that chilled my blood, as if she were silently attempting to read my soul. When she was not present, I fancied that I was an object of scrutiny by Mademoiselle Blanche, who seemed to be closely observing my every move.

One afternoon, when, owing to a headache, I excused my class early and returned to the dormitory to rest, I glimpsed a shadow beyond the curtains screening off my private quarters. The sound of a drawer being cautiously slid out struck my ear. Alarmed, I approached on silent feet; standing to one side, I was able to peer through a gap in the curtains.

I saw that the visitant—or should I say, the *spy*—was Madame Héger. She was standing before my small chest of drawers, coolly and meticulously examining the contents of my top drawer and work-box. I stood spellbound and aghast, as each succeeding drawer was opened in turn. She glanced at the fly leaves of every book; she unlidded every little box; she paid particular attention to each note and letter, which she carefully re-folded and returned to its place. Indignation and fury washed over me; yet I dared not reveal my presence. There would have been nothing in it but a scene, a sudden, violent clash, in which I would say things I would come to regret, and which would only have ended with my dismissal from my post.

Her next act truly stunned me: she pulled a set of keys from her pocket, and proceeded to unlock the long wardrobe drawer beneath my bed! She pulled from it a dress, and went through its pocket, fairly turning it inside out. Comprehension dawned: some night when I had been sleeping, Madame must have stolen in and borrowed my own keys to make a wax impression. How long, I wondered, had this surveillance been going on?

She put back the dress and began to glance through my other clothes. Her fingers seized the handkerchief which Monsieur Héger had once given me, a treasure which I had carefully pressed and folded. It was too much! I must put an end to this! I cleared my throat; I gave her an instant to collect herself, then pulled aside the curtain. Incredible woman! The drawer was shut; the work-box closed and in its place; Madame greeted me with a cool and tranquil nod.

"I have replaced your ewer and basin, Mademoiselle, with a new set. I saw that they were chipped. Good-afternoon." With that, she swept past me and out of the room.

Diary: when I wrote to Ellen and my family, I hinted at my sufferings and isolation, and admitted that Madame did not seem to like me any more. I said that I could not imagine why I had, unaccountably, lost the good opinion of the woman who had, with such kind affection, invited me to return to Brussels. What else could I say? Surely I could not admit to *them* the true reason for Madame's change in demeanour; just as surely, however, I could not hide it from myself. I knew. *I knew!* My employer suspected me, and perhaps her husband, of acts and feelings, the very nature of which were perfidious, depraved, and soul-polluting—suspicions that were entirely unfounded.

I *did* love Monsieur Héger; I could not deny it. However, I had no designs upon him; I did not wish him for myself. I only wished for a renewed enjoyment of the connection between our minds. My regard for him, simple and undemanding as it was, could do Madame no harm! Surely, I thought, if I could only wait a little longer, if I could prove to her that I posed no threat, she would come to see that she had been wrong, and things would return happily to what they once were.

Time wore on, however, with no improvement. August arrived. Exams were held; prizes distributed; by the 17th, the school broke up, the pupils went home, and the long vacation began.

On the eve of their departure, Monsieur Héger (I suppose without the knowledge or approval of his wife) presented me with a gift of another book, a two-volume edition of the works of Bernardin de Saint-Pierre, which he hoped "would help to occupy the lonely days ahead." With what gratitude I accepted this rare gift; but what a prophecy was in those words!

Oh! How I tremble when I recall that terrible, long vacation!

No students remained that year; the school building was empty, except for the cook and me. I wanted desperately to go home, but it was impractical to make such a long and expensive voyage for such a short visit. Five weeks, however, had never seemed such an eternity to me.

That summer was so different from the one the year before, when Emily and I had enjoyed every moment of our free time together. This time, the halls of the school building echoed, silent and desolate; the two rows of shrouded white beds in the dormitory mocked me in their hollowness, like taunting ghosts. My spirits, which had gradually been sinking ever since April, now plummeted. With all employment and company withdrawn, my heart seemed to almost die within me. I ate alone. I tried to read or write, but found the solitude too oppressive. When I visited the museums, the pictures held no interest for me.

The first weeks were hot and dry; then the atmosphere changed. An equinoctial storm raged for a week. I was imprisoned in that huge, empty house as the windows rattled and the tempest roared. Late one night, when I could bear the furious sounds no longer, I flung open the casement window beside my bed and crawled out onto the roof. From there, drenched and wind-blown, I felt and watched the spectacle in all its glory. The heavens were black and wild and full of thunder, and pierced intermittently by white and blinding bolts.

As I watched, I prayed to God to deliver me from my present misery and isolation; or if not, to at least send me direction; to show me His will. But nothing happened. No giant hand of God came down; no precious guiding word was whispered in my ear. I climbed back into my chamber, wet and shivering, and took to bed. When at last I slept, I dreamt.

In my dream, I was held captive by a cruel and scheming witch in a high castle tower. A storm raged without. Within I languished, starved and forgotten, waiting for my love to save me. My strength was nearly gone. Surely he still cared; surely he would come, before it was too late! A rap sounded at the window; I rushed thereto, and threw it open. A dark and dashing figure, richly clothed, leapt in through the gap, took me in his embrace, and kissed me soundly. It was he! It was my beloved Duke of Zamorna! But as he drew back, and gifted me with his adoring gaze, I gasped in dismay. It was not the Duke. *It was Monsieur Héger.*

The dream had lasted scarcely a minute or two, but it sufficed to wring my whole frame with mortification upon awakening. I had worked so hard to convince myself that I did not think of my master in a romantic way—that my love for him was innocent and entirely respectable. Oh, hopeless, hopeless Charlotte! What was I to do with such unwelcome thoughts and images?

The cook brought me tea in bed next morning. On beholding my ravaged countenance, she said, in concern, "Vous avez besoin d'un docteur, mademoiselle. J'appelle un."[45]

"Non, Merci," I replied; for I knew that no doctor could cure me.

The storm at last abated; the weather turned fair; I dressed myself and ventured out to clear my mind. For long hours, I traversed the boulevards and streets of Brussels. I wandered as far as the cemetery, and to the hills and fields beyond. As I walked, my thoughts turned towards home. I tried to picture what Emily might be doing at that moment: she was no doubt in the kitchen, cutting up the hash, while Tabby blew on the fire, in order to boil the potatoes to a sort of vegetable glue. Papa would be in his study, writing a letter of complaint to the *Leeds Intelligencer* on some matter of regional import. Anne was at Thorp Green, playing with the Robinson children, while Branwell recited some classic poem for his pupil. How divine were these imaginings to me! How dearly I missed them all!

When I looked up, I found myself back in the heart of the city, outside Saint Gudule. It was a church of the Catholic faith, a religion spurned by my father and alien to my nature, but which, living among its followers at the Pensionnat, had become increasingly familiar to me.

The bells began to toll for evening *salut;* they seemed to call me in. Against all precedent, I entered. Within, a few old women were saying their prayers. I hovered at the back of the cathedral

---

[45] You need a doctor, Mademoiselle. I'll call one.

until vespers were over. I saw six or seven people kneeling on the stone steps, in the open niches which served as confessionals. I approached, drawn by a force I could not name. The confessors whispered through a grating to a priest on the other side. A lady kneeling nearby urged me, in a kind voice, to go ahead, for she was not ready.

I hesitated; but at that moment, any opening for a sincere appeal to God was as welcome to me as a drink of water to the parched and dying. I went to a niche and knelt. After some moments, a little wooden door inside the grating opened, and I saw the priest lean his ear towards me. Suddenly, I realised that I was ignorant of the formula of confession. What should I say? How did one begin?

I fell back on the truth. "Mon père, je suis Protestante."[46]

The priest turned towards me in surprise. Although his face was obscured, I saw that he was an older man. "Une Protestante? En ce cas, pourquoi avez-vouz approché moi?"[47]

I replied that I had been perishing alone for quite some time, and that I needed comfort. He said, in a gentle voice, that as a Protestant, I could not enjoy the true blessings of a confession; but that he would be glad to hear me, and offer advice if he could.

I began to speak. At first, the words came haltingly; then they increased with speed and passion, until they became a flood. I told him everything—a vital outpouring of the long-pent-up pain that wrenched my heart—and I finished my oration with the question which preyed most deeply on my mind: "My father, if our thoughts and intentions are noble and unpolluted, are we held accountable to God for the sinful dreams that invade our sleep?"

The priest's visage, or what I could glimpse of it beyond the grate, appeared perplexed. At length he said compassionately, "My daughter, if you were of our faith, I would know better how

---

[46] My Father, I am a Protestant.

[47] A Protestant? In that case, why have you come to me?

to guide you; but I believe, in your heart, that you already know what course you must follow. I believe, too, that these feelings and afflictions under which you are suffering, are messengers from God to bring you back to the true Church. I would like to help you; but I need more time than I am able to give you here. You must come to my house, and we will talk again." He gave me his address, and instructed me to go there the next morning at ten.

I thanked the priest; I rose; I glided away, indebted to him for his kindness, but knowing that I had no intention of visiting him again. He seemed a worthy man; but in my weakened state of mind, I feared that, had I gone to him, his powers of persuasion would be so great, that I would soon end up counting my beads in the cell of a Carmelite convent.

I returned to the Pensionnat and faithfully reported this incident (which, dear diary, I later gave to Lucy Snowe in *Villette*) in a letter to Emily; although I carefully omitted the content of my confession. The act of communicating my suffering to my sister, however, as well as to the priest—a human being so intelligent, so worthy and consecrated—had done me good. Already I felt some measure of solace and relief.

"I believe, in your heart, that you already know what course you must follow." Those were the priest's words; the one and only true piece of advice he had given me. As I lay in bed that night, eddying darkness swam around me, and reflection came in just as black and confused a flow. Aloud, to the blank emptiness, I cried, "What am I to do?"

The answer came promptly from my mind, and the words it spoke—"You must leave Belgium!"—were so dreadful, that I stopped my ears. I hated to go home, to nothing—for no occupation awaited me there—and I hated more the idea of leaving Monsieur Héger decidedly, entirely, knowing that I would, in all probability, never see him again. And yet, the thought of staying was equally tormenting. How could I remain in that house, living on nothing but the hope of a mere glimpse of him day after day? How could I continue, knowing that my regard for him could never be openly expressed?

"If I must go, then let me be torn away!" I cried aloud. "Let another make the decision for me!"

"No!" cried Conscience tyrannically. "None shall help you, Charlotte. You must tear yourself away. You must cut out your own heart."

"No!" cried Passion. "Think of the long, lonely days at home, starved for a letter or a word, all contact with him reduced to memory and thought!"

For weeks, I was wrapped in an agony of tortured indecision. To stay, I had no will; to flee, I had no strength. At length, a voice within me averred that I must take action: I must abandon Feeling and follow Conscience. The secret love that kindled within me, unreturned and unknown, could only devour the life that fed it. One drear word comprised my intolerable duty—"Depart!"

Not long after school resumed, I gathered my courage. I waited for a moment when Madame Héger was alone in her salon, and—with apologies—I gave my notice. For an instant, surprise and relief flooded Madame's normally passive face; then the mask fell back in place. "Have no worries on our account, Mademoiselle," said she in the coolest of tones. "We shall get on. You may leave at once, if you wish."

The next day, Monsieur Héger sent for me. When I appeared in his library and took the seat he offered, I took great pains to repress my tears, and braced myself for what I believed was coming: his calm, measured words of farewell. Instead, to my surprise, he gazed at me with raised eyebrows and lifted hands, his eyes smarting with hurt and confusion.

"What is this madness? You are leaving? Whatever has possessed you? Are you not happy here?"

"Monsieur, I *have* been happy; it grieves me to leave this place, and to leave you. But I must."

"Why? Have you been offered another post?"

"I have not."

"Then to what do you return?"

"Nothing of consequence, Monsieur; but return I must."

"I repeat: why?"

How could I tell him? Even his own wife had, apparently, not dared to broach the truth. "I—I have been away too long, Monsieur. I miss my home and family."

"I understand if you are homesick, Mademoiselle. You should have gone home for the long vacation—I told you so. But to leave now, like this—the school year has only just begun! It is not so easy to find a good teacher of English. What shall we do?"

"You will find another teacher, Monsieur. You will forget me long before I forget you."

"How can you say that, Mademoiselle? After all this time, after all the dialogue that has been exchanged between us, I could never forget you. You are one of the brightest students I have ever had." The gentleness in his voice broke me down with grief, and at the same time turned me cold with dread, for this still voice was the pant of a lion rising. "Are we not good friends, Mademoiselle?"

I stifled a sob. His language was torture to me. "We are good friends, Monsieur."

"When you first came, you were afraid of me, I think. Look how far we have progressed. I believe you understand me now— you are able to read my moods—and I believe I understand you." (Diary: he did not.)

"Monsieur," said I, struggling to steady my voice as I dashed away tears, "I have achieved the attainments I sought in coming here. It is time for me to go."

"No! You have made great progress, but there is still much to be done. I tell you, it is too soon. You must not leave. I will not hear of it!"

The pain in his eyes and voice cut me to the quick. Oh! Why must he make this so much harder than it already was? It was clear that he still cared for me, in his way; that our parting would grieve him; that he saw me as a friend who was letting him down. Conscience and Reason turned traitors against me. I could not, at that moment, have persevered in my intention, any more than I could have leapt off a high cliff; but giving in, I knew, could only lead to equal doom.

I stayed through the end of December. Each day was a misery. When at last I announced my final determination, I was touched by the degree of regret expressed by my pupils. Monsieur Héger acquiesced with sad grace. The morning I left, I was called into the Hégers' sitting-room, where Monsieur placed a parting gift—an anthology of French poetry—into my hands, along with a diploma, testifying to my qualifications to run a school.

"You will let us know when your school is established, yes?" said Monsieur Héger, with great emotion, as he bade me good-bye, promising faithfully to correspond. "We will send one of our daughters to study with you."

Madame insisted on accompanying me to the boat at Ostend on that 1st of January, 1844, as if to ensure that I would have no opportunity to change my mind. Shedding bitter tears, I said good-bye to Belgium, believing in my heart, even then, that some day I would return.

I never did.

Eleven

Two years later, as I lay alone in the darkness of my chamber at the parsonage, the pain and heartache which seared my breast was still as fresh and agonising as it had been upon my return from Belgium. Two years later, I was still secretly in love with a man who resided on the other side of the sea; a man I had always known was unattainable; a man who had proved, by the cessation of his letters a year since (whether of his own accord, or at the insistence of his wife) that there was no possibility of pursuing even a distant friendship. How long, I wondered, did it take to stop loving another person? Was it possible to purposefully and permanently cut him out of one's heart? If so, how did one manage it?

My bedroom door opened and Emily came in, carrying a candle. I sat up, dried my eyes, and struggled to regain control over my emotions, as my sister sat down beside me on the edge of the bed.

"Charlotte, I am sorry for what I said to Branwell about Monsieur Héger. I meant well; but I now see that my attempt to give him comfort was a grave betrayal of your privacy. And I am so very, very sorry for everything I said to you. I spoke without thinking. I love you so much; you are my dearest sister; you are everything to me. I am deeply grieved to see how much my words hurt you. I never meant to cause you pain."

"I know you did not." I reached out to take Emily's proffered hand in the flickering darkness. Her cheeks, I saw, were streaked with tears. Emily wrapped her arms around me, and we clung to each other tightly for some moments, drawing comfort from each other's embrace.

When the hug ended, Emily said softly, "Charlotte, will you tell me now? Will you tell me what happened between you and Monsieur Héger?"

I shook my head. "Not yet. Some day, perhaps, I shall."

It was not until the following morning, when papa joined my sisters and me at breakfast, that I remembered, with sudden mortification, that he and Mr. Nicholls had been present during Branwell and Emily's verbal onslaught the night before.

After papa consumed his oatmeal and hastened off to his study with barely a word, I asked: "Did papa or Mr. Nicholls say anything about—about what they heard last night?"

"They were almost too shocked to speak," said Anne, with a sympathetic glance at me.

"Oh!" I cried, with fresh embarrassment.

"Do not worry," said Emily. "I told them it was all a great misunderstanding, that Branwell had twisted my words around, and none of it could be further from the truth. I am sure they will forget all about it."

Her explanation seemed very optimistic to me. People, in my experience, did not soon forget accusations of the type that Branwell had made, even if they were proved to be untrue. With burning cheeks, I wondered what Mr. Nicholls must think of me. For several days, I was too humiliated to look him in the eye. Then one day, my attitude changed. I had just finished teaching my Sunday school class, and had sent my young pupils on their way with a smile, when I nearly collided with Mr. Nicholls and John Brown in the doorway.

"Are ye going t' th' oratio a' th' church to-morrow night?"

John Brown was asking him. "We are t' hear th' celebrated tenor, Thomas Parker, sing wi' Mrs. Sunderland from Halifax, an' a great variety of instrumental and choral performers besides."

"I would never go to hear a *Baptist* sing," sneered Mr. Nicholls brusquely, as he stepped aside to let me pass.

I could only shake my head at this. Indeed, all the Puseyite curates refused to attend that concert, an event which filled the house of worship to suffocation, and proved to be one of the leading events of the year. As I listened to the glorious music ringing through the church that night, I reminded myself that Mr. Nicholls was a narrow-minded bigot. Why on earth did I care what he thought of me? I was guiltless of any real wrong-doing; he was not. Remember Bridget Malone, I told myself. Mr. Nicholls is the one who should be ashamed to hold his head up, not you!

I contented myself with this notion. If Mr. Nicholls no longer respected me, it was not my fault, nor my concern; for I had never really liked or respected him. I would simply go on avoiding him.

Avoiding Mr. Nicholls, however, was easier said than done. He lived next door; he met with papa every day; he conducted all three Sunday services and supervised the schools; he was everywhere. In fact, Mr. Nicholls's frequent visits to the parsonage gave rise to a dismaying rumour, which I first heard about in a letter from Ellen. She informed me that some one had inquired of her, with great solemnity and interest, if it was true that Mr. Nicholls and I were secretly engaged! I immediately replied in the negative, but her letter left me out of sorts for weeks.

My determination to think ill of Mr. Nicholls was sorely tested one afternoon in mid-March. It was a crisp, cold day: no longer winter, but not quite spring. Anne and I were making a round of visits to the poor to deliver the children's clothing we had sewn over the preceding months for those in need.

Our first stops were to the crowded little houses which clustered along Main Street in the village, a task we did not relish, for although the tenants were gracious enough, their houses were cramped and often very dirty, and so redolent of bad air that we could not bring ourselves to stay longer than a minute. More pleasant were our visits to the parishioners who lived farther afield—the mill-workers in the valleys, and the poor farmers who scratched out a meager living from the soil.

As Anne and I headed out in that direction beneath a glorious canopy of bright blue sky, the wind sounded through the leafless branches of the few scattered trees, and snow-drifts, still lingering in the hollows of the hills and dales, were fast melting beneath the sun. We soon came to the Ainleys' cottage, a tiny thatched and white-washed dwelling set just back from the road.

Three of the eight Ainley children, who were too young for school, were playing outside, attired in an assortment of old and ill-fitting, raggedy clothing. As Anne and I strode to the front door, the little ones surrounded us, making a clamour and fuss, tugging at our skirts and baskets and asking what we had brought them. Gently tousling their curly heads, I explained that they must be patient, for our deliveries must go into their mother's hands first.

"Ah! Aren't ye ladies angels t' bring me clothes for me childer," said Mrs. Ainley as she greeted us at the door and ushered us inside, carrying a one-year-old infant on her hip. A tall, kindly but tired-looking woman in a shabby brown dress, she was forty years old, but looked a decade older. "Th' Lord only knows, I've nought but two hands, an' wi' eight children, it's all I can do t' put food i' their mouths, mich less keep up wi' all th' sewing that be required t' clothe 'em, particular hard i' this cold weather, an' me so bad wi' th' rheumatiz i' me fingers an' all."

The children tried to follow us in, but their mother shooed them out. "Go an' play outside, th' lot o' ye! There's nought room for so mony bodies i' this wee house, and I crave a bit o' grown-up conversation wi' our visitors."

I shivered as we entered the little cottage; it was dark, close, and chilly, and smelled of smoke, but it was as tidy and clean as Mrs. Ainley could make it. She offered us ale, which we declined, aware that she could ill afford to share the beverage. Still holding the baby (a bonny, smiling lass with a head full of blonde curls), Mrs. Ainley quickly dusted off the two best chairs for us by the hearth; knowing that one of them was her favourite, I expressed a preference for sitting on a hard little stool in a corner near the window.

"I'm sorry it be so cold i' here," apologised Mrs. Ainley as she stirred the meager contents of the fire-place, which was no more than a few red cinders and a little bit of stick. "Our stock o' coals an' peat is finished, an' we're ill set t' get more. Sin' they lowered th' wages at th' mill, we've been i' desperate straits. Wi' th' prices o' bread an' potaters so high, me husband barely earns enought for us t' live on, for all he works from dawn till dark. Me oldest girl is a maid o' all work, an' she sends summat home every now an' again, but it's nought but a pittance."

Anne and I expressed our sincere dismay at the dismal working conditions in the township, which we knew were a source of misery and privation for many.

"Ah well, there's nought can be done about it, it's all th' poor state o' trade what's caused it, or so I'm told." Mrs. Ainley placed the good-natured infant on a blanket on the floor at her feet, where it lay quietly sucking its thumb. The woman then took a seat before us and exclaimed with enthusiasm over each new garment we presented her, thanking us profusely.

"Sich fine workmanship as ye ladies do is not often seen. Oh! How I wish I could sew like ye. I can still knit, praise God, when I find th' time, but me fingers can barely hold a sewing needle these days. There's a Sunday shirt I've been trying t' mak' these past four month for me son John; he needs it sadly, but God knows how I'll ever finish it."

"I would be happy to finish it for you," I offered.

"I can help," added Anne. "We can start working on it while we are here, if you like."

"Oh! Ye both are too good; I can never repay sich kindness."

"There is nothing to repay, Mrs. Ainley," said I. "If we can do something to ease your burden, it will give us great pleasure."

Mrs. Ainley gratefully brought the pieces of the unfinished garment to us, along with her sewing box. I found two brass thimbles within, which Anne and I fitted to our tiny fingers by means of a roll of paper. Anne and I were soon at work sewing the shirt, while Mrs. Ainley knitted a pair of stockings. Moments later, a large, brindled cat sauntered in from the next room and lay down before the hearth, lazily licking its velvet paws with half-closed eyes, as it gazed at the decaying embers in the crooked fender.

"That cat's nearly twelve year owd," commented Mrs. Ainley, looking down on the animal with affection. "Like one o' th' family, he is. I dunnut what we'd do wi'out him. He's a lucky one, too. Why, just th' other day, Mr. Nicholls saved his life."

"Mr. Nicholls?" said I in surprise.

"Indeed. T'wor about a week past, th' cat went missing. For four day we saw neither hide nor hair of him. Th' bairn were all beside 'emselfs with worry, crying like there wor no to-morrow. I shed a few tears, too, certain sure we'd never see th' likes o' 'at creature again. Then up th' walk comes Mr. Nicholls, wi' th' cat in his arms. It'd got trapped i' a storage closet at th' Sunday school, he says. He just happened by an' heard it mewing. Lord knows it would've died, otherwise. We're i' Mr. Nicholls's debt. An' not just about th' cat, neither. I bless th' day 'at gentleman arrived i' these parts, I can tell ye."

"Oh?" said Anne. "Why is that, Mrs. Ainley?"

"Mr. Nicholls has been so good t' us. He be so different from 'at last curate, Mr. Smith, who ye hardly ever saw except at church, an' who dinnut care nought for any one but hisself. Why, Mr. Nicholls stops by regular-like, t' read me my favourite passages from th' Bible, for ye know I can't read so well meself, an' we always have sich a nice chat abaat God an' life an' 'at. He talks t' me as kind as owt,[48] an' sits beside me jist like a son or brother. I get sich comfort from his visits."

As I listened to this discourse, I attacked the seam I was sewing

---

[48] Anything.

with barely restrained annoyance. Could I not go anywhere, I wondered, without hearing Mr. Nicholls's praises sung? My irritation turned to alarm when, a few minutes later, I heard a rattling cart pull up outside the cottage, followed by a knock at the front door. Mrs. Ainley answered it to find the aforementioned gentleman himself, standing with hat in hand.

"Good-afternoon to you, Mrs. Ainley," said Mr. Nicholls, patting the heads of the giggling Ainley children beside him, as they tried to poke their heads inside the door. "I couldn't help noticing the other day that your stock of coal was very low. I thought it might be a while before you could get more. So I took up a little collection from our parishioners and I've arranged to bring you some coal, which I hope will last until summer comes."

This sudden appearance by Mr. Nicholls so startled me that I inadvertently stabbed my finger with my needle. Stifling a cry, I shrank back into the corner, cursing the ill-timing of our visit, and hoping he would not see me.

"Mr. Nicholls, ye are goodness itself!" cried Mrs. Ainley, looking as if she might weep for joy. "What a great blessing this is!"

"Do you have a wheelbarrow about, so we can put it in the coal bin?" asked he; then, glancing in and catching sight of Anne and me, he froze in surprise.

"The wheelbarrow's out back, sir," replied Mrs. Ainley. "Let me show ye."

Some bustle followed in which Mr. Nicholls helped the carter transfer the coal to the bin, after which the horse and cart departed. As Mrs. Ainley and Mr. Nicholls returned to the front door I heard him say, "May I fill your coal scuttle, ma'am, before I go? It's a cold day, and your fire looked wanting."

"God bless ye, sir," cried the grateful woman, as Mr. Nicholls followed her into the house. As he passed me and Anne, he acknowledged our presence by an aloof, unsmiling nod, which I returned with a nod equally as cool. He then fetched the coal scuttle, filled it, and brought it back inside. Carefully stepping around the sleeping child and cat, he added a few pieces of fuel to the fire. I bent my head over my work. After a small pause, in which I felt Mr. Nicholls's eyes on me, he said, "Have you ladies formed a sewing circle?"

"No," replied Mrs. Ainley. "Th' Brontës jist come t' bring me them sweet new clothes they made for me bairn. They stayed t' keep me company, and t' sew a shirt for me son John."

"Did they?" said he, in a tone more gracious than before. Bending down to stroke the cat, who emitted a contented purr, Mr. Nicholls added, "Well, I won't interrupt your visit, ladies. Good day to you, Miss Brontë, Miss Anne."

My sister and I both responded in kind.

"I will see you in church on Sunday, Mrs. Ainley."

"Ye will for certain, Mr. Nicholls. Ye know we never miss a Sunday service."

"If you like, I can come by Monday next to read to you. Shall I?"

"Oh! If ye would, sir, I would so look forward t' it. An' thank ye again, for your most thoughtful an' generous gift."

"I did nothing but deliver a little coal, Mrs. Ainley. These good women are the ones deserving of your thanks. The garments they fashioned required a great many long hours to produce, making their gift far more thoughtful and generous than mine."

With a bow, Mr. Nicholls took his leave. Through the window, I saw him pick up one of the little Ainley children in his arms. He talked and laughed with her, the other children prancing happily at his side, as he walked away.

When Anne and I left the cottage half an hour later, carrying the pieces of John's shirt in our basket to complete at home, Anne said: "You see? I told you Mr. Nicholls was a good and amiable man. Do you believe me, now?"

"I do not know what to think. The man exhibits such wildly differing sides to his character! One day, he is spouting the most intolerant notions, or callously berating some poor church-goer for breaking a rule, and the next he is reading to them and delivering coal! Did it not infuriate you when Mr. Nicholls refused to attend the concert last week?"

"What business is it of ours if some one chooses to attend a concert or not?"

"It is the *reason behind* that choice, that tells us something about the man. It is a reflection of his prejudice."

"True; but we all have prejudices. It is a measure of our complexity as people, and some of the best people I know are the most complex," said Anne, with a look in my direction.

I sighed in frustration. "How does one reconcile the man that Mrs. Ainley just so reverently described, with the man who behaved with such cruelty a few years past, to Bridget Malone?"

"Mr. Nicholls was very young then. We should judge him for the man he is to-day, and not for his past misdeeds."

"I shall *try* to think of him in a better light. But in truth— even if Mr. Nicholls brought coal to every poor family in the township—to me, he will always be the man who called me an ugly old maid."

The spring of 1846 was a time of intense—albeit secret— creative output, as my sisters and I worked on our respective novels. Despite Emily's harsh critique of *The Professor,* I was not inclined to change or rethink it. It was what it was; if it turned out to be defective, I would have only myself to blame.

In early May, there was great excitement when the first three copies of our published book of poems arrived at the parsonage. The moment I saw the parcel, discreetly addressed to "Miss Brontë," I guessed what it contained. Giddily, I retrieved Emily and Anne from their piano practise and we raced upstairs, where we opened the package in the privacy of my bedroom.

"Oh!" we all cried in unison, when our eyes fell upon the book for the first time. It was very handsomely bound with an embossed bottle-green cloth cover, with its title and authorship— *Poems, by Currer, Ellis and Acton Bell*—prominently displayed in gilt letters. The pleasure I felt at actually holding the little volume in my hands cannot be described.

"It is so beautiful," exclaimed Anne.

"It is *published*!" I cried.

"You were right, Charlotte," said Emily. "There is something very satisfying in seeing our work in print, in such a well-bound volume."

Laughing with delight, we embraced each other repeatedly. It was the achievement of a dream. It was to be two long months, however, before our little book received any notice whatsoever from reviewers. In the meantime, a catastrophe of such enormous proportions engulfed our household, that any thought of literary attainment was banished from our minds.

The Reverend Edmund Robinson died. We learned of the event during the first week of June, just after Whitsuntide,[49] when Branwell received a letter from one of his informants at the Robinsons' household.

"At last!" he cried, wild with joy, clutching the epistle to his chest as he burst into the dining-room, where my sisters and I were all busy fair-copying our manuscripts in ink. We quickly covered our work, but Branwell was too enveloped in his own emotional frenzy to take any notice of our occupation.

"The old man is gone!" he continued gleefully. "Dead and buried! My Lydia is free! It is only a matter of time now. Ere long, my hopes and dreams shall all be realised. I will be the husband of the lady whom I love best in the world. I will no longer be pestered by any of the small and countless botherments, which like mosquitoes, sting us in the world of work-a-day toil. I will live the life of a gentleman at leisure, and be allowed to make myself a name in the world of prosperity!"

We hardly knew how to reply. Anything we said would have made little impression, however. Branwell was wrapped in such a fever of anticipation, that he neither ate nor slept for the next three days and four nights, throwing all about him into hubbub and confusion with the state of his emotions, as he eagerly awaited a word from "my Lydia."

---

[49] The week beginning on Whitsunday, the seventh Sunday after Easter.

When the word came, it was to dash every one of Branwell's cherished hopes. Mrs. Robinson sent her coachman, Mr. Allison, to explain the facts of the case, which were these: Mr. Robinson had recently altered his will; according to the new clause, his widow was precluded from having any further communication with Branwell, or else forfeit all interest in her estate. Furthermore, owing to remorse for her conduct towards her late husband, and grief for having lost him, Mrs. Robinson had become a complete wreck, and was—according to said Mr. Allison—contemplating retreat into a nunnery.

We could not be certain how much of this was true, particularly with regards to the will. It had never seemed likely to us that a wealthy, pampered woman like Mrs. Robinson, who spent money like water on frivolous items while on holiday (for so Anne had described her), would risk her comfortable style of life and incur the contempt of society by marrying a penniless, unemployed ex-tutor like Branwell. That lady had cast such a deep spell over my brother, however, that he had never entertained the concept.[50]

When the blow came, Branwell was already such a physical and emotional wreck, that he was driven to the brink of insanity. We, who had thought he could sink no lower than the state to which he had previously been reduced, were immediately proved wrong. For the rest of the day, he lay prostrate on the floor of the parsonage, bleating for hours on end like a new-born calf, shrieking that his heart had been broken beyond repair. That evening, when the household was gathered for prayers in papa's study, Branwell burst into the room, wild-eyed and shouting: "Give me some money, old man, and give it now."

---

[50] In fact, Mr. Robinson had *not* altered his will. He left his property in trust for his son, with his wife as trustee and executor; she received an income from the estate unless she married again—a standard provision at the time. Branwell's name was not even mentioned in the will. Nothing prevented Lydia Robinson from reopening communication with him; nor did she enter a nunnery; rather, two years later, she married a rich man, Sir Edward Scott.

He held papa's pistol in his hand. Martha, Tabby, and my sisters screamed in horror.

"Branwell," I cried, my heart thundering in fear, "what are you doing? Put down the gun!"

Papa's face went ashen. "Son, have you got my gun?"

"I have, and it is loaded, too, and aimed straight at your heart. Give me six shillings, or I swear I will blow your brains out, and my sisters' as well."

"Charlotte," said papa quietly, "you know where my coin purse is. Give him the money."

"Yes, papa." I slowly rose, my eyes glued to Branwell's. "I shall get your sordid money, Branwell, but not until you lower that weapon."

He lowered the pistol; as I issued past him from the room, Martha and Anne burst into tears. Not until I returned with the demanded coins did Branwell relinquish the weapon to me, along with the stolen keys to papa's bureau drawer, where the pistol had been kept. He then grabbed his hat and left the house. I sank down onto the entrance-hall's stone floor, trembling with such anxiety as I had never before felt, regarding the cold, steel element of destruction in my fingers with dread and disdain. At length, Emily issued into the hall, gently took the gun and keys from my possession, and restored them to their rightful places.

The next morning, Branwell knelt at papa's feet and begged his forgiveness in a torrent of anguished tears. My heart seemed to weep within me as I observed the look of shame, pity, and despair which diffused papa's countenance as he rose and tenderly took Branwell in his arms.

That night, as I lay on the edge of sleep, a childhood memory came back to me.

I was fifteen years old, in my first term as a student at Roe Head School. It was a week-end morning in May, and it had been four long months since I had been home or seen any of the members of my family. To my surprise, I was called into Miss

Wooler's parlour, where I found Branwell seated in one of her best chairs, waiting for me.

"Branni?" I cried, in stunned delight. "Is it really you?"

He rose to his feet, cap in hand, with a weary smile. "Hello, Charlotte."

He was just a lad then, a month shy of fourteen, but his face, with its handsome Roman nose and well-turned chin, was that of a man of twenty-five. He was taller than I remembered; his best shirt was stained with perspiration, and his bush of chin-length, carroty hair projected out at the sides of his head like two spread hands; indeed, he looked very flushed and fatigued; yet I had never in all my life seen a more welcome sight.

"Oh! I cannot tell you how much I have missed you!" I flew into his arms, where I relished the warmth of his tight embrace. "How on earth did you come to be here?" I said in astonishment, knowing that Branwell had rarely been away from home before.

"I walked."

"You walked *twenty miles*?"

"It is twenty miles by road, but I have been studying the map ever since you went away. I took a short cut across the fields and along the hilltops, just as a bird might fly. You should have seen me, Charlotte, cutting across the country, over pasture-fields and fallow and stubble and lane, clearing hedges and ditches and fences all the way. I am sure I cut out half the distance, or at least a third, for all it felt like twenty miles." He took a step back and studied me, up and down, with a teasing grin. "Now that I am here and have seen you—and am satisfied that you are just the same—I shall be saying good-bye and heading back."

"You will do no such thing!" I laughed and swatted him on the shoulder. "Oh! Such a long walk! You must be exhausted!"

"Not at all," said he bravely.

Knowing that he must return before dark—and that our time together must, by necessity, be short—I was determined to make the most of every moment. I took him first to the kitchen, where cook gave him some refreshment; I then showed him around the establishment, inside and out; then we stretched out on the wide front lawn in the shade of my favourite tree, where we chattered amiably for two precious hours.

He told me about his progress with his latest literary effort; I told him that I had been so busy with school, I had not had a single minute to even think of Glasstown; he promised to keep the saga going until I returned. He gave me all the little news of home, and of every one that I missed and held so dear; and before I knew it, it was time for him to leave.

"You will be coming home soon, will you not?" asked Branwell, as we said good-bye in the front drive.

"Yes. The term is over in five weeks." Tears streaked my cheeks, and I saw answering tears in his own gaze. We hugged each other tightly. "Thank you so much for coming," I breathed against my brother's ear. "It meant the world to me."

Now—fifteen years later—the memory of that golden day in May made me ache anew, and I sobbed convulsively. Those innocent, blissful days would never come again. It seemed that my darling brother—the boy who had once been our pride and joy, who had been so bonny and so filled with promise—was lost to us for ever.

Thank goodness my sisters and I had our writing endeavours to distract us from the somber atmosphere that pervaded the parsonage! On 4 July, 1846, two reviews of our book *Poems* at last appeared in the press. To our consternation, however, the first devoted a great deal of space to the mysterious identity of the "Bells."

"'Who are Currer, Ellis, and Acton Bell?'" I read aloud from the review in the *Critic* to my sisters, as we all lay stretched out in the meadow beyond the parsonage, beneath a rustling green tree. A west wind was blowing, and bright, white clouds flitted rapidly above. The moors stretched out in the distance, broken into cool dusky dells; but all around us, the great swells of long grass undulated in waves to the breeze, and larks, throstles, blackbirds, linnets, and cuckoos poured out music on every side in a glorious jubilee. "'If the poets be of a past or of the present age, if living or dead, whether English or American, where born, or where dwelling, what their ages or station—nay, what their Christian names, the publishers have not thought fit to reveal to the curious reader.'" I lowered the newspaper, somewhat disconcerted. "It seems that in our effort to conceal our sex, we have unwittingly created a mystery."

"Does he not say anything at all about the quality of the poetry?" asked Emily.

"He does, further down." I read on: "'It is so long since we have enjoyed a volume of such genuine poetry as this. Amid the heaps of trash and trumpery in the shape of verses, which lumber the table of the literary journalist, this small book of some 170 pages only has come like a ray of sunshine, gladdening the eye with present glory, and the heart with promise of bright hours in store. Here we have good, wholesome, refreshing, vigorous poetry—'"

Emily grabbed the newspaper from my hands and eagerly continued reading: "'They in whose hearts are chords strung by nature to sympathise with the beautiful and the true in the world will recognise in the compositions of Currer, Ellis, and Acton Bell, the presence of more genius than it was supposed this utilitarian age had devoted to the loftier exercise of the intellect.'" With a stunned expression, she repeated the one word which had most arrested her attention: "*Genius.*"

"Is the second review as good?" asked Anne quietly.

"Not quite," I replied, turning to the *Athenaeum,* which I had already perused. "He accuses Acton and Currer of 'indulgences of affection,' but highly praises Ellis, who he says possesses 'an evident power of wing that may reach heights not here attempted.'"

"Well," said Emily, lying back on the grass with a satisfied smile, "*that* is something."

"It certainly is," agreed I triumphantly. "It appears that the expense we incurred in publishing the volume was justified."

Appearances can be deceiving, however, as we soon discovered. Despite the fact that another positive notice appeared in October, and we spent a further £10 on advertising, our book of rhymes was not wanted. A year after its publication, only two copies had been sold! On that warm July day in 1846, however, my sisters and I could know nothing of the little book's fate. Even if some soothsayer had sagely warned us that our first foray into publishing would prove, in the end, to be an utter failure, I believe we would have refused to allow it to crush our spirits; for we had moved on to something bigger and bolder: we each had a novel, now completed and fair-copied, and ready to submit for publication.

Twelve

We did not intend, this time, to publish on our own account. In early July, I wrapped up our manuscripts and sent them off to the first name on a list of London publishers that I had compiled, explaining that the authors had already appeared before the public. As the three-volume set was the standard method of marketing a work of fiction, I described the works as "three tales, each occupying a volume and capable of being published together or separately, as thought most advisable."

While we waited to hear back about our novels, my attention necessarily became focused on my father. For a long while, papa had required assistance with all of the most basic activities of daily living, and his vision was now wholly obscured.

In August 1846, I accompanied papa to Manchester to undergo an eye operation with Mr. Wilson, an eye specialist of some renown, with whom Emily and I had consulted earlier that month. We moved into rented lodgings, where Mr. Wilson performed the operation on August 25th with two surgeons assisting. He decided to operate on only one eye, in case infection should set in. Papa displayed extraordinary patience and firmness throughout the ordeal. Afterwards, he was confined to his bed in a dark room with bandages over his eyes and a hired nurse in attendance, with instructions that he be bled with eight leeches at a time, placed on his temples, in order to prevent inflammation. He was not to stir for four days, or leave our lodgings for five weeks—and he was to be spoken to as little as possible.

The long wait now began.

Earlier that same morning, a letter had arrived from Emily, matter-of-factly stating that our three manuscripts had been returned, accompanied by a few curt words of rejection, by Henry Colburn, the first publisher to whom I had sent them. Although disheartened, I gave little thought to Emily's letter all day, my focus entirely directed to providing that comfort and support which papa required. Now that the surgery was completed, however, and I was left all alone in an airless, narrow, red brick, terraced house in Manchester in the heat of an August evening, I could not help but ponder our future.

I could not—*would not*—accept defeat. From my trunk, I retrieved the portable writing desk that I always took with me when I travelled, and unfolded it on top of a scratched little table by the window. I wrote a brief letter to Emily, instructing her to submit our work again. Restless, I then stood up and began to pace back and forth in the little sitting-room.

How strange it was to be living in an unfamiliar place, in such enforced seclusion! What was I to do with myself, I wondered, in the ensuing five weeks? To my disappointment, I was not even allowed to cheer papa by conversation. My days, I knew, would be long, filled with anxiety and no occupation. To make matters worse, I was suffering from a bad tooth-ache—a physical pain which was as agonising as my pervasive loneliness. I desperately needed some means of distraction.

The solution to my dilemma came to me in the form of an inner voice that was so unexpectedly sharp, and so distinct, that it stopped me in my tracks.

"There is one place," said the voice in my head, "where you

have always found consolation and refuge in times of need: your imagination."

"Yes! There is truth in that," I replied. Mentally, I further soliloquised: "*There* is my answer. It is insufficient to rely on the manuscripts we have completed, as our one and only ticket to success. My sisters must do as they please; but if I truly wish to be published some day, *I must keep on writing.* I must begin another book, the sooner the better—and what better time or place than now?"

What, I wondered, should I write about?

Emily had insisted that my novel *The Professor* was devoid of incident, a surface image with no depth. She had criticised me for employing a male narrator, and called the writing passionless and soulless. Perhaps Emily was right. Perhaps the self-control that I had been so determined to maintain ever since I left Brussels *had* proved injurious to my writing. Perhaps publishers, and the reading public, wanted something a little more wild, more passionate, and more wonderful and thrilling, than the homely tale I had written.

I proceeded up and down the room, deep in thought, endeavouring to come up with a fresh subject for a new book, but nothing that came to mind appealed to me. At length the sun went down, and I realised I was very hungry; in great frustration, I gave up the occupation. I went to the kitchen, lit a candle, and tried to take some nourishment, but the pain in my tooth was so severe, that I could take only a few wincing bites of the bread and cold meat that I had bought upon our arrival. I looked in on my father, who the nurse assured me was asleep; I then returned to my solitary musings.

It was nearly midnight. Famished, lonely, and out of sorts, I stopped and stared out the sitting-room window at the bright moon and the sprinkling of stars. All at once, an eerie sensation came over me, and I caught my breath. It seemed as if I had gazed out this same window once before; as if I had felt the exact same feelings that now possessed me, at some time in the past. I knew that was impossible; I had never entered these lodgings before in my life. Whence, then, did this peculiar feeling come from? What was it about my present, unpleasant circumstances which felt so uncannily familiar?

Suddenly, the answer came to me. I had indeed once been shut up in a similarly strange and lonely place, where I had felt equally ravenous and miserable. I had stood before a window just as I stood now, and gazed out at the night sky with desperate longing, wishing that the moon could send me home to Haworth on one of its beams. I remembered it as if it was yesterday:

It was when I was eight years old, and incarcerated at the Clergy Daughters' School.

Papa could not have known, when he escorted me to the Clergy Daughters' School at Cowan Bridge in August 1824, of the horrors that awaited me and my sisters there—or the devastating effects its tenure would have on my entire family. Indeed, he felt it providential that he had at last found an establishment where he could educate all his daughters for a reasonable price; for the new school, founded for the daughters of Evangelical clergymen, was sponsored by some of the most prominent people in the country, and the fees were kept low by subscriptions.

My sister Maria was ten years old at the time—only two years older than I—but with her lovely pale face and cloud of long dark hair, her devotion to study and family, and her brilliant mind (she could debate with papa on all the leading topics of the day), Maria had always seemed very old and wise to me, and had served as a model of good behaviour to the rest of us. It was seven-year-old Maria who had held me in her arms when our mother died; it was Maria who had comforted me when I was uncertain about the future. Although our aunt Branwell had selflessly left her native Cornwall to move in and take charge of us, she was a strict and exacting woman. It was my sister Maria who became our mother substitute in our affections, and I adored her.

Elizabeth, one year older than I, was also a sweet sister and dutiful child, whom I both loved and admired. Unlike Maria, Elizabeth was more outgoing: she loved active play, enjoyed helping in the kitchen, and her greatest dream at the time was one day to own a pretty dress.

All six of us children suffered from the measles and whooping-cough that spring. As Maria and Elizabeth were the first to recover, they were the first to be enrolled in school. A month later, papa brought me to join them. I knew nothing of schools then, good or bad; I only knew that at eight years old, I was at last to see something of the world beyond my own neighbourhood, and the prospect thrilled me!

The Clergy Daughters' School lay forty-five miles from Haworth in the tiny, isolated hamlet of Cowan Bridge. The large, two-storeyed building of stone and brick, situated beside a bridge and overlooking a stream and an endless vista of low, wooded hills, had been converted into a school from an old bobbin-mill. Its cold, grim interior now housed a vast, high-ceilinged schoolroom on the ground floor, with a large dormitory above, where more than fifty pupils slept two to a bed, in closely packed rows of narrow cots.

The school's founder and director, the celebrated Reverend Carus Wilson, was a towering block of black marble, with piercing grey eyes under bushy brows. He would appear without warning in the schoolroom, causing students and teachers alike to leap to their feet in silent deference, as he majestically uttered a string of criticisms regarding both teachers' and pupils' performance or appearance. To my horror, and my sisters' misery and distress, he sent for a barber and had their long, beautiful hair chopped off a few weeks after I arrived. The main point of his visits, however, was fiercely to issue whatever religious and moral lesson he deemed most appropriate for the day.

"The intent of this institution," Mr. Wilson sternly proclaimed one afternoon, "is not to pamper the body, or accustom you to habits of luxury and indulgence; it is devoted entirely to your spiritual edification, for that is the route to the salvation of your immortal soul."

I had not given much thought to heaven or hell before; but Mr. Wilson's severe approach, with its terrifying threats of damnation, was to produce in me an effect opposite to his intention: it created a passionate and lifelong resentment towards any religious doctrine which precluded freedom of individual thought or expression.

Our daily routine at the school was strictly regimented. We arose each morning in the dark to the loud ringing of a bell; we dressed by the dim, flickering glow of a rush-light, in identical, high-necked nankeen frocks and brown holland pinafores,[51] which were both uncomfortable and unbecoming. An hour and a half of tedious morning prayers was followed by an inedible breakfast, and then lessons began. The teaching methods were rudimentary: pupils gathered in groups by age around a teacher who orally presented a concept, which we were expected to learn by heart and parrot back aloud. I found this difficult at first, as I had little experience with memorisation, and the murmured cacophony of repetition from the other classes in the immense, echoing schoolroom was very distracting. I eventually mastered the tasks that were expected of me, however; schoolwork, I discovered, was something I was good at; it turned out to be the least of my worries.

It was a pity, I often thought, that papa had not stayed long enough when he delivered me or my sisters to school, to comprehend fully the dismal living conditions, the harsh disciplinary practices, and the many offences with regard to food to which we were daily subjected.

Indeed, the food was very bad, and in very short supply; we were kept in a constant state of near starvation. The cook was extremely dirty; she did not always clean out her pots before using them again. The typical daily meal was a watery stew called hot-pot, of boiled potatoes and bits of tainted, rangy meat, which had such an offensive taste and smell that I could not eat it, and was unable to stomach meat for many years thereafter. The

---

[51] Nankeen was a buff-colored cotton. Holland was a linen fabric.

porridge at breakfast was not only often burnt, but filled with fragments of other indefinable, greasy substances. The milk was often bingy,[52] and for tea, we were each allotted only a small mug of coffee and half a slice of brown bread—an offering which was usually stolen by one of the ravenous older girls. The only other food provided was a glass of water and a dreaded piece of oat cake before evening prayers.

As to prayers—although I firmly believe that religion is the life-blood of all existence, and should be the groundwork of all education—the unreasonably long hours dedicated to devotion, sermons, and lecture scripture lessons at the Clergy Daughters' School, particularly on an empty stomach, served more to hinder rather than promote the salvation of immortal souls.

In my second week at school, I was watching the other girls running about in the convent-like garden during the mid-day play hour, when I spied my sister Maria taking refuge from the sun in a quiet corner beneath the covered veranda. A book was open on Maria's lap, but she was not looking at it; instead, she stared off into space, to some point beyond the high, spike-guarded enclosing walls. I plunked down on the stone bench beside her and said, "A penny for your thoughts."

Maria looked up with a startled and embarrassed smile. "I was thinking of home."

"Oh! How I would love to be home right now. I hoped I would like this place, but now I do not think I shall."

"It does not matter whether or not we like it, Charlotte. It is only important that we do well and get a proper education, for this is the only school papa can afford. Did you know that he has paid an additional fee for you and me to be educated as governesses?"

"Governesses?" I made a face. "What about Elizabeth? Is she to be a governess?"

---

[52] A country expression for a kind of taint far worse than sourness, suggesting that it is caused by want of cleanliness about the milk pans, rather than by the heat of the weather.

"No. Papa said Elizabeth is more suited to be the mistress of the household when she grows up. You and I are lucky, Charlotte. We will learn so much more than the other girls. We must be as good as we can, learn everything that is assigned, be neat, tidy, and punctual at all times—and take care not to offend Miss Pilcher."

Miss Pilcher, who taught history and grammar to the third class, was a short, thin woman whose weather-beaten face and permanently-frazzled expression made her appear a decade older than her twenty-six years. She slept in a chamber adjacent to the dormitory; it was her responsibility to see to it that we were all properly clad and prompt in our arrival at morning prayers, a duty which she seemed to greatly resent. She also seemed to take a particular dislike to Maria, who, to my dismay, she persecuted on a regular basis for the most minor of offences.

When Maria's mind wandered in class, Miss Pilcher made her stand on a chair in the centre of the room for an entire day; for an untidy drawer, she pinned several undergarments to Maria's frock, and bound around her forehead a piece of pasteboard, upon which she had inscribed the word "Slattern." My heart burned with pain and fury at these injustices; but worse was yet to come. Twice, I saw Maria flogged with "the rod": a terrifying tool made from a bundle of twigs tied together at one end. The fear of that tool's sting was a great motivator to dutiful behaviour in every student; yet Miss Pilcher appeared to enjoy employing it for even the most cursory transgression. I watched in impotent horror, flinching as each of the twelve sharp lashes struck Maria's neck; but Maria remained calm and stoic throughout the ordeal, not giving way to tears until later, after she had quietly returned the despised rod to its place of storage.

Every day, I prayed that papa would come and release us from our prison; instead, when papa did return in late November, he brought six-year-old Emily to join us. His stay was brief, and we were only permitted a few minutes' audience with him. There was so much I wanted to tell him, but Maria made me promise not to breathe a word.

By now, Mr. Wilson had hired a new superintendent to manage the school. Miss Ann Evans was thirty years old, tall and lovely, and always impeccably dressed; she also had a sensitive nature. When I asked her to allow Emily to be my bed-fellow, so that I might more readily watch over her, my request was granted.

December came. The weather grew harsh and cold; we shivered in our beds, and the water in the ewers froze, making it impossible to wash. An early and deep snowfall made the road impassable, but we were still required to spend an hour every day in the open air of the frozen garden, and to walk more than two miles across the sweeping rise and fall of a snowy, exposed path every Sunday to church. Having no gloves, we arrived at church paralysed with cold, our hands numbed and covered with chilblains;[53] ditto our feet, for having no boots, the snow crept into our shoes and melted there.

We sat through the all-day service frozen, with wet feet. In late afternoon, as my sisters and I trudged back to school in the long line of dejected girls and teachers, we wrapped our purple cloaks tightly about us, squeezing our eyes to slits against the bitter winter wind, which cut through our clothing and flayed our cheeks raw. Upon our return, we were treated to further Bible study and a long sermon by Miss Pilcher, during which Emily and I, and many of the other younger girls, often dropped in exhaustion from the benches to the floor.

Maria had developed a little cough that autumn, which she insisted was a lingering remnant of the whooping-cough. By late January, however, her cough was worse, and she grew increasingly weak and pale. Then Elizabeth caught a bad chill on one of our Sunday walks, and developed a cough of her own. Several other pupils suffered from similar complaints, which the teaching staff attributed to typical winter colds. One afternoon, I was alarmed to see that Maria's handkerchief, after she

---

[53] An inflammation of the hands and feet caused by exposure to cold and moisture.

was seized by a coughing fit, was tinged with blood. I gave intelligence of the event to Miss Evans; she called in Dr. Batty, who examined my sister.

A few days later, when I rose to dress at the first morning bell, I noticed that Maria was not in her bed. I applied to Miss Pilcher, who informed me that Maria had been removed to Miss Evans's quarters during the night.

"Why?" I asked, filled with sudden, unspeakable dread.

"We believe she has consumption,"[54] said Miss Pilcher tersely, as she shut her door in my face.

I had never heard of consumption. The apprehension I had witnessed on Miss Pilcher's countenance implied that this was no simple childhood illness, from which one would easily recover. For the first time in my life, I was seized by the thought that my sister might die, and I felt a shock of horror and grief.

"I *must* see Maria," I told my sisters, as we headed towards the dining-hall that morning.

"How can you?" said Elizabeth. "She is with Miss Evans."

"Then that is where I shall find her."

When the teachers were looking the other way, I slipped out of line and out the door; with pounding heart, I dashed along the pebbly path to the cottage I knew belonged to Miss Evans. She admitted me with barely a word, explaining that I would find my sister in her bedroom. I crossed the apartment to the adjoining chamber, where, beside the larger bed, I saw a huddled form lying on a narrow cot. I advanced, terrified. Was it Maria? Was she alive or dead?

"Charlotte," said Maria in her gentle voice as I approached, "why are you here? Should you not be at breakfast?"

I sat down on the stool beside Maria's bed with relief. Although she was pale, and her eyes looked feverish, she was not much changed from the day before. "They told me you were ill. I was worried about you."

---

[54] Tuberculosis.

"Do not worry, Charlotte. Miss Evans has written to papa and asked him to come and take me home."

"I am glad. I shall miss you, but the fresh air of the moors will cure you." A coughing spell took hold of her; I winced at the effort it required for her to endure the lengthy spasms. "I wish there was something I could do to ease your suffering."

"There is. You can make me a promise."

"What promise?"

"If you hear that I have died, promise me you will not grieve."

A hot pang seared my chest and throat. "Maria, you are *not* going to die."

"I do not wish to. But if it is the Lord's will that I should die, I must accept it and be grateful for the time I have had on earth."

"How can you be grateful? You are far too young to die!"

"We all must die one day. My only regret is that I shall not have more time to spend with papa and you and all my family."

Tears welled in my eyes. "Are you very afraid?" I whispered.

Maria's eyes shone with courage and intelligence as she said softly, "No, I am not afraid. If I die, I will go to God. He will be revealed to me in heaven. He is our father and our friend, and I love Him."

A few days later, papa retrieved Maria from school. Over the next three months, while I clung to the belief that Maria was happy at home and getting well, conditions at the school turned from bad to worse. With the advent of spring, a new menace came to Cowan Bridge. The establishment lay in a low forest dell near a river, at times surrounded by dense fog, which brought moisture into the crowded schoolroom and dormitory, and became a breeding ground for typhus. By early April, nearly a third of the pupils, already weak from semi-starvation, had fallen ill. A doctor was called in. He condemned the preparation of the food, and the cook was dismissed. Ten more girls left school in declining health; I learned that six of them died soon after reaching home.

Emily and I somehow escaped the ravages of the typhoid fever, but Elizabeth did not. She was sent to the crowded hospital ward in the seminary, which I visited at every opportunity.

The second week of May, Emily and I were called in to a private meeting with Miss Evans in her study. I still remember what she wore that day: a lovely frock of deep violet silk, with a black lace collar and a black ribbon around her throat.

"Girls," said Miss Evans, in a solemn voice, "I received a letter from your father to-day. I am so sorry to tell you this, but your sister Maria has passed away."

Emily and I cried ourselves to sleep that night in each other's arms. Were we truly never again to hear our sweet Maria's voice? Were we never again to see her gentle smile, or feel the warmth of her motherly embrace? Of course, we could not go to the funeral; home was too far away.

Two weeks later, the doctor, upon examining Elizabeth again, determined that she had never suffered from typhus after all; she was in fact in the final stages of consumption, the same disease which had killed Maria. Emily and I watched helplessly as a servant lifted Elizabeth aboard the public coach to Keighley, which quickly drove away. Papa was shocked when a private gig drew up unannounced at Haworth parsonage with Elizabeth aboard. He took one look at her wasted face, the mirror image of Maria's only weeks before, and after remanding her to Aunt Branwell's care, he immediately came and rescued Emily and myself.

"You will never go back to that school," proclaimed a tearful papa as we journeyed home, "and that's the end of it."

How shall I describe the relief that Emily and I felt at leaving behind, once and for all, the hardships of the Clergy Daughters' School, and returning to our beloved home? It was a relief, however, that was tempered by enormous sadness: it was a home without Maria, and soon without Elizabeth. For Elizabeth's illness was so advanced, that she died just two weeks after reaching Haworth.

* ★ *

Tears stung my eyes as—twenty-one years later—I stood at the window of our lodgings in Manchester and reflected on the loss of my two beloved sisters. My grief and resentment was as fresh and deep to-day as if the harrowing events had only just occurred. If, at that moment, a genie had granted my dearest wish, I would have asked him to send me back in time to when my sisters were still alive, so that I might embrace them once more; I would have asked, too, for a private moment with my younger self, so that I might provide her with hope, solace, and comfort.

As I sadly processed these thoughts and memories, a realisation struck me; I was suddenly overcome by a chill that caused the hair on the back of my neck to stand on end; it was followed by a surge of heat, and the rapid pounding of my heart.

All at once, I knew what I should write next.

That anguished, lonely little school-girl, so miserable, starved and deprived—whose every thought and feeling I still recalled so vividly, to the depth of my very being—*I could write about her.*

Drawing on my own experience, I could fearlessly invest that little girl with all the emotion I wished, and deliver the kind of passionate story that I had so enjoyed writing in the past. The idea sent a thrill coursing through me, and my mind continued to work, all in a tumult. My main character should be motherless, I decided—*that* was something I knew about—and unwanted by the family who raised her. Perhaps she could grow up to be a governess; that was something I knew about, too.

There must be a romance, of course; I could add elements of the strange, the startling, and the harrowing, akin to the tales I had penned in my youth. But this would be no typical novel, I decided, about a young woman of great beauty—no! I would try something very different this time, from the stories I had written, and the books I had read: I would create a small, plain heroine, like myself. I could name her after one of my sisters; but no, that would be too blatant; instead, I would use Emily's middle name: Jane.

Whether or not such a story would meet with approval from a publisher or the reading public, I could not be certain; I only knew that I must proceed. *This* was the book I was meant to write next.

I sat down at my desk. I seized a sheet of paper. By the flickering light of a single candle, I dipped my pen in my ink pot.

And I began to write *Jane Eyre*.

Thirteen

The first chapters of *Jane Eyre* poured out in a frenzy. Over the next five weeks, as I waited for my father to recuperate from his surgery, I wrote all day, every day, and most of the nights as well. It was the first time I had ever written from a woman's point of view, and it felt so incredibly *right*.

The sense of extreme isolation and loneliness I had endured as a governess, I invested in my depiction of Jane as a child at Gateshead, unloved and unwanted by the Reeds. I re-created my life at the Clergy Daughters' School, and evoked the memory of my gentle, patient sister Maria in Jane's angelic but doomed friend, Helen Burns. Perhaps it was the intensely personal nature of these memories, bound up as they were by my terrible anger and grief caused by my sisters' deaths, that caused me to write *Jane Eyre* with a zeal that I had never before encountered in any of my earlier literary efforts. I wrote in a white heat; I wrote as if my very life depended on it; I wrote in a fervent articulation of all the pent-up emotion that had been fermenting in my soul for years. Every word I penned felt so real and true— as indeed it was, for it was inspired by fact—it seemed as if I were merely taking dictation from some otherworldly, magical source.

While I wrote, to my joy and relief, my father's health and vision improved daily. The surgeon continued to express his satisfaction at the success of the operation, and assured us that papa's eyesight would be perfectly restored in that one eye; ere long, he would be able to both read and write.

We returned home at the end of September with high hopes. Two months later, papa was so recovered as to be able to return to active duty. Meanwhile, I continued to write obsessively. Other memories and incidents from my own life, past and present, found their way into my novel. Thornfield Hall became a fusion of North Lees Hall and Ellen's childhood home, The Rydings. My fascination with attics and their mysterious occupants became a central theme, embellished by stories of the West Indies which I had been told by a friend at the Clergy Daughters' School, Mellany Hane, who had once resided in that exotic land.

The quiet, humble life enjoyed by my sisters and me was reflected in Diana and Mary Rivers and Jane at Moor House; the Rivers's good servant Hannah was the personification of Tabby. Many of the inner conflicts explored by the heroines in the stories of my youth found a new home in Jane Eyre's tale—and an alarming accident which occurred at home the very autumn of its composition inspired a similar mishap, allowing Jane to save Mr. Rochester from grave danger.

The mishap occurred on a mid-afternoon in early November. Papa was out. My sisters and I had just entered the parsonage after a walk on the moors with the dogs. Moments after Anne went upstairs, we heard a scream and a crash. Greatly frightened, Emily and I raced up after her, immediately aware of a strong smell of burning. As we reached the upper landing, I saw blue wreaths of smoke rushing in a cloud from Branwell's room.

"Branwell's bedclothes are on fire!" cried Anne frantically from his doorway. "He will not wake up!"

In an instant we were all within the chamber, which was close and dark. Great tongues of flame leapt at the curtains hanging around Branwell's bed, and had begun to incinerate the coverlets and sheets. In the midst of the heat and blaze, Branwell lay stretched and motionless, in his typical day-time stupor. His water-jug lay in pieces on the floor; I guessed that Anne had hurled its contents at the conflagration, to no good effect.

"Branwell! Branwell! Wake up! Wake up!" I shouted, shaking him, but he only murmured in his sleep and turned, oblivious.

"Get more water!" cried Emily. Anne raced out. While Emily dragged Branwell out of bed and flung him unceremoniously into the corner (where he awoke and shrank back against the wall, screaming in terror and confusion), I heaved the flaming bedclothes into the centre of the room and began beating them with a blanket. Emily seized my brother's coat from a chair and attacked the flames which enveloped the curtains. Anne and Martha both returned with cans of water from the kitchen; they joined the battle against the inferno, and at last we succeeded in extinguishing it. The hiss of the quenched elements surrounded us as we all stood in the small chamber, choking and waving away the vapour. I opened the window. Branwell continued to scream in the corner like an idiot.

"You stupid fool!" exclaimed Emily, whirling on him. "You know better than to go to sleep with a candle burning! You could have burnt the house down!"

It took all the rest of the afternoon and evening to clean up the mess, and some months before we managed to replace the damaged covers and curtains on the bed. From that day forward, Branwell was forbidden to have a light when left alone, and we hid all the candles, changing their storage place with regularity so that he could never find them. Furthermore, papa—who had always been deeply concerned about the dangers of fire—insisted that Branwell sleep in his room in future, so that he could prevent him from coming to further harm. The two men shared a bed every night thenceforth, for the remainder of Branwell's life.

★ ★ ★

As I wrote, a year sped by. During this time, the forlorn little parcel with our three other manuscripts made its rounds to a succession of publishers, meeting with rejection after rejection. Emily seemed to lose heart at this lack of interest in our work, but Anne did not; she began a new book of her own. As before, we met every evening to share what we were working on.

One night in midwinter 1847, when I had read aloud the latest chapter of my half-completed manuscript, Emily said with uncharacteristic enthusiasm, "It is very good, Charlotte. I believe this is the best thing you have ever written. The mystery is so compelling, I can barely wait to hear the next chapter."

"I love it, too," said Anne quietly. "Jane is so real; my heart goes out to her. I do worry a bit, though, about the way you portray religion in the novel. Sometimes it seems as if you wish to do away with morality."

"I take no stand on morality here. It is only a story."

"But in making Mr. Rochester your hero," persisted Anne, "you seem to be glorifying certain very base qualities. He is a very domineering man, with so many past mistresses, and he has an illegitimate child."

"Do not be such a prig, Anne," countered Emily. "I adore Mr. Rochester. Can you not see that he is, in every way, the embodiment of Charlotte's beloved Duke of Zamorna? It is those same *base* qualities that made the Duke so vital and interesting before, and they are no less fascinating to read about to-day." To me, she added, "I am amused, however, that you chose to make Mr. Rochester small, dark, irascible, and far from handsome. This, and his penchant for cigar-smoking, bears a greater resemblance to Monsieur Héger than your Duke."

I blushed at this observation. "I suppose I did model Mr. Rochester's *physical* likeness a bit after Monsieur Héger."

All the stories I had written in my youth contributed, in some way, to my new effort, and my sisters recognised each and every reference with enthusiasm.

When I revealed the truth about Bertha Mason, Anne cried,

"It reminds me of *The Fairy Gift*—but it is so much more thrilling!" I had quite forgotten that tale, which I had written at age thirteen, about a hero who was given four wishes. Although he wished to marry a beauty, he was given instead a horribly ugly and villainously strong wife, who haunted the corridors and stairways of a great mansion and tried to strangle him.

When I read the scene where Mr. Rochester tests Jane's love in the garden, Emily said, "That was very well done. The way he tortures her, step by step, before finally revealing his love—it is just like the Duke of Zamorna's jealous trial of Mina Laury, as well as that other story you wrote—where Sir William Percy begs Elizabeth Hastings to be his mistress."[55]

"Yes," agreed I, "and Anne, as always, should be pleased with the outcome—since Jane, like Elizabeth Hastings, takes the moral line and flees from temptation."

I completed *Jane Eyre* in early summer 1847, and had begun to make a fair-copy, but was obliged to put my work aside when Ellen came to visit us for a few weeks. My sisters and I always looked forward to Ellen's visits. In the sixteen years since Ellen and I first met at school, a warm affection had developed between her and Emily and Anne, and she was now considered almost as one of the family.

"I see no reason why I cannot tell Nell about the book," I said to Emily before Ellen arrived. "It would be easier on all of us if we could continue our work in the evenings, while Nell is here."

"No," insisted Emily. "I do not want her, or any one, to know about our writing. Our books have been rejected by every publisher to whom you sent them, and our book of poetry did so poorly—it is too humiliating!"

"We *will* sell our novels," I told Emily, despite the growing doubt that gnawed at me with each new rejection. "We have only to persevere and be patient."

---

[55] Emily refers to scenes from Charlotte's short novelettes *Mina Laury*, 1838, and *Henry Hastings*, 1839.

Papa had long since regained his health and eyesight in such full measure, that he had been able to resume all his usual duties in the parish. Mr. Nicholls, who had carried papa's entire burden for so long in duty, if not in title, was again relegated to his lesser role as curate. To his credit, Mr. Nicholls accepted this demotion with humility and grace, professing his continued delight and relief in my father's recovery. Every day, however, we expected Mr. Nicholls to accept a new post elsewhere, where he might take charge of his own parish—a promotion which, despite my own personal misgivings about him, I had to admit he certainly deserved. To my surprise, this never happened.

"I know why Mr. Nicholls does not leave," said Ellen during her visit in early July.

My sisters, Ellen, and I were relaxing lazily at one of our favourite spots, far out on the purple-tinged heath, hidden in an embankment along Sladen Beck, a place we called "The Meeting of the Waters." This secluded oasis of emerald green turf was dotted with small, clear springs that converged together in the stream, and at this season, it was festooned with clusters of brilliantly-coloured flowers. Since childhood, we had spent countless summer days dallying in this idyllic paradise, removed from all the world, basking in the pure joy of friendship, beneath a glorious canopy of cloudless blue.

All four of us were now seated or reclining, bonnetless, on one of the large, smooth grey rocks that lay scattered here and there within and beside the ponds, as if tossed by some giant hand; our skirts were hiked up indecorously to our knees, and our bare feet dangled in the sparkling, cold water.

"I caught a glimpse of Mr. Nicholls in the hall at the parsonage this morning, when he came to see your father," Ellen went on. "I think he stays in Haworth, despite the lack of advancement to his career, because he likes *you*, Charlotte."

"That is absurd," said I.

"It is not," replied Ellen.

"I tell Charlotte this all the time," said Anne, splashing her feet happily in the water, "but she will not listen."

"Did you see the way he looked at you, when he entered the house?" asked Ellen.

"I did not."

"He had the same expression on his countenance that I used to see on Mr. Vincent's, when he came to court me: awkward shyness and concealed admiration, all mingled with reserve and fear. He was hoping for a word or a look from you; yet you did not even glance his way."

I thought Ellen must be dreaming, and told her so.

"I *did* notice him lingering in the passage, eyeing you covertly," interjected Emily, who was lying, stomach down, on a large rock, sweeping her hand through the clear, shallow water and making the tadpoles dart about.

"Mr. Nicholls is always pleasant to me," observed Ellen. "He has been good to your father, and such a big help in the parish. Why do you dislike him so?"

I glanced briefly at my sisters, who caught my eye but remained silent. I had never told Ellen the story about Bridget Malone, believing it would be wrong to spread malicious gossip which could prove detrimental to Mr. Nicholls's career; neither had I told her about the mean-spirited comment Mr. Nicholls had made behind my back when he first came to Haworth, some two years before.

"I am afraid Mr. Nicholls is not the vision of perfection that you imagine him to be, Nell," said I, as I lay back on the rock and tilted my face up to revel in the warmth of the sun. "It would be indiscreet of me to say why; but not every one in Haworth loves him as well as you do."

A week later, Ellen had a chance to witness an example of Mr. Nicholls's unpopular behaviour first-hand. Ever since Mr. Nicholls's arrival in Haworth, he had been speaking out against the washerwomen's weekly practice of drying their wet laundry over the table-shaped tombstones in the Haworth churchyard. He was still complaining about it two years later.

"A churchyard should be a revered place of solitude and re-

spect, in remembrance of the deceased," I had heard Mr. Nicholls say to papa a few months earlier, when I served their tea.
"This spectacle is a mockery, akin to holding a weekly picnic on
holy ground."

"I think it rather charming," I had interjected. "All the
women gathered out in the churchyard with their baskets of
laundry, chatting away gaily in the breeze. It puts the graveyard
to practical use, and makes it seem less gloomy. It is a place for
them all to meet once a week."

"It gets them out of their back-yards," agreed papa. "I am
told they look forward to it."

"Well, I mean to put an end to it," Mr. Nicholls had said.

And so he did. He waged a long battle with the trustees of
the church, and at length achieved his aim. At services one Sunday in July, Mr. Nicholls made a startling announcement:

"From this day forth, the hanging of laundry shall no longer
be allowed in the Haworth churchyard. Ladies, you shall please
find a more suitable and respectable place to dry your wet garments."

A wave of protest rose up amongst the congregants, male
and female alike. Mr. Nicholls left the podium amidst boos and
catcalls. After the service, people huddled in groups in the
churchyard and lane, loudly voicing their complaints. My sisters
and Ellen and I were about to head back to the house, when Sylvia Malone strode up with a fierce expression on her face.

"Oh! That Mr. Nicholls!" Sylvia cried. "I'd sure and for certain loathe the sight of him to-day, if I didn't do so already!"

"I understand Mr. Nicholls's point about the laundry," said
Anne. "The practice has always seemed disrespectful to me."

"You would never see laundry hung out to dry in the Birstall
churchyard," agreed Ellen.

"Do you have trees in Birstall?" asked Sylvia.

"We do," replied Ellen.

"Well, there's barely a tree to speak of in *this* township," said
Sylvia heatedly, "so we can't very well put up a laundry line, can
we? Where are we supposed to dry our wet clothes now, I ask

you? Oh! How I wish that Mr. Nicholls would go back to Ireland where he belongs, and never return!"

Many parishioners echoed this view, expressing a desire, when Mr. Nicholls left on his annual, month-long holiday to Ireland, that he should not trouble himself to re-cross the Channel.

"This is not a feeling that ought to exist between shepherd and flock," I told Anne with a disgruntled sigh, after Mr. Nicholls's departure.

"It will all blow over in time," replied Anne with quiet assurance.

Anne's words proved true. The women of the community soon took to hanging their laundry over their own stone walls, or over the wall along Church Lane, which provided an equally fine meeting place.

That same summer, good news at long last occurred on the publishing front. Thomas Newby, the head of a small London firm, expressed a desire to publish Anne's *Agnes Grey* and Emily's *Wuthering Heights* together as a three-volume set—*Wuthering Heights* being a work of such length, they said, that it required two volumes of its own. To my disappointment, no interest was expressed in my novel *The Professor,* which was declared "deficient in startling incident and thrilling excitement."

My sisters were beside themselves with joy. I was delighted for them, but at the same time cautious; for the offer came only on condition that the authors paid for publication themselves, by advancing the sum of £50. We had already suffered a most disappointing experience with a self-funded publication, and I worried that no more good would come of this venture, particularly since only 350 copies were to be printed, at a fee that would nearly impoverish my sisters. After so many rejections, however, Emily and Anne were so relieved to have an offer of any kind, that they immediately complied.

This singling out of *The Professor* for rejection was a real blow. I was about to shove the cherished but dejected manuscript into my bottom drawer, when I recalled that there was one last publishing house on my list, to whom I had not yet applied: the firm of Smith, Elder & Co, of Cornhill, London. Although I knew my work had little hope of being accepted on its own, being too short for publication at one volume, I decided to send it to them anyway. I blush to admit it now, but in my naivete— (paper being so expensive—and having nothing else readily at hand)—I wrapped the manuscript in the same paper in which our works had previously been submitted and returned, simply scoring out the addresses of the other publishers, and adding the new.

I then went back to steadfastly copying out *Jane Eyre*. In due course, I received a reply from Smith, Elder & Co. I opened the envelope in dreary anticipation of finding two hard, hopeless lines, thanking me for my submission, and intimating that said publishers were not disposed to publish my manuscript. Instead, to my surprise, I took out a letter of two pages.

The letter was from a Mr. William Smith Williams, the literary advisor at Smith, Elder & Co. Mr. Williams declined, indeed, to publish *The Professor* for "business reasons," although he insisted that it had "great literary power." He then went on to discuss its merits and demerits so courteously, so considerately, in a spirit so rational, with a discrimination so enlightened, that this very refusal cheered me better than a vulgarly expressed acceptance would have done. He added that a work in three volumes would meet with careful attention.

I re-read the letter four times, my fingers trembling.

In great excitement, I wrote back to Smith & Elder to explain that I had a brand-new "work in three volumes" very nearly ready for submission, in which I had endeavoured to impart a more vivid interest than belonged to the previous one.

I wrote like the wind. At the end of August, I sent off the completed manuscript of *Jane Eyre* to Cornhill—and sat back to wait for their reply. I did not have long to wait; although at the time, those two weeks seemed the longest of my life.

Every day, I watched like a hawk from the dining-room window for the arrival of the postman. Since Tabby was now too deaf and lame to carry out more than the most simple kitchen tasks, it remained one of her few and most precious delights in life to accept and sort our mail; I would not take that pleasure from her; so I stood, with bated breath, listening as her halting steps sounded from the front door to papa's study, hoping against hope that she would turn back into the dining-room, and bring me a missive of my own.

When at last it came—when Tabby placed the envelope into my hands, from Smith & Elder to "Mr. Currer Bell, under cover to Miss Brontë, Haworth"—my heart nearly stopped.

"What be the matter, Miss?" cried Tabby in alarm. "Who's 'at letter from? Why, ye be as white as a ghost!"

"It is nothing," I said quickly (but loudly, so that she might hear.) Tabby's eyesight had grown so poor, that it was all she could do to make out the name of a letter's recipient, much less attempt to decipher the identity of its sender. "It is just an answer to an inquiry I made. I will read it upstairs." I then darted up to my room, where I ripped open the envelope, and with throbbing pulse, I rapidly took in the words written therein:

> *My Dear Sir: We are in receipt of your excellent manuscript, Jane Eyre, and would like to extend an offer for the copy and publication rights, in remuneration for which we are prepared to offer you the sum of £100 . . .*

I let out a shriek of excitement. Oh! It was too good to be true!

With sudden force, my door flew open and Emily rushed in. "What is wrong? What has happened?" With one look—the letter in my hand, the happiness written all over my face—Emily deduced at once what the missive must contain. "Do they want your book?"

"They will pay to publish! One hundred pounds!"

Emily—normally so staid, so placid, so matter-of-fact, when confronted by any situation in life, be it crisis or celebration—let out a scream, and threw her arms around me. An instant later, Anne blew in, eyes wide with fright, an expression which changed to jubilation when she heard the news. "Charlotte! This is too wonderful!"

"One hundred pounds!" exclaimed Emily.

"To earn something of my own—it is everything I hoped for—and look!" I cried, showing them the letter. "They want the first right of refusal for my next two books, for which I am to receive another one hundred pounds each."[56]

We cried out with such glee, that Martha poked her head in with concern, and even Branwell stumbled out of his room in a confused daze, wondering if something in the house had caught fire again. We were forced to grab our bonnets and race out onto the moors, where for several hours we behaved like silly school-girls, running and jumping up and down and hugging each other and emitting such great shrieks of laughter, that any one who saw us must have thought we had gone mad.

"Just think of it!" I exclaimed, throwing my arms wide, and gazing up with delight into the limitless expanse of blue heaven, "after all our hard work, after all the slaving and all the dreaming, we are all to be published at last, at the very same time!"

It was not until some years later, after I had met and become friends with my publisher, that I blushingly learned of the circumstances surrounding the acceptance of my novel. William Smith Williams, the first to read it, told me that he sat up half the night to finish the manuscript, and was enchanted; he then insisted that the head of the firm—the young and intelligent Mr. George Smith—read it for himself. Mr. Smith laughingly admitted that his colleague had evinced such high praises, he did not know how to believe him; but he, too, devoured the entire novel on a single Sunday, beginning after breakfast, cancelling an appointment to go riding with a friend into the country,

---

[56] With further editions and foreign rights, Charlotte actually received payments in the region of five hundred pounds per novel. Even so, the money on offer was low compared to the sums earned by many other popular novelists of the time.

bolting his dinner, and unable to retire for the night until he had finished the book.

I knew none of this, of course, at the time. I had barely processed the notion that I was to *be published,* before the act itself took place. *Jane Eyre* was rushed into print, from acceptance to publication, in a dizzyingly brief six weeks—so quickly, that it came out a full two months before Emily's and Anne's books, even though theirs had been accepted by Thomas Newby long before mine.

First, however, a letter arrived from Smith & Elder suggesting "some minor revisions" to *Jane Eyre.*

"They want me to excise the entire first section about Jane as a child at Gateshead," I told my sisters in dismay, "and revise, trim, or remove all the chapters about Lowood School."

"That is absurd. Those are important parts of the story," maintained Emily, "and of great interest."

"They establish Jane's background and character," agreed Anne. "They evoke one's sympathy."

"The publisher seems to think those scenes might prove too painful for some readers to peruse, and make the book too long." I put down the letter, distraught. "Why did they buy the novel, if they do not like it? I cannot imagine having to go back to retrench or change it now. If I make any alterations, I fear that I shall only injure the narrative. Every word I wrote contributes to the whole; and every word was true."

"Truth, I have to think, has a severe charm of its own," said Anne.

"And yet, had I told *all* the truth of my experience at the Clergy Daughters' School, I might indeed have made it far more exquisitely painful. As it is, I softened many particulars, to make the tale more pleasing."

"I would not change a word," insisted Emily. "Trust your instincts. Your book may suit the public taste far better than the publisher anticipates. Just write and tell them so."

I did just that. Smith & Elder acceded to my wishes. Then, not understanding how quickly my publisher would proceed, I left immediately for Brookroyd to enjoy a brief holiday with Ellen. To my astonishment, the day after my arrival in Birstall, Emily forwarded to me the first batch of proof pages of *Jane Eyre*, which I was required to proofread and return post-haste. Of necessity, I was obliged to conduct this operation in front of Ellen, sitting across from her in the same room. What a struggle it was to keep silent! Bound as I was by my vow to my sisters to keep our authorship a secret, I was obliged to pretend that I was working on some personal writing project of little importance. Ellen was canny enough to discern that something was up; but she honourably did not ask any questions, nor did she look to see to whom the parcel was addressed when we posted it back to London.

My novel debuted on the 16th of October. My first six, beautifully bound copies of *Jane Eyre, An Autobiography, Edited by Currer Bell* arrived on the 19th. If I had thought I felt great pleasure in seeing our book of rhymes in print, it was nothing compared to the elation that spread through me now. At last, my dream had come true: I held in my hands a published work of my very own: a tale which had sprung forth from my own experience and imagination, and was now, by the grace of God, the miracle of language, and the employment of the printing press, available for others to read!

Fourteen

I had kept my expectations low with respect to *Jane Eyre*'s success. I knew that critics were capricious, and popular goodwill was difficult to attain and even harder to maintain. The public was not interested in authors they had not heard of, and could be fickle; yet I did *so very much desire* that it should do well, if only so as not to disappoint the sanguine hopes of my gracious publishers, who had taken so much trouble about the work.

Hidden away at Haworth, I read with great interest the reviews in the newspapers and journals which Mr. Williams forwarded to me. Many found nothing to criticise.

"'A story of surpassing interest,'" I read aloud to my sisters from the *Critic* that October, "'which we can cordially recommend—It is sure to be in demand.'"

"Ha!" cried Emily. "I could have told you that."

"'This is an extraordinary book,'" I read, thrilled, in the *Era* a few weeks later. "'Although a work of fiction, it is no mere novel, for there is nothing but nature and truth about it. We do not know its rival among modern productions. All the serious novel writers of the day lose in comparison with Currer Bell.' Oh! Such lofty praise; surely I do not deserve it."

"But you do," said Anne.

I was dazed by the litany of commendations sent to me over the ensuing months. Not all were favourable; some reviewers proclaimed *Jane Eyre* to be coarse and immoral, a criticism which I have yet to understand, and which cruelly stung; others criticised Mr. Rochester's conduct as "hardly proper," and found certain incidents incredible or improbable. To my relief, however, the overriding opinion was resoundingly positive. One critic even called it "decidedly the best novel of the season." Mr. Smith wrote to inform me that demand was almost unprecedented; within three months of its appearance, all 2,500 copies had sold out, and *Jane Eyre* went into a second printing.

The question of my identity raised more than a few eyebrows. Numerous articles in the press, claiming to express the interest of the entire reading-world of England, clamoured to know: *who was Currer Bell?* Was it a real or assumed name? Was the book written by a man or a woman? Many little incidents in the book were verbally examined this way and that, in an attempt to answer this question of the author's gender—and all in vain. I laughed at their conjectures, and delighted in my anonymity.

Very quickly, I established a regular correspondence with Mr. Smith and Mr. Williams, who, although as yet personally unknown to me (and who regarded me, at the time, as the embodiment of my masculine persona), treated me with a courtesy and kindness, an intellectual acumen, and an expressed belief in my abilities, which greatly added to my personal confidence and happiness. Knowing that I had no access to a good circulating library, my publishers began sending me boxes of all the newest and best books to read, which my sisters and I devoured one after another. In this expansion of my contemporary literary knowledge, and in my ongoing and thrilling exchange of thoughts and ideas with my publishers, I felt as if a window had been opened, introducing light and life to the torpid retirement where I lived, and allowing me a glimpse of an entirely new and unknown world.

A new correspondence also began in an entirely unexpected quarter. The celebrated journalist, novelist, and dramatist George Henry Lewes, after publishing a generous review of *Jane Eyre,* wrote to Currer Bell (letters forwarded to me by Smith & Elder) exhorting me to "beware of melodrame" in my next book. This advice, while clearly well-intentioned, conflicted directly with what I had just experienced in my unsuccessful attempts to sell my less thrilling novel, *The Professor.* Mr. Lewes further advised that I should "follow the counsel that shines out of Miss Austen's mild eyes," a writer he claimed to be "one of the greatest artists, and one of the greatest painters of human character that ever lived." I knew that Jane Austen had died the year after I was born; but although her works had again become popular of late, I was not familiar with them. Intrigued, I obtained a copy of *Pride & Prejudice,* which my sisters and I read at once.

"Did you not just *love* the book?" said Anne, as we went about our floury kitchen duties one baking-day.

"It is charming," I replied. "I find Miss Austen shrewd and observant. At the same time, however, I find her writing subdued and contracted. One could never accuse her of windy wordiness. The novel is—how shall I put it—lacking in sentiment."

"Understatement!" cried Emily, as she forcefully kneaded the bread dough. "Miss Austen describes almost *nothing.* There is no physical affection between her lovers, and not a spark of passion in the whole novel! She is no poet!"

"Can there *be* a great artist without poetry?" I mused. "The book is like a highly cultivated garden: with neat borders and delicate flowers, but no glance of a bright vivid physiognomy— no open country—no fresh air—no blue hill—no bonny beck."

"I should hardly like to live with her ladies and gentlemen in their elegant but confined houses," said Emily.

"Well, *I* thought the characters delightful," countered Anne, "and the story enjoyable and extremely clever."

"I agree with your last point," said I firmly. "Miss Austen *can* be most amusing and ironic, and she employs the most exquisite sense of means to an end that I have ever read."

I did not tell my brother that my book had been published; he was too far gone, in any case, to notice or care. Now that I had met with some success, however, my sisters and I agreed that it was time to share the news with papa.

One afternoon in the first week of December, I brought into papa's study a copy of *Jane Eyre* along with several reviews, including, in all fairness, one notice which was not terribly praiseworthy. Papa was sitting in his chair by the fire, resting his eyes after his early dinner, which he often preferred to eat alone. I stopped beside him.

"Papa: I have been writing a book."

"Have you, my dear?"

"Yes, and I want you to read it."

"I had better not." (His eyes still closed.) "Your handwriting is too difficult for me to make out. I am afraid it will try my eyes too much."

"But it is not in manuscript, papa. It is printed."

"My dear!" Papa now looked up at me in alarm. "You should never have gone to such expense! It will almost surely be a loss, for how can you get a book sold? No one knows you or your name!"

"I did not pay for the publication myself, papa, and I do not think it will be a loss. No more will you, if you will just let me read you a review or two, and tell you more about it." I sat down with him and read some of the reviews aloud. He professed great surprise and interest.

"But who is this Currer Bell? Why have you not put your own name on the book?"

"Papa, you know that it is common practice for authors to adopt a pseudonym—and I think that authoresses are liable to be looked upon with more prejudice than their male counter-parts."

I gave him a copy of *Jane Eyre* and left him to read it. Later that day, when papa came into the dining-room where my sisters and I were having tea, he said, "Girls, do you know that Charlotte has been writing a book—and I think it is a better one than I expected."

My sisters and I exchanged a glance; it was all we could do to keep straight faces.

"Indeed?" said Emily. "A *book*?"

"Yes," said papa with enthusiasm. "Look here: it has already been published, three volumes in a fine binding, with paper of the highest quality, and a very clear type."

"I am pleased that you approve of its physical attributes, papa," I replied.

"Not only that," continued papa, "the story has quite got my attention. I have been reading it all afternoon. I see what all the critics are raving about."

"You will have to show me this marvelous book, Charlotte," said Emily, with a little sidelong glance.

"Perhaps I shall," I replied, smiling at both the comical look on her face, and at papa's praise. "But papa," I added, "I have struggled thus far to keep my work unknown to others, and I prefer to keep it that way. Please promise me that you will keep my authorship a secret."

"Why on earth should I do that? This is quite an accomplishment—a book published, and all of England singing its praises! Aren't you proud?"

"I am, papa—but I have no interest in becoming a public figure. I wish to keep my work a secret in Yorkshire, in particular. I should die if a stranger showed up at our door unannounced, prying into my private life. Far worse: were I to be ever conscious, in my writing, that my book must be read by ordinary acquaintances, it would fetter me intolerably."

"Well then, so be it," agreed papa with a deep sigh, "but I think it a great shame. How I should love to share this news with my colleagues. Mr. Nicholls, I'm certain, would be thrilled if he knew!"

"Mr. Nicholls?" said I, a sudden heat rising to my face. "Mr. Nicholls has no interest in literature, papa. I assure you, he would not care a fig about this. Please *promise me* you will not tell him."

Expressing great reluctance, Papa gave me his promise.

My sisters' publisher, Mr. Thomas Newby, sadly did not operate in the businesslike and gentlemanlike manner of Messrs. Smith and Elder. Emily and Anne suffered from the effects of exhausting delays, procrastination, and broken promises; yet they refused to move their work to Smith & Elder, insisting that they did not wish to impinge on my success.

To further add to my sisters' distress, when, in mid-December, their novels did at last appear—published together under their pseudonyms as a three-volume set, with *Wuthering Heights* comprising the first two volumes and *Agnes Grey* the third—the books were cheaply bound in a grey pasteboard cover. Instead of gilding, the titles and authors' names were simply printed in black ink on a tiny, cheap white paper square, glued to the cloth spine—the only strip of cloth in the entire production. The title-page of volume one misleadingly announced "Wuthering Heights, a Novel by Ellis Bell, in Three Volumes," as if Anne's work did not exist; and the books abounded in errors of the press. Nearly all of the mistakes that Emily and Anne had taken such pains to correct in the proof-sheets, remained unchanged in the final edition.

More troubling, however, was the way the books were received by the critics. The review of *Wuthering Heights* in the *Atlas* in January was so derogatory that I was almost afraid to show it to Emily, but it only drew from her a scornful laugh.

"'There is not in the entire *dramatis personae* a single character which is not utterly hateful or thoroughly contemptible,'" Emily read aloud one snowy afternoon from where she lay on the hearth rug by the fire, Keeper lazily stretched out at her

side. "Oh! I *knew* I should have never offered my book for publication." She threw the journal back at me in disgust.

"The *Britannia* praised *Wuthering Heights*," said I. "They
said your writing shows an 'original energy.'"

"They also said it struck them as 'proceeding from a mind of
limited experience,'" retorted Emily.

"You must concede, that much is true," said Anne, who sat
on the sofa dutifully sewing, with Flossy asleep beside her.
"None of us has much life experience to speak of."

"What is experience to imagination?" cried Emily. "And why
do they keep complaining that there is no purpose or moral to the
story? Must every book have a moral? Is there not value in examining the brutalising power and effect of unhindered passion?"

"There is, and others have said so," I replied. "Have you
forgotten the *Douglas Jerrold's Weekly* review?"

"He called it a strange book, baffling all criticism," answered
Emily tartly.

"He *also* said," (I quoted) "'it is impossible to begin and not
finish it. We strongly recommend all our readers who love nov-
elty to get this story, for we can promise them that they never
have read anything like it before.'"

"I hardly call that praise," scoffed Emily.

"You should be pleased, Emily, that your book has even been
noticed," commented Anne quietly.

I looked at Anne with a silent pang. Anne's book had been all
but ignored in the press. The few critics who did mention *Agnes
Grey* only remarked that it lacked the power of *Wuthering Heights,*
but was "more agreeable" in subject matter and treatment.
"Upon reflection," I said consolingly, "it was not perhaps the
best idea to present your works in tandem, as they are separate
stories, and so very different in nature."

"The critics have no power over me," declared Anne resolutely. "I wrote from my heart. That is all that matters; and in my
mind, I have already moved on to my new book."

"I still say, had *Agnes Grey* been published on its own, it
could be more fully appreciated for the sweet and gentle tale it

is. I fear that it has been overshadowed by Emily's more violent and dramatic story."

"We *both* lie in the shadow of your book, Charlotte," said Emily simply. "*Jane Eyre* is the darling of critics and readers alike. *It* can do no wrong."

"That is not true," I replied—but before I could go on, Emily rose to her knees, slid in front of me, and took my hands in hers, gazing at me with profound affection.

"Pray, do not let the dismal reception of our novels affect your own enjoyment of *your* triumph, Charlotte. *Jane Eyre* is a wonderful book, and we are both very proud of you."

Unlike the critics, papa—upon learning that all three of his daughters had been published—was universally enthusiastic in his delight and praise.

"I suspected *something* all along," said he with a laugh when confronted with the news, "but my suspicions could take no exact form. All I could be certain of, was that you girls were perpetually writing—and not writing letters."

Despite our objections, papa insisted on keeping the six volumes that comprised the works of the "Bells" displayed on a little table in his study. Papa proudly compiled a packet of extracts from every newspaper and periodical that reviewed our novels, carefully marked with the dates of publication. On more than one occasion, I found papa re-reading these reviews when I knocked on the door of his study and peeked in to announce the arrival of Mr. Nicholls. Quickly, papa was obliged to return his treasured clippings to their envelope, and stash them in their hiding place.

Over the past year, although I had had almost daily contact of some kind with Mr. Nicholls, it had always been brief, and we had rarely exchanged more than a few words. However, unlike our dissolute brother, and the simple, dutiful servants in our household, Mr. Nicholls was an intelligent, questioning, and observant man; this made it a challenge to keep our secret from him. On numerous occasions, Mr. Nicholls arrived at the parsonage at the same time as the post, when correspondence and parcels from our publishers in London were delivered. These mysterious bundles aroused curiosity in Mr. Nicholls's eyes, but my sisters and I always disappeared with our booty without a word of explanation.

One such morning in late January, when I heard Tabby call out, "Another parcel for ye, Miss Charlotte!" I came running to the front door, to find Mr. Nicholls returning the dogs from his walk. To my embarrassment, Tabby handed the package to me in Mr. Nicholls's presence. "Quite th' popular lady ye are, Miss! Who is it, keeps sending ye all them books from London?"

"A friend," I replied quickly, colouring as I tried to hide the return direction from Mr. Nicholls.

A week later, when I brought papa and Mr. Nicholls their tea, Mr. Nicholls asked my father why he gave such prominent placement in his study to the books by the Bells. Without missing a beat, papa answered that he merely admired their work. I was grateful to papa for his discretion, as was Emily, who continued to insist, *sine qua non,* on anonymity. I could see, by Mr. Nicholls's reaction, that he did not question the reply; nor did he express any interest in reading the works in question. I felt certain, at the time, that the notion of a woman penning a novel would have been astonishing to Mr. Nicholls—and the notion that the Bells were in fact *three women,* and the daughters of his parson, would have been the furthest thing from his mind.

I had long been an ardent admirer of William Makepeace Thackeray's work, and his newest effort, *Vanity Fair,* was a particular favourite of mine. When, not long after the publication of *Jane Eyre,* that worthy gentleman wrote in praise of my novel, I was so astonished, and so grateful for his generous tributes, that I dedicated the second edition of *Jane Eyre* to him—an act which caused an unexpected furour.

"Oh no!" I cried, racing into the dining-room, where Emily and Anne were both vigorously brushing Flossy's long, silky coat. "I have just heard from Mr. Thackeray, apprising me of the most surprising and distressing circumstances. Apparently it is public knowledge—although it was entirely unknown to me—that Mr. Thackeray, like my Mr. Rochester, had a mad wife whom he had been obliged to put away."

"You are joking," said Emily, putting down the dog's brush.

"I wish I were. A report is circulating in the press that *Jane Eyre* was written by a governess in Mr. Thackeray's family, and *that* is why Currer Bell dedicated 'his' book to him."

"Oh dear," murmured Anne. "What an unfortunate coincidence."

"Well may it be said that fact is often stranger than fiction," said I, as I sank onto the sofa with a sigh. "Mr. Thackeray's letter is so noble, and so uncomplaining; but to think that my inadvertent blunder has made him a subject for common gossip—oh! It is too awful."

The incident provoked a slew of comments in the press, calling further attention to the three mysterious Bells. Curiosity was aroused, not only by their undetermined sex, and by the content of their novels—(the "eccentricities of woman's fantasy" complained one critic)—people were now beginning to wonder if the Bells were not in fact one and the same person! Were *Agnes Grey* and *Wuthering Heights,* they asked, in fact early and less successful efforts by the author of *Jane Eyre*?

At first, Emily, Anne, and I just laughed at such speculations. As time wore on, however, and the prattle of the press continued, I found it less and less amusing. Emily tried to hide her pangs of disappointment at the savage reviews of her work behind a mask of resolute indifference and endurance; yet I knew what she truly felt, and I minimised my own achievement in every way I could. At the same time, whenever I heard my book praised, I felt chastened by a mixture of doubt and fear. I had poured all the best of me into *Jane Eyre*. Could I write another book that would be as well received?

The winter of 1848 was particularly severe, with a cruel east wind that whistled in from the moors. My brother and sisters and I all suffered from the influenza or a very bad cold twice over within the space of a few short weeks. Anne was the only one with whom it stayed long or did much mischief; in her case it was attended with distressing cough and fever, which left her chest weak, and brought on a severe recurrence of the asthma that had troubled her since childhood. For two days and nights, her difficulty of breathing was so painful and pronounced that I feared for her life. Anne bore it as she did all affliction: with heroic endurance and without one complaint, only sighing now and then when nearly worn-out.

Winter passed into spring, and all the while, I struggled to settle on a subject for my next novel. My publishers suggested that I adopt the installment technique employed by both Dickens and Thackeray, but I refused, insisting that I could not think of submitting a work for publication until I had written the last word of the last chapter, and was entirely satisfied with the whole that had preceded it; as such, I would stick steadfastly to the three-volume form. I submitted a plan for a manner in which I might rework *The Professor,* jettisoning the entire first part and revising and expanding the latter, but this was met with a polite and firm refusal. I made three different commencements on a new book, but they all displeased me. For a time, I was greatly stymied.

In my youth, I had been possessed by the *need* to record my vivid imaginings. Then, as with *Jane Eyre,* scribbling had been my joy and my tonic; entire weeks had passed in the blink of an eye while I was writing; I wrote because I could not help it. Now—to my dismay—the very success I had dreamt of, and the business-oriented expectation that came with it, had taken away some of the joy from the enterprise. The eminent writers of the day possessed a knowledge of the world, I felt, such as I could lay no claim to; in my view, this gave their writings an importance and a variety far beyond what I could offer. I felt a great responsibility to produce another excellent work. I did trust that I had the *power* to write; but I found it was not every day, nor even every week, that I could write what was worth reading.

At length, I settled on a topic. Notwithstanding the success of *Jane Eyre*, I was anxious to avoid a repetition of the charges of melodrame and improbability that had been levelled at me by some reviewers. The place in society of the unmarried woman was constantly and increasingly in my mind. At the same time, I was intrigued by the notion of writing a historical novel, and papa had told me many fascinating stories about the volatile conditions during the Luddite riots in the woollen and cotton industries in Yorkshire during the Regency era. With this in mind, I began to research and write *Shirley*.

Emily also began a new book of her own, although she refused to share what she was working on. "I do not know if I wish to publish again," explained Emily, when we met around the dining-table for one of our evening discussions that spring. "Even if I do, I work best in solitude. I wrote the greater part of the first draft of *Wuthering Heights* that way. I have a new book in progress; that is all I am willing to say at present. I shall show it to you if and when I am satisfied with it."

Anne, in spite of her weakening health, had been sitting stooped over her desk night and day for more than a year, hard at work on her second book, *The Tenant of Wildfell Hall*. So committed was Anne to the project, that it was only with difficulty that Emily and I could prevail upon her to take a walk, or induce her to converse.

"It is not good for you to lead such a sedentary life," I warned her, on a particularly glorious day in May. "You need the exercise, Anne. Come out with us!"

"I am almost done copying out my novel," insisted Anne. "Mr. Newby is expecting it. I want to finish."

The Tenant of Wildfell Hall was a daring novel, depicting a courageous woman who leaves her drunkard, dissolute husband in order to earn her own living, and to rescue her son from his bad influence. I applauded Anne's effort and her craft, and felt it was a powerful and well-written book; however, I thought the choice of subject a mistake.

"Your rich drunkard is not Branwell," I told her, "even if his drunkenness is clearly Branwell's. This painstaking rendering of his decay is disturbing to read, and the amorality of many of your central characters" (who were involved in adulterous affairs, like those she had witnessed at Thorp Green), "is, I fear, not something the public will take to readily. Think how they criticised me, for creating a character like Mr. Rochester—even though all of *his* affairs were in his past, and he regretted them."

"Yes, but Charlotte, if you had to do it over again, would you have written it any differently?"

I hesitated. "No, I suppose not."

"Your own publishers said that parts of *Jane Eyre* were too painful to read, and would alienate the public—and they were proved wrong. I believe it will be the same with my book. I feel it is my duty to tell this story. If, in my writing, I can do some good—if I can save one young woman from making the kind of foolish mistake that Helen makes in my story—I shall feel that I have achieved my goal."

Anne loyally gave her completed manuscript to her unscrupulous editor, Mr. Newby, from whom she secured better terms than she had for her first book: she was to receive £25 on publication and a further £25 on the sale of 250 copies, with payments increasing with the rate of sales. However, when Mr. Newby brought out *The Tenant of Wildfell Hall* in June 1848, he advertised it with a certain tricky turn in its wording, implying that it was by the same author (in the singular) of *Jane Eyre* and *Wuthering Heights*. Worse yet, he offered it on these terms to Harper's, the American firm that had published *Jane Eyre* in January (where it had a great run), and with whom my publisher had already made an agreement for Currer Bell's next novel.

"This is intolerable!" I cried, when I received a letter from Smith & Elder, apprising me of these underhanded dealings. "Mr. Smith is all alarm, suspicion, and wrath! He asks: was I aware that all this was going on? Did I submit my next novel to Harper's, without his knowledge? Of course I did not! How could he even dream I would do such a thing? How could Mr. Newby perpetrate such a *lie*?"

"I have written to Mr. Newby repeatedly on this subject," said Anne, greatly vexed, as she sank down on the rocking chair in the dining-room, where I had imparted the news. "I insisted that the works of the Bells are the production of three different authors."

"Yet Mr. Newby has written to Harper's," I exclaimed incredulously, "affirming that to the best of his belief, *Jane Eyre*, *Wuthering Heights*, *Agnes Grey*, and *The Tenant of Wildfell Hall* were all written by the same person!"

"He wants the public and the trade to believe he has got hold of Currer Bell," said Emily in disgust. "He is trying to cheat Smith & Elder by securing the American publisher's bid. You were right, Charlotte. He is a despicable man! I am sorry that I ever gave my book to him."

"Now Smith & Elder are questioning my loyalty and honesty, as well as my very identity," said I, pacing back and forth before the hearth. "We must do something at once, to prove to my publisher that we are three separate persons, and we must confront Mr. Newby with his falsehood."

"How?" said Anne.

"There is only one way. They must see us in the flesh. We must go to London in person—all three of us—without delay."

"To London!" cried Anne, with a thrilled and terrified expression.

"If we go in person," argued Emily, "all our efforts at anonymity are lost. They will learn that we are women."

"What shame is there in revealing the truth?" I replied heatedly. "Our books have already been published and long since reviewed. Let the public know that we are of the nobler sex!"

"No!" cried Emily. "I cannot allow that. I never would have agreed to publish in the first place, had I thought there was any chance of giving up my privacy."

"Then we will only tell our publishers," said I, "and make sure they do not reveal our secret to any one else. Will that do?"

Emily heaved a sigh. "If you *must* go to London in person, then *go*—but I want no part of it. This is all about your book,

Anne, and your name, Charlotte. Two authors will prove your point quite as well as three; but Ellis Bell shall remain a man, and *he* shall stay home."

The outing proved to be an exciting adventure. It was Anne's first visit to London (she had never left Yorkshire in her life), and only my second. I had spent three thrilling days touring London's most famous sights with papa and Emily en route to Belgium six years earlier, but I had taken no time to stop there before my last voyage.

Anne and I immediately packed a small trunk, sent it to Keighley, apprised papa of our plans, and boldly set out that very afternoon after tea. It was the 7th of July. We walked to the train station through a thunderstorm; we got to Leeds, and were whirled up by the night train to London. We arrived—after a sleepless night—at eight o'clock in the morning at the Chapter Coffee-House in Paternoster Row, where I had stayed before. We washed ourselves, ate some breakfast, and set off in queer inward excitement to find 65 Cornhill.

For Anne, who had been in delicate health all year, the long journey and the walk through town proved both exciting and taxing. I thought she looked very pale when we arrived, although she insisted she was fine. Smith & Elder, it turned out, was housed in a large bookseller's shop, in a street almost as bustling as the Strand. We went in and walked up to the counter. It was a Saturday—a full working-day—and there were a great many young men and lads here and there in the small room. I said to the first I could accost: "May I see Mr. Smith?"

He hesitated, looked a little surprised, and asked for our names. I declined to give them, explaining that we had come to see the publisher on a private matter. He bade us to sit down and wait. As we waited, my apprehension grew; what would Mr. George Smith think of us? He had no idea we were coming; he had believed, for the past eleven months of our association, that Currer Bell was a man; and my sister and I did not, I knew, make a very impressive picture, both being so small of stature, and attired as we were in our homemade, provincial dresses and bonnets.

At length a tall, handsome, gentlemanly young man came up to us. "Did you wish to see me, ma'am?" said he dubiously.

Anne and I stood. "Is it Mr. Smith?" I said in surprise, looking up through my spectacles at a dark-eyed, dark-haired youth of twenty-four, with a pale complexion and a trim, athletic figure, who appeared far too young and far too good-looking to be the head of a publishing house.

"It is."

I put his own letter into his hand, directed to Currer Bell. Mr. Smith looked at it, and then at me again. "Where did you get this?" he asked.

I laughed at his perplexity; after a moment, as a silent, astonished recognition crossed his countenance, I said, "I am Miss Brontë. I am also Currer Bell, the author of *Jane Eyre*. This is my sister, Miss Anne Brontë—otherwise known as Acton Bell. We have come from Yorkshire to put to rest any doubts you may have about our identities, and our authorship."

Fifteen

You are the Bells?" exclaimed Mr. Smith, absolutely stunned. "But I thought—I assumed you were three brothers!"

"We are three sisters!" I replied—instantly regretting the avowal, for in those four hastily spoken words, I had inadvertently broken my promise to Emily. "I am pleased that you thought as you did, sir," I went on quickly, "for that is indeed the impression we wished to impart."

Mr. Smith let out a great laugh, a mixture of surprise and apparent delight. "And what of Ellis Bell?"

"*He* could not come with us." I rapidly launched into a brief explanation of the situation with Mr. Newby, anathematising Newby with undue vehemence.

"Your charges are all well-founded," said Mr. Smith. "We call Newby's establishment the 'Nubian Desert.' Manuscripts and correspondence can languish there for an eternity. Will you be so good as to wait a moment? There is some one to whom I must introduce you." He hurried out and promptly returned with a pale, mild, stooping gentleman of fifty: Mr. William Smith Williams. It was a great pleasure finally to meet the other man with whom I had been corresponding with such intimate regularity for nearly a year.

There followed a great shaking of hands, and an hour or more of talk as we sat in Mr. Smith's bright little office (only large enough to hold three chairs and a desk, but ceiled with a great skylight.) The young Mr. Smith was the most loquacious, while Mr. Williams and Anne said almost nothing at all. Mr. Williams had a nervous hesitation in speech, and seemed to have a difficulty in finding appropriate language in which to express himself, which threw him into the background in conversation; but I knew with what intelligence he could write, so I could not undervalue him.

I also liked Mr. Smith immediately. I saw that he was a pleasant, practical, intelligent, and shrewd man of business; and he was gracious and generous as well. Once he recovered from his initial shock at learning the true identities of Currer and Acton Bell, he responded gallantly, by inviting us to stay at his house—an invitation I declined.

"We only intend to stay in town for the night, Mr. Smith. We will return home to-morrow."

"Oh, no; that is impossible, Miss Brontë," rejoined Mr. Smith, from his seat behind his desk. "You have come all this way, you must stay a few days at least. Is this your first time in London? Have you seen its sights?"

"I have been here once before, and saw a great deal. My sister has not."

"You must allow me to show you around. You must make the most of your time! I will take you to-night to the Italian opera; you must see the Exhibition; Mr. Thackeray would, I know, be very pleased to meet you. If Mr. Lewes knew Currer Bell was in town, he would have to be shut up! I will ask them both to dinner at my house, and you will meet them."

I said firmly, "Mr. Smith, with all these invitations, you make my head spin; but I am afraid I must say no to all of them. My sister and I have come here to-day with one idea only: to introduce ourselves quietly to you, and to pay our 'respects' to

Mr. Newby. We have no desire to meet any one else. In fact," I added gravely, "we must insist, sir, that you tell no one else we are here, and let not a single other soul into the secret of our identities. To the rest of the world, we wish to remain as gentlemen—the same, elusive Bell brothers."

Mr. Smith's face fell. "But surely not—that is to say—you will be missing out on such an opportunity! Do you realise what a sensation you will cause, Miss Brontë, if you allow me to introduce you to London society? People will simply fall over themselves to meet the author of *Jane Eyre!*"

"That is precisely the sort of spectacle, sir, that I wish to avoid."

"I understand you completely, Miss Brontë," interjected Mr. Williams, with a kind and sympathetic look.

"Thank you, Mr. Williams."

"You cannot wish to leave so quietly as this," insisted Mr. Smith unhappily. "Surely you can attend one dinner party. I will introduce you as my 'cousins from the country.' I will invite Mr. Thackeray and Harriet Martineau and Charles Dickens. You wish to meet them, do you not?"

At the mention of these names—all heroes of mine—I was infused by a sudden thrill; the desire to see them kindled in me very strongly. "It is a tempting offer. But—could we truly remain incognito?"

"I will do my best—although I admit, I cannot ask men like Thackeray without a *hint* as to whom they are to meet."

I glanced at Anne; she shook her head silently. I knew she was right. Such an evening, I realised, would only make a show of us, to no good effect. "I am sorry, Mr. Smith. I should very much like to meet these literary giants; but it is far better that the world should think of us as the 'coarse Bell Brothers,' than as two tiny, shy, country women from Yorkshire, cowering in a corner, too nervous to say a word—for I assure you, that is what would occur." I rose. "Now we really must go; I fear we have taken up too much of your time."

"Miss Brontë," said Mr. Smith, as he hastened around his

desk to our side, "if you insist on declining all my other offers, at the very least, you must allow me to introduce you to my sisters. I promise they will not reveal your identity to any one. Tell me: where are you staying?"

I did not have the heart to refuse again, and gave him the information he desired. To our astonishment, when Mr. Smith called on us that evening at our inn, he was attired in evening costume, accompanied by two elegant young ladies in full dress, prepared for the opera. Anne and I were not expecting to go out; we had no fine, elegant dresses with us, or in the world; but we quickly attired ourselves in the best of what we possessed, and went with them. I was struck more by the architectural brilliance of the Opera House itself and the brilliant throng there assembled (I had only witnessed such splendour and spectacle once in my life, in Brussels), than by the performance of Rossini's *Barber of Seville* (I have seen stories, since, that I like better); but the entire evening was a genuine thrill, which my sister and I would never forget.

On Tuesday morning, before leaving town—having made our way around the art galleries by day, and taken meals with Mr. Smith and the Smith Williamses in the evening—we went to see Mr. Thomas Newby. That interview began with the same reception of shocked disbelief that we had received at Smith & Elder, but there the similarity ended. Mr. Newby's establishment at 72 Mortimer Street, Cavendish Square was as gloomy and cluttered as Mr. Smith's had been light and neat, and the man himself matched his surroundings: small, dark, aloof, shuffling, and vaguely unkempt as to his person. Moreover, the discovery that his client Acton Bell was a woman, induced in him a clear and new-found attitude of condescension and contempt.

"I do beg your pardon," said Mr. Newby haughtily from behind the dusty counter (he did not invite us into his back office, for which I was unspeakably grateful), "if I have misinterpreted the situation, but I was operating on intelligence as to the identity of this Mr. Bell, which I believed to be valid. I shall withdraw my offer to Harper's, of course, and let us hope for the best with your current book, *Miss Anne.*" The shifty gleam in his beady eyes and the condescending, deceitful cast to his voice verified every concern I had ever held as to his character.

"I have done with Newby," resolved Anne later that morning, as we dropped into our seats on the train bound for home, laden with books which Mr. Smith had given us. "I will never more have him for a publisher."

"Let us hope that he at least keeps his end of the bargain," said I.

Newby did, in fact, emit a full disclosure to Harper's; but it was not long before he began leaking the secret of our true names and gender; and it was years before he paid even a small part of the money owed to my sisters.

As Anne and I sat on the train, we re-read the first notices for *The Tenant of Wildfell Hall,* which had come out on the very day we had arrived in London. The reviews were mixed, praising the writing but complaining about the novel's graphic depiction of human vices, and the writer's "morbid love for the coarse, not to say the brutal."

I felt badly for Anne. Although she did not say much, being of such a naturally taciturn, still, and reserved nature, I could see that she felt the effects of the unfavourable notices most keenly. However, despite (or perhaps because of) the reviews, Anne's novel sold very well, and Newby published a second edition just six weeks after the first.

We were no sooner in the door of the parsonage than Emily made us sit down by the fire in the study and give her and papa a precisely detailed description of everything we had seen and done over the past five days. Although Emily had professed no interest in going to London, the gleam in her eyes as I gaily told our story (with Anne interjecting a thought here and there), revealed the enjoyment she derived from living the experience vicariously. I told her all, refraining only from mentioning that I had inadvertently betrayed the truth of her identity to Mr. Smith and Mr. Williams. The facts came out two weeks later, however, when Emily read a letter to me from Mr. Williams, in which he alluded to my "sisters" in the plural.

"How could you?" exploded Emily, waving the letter in front of my face with the same wrath she had brought down upon my head when I first discovered her poems. "I was explicit about my feelings on this issue!"

"I am very sorry," I replied, shame-faced. "The words 'we are three sisters' escaped me before I was aware. I regretted the admission the moment I made it."

"You shall write back to Mr. Williams immediately, and inform him that henceforth, *Mr. Ellis Bell* shall not endure to be alluded to under any other appellation than his nom de plume."

I did as Emily ordered. I am not certain if she ever forgave me.

Six weeks after my return from London, an incident occurred which dramatically altered my relationship with Mr. Nicholls. It began when Martha told me the sad news that the Ainley family, after being beset by illness all summer, had just lost their newest infant. It had been a blistering, brutal month, with my father sick in bed all the past week with a severe case of bronchitis; Mr. Nicholls had been handling all of papa's duties in his stead. I wanted to pay my respects to the Ainleys. As Emily never made such calls, and Anne was busy with other things, I decided to go on my own.

It was a hot morning in late August. Children of all ages were milling aimlessly outside the Ainleys' cottage as I approached; only the youngest ones were playing, but not with their typical muster, nor did they gather around me as I walked up to the front door. From within the house I could hear the murmur of conversation, and the sound of people crying. With a heavy heart, I knocked. The door was opened by Mr. Ainley, a tall, hardy-looking man with thinning, sandy hair and a prematurely lined face.

"Miss Brontë," said he with a nod, as he wiped his red and brimming eyes on his sleeve, and gestured for me to enter.

Inside the small, dark room, a sparse crowd of sad-faced people were gathered, all dressed in black or whatever dark-coloured clothing they possessed; many of the women were sobbing. Mrs. Ainley sat in her rocking chair, weeping softly. Their eldest son John, wearing the very shirt that Anne and I had sewn for him the year before, stood over the tiny coffin which rested beside the hearth.

"I am so sorry for your loss, Mr. Ainley," said I, after which I made my way to Mrs. Ainley's side. A chair was produced for me; I sat and took Mrs. Ainley's hand. "My heart goes out to you, ma'am. I can only imagine how difficult it must be, to lose a child so young."

"Our Albert wor sich a good little bairn," said Mrs. Ainley brokenly. "He ne'er gave us a single care. Then two nights past he took wi' a fever, an' before I knew it, he wor gone." She burst into fresh tears.

"His loss hit us ever so hard," said Mr. Ainley, "but we must accept it, for 'twas clearly th' Lord's will. We be sorely grieved, howsoever, by what has happened sin', for Mr. Nicholls has refused t' bury him."

"Refused to bury him?" I repeated, stunned. "How can that be?"

"Mr. Nicholls said 'at, seeing how th' baby was unbaptised, 'twould go against God an' be against all his principles t' bury him," said Mr. Ainley.

"Against his principles?" I cried. "To bury an infant?"

"We surely meant t' have th' baby baptised!" said Mrs. Ainley. "But I wor poorly for th' first two months after his birth, an' then Mr. Ainley an' all th' other childer got sick, an' then 'twas too late. We asked him if th' parson could perform th' service, but Mr. Nicholls said he wor confined t' bed—an' that Mr. Brontë would be of no different mind, in ony case."

This much was true, I thought, fuming inwardly. I had argued with papa many times over this same, infuriating clerical obstinacy; it was one of the few, rigid teachings of Puseyism to which papa stubbornly adhered.

"Mr. Nicholls says th' bairn cannot be buried i' th' church-yard," Mrs. Ainley went on. "So now our poor Albert be condemned t' an eternal life o' damnation, 'cause we'll have t' bury him ourselves, without th' blessing o' a man o' God!"

I could hardly contain my anger and dismay at this news. I bade the Ainleys good-bye, conveying my deepest sympathies, and promised to make some inquiries, to see if I could do something on their behalf. I then made immediately for home, intending to unleash my fury on papa. However, as I turned into Church Lane, I saw Mr. Nicholls exiting the schoolhouse. I strode directly up to him, my heart pounding.

"Sir! I have just been to see the Ainleys. They told me of your unconscionable behaviour—that you have refused to bury their child! How can you call yourself a Christian, sir, and treat them so cruelly?"

"Miss Brontë," responded Mr. Nicholls, clearly taken aback. "I am grieved if I have given you offence in this matter, but I was only doing my duty."

"Your duty? How can it be your duty to ignore the needs of a poor, innocent child? It is sad enough that he met such an untimely end—but to be banished from the churchyard? Now his parents think he will suffer eternal damnation!"

"So may he, regardless of any action I take. The Ainleys' infant was not baptised. The parents had fulfilled their secular duty in registering the child's birth with the district registrar, but they failed in their *divine* duty to have the religious rite performed."

"Oh! I suppose I should have expected such a self-serving, hard-headed, righteous response from *you*!" I cried, my blood boiling. "You are not a minister, Mr. Nicholls—you are a machine! An unthinking automaton, that performs its job without an ounce of thought or sympathy for the people for whom it labours!"

"Miss Brontë—" he began, alarmed.

"My heart bleeds for the Ainleys, but you! You feel nothing for their plight. You cast them off as a matter of *principle*!" I shook my head, my mind veering off to another arena in which he had also given offence. "This 'casting off' of those who do not meet your high standards seems to be a habit with you, Mr. Nicholls. How you can live with yourself, sir, is a mystery to me—for you callously cast off women who do not serve your purpose in the same indiscriminate manner!"

Mr. Nicholls now stared at me in stunned consternation. "I beg your pardon? Women?"

"*Women* are mere objects to you, sir, to be discarded when you are finished with them!"

"Why do you say that?"

"Did you not imagine, sir, when I met Miss Bridget Malone all those years ago, that she would tell me everything that happened between the two of you, back in Ireland?" I shot back.

Mr. Nicholls went deadly pale; for a moment he seemed incapable of speech; then he said quietly, "What did Miss Malone say?"

"She told me the whole story: how you led her on and promised to marry her, then coldly dropped her when her father refused her a dowry."

"She said that?"

"She did! What a cad you are, Mr. Nicholls. An insufferable cad! Miss Malone's admission did not surprise me at all, however, for I have been subjected to your views with regard to womankind in general, and single women in particular, on many occasions before—and since. May I be the first to inform you, sir, that not all unmarried women are husband-hunting old maids, however deeply that false impression may be ingrained in your brain, and in the brains of your colleagues! Many of us are quite satisfied not to marry. We would not trade our valued independence for a life of bondage and servitude to a self-centred fool like yourself, no matter how destitute our fortunes! The fact that we are obliged to put up with your narrow-minded smugness as our curate is hard enough! Which brings me back to my original point: the Ainleys. They are church-goers, sir! They have always spoken so highly of you—yet you have let them down in the hour of their greatest need! How hard would it be for you to say a few prayers over their poor child's grave?" With that, I stomped away without a backwards glance, yanked open the parsonage door, and slammed it behind me.

I immediately went up to see my father, intending to express my opinion with regard to the Ainleys' plight; but papa still looked so weak and feeble, and his cough sounded so terrible, that I did not have the heart to distress him further.

That evening, I poured out my heart to my sisters. Emily was aghast at Mr. Nicholls's callous handling of the Ainleys' predicament. Anne, ever devout, was filled with conflicting emotions; in the end, despite all arguments put forth by Emily and myself, she declared that Mr. Nicholls had only acted according to the teachings of the church, and that his decision had been right and proper.

"You should not have criticised Mr. Nicholls so harshly," insisted Anne.

"I spoke my mind, and I am not sorry for it. I can never forgive Mr. Nicholls."

The next morning, as I left the house on my way to the village, I saw a small group of mourners gathered at the far end of the churchyard. On a second look, I recognised them as Mr. and Mrs. Ainley and their eight children, along with a few of their neighbours; they were all standing over a grave. When one of the mourners changed his position slightly, I saw that the officiant reciting the funereal prayers was Mr. Nicholls himself.

My heart gave a little leap. Clearly, my outburst the day before had produced a good result. Mr. Nicholls had listened and taken heed! Despite his other faults, it spoke well of him that he was not too proud to admit that he had made a mistake, and to rectify it. I hastened over to join the little group, just in time to hear Mr. Nicholls pronounce the final words over little Albert Ainley's casket. Upon finishing, Mr. Nicholls looked up; noticing me, he glanced away, his countenance clouding over with an expression so bitter, and so wrathful, that it took me by surprise. Was all that anger directed at me? I wondered in dismay.

I paid my respects to Mr. and Mrs. Ainley, who told me how grateful they had been when Mr. Nicholls stopped to see them early that morning, to say he had changed his mind about their infant's final disposition, if they would keep to a small mourning party. It did my heart good to see that at least a portion of their suffering had been relieved. When I looked up again, determined to brave Mr. Nicholls's foul mood and offer my thanks, he was gone.

Half an hour later, I had just left the cobbler's shop, where I was measured for a new pair of shoes, when I ran into Sylvia Malone, coming out of the post-office.

"Good-afternoon, Miss Malone," I said, greeting her with a smile.

"Miss Brontë!" An odd look crossed Sylvia's countenance; her features soon composed themselves, and she walked up to me with a firm step and a smile. "How are you? It seems a great while since I last saw you."

"It does indeed." I had not observed Sylvia at church in several weeks; but then, she was not a regular attendant. "I hope you and your family are well."

"We are." Sylvia went on to give me a brief account of various events that had occurred in her life since last we met, and I shared such news as I was willing to impart about my own family. I was about to say good-bye, when—the incident with Mr. Nicholls being fresh in my mind—it occurred to me to ask: "What news have you heard from your cousin, Miss Bridget? Has she a new beau?"

"Indeed she has, Miss Brontë. I received a letter from her just a few weeks past. It seems she's engaged to be married."

"Engaged? How nice. I hope he is a good fellow?"

"I couldn't rightly say, having never met him; but he has money, apparently. He's in trade, she said, like my uncle—and Bridget seems happy enough."

"Then I am happy for her."

Sylvia hesitated, then said, "Bridget told me something else in her letter, Miss Brontë. She said I could tell you if I want, if you didn't know already. But—it happened so long ago, perhaps you've forgotten all about it."

"Forgotten about what?"

"Do you recall all that bile my cousin spewed against Mr. Nicholls when she was here, three years ago? Her telling of how he courted her and then abandoned her, and that?"

"I do recall it."

"Well, it seems that Bridget was not entirely truthful."

I stared at her. "What do you mean?"

"Now that Bridget's engaged, and about to be married in the church, she said she feels the need to bare her soul of any misdeeds she may have committed in the past. She said she's ashamed to admit it now, but everything she told you against Mr. Nicholls didn't really happen."

"Didn't happen?"

"No. Mr. Nicholls did nothing wrong at all, it seems. The only wrong was done by Bridget herself. Mr. Nicholls *did* often call at their house, as she said, but it was to see her brother, not her. Mr. Nicholls was so tall and good-looking and kind, that Bridget fell in love with him from afar. One day, she revealed her feelings to him, but he admitted he did not return those feelings. He gave her no hope whatsoever. This so enraged her, that she spitefully told her brother some lies about Mr. Nicholls, insisting that he had taken certain unwanted liberties with her person—nothing unlawful, mind you, for she was already of age—but enough to result in Mr. Nicholls's dismissal for a time from Trinity College while he fought the charges, and apparently causing him untold grief."

I stood frozen to the spot. How to explain what I felt on hearing this admission: astonishment! Horror! Mortification! Chagrin!

"Bridget knows that her behaviour then was wicked. She felt sorry for it afterwards, and she took it all back two years later. When Bridget saw Mr. Nicholls in Keighley, she was taken by surprise. So afraid was she that he'd speak out against her, and make me think less of her, that she told me that story to poison my mind against him. If you ask me, she is just too, too horrid, Miss Brontë, and I suppose I ought to be ashamed to call her cousin; but thank goodness it doesn't seem to have done Mr. Nicholls any permanent harm. I was so sure you would have forgotten all about it by now, that I almost didn't tell you."

"I am glad you did."

"I must go now; I have a new young man myself, and he is expecting me. Good day, Miss Brontë!"

"Good day, Miss Malone."

As I watched Sylvia dash away down the street, every fibre of my being seemed to cry out with silent shame and alarm. This new information put Mr. Nicholls into a very different light, indeed! It put an end to the very basis of the negative opinion I had cherished, for nearly three long years, with regard to his worth.

Anne had insisted, from the start, that there must be more to Bridget Malone's story than first appeared—but it had never occurred to me that she had entirely invented it. The look on Bridget's face as she had told her tale, and her tearful tone of voice and manner, had evoked every sympathy from me. It had all been a performance, I now realised, to my utter dismay: a performance which that young lady had perfected on many previous occasions, apparently with far greater detriment to Mr. Nicholls than the loss of my good opinion.

Oh! How imprudently I had acted! How foolish I had been, to accept the word of some one of whom I knew so little! Bridget Malone had been the acquaintance of but a few hours, whereas I had known Mr. Nicholls, at the time of the telling, for many months. Since then, I had seen every evidence of Mr. Nicholls's good nature; I had witnessed all manner of good deeds that he had done; yet I had ignored them all. Based on my injured pride over something he had once said to me, and my distaste for his stricter religious principles, I had thought the worst of him, blindly accepting the words of a spurious, recalcitrant stranger. All that time, Mr. Nicholls had been blameless! Entirely blameless!

I went over, in my mind, all the angry accusations that I had hurled at him the day before. What I had said about the Ainleys, although stridently worded, had at least been based on truth, and Mr. Nicholls had found it in his heart to address it. My diatribe on spinsters was also based on fact; I had heard him utter those views many times; but what I had said with regard to Bridget Malone—oh! How I wished I could take those words back!

I turned up the lane, determined to knock on the sexton's door, ask for Mr. Nicholls, and offer an apology; to my surprise, I saw that gentleman up ahead, just passing through the far gate leading out to the meadows and moors.

"Mr. Nicholls!" I called out. He paused and turned. He did not have the dogs with him; no doubt he had avoided stopping at the parsonage, in case he might encounter me. With thundering heart, I hurried up to where he stood. "May I speak with you a moment, sir?"

He had the same bitter, angry expression on his countenance that I had observed earlier at the graveyard. Still, he looked down at me steadily and said in a low tone, "Of course."

"I wish to apologise, sir, for something I said yesterday."

"You need not apologise, Miss Brontë. It pained me to hear what you said, I admit, but I thank you for your honesty. I lay awake all night pondering it, and—" (after a slight hesitation)— "with regard to the *Ainleys*—I came to see that I might be allowed to make an exception to the rules of the church in this one case, because they had faithfully baptised all eight of their other children, and would have done so again had illness not befallen the family. I told them, however, that I should not be inclined to be so lenient in the future, towards them or any other parishioner."

Oh! What an infuriating man! I thought, my ire rising again, as my fledgling respect for him instantly fled. "I see. I should have realised that your actions did not signify a permanent change of heart, sir. Your beliefs are indeed far too ingrained for such radical alteration."

He scowled. "Perhaps they are. Good day, Miss Brontë." He was about to turn back towards the gate, but paused when I called out:

"Wait. Please wait, sir." I took a deep breath, silently chastising myself for losing my temper, and steeling myself not to be swayed from my task. "I am sorry. I am generally a very reticent person, I assure you; yet for some reason, with you, I seem to speak my mind. Please know, sir, that I am grateful for what you did for the Ainleys, and I regret the *way* I spoke to you on that subject; but that is not the main reason for my chagrin. I wish to apologise for another accusation that I so callously—and incorrectly—vocalised. You see, I have just spoken to Miss Sylvia Malone."

"Have you?"

"Yes. Her cousin Bridget wrote to her recently from Ireland, with certain revelations about—about the truth in your past association with her. I understand now that everything Miss Bridget Malone told us was a lie—that your behaviour was irreproachable, sir, and that all blame in that affair belongs to the young lady herself."

Relief washed over Mr. Nicholls's face. "I am so glad to hear that you know the truth, Miss Brontë. Despite all the troubles I endured at Miss Malone's hand, I was stunned to hear that she would stoop to spinning an entirely new lie about me, for her cousin's and your benefit. To think that all these years, you have thought me guilty of such behaviour! I had no idea, and the notion grieves me more than I can say."

"It grieves me to think that I believed it, sir. I should never have taken her word on the subject. I truly regret my choice of words yesterday. I called you a name—oh! I blush to think of it now."

"Please do not berate yourself, Miss Brontë. You were acting on information you believed to be true, just as you did with regard to the Ainleys. You spoke what was in your heart, and only good can come from speaking the truth."

"I have always thought so, until now," said I, with a rueful smile.

A small pause ensued. He eyed me uncertainly, then glanced over his shoulder at the heath beyond and said, "I was about to take a walk, Miss Brontë. May I inquire—are you free at present? Would you care to join me?"

I had never—not once—taken a walk with Mr. Nicholls; a day ago, I would not have even considered such a thing. To my surprise, I heard myself say: "Where are you headed?"

"Any place my feet take me. It is a beautiful day, and I can think of no better place to enjoy it than out on the moors."

I hesitated. "I could not agree more. I would be pleased to accompany you, sir."

With a hint of a smile, Mr. Nicholls opened the gate and stood aside to let me pass before him.

VOLUME III

Sixteen

The day was warm and fair. Mr. Nicholls and I followed the pebbly path leading away from the gate, as it descended amongst the wild pasture fields, passing by the bleating flocks of grey moorland sheep and their little mossy-faced lambs. The soft breeze was from the west; it came over the hills, sweet with scents of heath and rush; the sky was of stainless blue; the air was filled with the buzzing of insects and the intermittent twittering of birds.

Despite the beauty of the day, it felt awkward, at first, to be walking alongside Mr. Nicholls. After all the years of distance between us, and my own long-cherished animosity towards him, it was difficult to know how to begin a conversation. I was afraid of saying the wrong thing, which might lead us once more into dangerous waters; he seemed equally tentative; and for some time, we walked in uncomfortable silence. As we left the fields and set out across the purple wilderness of heath, however, I drew courage and said, "Sir: I wish to again express the distress I felt, when I learned of your past sufferings at the hands of Miss Malone. Is it true that you were forced to leave Trinity College on her account?"

"It is. I returned home and became a school-teacher for the next two years, while fighting to clear my name."

"You were a school-teacher?" said I in surprise. "So was I."

"I know. Your father said. From all accounts, I liked the occupation far more than you did, Miss Brontë; but it was never my true aim. When, at last, Miss Malone saw the error of her ways and recanted, I was reinstated at the university."

"Thank goodness for that. I hope the institution accepted your complete innocence in the matter, sir, and issued an apology?"

"They did. They promised me as well that the incident would be permanently expunged from my record and never mentioned again. It is the reason, however, that it took me seven years to graduate from Trinity with my Divinity degree, instead of the usual five."

"Oh—I see. I knew, when you came to Haworth, that you were twenty-seven and newly ordained, but I just assumed that you had started university later than most."

"No."

"What brought you to England, Mr. Nicholls, after you graduated?"

"Curacies in the Church of Ireland are few and far between these days. I was obliged to cross the Irish Sea to seek my fortune."

"It must have been difficult to leave your native country, sir, and your family."

"It was; but it turned out well enough, I think." He glanced at me with a little smile as we walked. "Enough on that subject, however. I'd much rather talk about you, Miss Brontë. Your father said that you attended school yourself."

"Yes—three times, in fact."

"He told me about the first school you attended—that you suffered great privations, and about what happened to your sisters Maria and Elizabeth. Ever since I've known about it, I've wanted to say how very sorry I am for your loss."

"Thank you, Mr. Nicholls."

"I lost a sister myself at a very young age."

"Did you? I am sorry. What was her name? How old was she?"

"She was called Susan. She was four years old when she got sick and died. She was such a bright-eyed, bonny lass, full of life and sparkle. I was only seven at the time, and I was very angry. I couldn't understand how the Lord could take my perfect, lovely sister away from me."

"I had just turned nine when my own sisters died," said I, glancing up at him with sympathy and an unexpected feeling of connection, with the discovery that we shared this same sad history. "It would be hard to lose a beloved sibling at any age, I imagine, but I think it is particularly hard on the very young. In some ways, I never got over it."

"I feel the same. It was the loss of Susan, I think, that eventually led me to the clergy: I was struggling to gain a better comprehension of God and our place in the world, and I wanted to be able to provide comfort and solace to those who suffered as I did."

"We are fortunate in Haworth that you chose that calling, sir, and that your path led you to us."

"You wouldn't have said so yesterday, I fear; but I'm glad you think so now." There was a teasing lilt to his voice. It was the first time I had ever heard him speak thus to me—with gentle amusement, leaving his usual sense of gravity and seriousness behind—and it caught me off guard. I found myself smiling, and responded in an equally teasing tone:

"Am I safe in believing, sir, that you hold no rancour towards me on that score?"

"Perfectly safe."

"I am glad of it."

We were treading the wild track of the glen now. We descended the ravine to the stream, which, swelled with past spring rains, poured along plentiful and clear, catching golden gleams from the sun, and sapphire tints from the firmament. Leaving the track, we trod a soft, mossy fine and emerald green turf, minutely sprinkled with tiny white and yellow star-like blossoms. The hills above, meantime, shut us quite in.

"Shall we rest here?" asked Mr. Nicholls, as we reached the first stragglers of the battalion of rocks, guarding a sort of pass, beyond which came the rushing sound of a nearby waterfall.

I nodded and took a seat on one of the large stones. Mr. Nicholls sat on a rock a few feet away and removed his hat. For the first time, I was struck by how handsome he was, sitting there with the breeze stirring his thick, dark hair and kissing his brow, and his countenance glowing pleasantly in the afternoon light.

"Wouldn't it be grand, Miss Brontë, if we could wipe the slate clean and start afresh, as if we had only just met?"

"It would," I agreed. I thought—although I did not speak it aloud—that there was one memory I should like to obliterate from Mr. Nicholls's mind for ever: the false, salacious words he had overheard my brother pronounce, about my attachment to a certain person in Belgium; but I dared not bring that up. Instead, I added: "With that in mind, I would be most appreciative if you would endeavour to forget the stinging remarks I made yesterday."

Mr. Nicholls looked at me. "Does that mean—in your view—I might be worthy of calling myself a Christian, after all?"

"You might indeed, sir."

"And a minister?"

"Yes."

"You do not consider me an automaton?"

My lips twitched. "No. You do hold some very rigid views, sir, which I will never agree with—but it means you have principles and you stick to them. This only makes you a thinking man, not a machine."

"A thinking man—*that* I can live with—but not, I hope, an insufferable cad?"

"No; at least, not to my present knowledge." I laughed.

Mr. Nicholls joined in my laughter: a deep, loud, joyous sound that seemed to spring forth from his very centre. Then, unexpectedly, a slight blush crept across his countenance; his smile faded and his glance wandered away, fixing itself on some distant point along the stream. "Speaking of wiping the slate clean, Miss Brontë: there's something I should very much like to take back—a remark I made not long after we first met, which has greatly troubled me, and which I think gave you pain."

"Oh?" I replied with enforced casualness, fairly certain I knew the very remark to which he referred. "What remark was that, sir?"

"Perhaps you do not recall it. I sincerely hope as much; but I cannot forget. It was three years ago, the day Branwell and Anne came home from Thorp Green, and Mr. Grant and I came to tea. We'd been aggrandising ourselves, and disparaging women in a most disgraceful manner, and you forcefully—and rightly—spoke your mind. I was too young and foolish, then, to understand how insensitively we'd behaved, and as you left the room—I truly thought you were out of earshot—I said something that brings me regret and shame every time I've thought about it since." In a low voice, he said, "I called you an angry old maid."

I stared at him. "An *angry* old maid?"

"So you *had* forgotten it?"

"No! Mr. Nicholls, *no,* I had not forgotten it," said I, unable to conceal my astonishment. "Your words were emblazoned in my mind, and I admit, they caused me many painful hours, but—*angry?* Are you quite certain that is what you called me? An *angry* old maid?"

"Oh! Pray, don't keep repeating it," cried he, blushing to the roots of his dark hair as he turned back to meet my gaze. "I saw the look that crossed your face when I uttered those words; such a black, angry, mortified and anguished expression I have never witnessed, before or since. I shudder to recall it, and to think that I was the cause of it—and to think that *this* blunder might have been part of the reason you have so disliked me all these years."

My thoughts continued in a whirl; I had a brief impulse to

contradict him on this point, if only to ease his conscience; but we were speaking truths now, and every word of it was true.

"I am convinced—*now*," he went on, "that you're entirely comfortable with your unmarried status. Perhaps this wasn't so at the time. In any case, my choice of words was clearly most insulting, and I regret them."

I could contain myself no longer. I burst out laughing.

Mr. Nicholls stared at me, completely baffled. "My confession amuses you?"

I nodded, tears of laughter filling my eyes, so overcome with mirth that, for a good long while, I was incapable of speech. Mr. Nicholls, seeing me thus engaged, became similarly infected, and in great bemusement joined in my laughter without understanding its cause.

"I am sorry, sir," said I, taking off my spectacles and drying my eyes with my handkerchief, when at last I caught my breath and was able to speak. "I am not laughing at *you*, or in any way denigrating your confession. I am laughing at myself, and my own folly."

"Your own folly? What do you mean?"

Could I tell him? My cheeks burned as I imagined pronouncing aloud the thoughts that rang within my head: *It was not the term "old maid" that gave me such offence. It was the word which preceded it. I did not know that you said "angry." I heard "ugly." I thought you called me an ugly old maid.*

"Suffice it to say, Mr. Nicholls, that I heard you incorrectly. Perhaps it was your accent; perhaps it was my own misconception, predisposed as I was to hear only ill from you, and about myself; but I thought you said something else. *What* I thought is not important; I am pleased, however, to hear that it was no worse than what you have just expressed. Believe me when I say that you are entirely forgiven, and please do not feel any further remorse on that account."

"You're truly no longer angry with me?" said he uncertainly. "You're not offended by what I said?"

"I am not; and had I known your *actual phraseology,* I should not have been so angry in the first place. There are other things you said then, and since, which I could quibble with—but you have admitted that you behaved insensitively that day, sir, and that is enough for me. Now let us drop the subject, shall we, and never refer to it again."

Some time later, when Mr. Nicholls and I returned from our wanderings and stood in parting at the door to the parsonage, he said with a smile, "Thank you for accompanying me to-day. I enjoyed it."

"So did I." Over the course of the past two hours, I had learned more about Mr. Nicholls than I had in the entire three years of our acquaintance combined. Despite our differences, I now knew that we had a few things in common. He had made a very satisfactory apology, besides. As I returned his smile and said good-bye, I realised that I might not mind taking other such walks with him in the future.

That thought, however—and any possibility of pursuing it—was cut short with terrible finality by the string of events which engulfed my family in the ensuing weeks and months to come.

Branwell's constitution had been failing quickly all summer. Indeed, his health had worsened steadily over the previous eighteen months, but he had so often been drunk, or ill from the effects of that intoxication, that we did not truly perceive how dangerously feeble he had become. Branwell's fainting fits, and the *delirium tremens* from which he had been suffering, combined with the bouts of influenza which had afflicted our entire household, had served to mask the symptoms of the more prevailing, ravaging disease which had taken hold of his abused physical frame: consumption.

That September, my brother was confined to his bed for three weeks. He only struggled to his feet twice: once, to stagger into the village; and again, when I brought him a message from Francis Grundy, his friend from his days working on the railway at Luddenden Foot. Mr. Grundy was in town unexpectedly, and hoped Branwell would meet him for dinner in a private room he had reserved at the Black Bull.

"It cannot be Grundy," cried Branwell in alarm as, with great effort, he rose trembling from his bed and pulled on a shirt over his emaciated frame. His sunken eyes glared with the light of madness, and his mass of red, unkempt hair, which he had not allowed us to cut for months, floated wildly around his great, gaunt forehead. "Grundy has written me off. He would never come to see me. It must be a call from the Devil! Satan is trying to get his grip on me!"

"Branwell, be still," said I, in a soothing tone. "It is no message from Satan. It is your friend, Mr. Grundy, who only wants to have dinner with you—but you are unwell. I will tell him so, and bid him come to the house. Go back to bed." I gently took his arm, but he roughly shoved me off of him.

"Get out of the way! I must go and face him myself!" exclaimed he, and somehow he summoned the strength to do it.

I did not find out until later that Branwell had stolen a carving knife from the kitchen and hidden it in his sleeve, prepared to stab his "otherworldly visitor" at first sight. Thankfully, when Branwell entered the dining-room where Mr. Grundy awaited, the latter's voice and manner brought Branwell home to himself, and he dropped into a chair in tears.

On the 22nd of September, a most propitious change came over my brother: a change which, I am told, frequently precedes death. His demeanour, his language, his sentiments were all singularly altered and softened, and the calm of better feelings filled his mind.

Branwell had, for most of his life, rejected the comforts of his religion, and refused to repent of his many sins; this had caused papa and all our family untold heartbreak. In this, his darkest hour—to our relief—Branwell at last gave himself up to repentance: for two full days, he talked with compunction of nothing but his misspent life, his wasted youth, and his shame.

"In all my past life, I have done nothing either great or good," mused he with deep regret, as I took my turn at his bedside, "nothing to deserve the affection that my dearest family has shown me." Seizing my hand, he cried, "Charlotte, if only I could make amends, I would; but if love and gratitude could be measured by the beats of a dying heart, you would know that mine beats only for you, our father, and my sisters. You have been my only happiness."

As we all gathered around Branwell's bedside on that Sunday morning, the 24th of September, it was with painful, mournful joy that I heard him praying softly; and to the last prayer which my father offered up, Branwell added "Amen." How unusual that word appeared from my brother's lips—and yet what comfort it gave us all to hear it! I can only hope it brought a similar measure of comfort to my dying brother; for twenty minutes later, he was gone.

Till the last hour comes, we never know how much we can forgive, pity, and regret a near relation. Many, after the circumstances we had endured, might regard our brother's death as a mercy, rather than a chastisement; at times, my sisters and I considered it as such. However, when I saw my brother draw his last breath—the first time I had yet seen a death take place before my eyes—when I saw his features begin to calm, succeeding the last dread agony, I felt a sense of loss that would not be assuaged by any amount of weeping.

I wept for the wreck of talent, the ruin of promise, the untimely, dreary extinction of what might have been a burning and shining light; I wept for the brother that I had once loved with all my heart, and would never see again. All my brother's errors, all his vices, felt nothing to me in that moment; every wrong he had done seemed to vanish; his sufferings only were remembered. I prayed that there was peace and forgiveness for him in heaven.

Papa was acutely distressed for days; he kept crying out, "My son! My son!" His physical strength did not fail him, however, and in time he recovered his mental composure.

It rained on the day of Branwell's funeral. Autumn set in with a vengeance; we all caught colds, and in the ensuing weeks, we sat muffled at the fireside, shrinking before the frigid east wind that blew wild and keen over our moors and hills.

Emily's cold turned into a persistent cough, which worsened day by day, soon accompanied by pain in her chest and side, and a shortness in breathing. A stoic in illness, Emily neither sought nor accepted sympathy; but she wasted away before our eyes, becoming increasingly thin and pale. Weighed down with unspeakable dread, I implored Emily time and time again to allow me to call a physician, but she would have none of it.

"I will have no poisoning doctor," she insisted obstinately, "trying to drug me with quackery and remedies that will only make me sicker. I will rally on my own."

But Emily did not rally.

She declined.

The details of Emily's illness are deep-branded in my memory: the deep, tight cough, which echoed throughout the house, day and night; the rapid, panting breathing after the least exertion; the intermittent fever; the trembling hand; the dwindling appetite; the hollow, wasted aspect of her frame and countenance; all the signs of consumption. As I watched her stubbornly toil every day to complete her ordinary household chores, even when it was clear that she was unfit to do them, I nearly went mad with worry. The tie of sister is no uncommon bond, and my sister was as dear to me as life itself; I could not bear the thought of losing her. For three months, I sought counsel from all sides; I suggested remedies; I strove to take Emily's burden from her, and encourage her to rest; all these efforts my sister met with annoyance and refusal.

There was, in Emily, a simple and primitive streak. Like the gipsies and the hill-folk she so resembled, and the wild creatures she so dearly loved and championed, she tenaciously clung to her natural habitat and instinctive ways. She handled her illness, I thought, as would a sick animal: she would rather retreat into a corner with which she was familiar, to recover or not, than to be prodded and handled by strangers or strange methods. Emily had always been a law unto herself, and a heroine in keeping to her law. She did not wish to die; but she had a super-stitious belief in natural forces, and to those forces she now com-mitted her life.

Never in all of Emily's life had she lingered over any task that lay before her, and she did not linger now. She sank rapidly. She made haste to leave us. Yet, while physically she perished, men-tally she grew stronger than we had yet known her. Day by day, when I saw with what a front she met suffering, I looked on her with an anguish of wonder and love. I have seen nothing like it; but, indeed, I have never seen her parallel in anything.

On the evening of the 18th of December I saw Emily issue from the warm kitchen into the cold, damp hall, on her way to feed the dogs. Suddenly she staggered, nearly colliding with the wall as she struggled to keep hold of her apronful of broken meat and bread. Anne and I cried out in alarm and rushed to help her.

"I am fine," insisted Emily, brushing us aside as she went about her task, giving Flossy and Keeper their supper from her hands. It was the last time she would ever feed them.

Owing to the harsh onset of winter, and the fact that Emily's little bedroom had no fire-place, she had a few weeks previously moved into the room that Branwell had long since vacated after his misadventure with the candle. That night, as I passed by said chamber, I observed Emily crouched before the hearth, this time feeding something very different: she was placing pages from a thin stack into the roaring blaze.

Curious, I entered the room. The fire-place was suffused with a thick layer of feathery ash. I glanced at the few pages left in Emily's grasp, and recognised the handwriting thereon as her own. These last sheets she quickly added to the fire and stirred it, watching as they burst into flame. "What are you burning?" I asked, in sudden alarm.

"Nothing of import."

"If it is something you wrote, it would be important to me. What is it?"

"Just my old Gondal writings, and my book."

"Your book? No! What book?" Desperately, I tried to grab the poker from Emily's grasp, to rescue from the fire what little remained of her offering, but she held on to the tool with surprising tenacity. As I watched helplessly, the last of the curling pages withered into ashy oblivion. "What book?" I repeated quietly, although I already guessed the terrible answer. "Surely—not the one you have been working on these past two years?"

"Yes."

"Oh, Emily!" The cry of woe was wrenched from the depths of my very soul. Tears sprang forth at the thought of losing such a precious document, and I sank down upon her bed, feeling faint. "You never even let us read it, Emily! It is hard enough that you never shared so many of your Gondal stories—and now they are gone—*gone*! But your new book! Why did you burn your new book?"

"I was not satisfied with it. I saw what people thought of my work when I *was* satisfied. I could not bear to have them scrutinise something so unformed and incomplete, after I am dead."

"Emily," said I, with more hope than conviction—eerily echoing the anguished words I had once spoken to my sister Maria—"you are *not* going to die."

Emily sighed and sank down into her chair, the poker dropping to the floor with a clatter. "I do not wish to, believe me; but that is for God to decide."

The next morning, I rose at dawn, bundled up in my cloak and gloves, and strode out across the moors, weeping in despair, all the while searching in every little hollow and sheltered cranny for a lingering spray of heather to take in to Emily. Emily loved the moors. Flowers brighter than the rose bloomed in the blackest of the heath for her; and heather was her favourite flower in all the world. There were times when she had spent entire days lying about and day-dreaming in the heath; surely the sight of that familiar bloom would bring her pleasure, I thought.

At last, with a cry of joy, I found what I was seeking: one

wee, hardy spray, withered yet still recognisable. I ran all the way back to the parsonage, my heart pounding, for that small, resilient piece of heather seemed to me a symbol of hope, of life expectant, of promise renewed. I flew inside the house and up the stairs, where I found Emily in her bedroom, already up and dressed and sitting by the hearth, her long brown hair hanging loosely about her shoulders as she stared into the fire. The acrid odour of burning bone filled the room.

"Charlotte," said she listlessly, as I entered, "my comb is down there. It fell from my hand. I was too weak to stoop and pick it up."

Alarmed, I hastily retrieved the comb from the embers. A large piece of it was melted out. Tears filled my eyes; I thought that damaged comb the saddest, most heart-breaking sight I had ever witnessed; but I only said, "Never mind, Emily. You can have my comb, or if you like, I will buy you another." Then, wiping my eyes, I said, "Look what I have found for you," and I offered her the tiny sprig of heather.

To my grief and distress, Emily only glanced at it with dim, indifferent eyes and said, "What is that?"

I will never be able to erase that terrible day from my mind. Emily weakened steadily. Refusing all help, she faltered downstairs, where she sat on the sofa and struggled to pick up her sewing; but her breathing became so laboured, that Anne and I grew increasingly alarmed. At one o'clock, Emily finally whispered: "If you will send for a doctor, I will see him now." I sent for him; the doctor came; but it was too late. An hour later—with faithful Keeper lying at the side of her dying-bed, and Anne and I, weeping, holding both her hands—Emily was torn, conscious, panting, and reluctant, out of a happy life.

Emily—the light of my existence, now extinguished forever—was taken in her prime. She was only thirty years old.

To lose Emily was akin to losing a part of myself. Her death, particularly coming so hard on the heels of Branwell's, was such a heart-breaking blow to all in our household that we were stunned into inaction for many days. Keeper kept a vigil at her bedroom door, where he howled piteously. Anne, Martha, and Tabby sat in the kitchen and wept. Papa, broken-down with grief, said to me almost hourly, "Charlotte, you must bear up; I shall sink if you fail me."

In fact, I did fail him; I became so ill that for a week I could barely rise from my bed. Some one had to remain strong, I knew, to try to cheer the rest; but I knew not where this strength would come from.

That strength, as it turned out, came from Mr. Nicholls.

Our curate was the first person to call at the house to offer his condolences, less than an hour after Emily's death. Over the previous months, I had seen in Mr. Nicholls's eyes the concern and sympathy with which he had observed the rapid decline of both my brother and my sister. He now stepped in with kindness, consideration, and proficiency when he was most needed: he offered to assist with the arrangements for Emily's funeral service, and to perform the ceremony. Papa, too overcome with grief to consider any other option, accepted gratefully.

On the appointed day, with a hard December frost covering the ground and a keen east wind cutting cruelly through the churchyard, Mr. Nicholls and papa led our small, mournful procession from house to church. My now-diminished family and I sat in our pew with Keeper lying at our feet, while Mr. Nicholls spoke to the sizeable congregation in his strong, clear Irish voice from the pulpit.

After he read the burial prayers, and Emily's coffin was laid to rest in the family vault beneath the church, we all gathered outside, our neighbours paying their respects with gentle honesty and sympathy, despite the frigid temperatures and biting wind. When most of the villagers had gone, I went up to Mr. Nicholls with gratitude in my heart, and offered him my gloved hand.

"Thank you, sir, for all you have done, and for all you said on my sister's behalf. Your words meant a great deal to me, and I know they brought comfort to my grieving family."

Mr. Nicholls took my hand and squeezed it warmly, letting it go with apparent reluctance. "I was honoured to do what little I could; but you are the true strength in your family, Miss Brontë. You are their rock and their foundation. You will be their comfort now, and they are most fortunate to have you."

"Thank you, Mr. Nicholls." As I turned back to join my grieving sister and father, fresh tears stung my eyes. I vowed that somehow, in the days to come, I would rise to earn Mr. Nicholls's faith in me. In that hour of desperate need, however, I felt I could not go on without the comfort of a friend.

I wrote to Ellen. Ellen came after Christmas and stayed for a fortnight. I sent a coach to meet her train at Keighley; no sooner had she stepped across our threshold, than we fell into each other's arms.

"I am so sorry, Charlotte. I loved Emily dearly."

"I know."

"At least we can be thankful that her suffering is over."

I nodded, unable to reply.

Ellen was the picture of serenity and consolation; the constancy of her kind heart was a great blessing to me. A few days after her arrival, we were sitting round the fire in the dining-room with Anne, our mutual companionship all we needed to celebrate the last day of the year. Ellen sat in Emily's old chair, the firelight gleaming on her brown curls as she worked away at some embroidery; Anne and I sat side by side on the sofa, reading the newspapers. I noticed a sudden, small smile steal over Anne's gentle face.

"Why do you smile, Anne?" I asked.

"Only because I see that the *Leeds Intelligencer* has inserted one of my poems," replied Anne happily. As soon as she said it, Anne caught her breath and looked at me, alarmed by what she had given away in speaking thus.

I glanced at the paper Anne held, and saw the item to which she referred. The poem, "The Narrow Way"—an earnest and lovely expression of Anne's devotion and beliefs—had first been printed that August in *Fraser's Magazine* under her pseudonym

Acton Bell, and was now reprinted here. Before I could comment, Ellen looked up from her fancy work and said, "I did not know that you wrote poetry, Anne. Is your poem truly published?"

"It is."

"May I have the honour of reading it?"

Anne turned to me with raised eyebrows and a silent nod, whose meaning I understood. I rose and said, "You may, Nell. But first, I have a gift for you."

"A gift? Why? Christmas is past, and I thought we agreed not to exchange presents."

"This is not a Christmas gift. It is a gift in honour of Emily's memory." I fetched a set of books from the shelf, and handed them to her. It was the three-volume edition of *Wuthering Heights* and *Agnes Grey*.

Ellen studied the volumes in surprise. "Thank you. I have heard of this book. Was it one of Emily's favourites?"

Anne and I exchanged a little smile—the first smile that had curved *my* lips, I think, in many months. "I believe it was," said Anne.

"Emily would have been the last to openly admit it," I added, "but she loved this book dearly, for the first two volumes are the work of her very own pen. In fact, she named the character of Nelly Dean after you, Nell."

"After me?" Ellen stared first at the book, and then at me. "Do you mean to say that *Emily* wrote *Wuthering Heights*?"

"She did," I replied.

"*Emily* was *Ellis Bell*?"

"She was."

Ellen's eyes widened in sudden, stunned comprehension. She quickly glanced at the third volume, then looked from me to Anne and back again. "Then who is Acton Bell?"

"I am," admitted Anne.

"Oh!" exclaimed Ellen, her astonishment and deep esteem all contained in that single word. "Oh, Anne!" Now Ellen slowly turned and stared open-mouthed at me. "Then surely *you*, Charlotte—you must be—"

"Yes!" said I, blushing, as I struggled to withhold another smile. "I am."

Ellen leapt from her chair in excitement. "I knew it! I knew it! I have never forgotten, Charlotte, how you excelled at telling stories when we were at school. I saw you working on that manuscript at my own house! How many times did I ask you, 'have you published a book?' You always rapped my knuckles and said no! When I visited my brother John in London last summer, the whole household was in an uproar to get a copy of *Jane Eyre,* and from the moment the book arrived and the first half page was read aloud, I felt instinctively that it was yours. It was as though *you* were present in every word, your voice and spirit thrilling through and through, with every outlet of feeling. Oh! How I longed to know the truth—I wrote and begged you to tell me the truth—yet still you denied it!"

"I am sorry, Ellen dearest. I did not wish to lie, but Emily forbade me from telling any one. Because we chose pseudonyms with the same surname, I could not admit my identity without revealing hers. Now that she is gone, although Anne and I still wish to preserve our anonymity, we could see no reason to keep the secret from *you* any longer."

"What can I say, except: I am *so* proud of you." Ellen wrapped first me and then Anne in her warm embrace. Shaking her head in wonder, she said: "You are both so clever. I cannot even *imagine* writing a novel. Now you must tell me every single detail of how it all came about."

In the waning months of 1848, our entire attention had been focused on Emily's illness and decline; at the same time, however, I could not ignore my growing fears on Anne's behalf. Every day and every night, Anne's deep, hollow cough echoed through the parsonage. As the new year dawned, papa, determined to obtain the best possible advice, summoned to the house a respected physician from Leeds who specialised in cases of consumption, to examine Anne with the stethoscope.

"It is, I am afraid, a case of tubercular consumption with

congestion of the lungs," Mr. Teale matter-of-factly told papa and me in the privacy of papa's study, after he had completed his exam.

I was too choked with dread to speak. Papa asked softly: "Is there nothing that can be done?"

"I believe there is," said Mr. Teale. "The malady has not yet reached too advanced a stage. A truce and even an arrest of the disease might yet be procured, if your daughter takes my prescriptions and adopts a strict regimen of rest and avoidance of cold."

Hope surged through me; I could breathe again. Could Anne be saved? Oh! If only it were true! "Tell us exactly what to do, doctor. We will put ourselves in your hands."

At Mr. Teale's recommendation, I gave up sharing a bed with Anne, and moved instead into Branwell's old chamber. We took every care to ensure that the temperature of Anne's room remained constantly equal. Anne—knowing what helpless agonies we had all suffered in watching Emily forgo all medical advice and treatment—was very patient in her illness, and dutifully followed the doctor's regimen for as long as she was able. At his direction, she did not stir from the house all winter, even though it meant giving up her beloved Sunday services at church. Papa and I prayed with her at home every Sunday afternoon instead, and he repeated the gist of his sermon for her benefit. However, the blister[57] that Mr. Teale insisted we apply to Anne's side induced only pain but no relief, and the daily dose of cod-liver oil, which Anne said tasted and smelled like train oil, only made her too sick to eat; at length, we were obliged to give these treatments up. Our local medical man strongly advised hydropathy;[58] this was attempted with no better result.

A second opinion was sought and received, with Mr. George

---

[57] A hot compress, usually containing various toxic substances which intentionally blistered the skin, hoping to draw the disease to the surface of the body.

[58] The curing of disease by the internal and external use of water.

Smith's assistance, from the renowned physician to the Queen's household, and the foremost authority in England on consumption: Dr. John Forbes. To my disappointment, although Dr. Forbes replied by post with speed and kindness, it was only to express his faith in Mr. Teale, to reiterate advice that we had already received, and to caution me against entertaining any sanguine hopes of Anne's recovery.

The days of winter passed by as darkly and heavily as a funeral train, each new week reminding us that the same messenger who had snatched Emily from us with such haste was at his evil work again. By the end of March, there was a wasted, hollow look in Anne's pallid face and eyes—a look too dreadful to witness or describe.

"I do wish it would please God to spare me," said Anne one morning, as she stared wistfully out the window at a flock of birds soaring above the church steeple, "not only for your sake, Charlotte, and for papa's, but because I long to do some good in the world before I leave it. I have many schemes in my head for future practice—ideas for stories and books I should like to write. Humble and limited though they may be, I should not like them all to come to nothing, and myself to have lived to so little purpose."

"You have lived to great purpose, Anne," said I, fighting tears as I squeezed her hand with deep affection, "and you *shall* get well. You are too precious to give up without a fight."

In the six months since the day of my walk on the heath with Mr. Nicholls, our household had been so overtaken by death and relentless illness, that he and I had barely exchanged more than a few hurried sentences here and there. The last Sunday in March, however, Mr. Nicholls strode purposefully up to me after services to inquire after Anne.

"Your father has given me regular reports, but I was not sure I believed them. I wanted to hear from *you* how she is faring."

I opened my mouth to reply, and suddenly, unexpectedly, burst into tears. Mr. Nicholls stood silent and grave before me, deep sympathy and concern etched on his countenance. He drew a handkerchief from his pocket and offered it to me. I had a fleeting memory of another man, years ago, in Brussels, who had offered me his handkerchief at a time of grief. How my life had changed since the years I passed in Belgium! I felt almost a completely different person now. Although I had a perfectly good handkerchief of my own in my pocket, I took that which Mr. Nicholls offered, and struggled to regain control of my emotions as I dabbed at my streaming eyes.

"Is she so very ill, then?" asked Mr. Nicholls softly.

I nodded. "When we lost Emily, I thought we had drained the very dregs of our cup of trial, but I greatly fear that there is yet exquisite bitterness to taste. Anne is only twenty-nine years old, sir; yet already, she is weaker and more emaciated than Emily was at the very last."

"I am sorry. Is there any service that I can perform for Miss Anne, or for you and your father? Anything at all?"

"Thank you, Mr. Nicholls, but we are doing all that is humanly possible; that is our only consolation, I suppose."

He said good-bye, then; but to my surprise, he called at the house the very next afternoon.

"I have brought you something, Miss Anne," said Mr. Nicholls, after Martha showed him into the dining-room where Anne was resting, and I was setting the table for dinner.

"Have you, Mr. Nicholls?" replied Anne, as she slowly began to rise from her chair by the fire.

"Please, do not get up." He hastened forward. "One of my parishioners told me that Gobold's Vegetable Balsam is an excellent remedy for the type of ills from which you suffer. I thought it might be worth a try. I have taken the liberty of fetching you some from Keighley, in case it might be of benefit." He placed into her hands a small jar.

"How kind of you. I shall indeed try it. Thank you, sir." Mr. Nicholls bowed, and was about to depart, when Anne added: "Would you care to join us for tea, Mr. Nicholls?"

"Oh, no—I would not think of intruding on your family meal."

"It is no intrusion, and it would please me greatly."

Mr. Nicholls appeared uncomfortable. With a sudden pang, I realised that, in all the years that Mr. Nicholls had resided next door, he had only joined us at table a handful of times, usually when a visiting clergyman was in town, or at his own invitation, in the company of one of the other local curates. On every one of those occasions, I had been less than gracious, still prejudiced by my misconceptions about him. I turned to him now with a smile. "Do join us, Mr. Nicholls. We would be very happy to have you."

He glanced at me in surprise and gratitude, and bowed again. "Thank you. I will."

The meal of roast lamb and turnips progressed quietly at first. I made an attempt at small-talk with papa and Mr. Nicholls, but Anne's lack of appetite and frequent, deep cough was a continual reminder to all at table of her weakened state.

"Papa, Charlotte: I have been thinking," said Anne, as she laid down her fork. "You know my legacy from Miss Outhwaite?"

I nodded, providing a hasty explanation to Mr. Nicholls: "Anne's godmother died just last month. She left Anne £200."

"I would like to use part of it to pay for a holiday," said Anne.

"A holiday?" was papa's surprised rejoinder.

"I would like us all to go away for a few weeks. I have read that a change of air or removal to a better climate hardly ever fails of success in consumptive cases, if taken in time."

"My first impulse was to hasten you away to a warmer climate," I admitted, "but the doctor strictly forbade it. He said you *must not travel.*"

"He said I must not leave the house until winter is over," corrected Anne, "and it is now spring. I feel that there is no time to lose."

"You might go to the coast," suggested Mr. Nicholls. "The sea air is supposed to be particularly beneficial."

"Yes!" cried Anne, her eyes sparkling with a zest I had not seen in months. "Oh! How I should love to go to the sea! If only I could see Scarborough again. I so enjoyed my summers there with the Robinsons. You would love Scarborough, papa; and Charlotte, I see how weary you have become from nursing me. The sea air would do us both good."

"I am seventy-two years old, my dear," said papa. "My travelling days are over. But you two may go, if you wish."

I gave Anne my promise to take her to Scarborough if the doctor would allow it; but after dinner, when I walked Mr. Nicholls to the door, I expressed to him my grave misgivings: "I would do anything for Anne; but do you truly think she has the strength for such a journey?"

"The journey may help her regain her strength," said Mr. Nicholls.

I nodded; but as he dipped his head and studied my expression, he guessed the fears that I could not put into words. Gently, he said, "If the Lord wishes to take her, Miss Brontë, he will do so, whether she's here or in Scarborough. It's clear she wants this very much. She deserves this one last pleasure, don't you think?"

I nodded tearfully.

"Don't worry about leaving your father," added he, astutely naming my second fear, as he crossed the threshold. "I will watch over him while you are gone."

Seventeen

Anne knew of a particular lodging house at No. 2 Cliff, where she had stayed before with the Robinsons, and which she said was one of the best situations in Scarborough. I booked a room there accordingly, insisting on a sea-view, for I wanted Anne to have every possible advantage. Anne, determined that I should have a companion in the dreadful event that something should happen to her, invited Ellen to accompany us, and Ellen readily agreed.

The three of us travelled by train to the Yorkshire coast, breaking our journey with an overnight stay in York, where Anne was able to go out in a Bath chair.[59] Upon seeing the imposing York Minster, which Anne had so admired in the past, she was moved to tears.

"If *finite* powers can build such a cathedral as this," said she with great emotion, "what might we expect from the infinite?" Ellen and I, seeing Anne's enraptured face, were so choked up as to be incapable of speech.

Anne's happiness increased upon our arrival in Scarborough,

---

[59] A wheeled and hooded chair, used especially by invalids.

where she was eager to share its delights with us. She took us along the bridge across the ravine in the middle of the bay, from which vantage point we were afforded a spectacular view of cliffs and sands; she then insisted that Ellen and I walk on ourselves, while she rested. She even drove out on the beach for an hour in a donkey cart, taking the reins herself when she felt the boy driver was not treating the animal well.

On Sunday evening, the 27th of May, we wheeled Anne's chair to the window of our sitting-room, whence we three viewed the most glorious sunset I have ever witnessed. The sky was awash in shades of pink, purple, blue, and gold; the castle on the cliff stood in proud glory, gilded by the declining luminary; the distant ships glittered like burnished gold; and the little boats anchored near the shore heaved pleasantly with the ebb and flow of the tide.

"Oh!" was the single word Anne spoke, her sweet, angelic face illumed nearly as brilliantly as the scene we gazed upon.

The next morning, feeling much weaker, Anne asked if she might see a doctor to learn if there was yet time to return home. A medical man was summoned—a stranger—and he told her with poignant honesty that death was close at hand. I was stunned; I did not think it would be so soon. Anne thanked him, and bade him to leave her to our care. She lay on the sofa, praying softly to herself, while Ellen and I sat silently at her side, unable to stem our flow of tears.

"Do not weep for me," said Anne quietly. "I am not afraid to die." In between laboured breaths, she said: "Do you remember, Charlotte, before we came here, when I told you how much you would love Scarborough, and described its many splendours? I painted for you a mental picture of these very lodgings, and told you of the beautiful view. You had to take my words on faith, then, for you had not yet seen it yourself. But has it turned out to be just as I said?"

"It has," said I brokenly.

"So it shall be with the kingdom of heaven. We must take it

on faith, be thankful for release from a suffering life, and trust in God that a better existence lies before us."

Had I never believed in a future life before—seeing my sister's radiant and tranquil face, and hearing those serene and measured words from her lips—I would have felt assured of it now.

To Ellen, she said, "Be a sister in my stead. Give Charlotte as much of your company as you can."

"I will," replied Ellen tearfully.

I took Anne's hands in mine, shaking with the effort to restrain my grief. "I love you, Anne."

"I love you, too. Take courage, Charlotte. Take courage," were Anne's last whispered words.

A year before, had a prophet warned me of the suffering that lay in the long months ahead—had he foretold how I should stand in June 1849—how stripped and bereaved I should be—I should have thought: this can never be endured. They were all gone: Branwell, Emily, Anne—all gone like dreams within an eight-month period—gone as Maria and Elizabeth had gone more than twenty years before. Why younger and better souls than I had been snatched from life, while God chose to spare me, I could not comprehend; but I believed that the Lord was wise, perfect, and merciful. I vowed to somehow remain strong, and to be worthy of his gifts.

To spare papa the grief of a funeral for yet another child, we buried Anne in Scarborough, in the churchyard of St. Mary's, high above the town. Although I was sad that she would not lie in our own church vault with the rest of the family, it gave me comfort to think that Anne was laid to rest in her favourite place, overlooking the dramatic sea-side view that she so loved.

When I returned to Haworth, papa and the servants received me with such warm affection that I should have felt consoled, but there is little consolation for such a grief. The dogs greeted me in a strange ecstasy. I am certain they regarded me as the harbinger of others; they thought that as I had come back, those who had been so long absent were sure to be not far behind. Mr. Nicholls assumed many additional duties in the parish to assist my grieving and aging father, and he expressed his sympathy to me; but I was too deep in my own misery to do more than acknowledge his attempts at solace.

Oh! How quiet the parsonage was. The rooms, once so full of drama and life, were all empty and silent; all day long, the only sound was the ticking of the clock. When I dared to venture out, the resounding chip, chip of the stone-cutter's recording chisel, as he engraved the endless headstones for Haworth parish, was such a painful reminder of my own fresh grief that it sent me scurrying back inside. I felt like a prisoner in solitary confinement, with only a church and a gloomy graveyard for my prospect. I began to thirst for other society, but at the same time, I doubted my capability of pleasing or deriving pleasure from it. For a full week, I was incapable of performing any useful occupation, and could not lift a pen for any more formidable task than the writing of a few lines to an indulgent friend.

At length, after an inner struggle, I rallied. The struggle came on a dim June morning; my first thought upon awakening had been a dour repetition of the same grim words that had plagued me all week: "Your youth is past. You shall never marry. The two human beings who understood you, and whom you understood, are gone. Solitude, Remembrance, and Longing are to be almost your sole companions all day through. At night you shall go to bed with them; they will long keep you sleepless; to-morrow, you shall wake to them again, and every day thereafter, for the rest of your life."

I wallowed for a few tearful moments in this state of self-pity, when a new voice spoke up with sudden force—a sweeter, purer voice—the voice of an angel, who sounded (I thought) like Anne: "Lonely sufferer, these are dark days indeed; but there are thousands who suffer more than you. Yes, you are lonely, but you are not alone; yes, you have lost most of those you loved, but you still have one near relative left, who is very dear to you. Yes, you reside in an isolated moorland parish, but you are no desperate old maid, without hope or motive; nor are you like the raven, weary of surveying the deluge and without an ark to return to. No! You *have* hope! You have motive! *Labour* must be the cure, not sympathy! Labour is the only radical cure for rooted sorrow!"

I sat up in bed, my heart pounding as I threw off the covers and dried my eyes. My new-found course was clear. To ease my grief and loneliness, I must go back to work.

My novel *Shirley* had been almost two-thirds completed when my brother died and my sisters became ill. I had barely looked at it since. It was hard going now, trying to write in unaccustomed isolation; it seemed useless to attempt to create what there no longer lived an Ellis and Acton Bell to read. I dearly missed their congenial, bantering support; and at first the whole book, with every hope founded on it, seemed to fade to vanity and vexation of spirit.

At length, however, the occupation of writing became a boon to me; it took me out of dark and desolate reality to an unreal but happier region. I could pour out my own feelings onto the page, with words wrung straight from the pain at the aching centre of my heart; but I could be kinder to my own characters than God had been to me. I could strike my fictional Caroline with a fever, take her into the Valley of the Shadow to the very brink of death, and then—like the powerful Genius Tallii[60] of my childhood—I could restore her to health, find her a longed-for, long-lost relative, and give her in marriage to the man she loved.

You can write nothing of value unless you give yourself wholly to the theme, and when you so give yourself, you lose

---

[60] The four Brontë children adopted pseudonyms they used among themselves in connection with their play and their early fantasy writing. Inspired by the *Arabian Nights* and James Ridley's *Tales of the Genii*, they imagined themselves as powerful "geniuses" (another word for genii.) Charlotte's name was "Genius Tallii."

appetite and sleep—it cannot be helped; and so it was with *Shirley*. I put great effort into the novel, completing it at the end of August 1849; again, the book was rushed into print, appearing in late October. It was for the most part well received by the press and public, though not with such acclaim as *Jane Eyre*. It seemed that those who had spoken disparagingly of *Jane Eyre* liked *Shirley* a little better than its predecessor; while those who were most charmed with *Jane Eyre,* were—ironically—(despite certain critics' stern admonitions to avoid melodrama in future) disappointed at not again finding the same level of excitement and stimulus. What I did not foresee was the way in which my new book would change my life:

Shirley took away, once and forever, my precious cover of anonymity.

In writing *Jane Eyre,* although I based the Lowood School and its populace on true events, those events had occurred so long ago, that a connection was not made to the author's life. My new book changed all that.

Shirley was set in the past, against a backdrop of social and economic unrest, during the Luddite riots in the West Riding of Yorkshire in 1811–12. However, I had modelled many of the characters on people who were nearly all still living in the close-knit communities of Birstall, Gomersal, and our own neighbouring parishes. Perhaps it was naive of me, but I entertained no fear of discovery. I was so little known, I thought it inconceivable that I should be identified with the work; that any one should suspect the quiet, unmarried daughter of Haworth's parson of writing a novel, was the furthest thing from my mind. How wrong I turned out to be!

The unveiling of my secret began quietly. My correspondence from Smith & Elder occasionally arrived unsealed; it had been opened and examined, I suspected, at the Keighley post-office. Joe Taylor, to whom I had applied for advice in the writing of *Shirley,* had told so many people in Gomersal about my authorship, that when I visited Ellen there, I was met with a new deference and augmented kindness from people from all over the district.

The critic Mr. George Lewes, upon hearing from a former schoolfellow of mine who recognised the school in *Jane Eyre* as the Clergy Daughters' School, and Currer Bell as Charlotte Brontë, announced that the author of *Shirley* was a spinster and the daughter of a clergyman, who lived in Yorkshire! The news spread to the London newspapers. Mr. Smith assured me that it was best to fight fire with fire, and so in December 1849 I went to London to stay with him and his mother, where I was formally introduced at a dinner party to the literary Rhadamanthi:[61] the five most respected and dreaded critics in the world of letters. Although I trembled at first to meet these great men, I discovered them to be prodigiously civil when met face to face; and in perceiving their flaws, and finding them to be mortal after all, I lost my awe of them.

Mr. Nicholls was one of the first people in Haworth to learn of my authorship. It was a bright, brisk January day, just after the commencement of the new decade. A winter cold had kept me inside ever since my return from London. Now recovered, and bundled up in cloak, hat, and muff, I was taking advantage of a respite in the weather to walk a well-trodden path in the snowy churchyard, with no one else about. After some minutes, I heard the crunching of footsteps on the snow behind me. Mr. Nicholls approached and stopped before me, his hands jammed in his coat pockets, his cheeks bright red from the cold, and a peculiar, half-smiling, half-flustered look on his face.

"Miss Brontë."

"Mr. Nicholls."

He glanced at me, then away, then back at me again, in a look that was part awe, part shyness, part stunned disbelief. "I was hoping to see you. I wanted to congratulate you. I've learned

---

[61] In Greek myths, Rhadamanthus was a wise king, the son of Zeus and Europa, who ruled Crete before Minos, and gave the island an excellent code of laws.

from your father the most astonishing news—that you've had two books published."

"Papa told you? I shall have to scold him, Mr. Nicholls; that was very wrong of him. It was meant to be a secret."

"Why keep such an accomplishment a secret, Miss Brontë? Two books! You should be very proud. The moment he told me, I went out and got hold of a copy of *Jane Eyre*."

I felt a strange fluttering in the pit of my stomach. "You have read it?"

"I read it in two sittings. I could not put it down."

I felt a heat rise to my face and I looked away. I was pleased by his response, yet at the same time aghast. It was one thing to lay bare one's soul under cover of anonymity; it was quite another when that safety shield was removed, exposing oneself, naked and open, to the world. *Jane Eyre* revealed some of my most personal thoughts and feelings with regard to love, morality, and a woman's place in society; it revealed a side to my nature which (as an unmarried woman, and one whom Mr. Nicholls had admittedly called an old maid) I felt could be construed as the passionate ravings of a lovelorn spinster. Did Mr. Nicholls view me as such? I could not tell.

"I would never have guessed that you would be interested in reading such a novel, sir," was my quiet reply.

"I was educated with the classics, I admit, and I've never read this sort of book before; nor have I ever read a book written by some one I know. It was a new and thrilling experience to read your story, Miss Brontë. It was—it *is* a very good book."

"Thank you."

He shook his head, awe-struck. "I understand your sisters are published, as well."

"They are."

"The whole Brontë family, a pack of authors! I wish I'd known it while they were alive. To think that all this was going on, right under my nose, and I never suspected it. At least this solves the great mystery, as to the purpose of all that writing paper you devoured."

His eyes twinkled so gaily, that I could not help but smile; then he laughed out, and I found myself laughing along with him. "I still feel very badly about that affair," said I, in between bursts of merriment. "It was so kind of you to go all the way to Bradford to procure paper for us in our hour of need; yet I was so pig-headed, I could not appreciate it."

"No harm done. That was long ago. I look forward to reading your other book, by the way, but I can't seem to find it anywhere. Would you consider loaning me a copy?"

This request filled me with new-found anxiety, and brought another blush to my cheeks. I had written many scenes in *Shirley* that came from personal experience, and I had included a trio of self-important, buffoonish curates, based on the clergymen in my neighbourhood—two of whom were Mr. Nicholls's particular friends. I had also briefly introduced a character who was Mr. Nicholls's mirror image at the end. As my feelings towards Mr. Nicholls had softened considerably of late, I had portrayed him in a far better light than his colleagues; still, I was concerned about his reaction.

"I would be happy to loan you the book, sir, but I should warn you: when I wrote *Shirley,* I could not conceive that anyone in my neighbourhood would ever read it. It seems that I was foolish in that regard. You may find certain characters and events in the book a bit—familiar. I hope I did not offend."

"Duly noted. Now when can I have it?"

I gave him the book. The next day, his landlady Mrs. Brown told me she seriously thought Mr. Nicholls had gone wrong in the head, for she had heard him alone in his room, giving vent to great roars of laughter, clapping his hands, and stamping his feet on the floor. The evening after *that,* when Mr. Nicholls came to see papa, I heard him reading aloud all the scenes about the curates; he read the scene about the wayward dog and the frightened curate twice, laughing his head off.

Afterwards, he knocked at the door to the dining-room, where I sat reading. I bade him come in; he entered and said hello.

"Would you care to sit, sir?"

"Regrettably, I cannot stay. I wanted to return your novel, and thank you for the loan." He laid the book on the dining table. "It is a delightful book, Miss Brontë."

I thanked him. As he made no move to leave, yet seemed to wish to say more, I prompted eagerly, "Please feel free to share any thoughts you may have about the novel, sir. Not all the critics have appreciated it. I no longer have any one, save papa and my publishers, with whom to discuss such matters, and I am most interested in your opinion."

He fell silent for a moment, then said, "Well: I am no expert in these things, but I don't know what the critics could find to complain about. I thought it well done. I liked your descriptions of the Yorkshire country-side. I recognised Keeper in your 'Tartar.' You captured Mr. Grant and Mr. Bradley to perfection. I've never laughed so hard in all my life! I intend to order my own copy."

"I could hardly ask for a better recommendation."

After some further hesitation, he added, "Would it be presumptuous of me to inquire, Miss Brontë—by any chance—am I meant to be your Mr. Macarthey?"

My cheeks grew warm. "I admit I did have you in mind, sir, when I wrote that little piece about him at the end." At his laugh, I added, "Believe me, I should never have written it, had I thought you would read it."

"Well I am honoured," said he triumphantly, "to find myself in your book, however small my part might be."

A few days later, I was writing a letter when Martha rushed in from the kitchen, puffing and blowing and much excited.

"Oh ma'am, I've heard sich news!"

"What about?" said I, but I could guess what was coming.

"Please ma'am ye've been an' written two books—th' grandest books 'at ever was seen! My father has heard it at Halifax an' Mr. George Taylor an' Mr. Greenwood an' Mr. Merrall at Bradford—they're going t' have a meeting at th' Mechanics' Institute an' t' settle about ordering 'em!"

I calmed Martha down and sent her off, then fell into a cold sweat. *Jane Eyre* and *Shirley* to be read by John Brown, our sexton—and no doubt every man and woman in Haworth— God help, keep, and deliver me!

The word spread like wild-fire. I no longer walked invisible. Soon the entire village was clamouring to read my books, making great fools of themselves over *Shirley* in particular. They cast lots for the three copies on loan at the Mechanics' Institute, fining borrowers a shilling per diem if they kept the volumes longer than two days. Ellen wrote to tell me that *Shirley* was experiencing a similar interest in her own district, many of whose inhabitants recognised themselves, and were thrilled to find the Yorkshire people and country-side portrayed in print by one of their own. Even the local curates—poor fellows!—showed no resentment, each characteristically finding solace for his own wounds in crowing over his brethren.

It would be mere nonsense and vanity to repeat any more of what I heard at the time, particularly since the positive was balanced by an equal weight of negative from the press. Nevertheless, I was grateful for our neighbours' enthusiasm, as it was a source of reviving pleasure to my aging father, whose pride in my work now knew no bounds.

One morning, an incident happened which curiously touched me. Papa put into my hands a little packet of old, yellowed letters.

"Charlotte," said he gently and gravely, "it occurred to me that you might like to see these. They are your mother's letters."

"My mother's letters?" I replied in great surprise.

"She wrote them to me before we were married. I have always treasured them. You may read them if you like." With that, he left the room.

My mother's letters! I had had no idea that such letters existed. I understood at once what must have inspired papa to share them with me, after all these years: in reading about my character Caroline's longing for her mother in *Shirley*, he no doubt recognized the depth of loss I had sustained when my own mother died at such a young age. My stomach quavered as I opened the first fragile epistle; my heart gave a little leap when I beheld the delicate, unfamiliar handwriting on the pages therein. How strange it was to peruse now, for the first time, the records of a mind whence my own sprang! How sad and sweet it was to find that mind of a truly fine, pure, and elevated order! There was a rectitude, a refinement, a constancy, a modesty, and a sense of gentleness about them, that was indescribable—and a sense of humour, too—she addressed my father as "Dear saucy Pat." Oh! I thought, as tears sprang into my eyes, how dearly I wished that she had lived, and that I could have known her!

When I returned the precious documents to papa, I thanked him for his generosity and sensitivity in sharing them with me.

"She was a dear and wonderful woman, and you are a lot like her, Charlotte," said he, as he squeezed my hand affectionately. "You are my solace and my comfort now; I do not know how I should survive without you."

"You will never have to, papa," I promised.

My life over the next three years was a strange amalgam of solitude and society. I used part of my earnings to do a little interior remodelling in the parsonage, widening the dining-room and bed-chamber above, adding curtains here and there and refurbishing upholstery. Restless and unable to commit to a theme for a new book, I made several visits to London, where I was wined and dined at the home of Mr. Smith and met several prominent writers, including William Makepeace Thackeray. I visited the city's many attractions, and I saw the celebrated actor Macready in *Othello* and *Macbeth*.

At the urging of Mr. Smith ("you are a famous author now, Miss Brontë," said he; "it is *de rigueur* to have one's likeness painted") I reluctantly had my portrait done by the fashionable artist George Richmond—a subtle drawing in coloured chalk which Mr. Smith sent to our house, along with a framed portrait of my childhood hero, the Duke of Wellington, as a gift for me. I thought my picture a flattered likeness, which more resembled my sister Anne than myself. Tabby insisted that it made me look too old; but as she, with equal tenacity, asserted that the Duke of Wellington's picture was "a portrait o' th' Maister" (meaning papa), not much weight could be ascribed to her opinion.

Martha said, "Th' eyes be very like. 'Tis like ye're staring down at me, ma'am, forming an opinion like, an' looking at me through an' through, right t' me very soul."

Papa proudly hung my portrait over the fire-place in the dining-room, pronouncing it a correct likeness. "It captures you entirely," said he with an uncharacteristic grin. "Such a wonderfully good and life-like expression! It succeeds, as well, as a graphic representation of both mind and matter. I fancy I see within it strong indications of the author and the genius."

"I fancy *I see* strong indications of bias in your opinion," said I with a laugh.

When Mr. Nicholls saw the portrait, he stood staring at it, speechless, for a very long while, with twinkling eyes and a smile that he seemed determined to hide. When papa asked his estimation of the work, Mr. Nicholls only said that he thought it very good.

In the summer of 1850, I went to Edinburgh for several days to meet with George Smith and his siblings, a trip which elicited numerous shocked remarks from Ellen about propriety and such. She soon began to entertain notions about a match between us. I laughed at the idea. While I enjoyed a regular correspondence with my handsome, intelligent, and charming young publisher, in truth I felt only friendship for Mr. Smith, and he for me. Mr. Smith would only marry a beauty—I knew this instinctively—and the disparity between our ages and our positions in society, in any case, would make any such pairing quite impossible.

From Edinburgh, I proceeded to Windermere in the Lake District, to stay with my new friends, Sir James and Lady

Kay-Shuttleworth (literary enthusiasts who had sought me out, and had deliberately taken me under their wing), in a house they had taken for the summer. There, most memorably, I met Mrs. Elizabeth Gaskell[62]—a woman six years my senior, and a writer of genuine talent, whose work I admired. She had written to me (through my publisher) with such praise and affection on the publication of *Shirley,* that I had felt obliged to reply to express my gratitude. In person, I found Mrs. Gaskell to be highly intelligent, wise, cheerful, and pleasing, with cordial manners and a kind and good heart. The two of us discovered we had much in common and became quite close, beginning a friendship which increased yearly in importance.

One of my greatest solaces upon returning home was reading. Great boxes of the newest books were sent like clockwork from Cornhill, and I spent long hours every day decadently devouring them. My other avid pursuit was a devotion to correspondence. I regularly exchanged newsy letters with Ellen, Mr. George Smith, Mr. Smith Williams, and my friend and former school-teacher Miss Wooler (with whom I had been corresponding ever since my years as a teacher at Roe Head School)—communications which were the bright spot in my week, and provided a welcome relief from the isolation of Haworth. The infrequent letters that came from Mary Taylor in New Zealand were equally diverting; she seemed happy and fulfilled in her new life in that distant colony, despite occasional loneliness, and the hard work involved in managing her store.

On occasion, when painful memories struck too rife, or my own loneliness seemed too difficult to bear, I would take out my letters from Monsieur Héger from their rosewood box, and read them again. I knew full well that the act was foolish; there was no longer any place in my mind or heart for my old master; I had made peace with that fact long ago. Yet, for some reason I could

---

[62] Eilzabeth Gaskell—who became one of the most admired and widely read novelists of her day—would later write a famous and groundbreaking biography of Charlotte Brontë.

not name, whenever I re-read those fragile documents in the flickering candlelight, Monsieur's thoughts and words brought me comfort.

A warm friendship had developed through correspondence between myself and Mr. James Taylor, my publishers' managing clerk. I had met the man in person on several occasions, and I sensed that Mr. Taylor had become enamoured of me. When Mr. Taylor wrote to inform me that he wished to visit me at Haworth in April 1851, I had a presentiment as to what the nature of his call might be, and I was predisposed to think well of him. As I anticipated, Mr. Taylor did propose to me; however, there was a catch: he intended to leave immediately for India for five years to run a branch of Smith, Elder & Co there, and requested that I promise to marry him upon his return.

An absence of five years—an expanse of three oceans between us—it was equivalent in my mind to an eternal separation! There was, additionally, a barrier even more difficult to pass: upon that visit, no matter how hard I tried, I could find in Mr. Taylor nothing of the gentleman—not one gleam of true good breeding. Moreover, his resemblance to my brother Branwell (he was small in stature and red-headed, with a determined, dreadful nose) was very marked; as he stood near me and fastened his eyes on me, my veins ran ice. Papa seemed to think that a prospective union, deferred for five years, with such a decorous, reliable personage as Mr. Taylor, would be a very proper and advisable affair; but marry him I could not, even if my refusal condemned me to spinsterhood and a life of loneliness.

In London, as a lark, George Smith and I—adopting the names of Mr. and Miss Fraser—visited a phrenologist[63] in the Strand, a Dr. Browne, who provided us with written analyses of our

---

[63] Phrenology was a psychological theory popular in the nineteenth century (and enthusiastically embraced by the Brontës), based on the belief that the shape and configurations of the skull revealed character and mental capacity.

natures and abilities. Mr. Smith was deemed "an admirer of the fair sex, affectionate and friendly, fond of the ideal and romantic, and not prone to procrastinate"—a reading which was like as the very life itself. I was professed to be "in possession of a fine organ of language," one who can "express her sentiments with clearness, precision, and force," and is "endowed with an exalted sense of the beautiful and ideal." My attachments, he maintained, were "strong and enduring," and "If not a poet, her sentiments are poetical or are at least imbued with that enthusiastic glow which is characteristic of poetical feeling." This reading delighted me, for its most flattering points described the woman that I aspired to be.

I believe I stayed in London longer than I ought, simply to avoid returning home, to an emptiness I found difficult to bear; I then spent several delightful days with Mrs. Gaskell and her family at her cheerful, airy house in Manchester. Upon my return to Haworth, Ellen came to visit; but after her departure, the solitude of my life at Haworth seemed overwhelming. I missed my sisters with a physical ache that—although lessened somewhat with time—still haunted my days, and kept me lying awake far into the night.

When I walked on the moors, everything reminded me of them, and the times when they were there with me. There was not a knoll of heather, not a branch of fern, not a young bilberry leaf, not a fluttering lark or linnet, but reminded me of Emily, who loved them so. The distant prospects had been Anne's delight, and when I looked round, she was in the blue tints, the pale mists, the waves and shadows of the horizon. If only, I thought, I could taste one draught of oblivion, and forget much that my mind retained; but I could not forget.

I was harassed, too, by the knowledge that my publishers expected another novel. All my fits and starts at a new creative attempt had so far proved unsatisfying; but I could put off the inevitable no longer.

Since Smith & Elder had made it clear that they did not want *The Professor,* I locked up that martyrised manuscript in a cupboard, and decided to begin a new book—a book which would examine my experiences at the Pensionnat in Brussels in a different light, from the female point of view. I called it *Villette*. My charming Dr. John Graham Bretton and his mother, Mrs. Bretton, I patterned unashamedly after Mr. George Smith and his mother. My memories of Madame and Monsieur Héger I poured into my characterizations of Madame Beck and the professor, Paul Emanuel, who would ultimately win the heart of my heroine, Lucy Snowe.

My progress on the novel was achingly slow, disrupted by bouts of serious illness and loneliness. At times I despaired, hungering for some opinion beyond my own, but there was no one to whom I could read a line, or of whom to ask a counsel. Furthermore, Currer Bell could not apply himself solely to writing; he was also a "country housewife," with sundry little matters connected with the needle and kitchen to attend to, which took up half his day, especially now when, alas! there were but one pair of hands to come to Martha's aid, where once there had been three.

The months ticked by. Keeper died, and we buried him in the garden. Flossy grew old and fat. The silence in the parsonage was deafening, broken only by Mr. Nicholls's regular visits to see papa. When Anne had asked Mr. Nicholls to tea that night so long ago, just two months before her death, she had unknowingly (or *was* there method in it?) planted a new idea in my head. The dining-table being too large and empty for just papa and myself, we had begun to take our meals together in papa's study. On occasion, after Mr. Nicholls's business with papa was concluded, I asked him to stay for tea.

Mr. Nicholls was no longer the boyish youth who had first come to Haworth; the years had changed and mellowed him. I thought him an even-better-looking and more-solidly-built man now, in his mid-thirties, than he had been before: his face and torso had filled out a bit, and the thick but neatly trimmed black whiskers which ringed his face and chin gave him a more mature appearance. Moreover, when he stayed to tea now, Mr.

Nicholls comported himself in a manner I found far more agreeable, mild, and uncontentious than in the past. Only rarely did
he make a bigoted remark or espouse some Puseyite religious
principle which made me wince, and I heard no more utterances
from his lips that were disparaging to womankind. In fact, he
admitted that he had changed his mind about some of his former views where women were concerned.

"I was raised to believe in a particular hierarchy between the
sexes," Mr. Nicholls explained one evening, "but you have
caused me to rethink all that, Miss Brontë—or should I say, Mr.
Bell."

"You do not still think, then," said I with a little grin, "that a
woman's place is in the kitchen?"

"Not if she can afford to hire a cook," replied he, to which
we both laughed.

During these infrequent visits, Mr. Nicholls and papa generally spent the hour discussing the needs of the parishioners,
what could be done to ease the plight of the poor, how best to
solve the issues that arose at the Day and Sunday schools, and
the never-ending topic of Haworth's health and sanitation woes.
The three of us also talked about my brother and sisters, sharing fond or pleasant memories. Mr. Nicholls occasionally asked
with interest about the novel I was working on; I found it was
not a subject he could discuss in any depth, but I sensed that he
was proud of me and my achievements. He seemed equally interested in the manner in which my life had changed, as a result
of my writing.

"Your father says you have met a great many famous people,
Miss Brontë," said Mr. Nicholls one night.

"I would not say a great many, sir, but I have been so fortunate as to form a few new acquaintances."

"Who among them is your favourite?"

Without hesitation, I replied: "Mrs. Gaskell. She is not only
a very good writer, but a good and genuine person. Are you familiar with her work?"

"No."

"She is a regular contributor to Dickens's magazine *Household Words*. Her *Mary Barton* is an excellent novel. If you like, I can loan it to you."

"I would appreciate that," responded Mr. Nicholls, adding, "I understand you also hold Mr. Thackeray in high esteem. What is he like?"

"Well, he is very tall."

Mr. Nicholls laughed. Papa said: "*Every one* is tall in comparison to you, my dear."

"Despite Mr. Thackeray's height," said Mr. Nicholls, "did you enjoy his company?"

"Not really, sir."

"No?"

"No. The first time I met him, I was such a trembling spectacle, viewing him as such a Titan of mind, that I just shook his hand and barely said a word. What little I did say, as I recall, was irretrievably stupid. The second time we met was at a dinner party at his house in Young Street. Mr. Thackeray had invited a brood of society women to meet me, who all seemed to expect some sort of brilliant literary lioness. I fear I greatly disappointed them all. I knew no one; I was shy and awkward; I could not supply the kind of thrilling conversation which they seemed to expect. When we ladies left the gentlemen to their port and returned to the drawing-room, I retreated to a corner and spent the better part of the evening exchanging a few low words with the only person with whom I felt comfortable: the governess."

Mr. Nicholls laughed again. "It sounds a bit dreadful."

"It was. I am afraid I do not possess the ease and confidence required to fit in with London society, sir, and I suspect I never shall."

My answer seemed to please him. It was only months later that I understood why.

Mr. Nicholls left to spend his month-long holiday in Ireland. Whereas I had once given his annual absences no more than a passing thought, I found I missed his smile and genial laugh at tea. In time, I came to consider him a valued member of the household circle, like a favourite cousin or a brother. In time, he did not bother to wait for an invitation to tea; he began inviting himself.

On my birthday in 1852, Mr. Nicholls surprised me with a gift—the first such offering since the writing paper he had so infamously purchased seven years before.

"I noticed that your copy of the *Book of Common Prayer* is rather worn," said he, just before we sat down to dine that April afternoon.

"Indeed it is, Mr. Nicholls. My prayer book is so old, and has been read at so many Sunday services, it is nearly falling from its cover. I think that faith alone holds its pages together."

He produced a brand-new edition in a handsome binding, which he placed into my hands. "I hope this will serve in its stead."

I was both surprised and grateful. "Thank you, Mr. Nicholls. How thoughtful of you."

"Happy birthday, Miss Brontë," said he with a modest smile.

In the ensuing months, while I was still hard at work on *Villette,* I perceived a change in Mr. Nicholls's behaviour towards me. I felt his eyes on me at church, when he sat across from me at tea, when he glanced into the Sunday school class I taught, or encountered me in the lane. He was often in low spirits now when we were together, and spoke of expatriation[64]; and I saw that he was often held back in our conversations by a strange, feverish restraint.

For a long while, I scarce ventured to interpret to myself, much less hint to any other, the meaning behind his altered manner. Emily, Anne, and Ellen had all once insisted that Mr. Nicholls cared something for me, and wanted me to care for him. In my rancour towards him during those early years, I had

---

[64] To withdraw or exile oneself from residence in one's native country.

not perceived any truth in their assertions; now, I told myself I was wrong, or must be imagining it.

That autumn, Mr. Nicholls inquired repeatedly about the progress of my novel. It seemed to frustrate him, as much as it did Mr. Williams and Mr. Smith, that the work was taking longer to complete than anticipated. At last, I finished the third volume of *Villette* and sent the manuscript to my publisher, with instructions that its release be delayed until after Mrs. Gaskell's new novel *Ruth* came out, so that the two books would not be in competition with each other. I then went to Brookroyd to visit Ellen for a much-needed, two-week respite. I had only just returned to Haworth, still much caught up in my concerns as to how that novel would be received, when an event occurred which created sudden havoc in my life, as completely and effectively as the most cataclysmic storm or earthquake:

Mr. Nicholls proposed.

Eighteen

It was Monday evening, the 13th of December, 1852. Mr. Nicholls came to tea. As always, the three of us gathered in papa's study, seated in our customary chairs by the fire, our plates in our laps. Flossy, now very old and as gentle and sweet as ever, lay curled up on the floor beside us.

As we dined, I could not help but notice that Mr. Nicholls suffered from a nervous disquietude of manner more pronounced than any I had yet witnessed. He barely touched his food or sipped his tea, and replied to my questions in monosyllables.

"Your father tells me," he said at last, with a strange, eager apprehension in his tone, "that you finished your new book."

"I did. I sent the manuscript off just before I left to visit Ellen. It is quite a relief to have it off my hands, I can tell you. I have had my fill of writing for a while. I look forward to a long break."

My answer seemed to both please and worry him. "You are happy with the book, I hope?"

"I am content that I have done my best. Unfortunately, my publisher is not *quite* as satisfied. Although Mr. Smith accepted the manuscript without revisions, he made it clear that he would have preferred a different romantic solution."

"I do not disagree with him," interjected papa. "I have problems with the ending of that book myself."

Papa was unhappy, I knew, that his favourite character, Dr. John, dropped out of sight in the third volume, while the story pursued the growing relationship between the heroine and her professor, Monsieur Paul Emanuel. "I could not unite characters who are so totally unsuited to each other, papa." At this pronouncement, I saw Mr. Nicholls's face fall. I added quickly: "Forgive me, Mr. Nicholls. We ought not to discuss the ending of a book you have not yet read."

He only nodded, and then fell silent for the next quarter of an hour, until I said good-night and withdrew from the room.

I adjourned, as was my habit, to the dining-room, where I sat reading in my chair by the fire. I heard the renewed murmur of conversation from behind the closed study door. At half-past eight I heard the door open, as if Mr. Nicholls meant to leave. I expected to hear the usual clash of the front door, since Mr. Nicholls and I had already said our good-nights; instead, to my surprise, he stopped in the passage and tapped at my open door.

"May I?" His deep voice, normally so sure and steady, quavered slightly.

I looked up from my book and beheld a peculiar, agitated look on his countenance, which was deadly pale. Like lightning, it flashed on me what was coming, and my heart began to pound with alarm. "You may. Please sit."

Mr. Nicholls entered, but he did not sit. He stopped a few feet before me with downcast eyes and clasped hands, as if gathering his courage. When at last he raised his gaze to mine, he spoke low and vehemently, yet with difficulty. "Miss Brontë. Ever since I came to Haworth, almost from the first moment of our acquaintance, I've felt the greatest respect and admiration for you—for your remarkable intelligence, your strength and spirit, and your fine and giving heart. Over these many years, that admiration has grown into something deeper and more powerful. You are, and have been for quite some time, the single most important and valued person in my life."

My heart thundered in my chest. To see this normally stoic man so diffused with emotion affected me deeply; but before I could gather my thoughts to speak, he went on, with great humility:

"I've longed for many years to express my feelings to you, but I was fully aware, in those early days, that you were not at all of like mind. Not only that, you were—and still are—so far above me: I'm only a poor curate, and you the parson's daughter; and so I said nothing. The day we took that walk to the beck, some four years past, I thought the tide might turn in my favour; but then all that sadness happened in your dear family. I saw you needed time to heal and mend. And so I waited. Just as I gathered my courage to speak, I discovered, to my great surprise, that you were not only the Miss Brontë I had come to know and love so well—you were, in fact, a famous author. You met with great celebrities in London; you had the very world at your feet. Who was I, I asked myself, to dare approach you now on such a subject? How could I even hope that you might be interested in the likes of me?"

"Mr. Nicholls—" I began, but he raised a hand to stop me.

"Please; I must finish, before I lose my nerve again." He glanced briefly into the fire, then back at me. "For many a moon, I tried to put the thought out of my mind. I tried to tell myself I must be satisfied to be Miss Brontë's friend, and only a friend. I tried in vain. To be your friend, I knew, would never be enough. And so I've waited and I've watched, every day for the past three long years, silently hoping, yearning, to see some small sign from you—some tiny hint that you might in some way come to reciprocate my feelings. I felt a growing friendliness between us, and I thought: perhaps that is enough. I told myself: I must speak; but I saw how engrossed you were in your writing. Fearing to disturb your peace of mind, I resolved to wait until you'd finished your new book."

He was trembling now, his eyes alive with such a desperation of hope and fear and affection, as I had never witnessed in my life. "These last few months I've endured such tortuous suffering and agitation of mind and spirit, as I cannot begin to describe—afraid to admit to my feelings, yet unable to bear the agony of not knowing. I must say it now: I love you, Miss Brontë. I love you with all my heart and all my soul. I can imagine no greater honour on this earth, than if you were to agree to be my wife. Will you consider it? Will you have me? Will you marry me, and share my life with me?"

I was stunned—overwhelmed—speechless with confusion. For the first time, I felt what it costs a man to declare affection where he doubts response. I had begun to suspect that Mr. Nicholls harboured feelings for me, but I'd had no conception of the degree or strength of those feelings. He stood before me now, anxiously awaiting my reply. How was I to answer? How did I feel? I hardly knew.

"Have you spoken to papa?" I said at last.

"I dared not. I thought it best to speak to you first."

I stood. "Mr. Nicholls: I am honoured and humbled by your offer, and from my heart, I thank you for it most respectfully. I can give you no answer, however, until I speak to papa."

He looked at me desperately. "I understand; but surely, you can say how you feel. Do you return my affections? At least tell me that! I crave leave for some hope."

"I think it best that I say no more at present, sir, for I do not yet know what I think or feel. I promise a reply on the morrow." Still, he did not move. I took him by the arm and half led, half put him out of the room and into the hall. "Good-night, sir. Again, I thank you."

Once I saw the front door close firmly behind him, I leaned back against the passage wall, my mind in a whirl, my heart pounding wildly. What had just happened? Had I imagined it— or had Mr. Nicholls truly just proposed marriage to me? I was thirty-six years old; I had given up any thought of marriage, sure in the belief that no one *I* could love would ever love me. I had long vowed that I would rather remain single all my days, than to marry a man who did not adore me, and whom I could not adore in return with all my heart; yet here was a conundrum.

Here was Mr. Nicholls, declaring his affection with as much passion and feeling as any romantic hero I had ever imagined in a story or a novel.

How did I feel about Mr. Nicholls? Did I love him? No; but whereas I had once despised him, I had, over the years, gained a true respect for him; I had grown to like him, and to consider him a trusted and valued friend—almost a member of the family. In his startling declaration, his entire being seemed to proclaim his love for me—a love he had kept hidden. Who could say if, in time, an answering love could blossom in my own heart?

Oh! If only my sisters were alive, I thought. How dearly I would have liked to share this news with them, and to obtain their counsel. I did not even have a close friend with whom to speak; the only women with whom I shared my confidence—Ellen, Mrs. Gaskell, and Miss Wooler—lived many miles away; and this was not a matter which could be deferred for a time-consuming deliberation by post. There was no one but papa; and I required his consent in any case. Surely, I thought, papa would share his wise and impartial views on the subject, and help me understand what I ought to do.

I took several deep breaths to steady myself, knocked at the study door, and entered.

Papa sat beside the fire-place, erect in his chair, reading the newspaper with the aid of a magnifying glass and the light of hearth and candle. Too unnerved to sit, too stunned to consider how best to choose my words, I strode to papa directly and simply said, with shaking voice: "Papa. I have just had a proposal."

"What's that?" said papa, his attention still fixed on his paper.

"Mr. Nicholls has asked me to marry him."

Papa's head shot up; his mouth fell open; he stared at me, aghast. The magnifying glass nearly slipped from his grasp; he caught it with both hands, recapturing the newspaper which threatened to slide from his lap. "What do you mean? Are you trying to provoke me? Or is this some kind of a joke?"

"No, papa. Mr. Nicholls came in to see me after he left you.

He has only just said the words. He declared that he loves me, and he asked me to be his wife."

Papa's voice rose in sudden anger. "That's preposterous! *Mr. Nicholls?* Who does he think he is, to be making such an outrageous declaration—and to you, directly? How dare he? Such a question must be put to the father! I hope you gave him a flat refusal!"

"I made no answer, papa. I said I needed to speak to you first."

"Well, you can tell him for me that he can go straight to the devil!"

"Papa!"

"*Mr. Nicholls?* Asking you *to marry him?* Is he mad? The man is my curate! A lowly curate! Did you know this declaration was coming?"

"I did not, but—I have seen signs. My reason tells me it has been long brewing."

"How long? How long has it been brewing?"

"He said he has loved me for many years, but was afraid to come forward."

Papa stood and strode to his desk, where he slammed down his newspaper and magnifying glass with such fury, it was a wonder the instrument did not shatter. Flossy, who had awakened with a start at papa's first outburst, now scampered from the room in terror. "For many *years?* The ingrate! The bastard! All this time he's been living amongst us, and working by my side—I thought him to be so diligent, so upstanding, so devoted to the community—all the while he's just been plotting and planning behind my back, to steal away my only living daughter!"

I was stunned and affronted to hear papa speaking against Mr. Nicholls in this way. "Papa, that is not true. This was no plot. If Mr. Nicholls has feelings for me, they do not take away from the work he has done for you and for this parish."

"Don't argue with me, girl!" Papa whirled to face me, his eyes flashing behind his spectacles, with a growing anger and agitation that I thought most disproportionate to the occasion.

"The man is a cunning, devious liar. To think, after all the hours and weeks and *years* I've spent in the man's company, he never breathed a word about this to me—not even a hint. For years, he has purposely concealed his aims from the both of us!"

"If he did, papa, I believe it was not out of cunning or disingenuousness—but because he feared this very reaction from you, and feared I might reject him."

"And reject him you must, in no uncertain terms! I wouldn't hear of such a match, not in a thousand years, I tell you! That man has nothing. Nothing! A measly ninety pounds a year, no expectation of a penny more to come, and no house of his own. Where does he expect to keep a wife? In that single room in which he lodges at the sexton's house?"

"I do not know. I did not think of that. I suppose it is true that Mr. Nicholls does not have a great deal of money, papa— but should not the main consideration in my decision be more about my feelings for the man himself, rather than the size of his income?"

"The size of a man's income tells you a great deal about the man, Charlotte. Marrying him would be a degradation! Clearly, he is only after your money."

"My money?" I cried, aghast. "My *money*? Is it so inconceivable to you, papa, that a man could love me for myself?"

"Of course not!"

"You do not want any one thinking of me as a wife!"

"Don't try my patience! You are a brilliant and successful woman, Charlotte—a celebrated author. If you wish to marry, then marry well! Had you said yes to James Taylor, I would have been proud!"

"Why? Because Mr. Taylor was leaving the country, and asked me to wait? That was a safe choice, was it not, papa? It would have kept me here as your housekeeper for another five years!"

"It has nothing to do with that!"

"Doesn't it? What are you afraid of, papa? Do you think if I married, that I would go away and leave you, to live and die alone? I promised I would not—and I will not break that promise. Mr. Nicholls lives here; if I married him, I would not be going anywhere!"

"To even *consider* that you should so lower yourself, as to fall prey to the common lot of any ordinary clergyman's daughter—to marry your father's *curate*—and such a lowly, ungrateful, lying wretch as this one is—it is unthinkable! You would be throwing yourself away!"

My blood boiled with a sense of injustice, but papa had worked himself up into a state not to be trifled with: the veins on his temples started up like whipcord, and his eyes became suddenly bloodshot, the same symptoms which had preceded the dangerous apoplectic seizure he had suffered earlier that year. The doctor had warned me, then, that extreme anxiety could produce a relapse of that condition, which could prove extremely debilitating, or even fatal.

"Papa, please calm yourself," I said hastily, my anger mitigated by sudden concern.

"I shall calm myself when you give me your word that you will refuse him!"

I hesitated, then with a confused nod, I said, "I will write to him on the morrow."

Diary, I had spent many sleepless nights before, but the hours of darkness following Mr. Nicholls's proposal proved to be the longest and most tortuous of all. I was astonished and deeply touched by the outpouring of emotion he had displayed, and his admission of the sufferings he had undergone; it grieved me to think that I would be the cause of his further suffering. Had I been in love with Mr. Nicholls, even my father's violent opposition to the union, and my fears for his health, could not have prevented me from accepting him on the spot. But I did not love Mr. Nicholls—at least, I did not love him *then*—nor had I, up until that time, ever entertained an attachment to him. I liked him very much; I knew his worth; but I also knew that a disparity existed between us, not only in terms of this explosion of feeling, but in key religious attitudes and principles which were central to my heart.

As I tossed and turned, I suddenly realised that, although I had come to know Mr. Nicholls better in recent years, I still did not know all that much *about* him. Although he went home to Ireland every autumn to visit his family, he had never spoken about them, except telling me about the death of his sister. He had never talked about his life before he came to Haworth, and I had never asked. How strange it was, I thought, that one could live next door to a person for nearly eight years, and see him nearly every day, yet still know him so little!

What I did know, convinced me that Mr. Nicholls was a man of action: he devoted himself to the realities of the present, whereas I was often miles away in thought. Was I some one that Mr. Nicholls could truly put up with for a lifetime? I feared not. I could not enter into such a binding contract as marriage without an equally binding and mutual affection; and I doubted I could ever return Mr. Nicholls's affection with the fervour he had expressed to me.

A part of me wished I could have a chance to explore the matter further: that I might be allowed the time to experience a real courtship with Mr. Nicholls, to discover whether or not we could be compatible, despite our many differences. Papa's vehement antipathy to the union, however, made *that* an impossibility. It greatly angered me that papa had so verbally abused him, and applied such unjust epithets against him. I hated to think that, in refusing Mr. Nicholls, I would seem to only be blindly following papa's dictates; yet refuse him I must.

I wrote and tore up at least six drafts of my letter to Mr. Nicholls, before settling on the following brief note, which I had Martha deliver to him the next morning:

December 14th, 1852

My Dear Sir,

Please know that I hold you in the highest esteem, and am sensible of the great honour you bestow upon me by

the declaration which you made last night. However, af-
ter giving the matter a great deal of thought, it is with
sincerest regret that I must decline your proposal. I con-
sider you a valued friend, Mr. Nicholls, and I do hope
that friendship can continue.

> *Believe me to be, yours truly,*
> *C. Brontë*

Within the hour, I received the following note in reply:

December 14th, 1852

My dear Miss Brontë,

I am deeply, deeply grieved. I can imagine no future pros-
pect of happiness in this life without you at my side. I
accept your offer of friendship; but please know that my
abiding affection for you remains, and will ever remain
unchanged.

> *A. B. Nicholls*

This avowal of Mr. Nicholls's distress filled me with pain. I was equally pained by papa's continued, vociferous hostility towards him—which, despite papa's insistence to the contrary, I believed stemmed as much from the bare thought of any one thinking of me as a wife, as it did from his objections to the gentleman in question.

To my surprise, my father was not the only one who thought Mr. Nicholls to be beneath my notice.

"What on earth can Mr. Nicholls have been thinking?" snapped Martha the next morning as she angrily dusted the dining-room. "I dunnut blame ye one whit for refusing him, ma'am. He has some nerve, t' think 'at he could win *yer* affections—ye, a famous author an' such like, an' him nought but a poor curate—why, he's overreached his station, an' 'at's a fact."

"Please do not speak ill of Mr. Nicholls," I said firmly, looking up from the table where I was scribbling a letter to Ellen, elucidating all that had happened. "He is a good man."

"I once thought so, but I dunnut ony more," replied Martha. "Mama says he be so downcast, he entirely rejected his meals yesterday an' again this morning, but refused t' say why. I told her all 'at happened, an' she be quite horrified. She said he be a man o' great presumption."

Oh no, I thought, my cheeks burning; Martha's mother—Mr. Nicholls's landlady—was a very garrulous individual; now that she had been apprised of the news, there would be no way of stopping it from spreading throughout the village.

To my further mortification, that same morning, papa wrote a very harsh note to Mr. Nicholls, cruelly deriding him for concealing his intentions with regards to me, citing all the objections he had to him as my suitor, and berating him for daring to make a declaration. I begged papa to revise said note, or not to send any note at all.

"I *will* send it," insisted papa. "I intend to put that ungrateful, devious, lying bastard in his place."

I could not stop Martha from delivering the pitiless dispatch; I felt, however, that the blow must be parried; so I wrote a softening note to accompany it.

December 15th, 1852

My Dear Sir,

I apologise profusely for the words expressed herein by my father. I find his missive so cruel and unjust, that I could not refrain from sending a line or two of my own. Please believe me when I say that, while you must never expect me to reciprocate the strength of feeling you expressed on

Monday night, at the same time, I wish to disclaim par-
ticipation in any sentiments calculated to give you pain. I
wish you well, and do hope that you will maintain your
courage and spirits.

Yours faithfully and most respectfully,
C. Brontë

I could not discern if my note in any way lessened Mr. Nicholls's distress. For the next few weeks, he kept mainly to his
rooms, deliberately avoiding any contact with me or my father.
He occasionally took Flossy for a walk, but we did not see him
then, as Flossy had, for many years, been going directly to the
sexton's house on his own every morning. Mr. Nicholls took
care of his most important clerical duties, but for a time sent
Mr. Grant to preside for him in church. On Christmas, papa
and I dined in virtual silence; Mr. Nicholls, who had amiably
joined us for the past few years, naturally stayed away.

A few days after Christmas, Mr. Nicholls attempted to call
on my father, but papa refused to see or speak to him. To my
dismay, Mr. Nicholls then delivered a note to papa, offering his
resignation, and insinuating that he intended to apply to the
Society for the Propagation of the Gospel, as a missionary to
one of the colonies in Australia.

Australia! Was Mr. Nicholls indeed going to leave us, and
emigrate to Australia?

"Let him go to Australia, if he can!" declared papa contemptuously, as he tossed Mr. Nicholls's note into the fire. "It is best
for all concerned."

"You are very hard on Mr. Nicholls," said I.

"As a man sows, so shall he reap. I can never trust Mr. Nicholls any more in things of importance. His conduct might have
been excused by the world, in a confirmed rake or unprincipled
army officer, but in a clergyman, it is justly chargeable with base
design and inconsistency!"

"For seven and a half years, papa, you always praised him to the skies. In all that time, he has conscientiously performed his parish duties as your most valued curate. Yet overnight, he has become an object of your greatest derision. I do not understand you—and I feel very badly for him."

"Feel badly all you like. He's leaving the country, and good riddance."

From that day forward, my father treated Mr. Nicholls with a hardness not to be bent, and a contempt not to be propitiated. They never met in person; all communication was done by letter. News of Mr. Nicholls's proposal and my refusal had now circulated throughout the village. Every one seemed to presume that I had scornfully refused him, and immediately took papa's side against him, insisting that Mr. Nicholls had overstepped the bounds of decency and propriety in proposing to me, and stirred up trouble. In refusing his meals, Mr. Nicholls was driving his landlady to distraction, and incurring the wrath of his landlord, who said he would like to shoot him! Papa heartily agreed.

I was mortified and distressed by the whole business, and wondered how on earth it had got so out of control. Whence came this turbulence of emotion? Nobody seemed to pity Mr. Nicholls but me. I thought they did not understand the nature of his feelings—but I now saw what they were: he was one of those who attach themselves to very few, but whose sensations are close and deep—like an underground stream, running strong in a narrow channel.

One morning in late December, just before the new year, I chanced to glance out the parsonage window and see Mr. Nicholls greeting Flossy on his doorstep before their daily walk. He looked very ill and seemed encompassed in a dark gloom. My heart went out to him; I grabbed my shawl, hastened out, and met him in the snow-encrusted lane, as he was heading towards the gate.

"Mr. Nicholls."

He stopped and turned; his eyes met mine; his face hardened. "Miss Brontë."

It was freezing cold; I shivered; I hardly knew what to say. I blurted: "I am so sorry for everything that has happened, and sorry to hear of your resignation, and your intention to leave the country."

He was silent for a moment; his voice caught as he murmured: "Are you?"

"I am. Life is filled with sadness and uncertainty, Mr. Nicholls, but also many blessings. Australia is a world away; the journey there is long and dangerous. I believe, sir, that a good life can lie in store for you here in England, if you will only rally."

An awkward silence fell. He said quietly: "Thank you, Miss Brontë. You are cold; you must go in, lest you become ill. Goodday." He tipped his hat and quickly passed through the gate, Flossy trotting quietly at his side as they headed down the path crossing the snow-encrusted fields. I hurried back into the house, wishing there was something else I might say or do to ease his suffering.

This brief conversation apparently instilled in Mr. Nicholls a flicker of new hope, for the next day he wrote to papa, requesting permission to withdraw his resignation. Papa answered that he should not give back Mr. Nicholls his post unless he gave a written promise "never again to broach the obnoxious subject" either to him or to me. This, Mr. Nicholls was apparently not prepared to do. While I was off in London making corrections on the proofs for *Villette,* to my dismay the two men continued to exchange vitriolic letters. I returned home to discover that, although Mr. Nicholls had decided not to emigrate to Australia, he was still determined to leave, and had given notice that his present engagement as curate of Haworth would be concluded at the end of May.

I realised, with a pang, that I would be very sorry to see him go.

At the same time as this drama was unfolding, the reviews for *Villette* came in. They were generally very favourable, except for a few harsh criticisms from people I had considered my *friends*; they seemed to be reviewing my life as they saw it reflected in the novel, rather than the novel itself. Papa was full of praise in my accomplishment, but I could find no pleasure in it. My father's enthusiasm appeared to me as nothing more than a tactic to divert my thoughts from any consideration of marriage, to that subject which he so highly valued: career.

The months that followed were a period of smouldering mutual resentment between Mr. Nicholls and my father. Mr. Nicholls grew so gloomy and reserved that people in the village began to shun him. At times, I thought he might be almost dying and they would not speak a friendly word to him or of him. I was told that he discharged his duties faithfully, but afterwards sat drearily in his rooms, avoiding every one, seeking no confidant, scarcely speaking even to his own friends when they came to visit. I own, I very much respected him for this. How mortified I should have felt if he had vilified me in the bitter and unreasonable manner in which papa continued to vilify him!

Was there truth and true affection at the bottom of his chagrin, I wondered—or only rancour and corroding disappointment? I could not be certain. It seemed ironic, but in all the years that I had known Mr. Nicholls, I had not really come to *understand* him—to penetrate his mind. Every time I convinced myself that I should defy my father and give Mr. Nicholls another chance, I observed him behaving in such a displeasing manner— flashing dark looks at me, getting into a most pertinacious and needless dispute with the school inspector, and losing his temper when the bishop came to visit—that all my old, unfavourable impressions strongly revived. One evening during the bishop's visit, when Mr. Nicholls stopped in the passage, I drew away and went upstairs; Martha said that, in perceiving my manoeuvre, a dark, flaysome[65] look crossed Mr. Nicholls's face that filled her soul with horror. No sooner had I reached the upper landing than I was filled with guilt and remorse for my cowardice.

Mr. Nicholls was, I believed, a good man who was suffering much on my account; could I not make a single overture to ease his pain? What compelled me to remain so aloof to him? In refusing him, I wondered, was I losing the purest gem—and to me, far the most precious thing that life can give: genuine attachment—or was I escaping the yoke of a morose temper?

In spring, an event occurred which made it impossible for me to harbour any further doubts as to the nature and truth of Mr. Nicholls's regard for me.

It was Whitsunday, the 15th of May. At services, I ventured to stop to the sacrament. Papa was ill, at home. As I sat in our family pew, I realised with a pang of regret that this would probably be the last time Mr. Nicholls would conduct a service in this church, the last time he would be a member of this parish. Mr. Nicholls seemed keenly aware of this fact as well, for as he stood before the congregation, and his eyes briefly found mine, an expression of grief crossed his countenance; he struggled against it—faltered—and then lost command over himself. For a long moment, he stood white, shaking, and voiceless before my eyes and in the sight of all the communicants. Joseph Redman, the parish clerk, spoke some words to him in a low tone. Mr. Nicholls made a great, rallying effort; with tears in his eyes, and with the greatest difficulty, he whispered and faltered his way through the service.

Oh! What a great heat of misery enveloped me at that moment! I never saw a battle more sternly fought with feelings and emotions than Mr. Nicholls fought with his. All at once, I felt many eyes turned in my direction; all assembled seemed to guess at the meaning behind his grief. Women began sobbing

---

[65] Fearsome, terrifying.

around me; I felt the tide of the congregation change as one in Mr. Nicholls's favour, and I could not check my own tears from spilling down my cheeks.

All the negative feeling which had built up against Mr. Nicholls in the preceding months seemed to vanish in the last week of his residency. The congregation presented him with a handsome, inscribed gold fob-watch at a public meeting held in his honour—a meeting from which papa remained conspicuously absent. I felt as if a great tide was sweeping life's events down an inexorable and painful path, over which I had no control. Mr. Nicholls was to go, it was all my fault, and I was powerless to stop it.

On Mr. Nicholls's last night in Haworth, he called at the parsonage to say good-bye, and to render into papa's hands the deeds of the National School. Martha and two workers were busy with spring cleaning in the dining-room, where I normally would have been sitting, so I knew he could not find me there, even if he had wished to. I waited in the kitchen, unwilling to go into the study to speak to him in papa's presence; indeed, until the very last moment, I thought it perhaps best that he not see me. When I heard the front door close, however, I went to the front window. I perceived Mr. Nicholls leaning against the garden gate in a paroxysm of anguish—sobbing as I have never before seen a person sob. My heart turned over; a great sob caught in my own throat, and sudden tears sprang to my eyes.

I took courage and rushed out, trembling and miserable. I went straight to him. For some moments we both stood in silence, overcome with grief. I could not think what to say. I did not wish for Mr. Nicholls to leave, but as things stood—it would be unfair to give him false hope—neither could I ask him to stay.

"I am so sorry," I finally whispered. "I shall miss you."

He lifted his eyes to mine—eyes which even now, ravaged as they were with grief, brimmed over with undisguised affection. "I wish—" he began; but he could proceed no further.

Tears coursed down my cheeks. I saw, in his look, a plea for such encouragement as I could not then give him. "Be well," was all I could manage.

"And you," he replied. He quickly passed through the gate and walked away.

It was only early the next morning, after a miserable night, that I realised I had never asked Mr. Nicholls where he was going.

Nineteen

In a panic, I dressed at dawn and rushed next door to Mr. Nicholls's lodging-house. The sexton answered the door in his night-shirt and cap, wiping sleep from his eyes. "Mr. Nicholls left before sunrise. We'll not be seeing him ony more, an' more's th' pity."

I found Mr. Brown's remark most interesting, considering the fact that just five months previously, he'd wanted to shoot the gentleman. "Do you know where he went?" I asked.

"Th' south o' England for a few weeks, he said. Then he'll be seeking a new curacy somewheres, I suppose."

"You suppose? Do you mean to say that Mr. Nicholls left without the security of another position?"

"He did. But I woudn'a worry abaat Mr. Nicholls, ma'am. He'll land on his feet somewheres. He's been given fine references, an' he'll be an asset t' ony community. An' ye can rest yer mind: for all his pain, he never gave a hint t' onyone why he was leaving, an' never breathed a single word against ye or yer father."

"Didn't he?" said I, as a little pain clutched at my heart.

"No. Indeed, when I pressed th' matter, he insisted 'at there never was ony quarrel betwixt Mr. Brontë an' hisself, 'at they parted as friends, an' he left solely on his own account—an' he expressed only th' highest praises concerning ye, Miss Brontë."

For three weeks after Mr. Nicholls left, I was ill and restless. The stress from the previous months took its toll on papa, and the very thing which I had most feared occurred: he suffered a stroke which rendered him, for a few days, completely blind. I tended to him; he rallied; but he did not completely regain his sight, and his dependence on me and on his new curate (Mr. de Renzy, a man ill suited to the job) again increased.

Then a letter came from Mr. Nicholls.

"Mr. Grant were jist here," said Martha, handing me an envelope. "He says this letter be enclosed i' a missive to him, an' I mun promise t' deliver it quietly t' ye, when yer father weren't i' th' house."

I took the letter and thanked her; as soon as she quitted the room, I opened it.

June 21st, 1853—Salisbury

My dear Miss Brontë,

Please forgive me for resorting to subterfuge to deliver this missive, but knowing your father's antipathy to me, I feared that any direct communication might not reach you.

I hope you will not find this letter unwelcome. For three weeks, I have wrestled with my conscience as to whether or not I could or should write to you. At length, I found courage in one small thing: the look in your eyes as we stood at the parsonage gate, the night before I left. I beheld in your gaze such empathy—at least so it appeared to me—as if you wished me to know that you understood all I had felt and suffered over the past few years, and in the past six months in particular. Was I imagining it? If so, you may discard this letter and think

*no more about it. If not—if you could offer me some mea-
sure of hope, some indication, however small, that you
have experienced an alteration of feeling, it would mean
everything in the world to me.*

*My decision to leave Haworth was undertaken only
under the greatest duress and oppression of mind and
spirit. Under the circumstances, no other course of action
seemed open to me. Now that I find myself finally and
completely severed from all contact with you, however—
without even the chance of glimpsing you from time to
time, as you walk from house to church, or in the garden,
or out upon the moors—I find myself tormented and bereft, my heart ripped in two by deepest pain and searing
regret.*

*I have spent my time these past few weeks touring in
the south—beautiful country, but I can take no pleasure
in it. I visited the cathedrals at Winchester and Salisbury; the latter is especially magnificent; but all I could
think of was: how I wish Miss Brontë were here to see this
with me! You would find it an amazing architectural
feat, equally as impressive as the York Minster.*

*Please do not ask me to forget you. That I cannot do.
My love for you burns eternal; it will never change. I
think of little else. I dream of none but you. My association with you has been, for me, one of life's greatest and
purest joys; I cannot accept its total loss. I understand
that you do not return the same degree of affection that
I feel for you. We needn't discuss the issue of marriage
again if you prefer—but if you could only find it in your
heart to offer me, at least, the fruits of our former friendship, I would accept it happily and with more gratitude
than you can imagine.*

*Would you consider allowing me to write to you
again? Please be assured that a letter from you, Miss
Brontë, would not only greatly cheer and encourage its
infinitely grateful recipient, but would provide one of the*

*only pleasures now extant in a life which now seems de-
void of purpose and meaning.*

*I shall remain at this address for another week. Fol-
lowing that, I return to Yorkshire, in the hopes of securing a new position. Please give my best to Martha and
Tabby, if you can do so without your father's knowledge;
and may I express my most sincere wishes for that gentleman's continued good health, as well as your own. I remain, yours most faithfully and respectfully,*

A. B. Nicholls

I read the letter once; twice; a third time; each time, with
marked astonishment. Oh! How familiar did the anguished
words seem! Years ago, I had written countless such letters myself to Monsieur Héger, filled with a similar force of feeling, and
a similar agony of hope and despair. Here, I thought, was a spectacle of emotion that mirrored my own! Mr. Nicholls appeared
to me very differently now, on the page.

It seemed incredible to me that the reserved curate I had
known for eight years—the man who had so quietly and steadfastly gone about his duties, masking his feelings behind a façade
of iron masculinity and proper, socially correct politeness—was
the same man who had written this impassioned letter, who had
proposed to me with such emotion, and who had broken down
in front of the entire congregation and again at the parsonage
gate. Clearly, I thought, still waters did run deep.

I responded the same day, apprising Mr. Nicholls that I
would welcome a correspondence with him, but it would be best
if he continued to send his letters via Mr. Grant.

Two weeks later, Ellen came to visit. For the first time in our
long history, we quarrelled. Ellen seemed determined, in everything she said, to verbally undermine Mr. Nicholls.

"You are lucky to be rid of him," asserted she one morning
over coffee.

"Lucky? Why do you say so? You used to sing Mr. Nicholls's praises. What has caused this sudden change of heart?"

"He was so gloomy when I was here a few months ago. I cannot abide a gloomy person."

"He had reason to be gloomy."

"He should have risen above his unhappiness, and not infected others with it. But there are other reasons why I have changed my mind about him. He does not suit you, Charlotte. He is a curate—you have long insisted that you would *never* marry a member of the clergy—and he is *Irish*. Even your own father says the Irish are a very slack, ill-mannered, and negligent people!"

"Mr. Nicholls is hardly slack or ill-mannered, Nell—quite the reverse, in fact."

"But *his family* will be. Think of it: had you married him, you would be obliged to visit his poor, illiterate relations back in Ireland."

"I am certain I could survive a visit to Mr. Nicholls's Irish relatives without permanent scarring."

"You joke—but I am serious. You said you would never marry, Charlotte. 'We will be old maids together, and live very happily on our own,' you said."

I stared at her. "Your primary objection, then, is not so much to the man himself—but to the idea of me marrying at all?"

"It would be inconsistent with your very nature for you to marry now."

"Inconsistent? Why would it be inconsistent, Ellen? When you entertained the notion of Mr. Vincent's proposal all those years ago, I strongly urged you to accept him. I wanted you to be happy, if you could find happiness with him. Yet now you begrudge me the same opportunity!"

"*You* are the one who refused Mr. Nicholls's proposal, not I! Are you saying that you wish you had accepted him?"

"No! I do not know *what* I want. But—"

"I am only trying to reassure you that you made the right decision. I could not abide it if you married now, Charlotte. I would hardly ever see you. If we are to be old maids, we must bear our position, and endure it to the end."

"Endure it? Oh, this is too much, Ellen! I thought you were my friend! Yet you wish to doom me to eternal spinsterhood, just so that I will be more *available* to you? This is unacceptable. You are no better than my father!"

The discord between us reached such a pitch, that Ellen left the next morning, a full week earlier than intended, and all correspondence between us abruptly ceased for a time.

Miserable, and fed up with papa's company, I left papa in Martha and Tabby's care and took every opportunity to go from home. I left for Scotland with Joe Taylor and his wife in August, but that journey was curtailed by their sick infant, and we ended up in the nearby spa town of Ilkley instead. I returned to Ilkley again to meet Miss Wooler for several days; despite the disparity in our ages, we had maintained a friendship that I greatly valued.

I continued to correspond with Mr. Nicholls. By now, he had taken a curacy with the Reverend Thomas Cator at Kirk Smeaton, about fifty miles away near Pontefract, still in the West Riding of Yorkshire. In early September, he requested leave to visit me. I replied that he could, but—although I felt miserable in the deception—I insisted that we keep his visit a secret from papa.

Not wishing the eyes and ears of the neighbourhood to gain appraisal of our rendezvous, we decided that I should call at Oxenhope vicarage, where Mr. Nicholls would be staying with the Grants. (Mr. Grant, despite his long-ago assertion of disinterest in the fairer sex, had six years previously married a lovely woman, Sarah Ann Turner, with whom he appeared very happy.)

The day of our meeting it poured down rain. When I arrived at Oxenhope vicarage (filled with guilt that I had lied to papa, and drenched to the bone after my long walk), the housekeeper graciously took my wet cloak, bonnet, gloves, and umbrella and showed me into the parlour, where Mr. Nicholls and Mr. and Mrs. Grant instantly rose to receive me. The look in Mr. Nicholls's eyes was so filled with nervous apprehension, that it instilled in me a similar anxiety. A few words of greeting were exchanged; Mr. Nicholls apologised profusely that I had been obliged to walk out in such bad weather. I was ushered to a chair by the hearth, where I warmed myself by the glowing fire. A maid brought tea and refreshments.

Mr. Nicholls inquired as to my health, and that of my father. I briefly mentioned papa's recent stroke and difficult recovery, which seemed to fill him with alarm. "He is much better now," I added reassuringly, "but I fear his sight will never again be as good as it was."

"I am sorry. I do hope he improves."

"Thank you." An awkward silence fell. "Mr. Nicholls: I hope you are enjoying your new position?"

"I am, thank you."

"Isn't it wonderful," observed Mrs. Grant, as she sipped her tea, "that Mr. Nicholls was able to find something so close by?"

"Indeed," said I, although in fact, I thought fifty miles a very great distance away.

Another silence fell. Mr. Nicholls blurted, "I read *Villette.*"

"Did you?" *Villette* had come out eight months before. The fact that Mr. Nicholls had never had an opportunity to mention it—considering that he had read both *Jane Eyre* and *Shirley* in two days, immediately after receiving them—was a poignant reminder of the gap that had grown between us.

"I loved it. The school was well described," said Mr. Nicholls with a hint of his former enthusiasm. "The country—you used another name, but—was it meant to be Belgium?"

Unaccountably, I felt myself blush. "It was."

"I was a little puzzled about the ending. What did you mean when—" He broke off and turned to Mr. and Mrs. Grant. "Have you read Miss Brontë's new novel?"

"I am afraid not," admitted Mrs. Grant.

"I am not fond of novels," interjected Mr. Grant with a frown. "But see here, Nicholls: how's the fishing up at Kirk Smeaton? Have you had any luck tickling the trout?"

A long discussion followed about fishing, after which Mr. Grant said, "Are the Dissenters as annoyingly vocal at Kirk Smeaton as they are in this community?"

"They are," replied Mr. Nicholls. "Last week I was obliged to spend a full half-hour arguing with a gentleman about the merits of the true church, and defending compulsory church rates."

"Where will it end?" exclaimed Mr. Grant, shaking his head. "Ladies: did you know they actually *considered* opening the universities to non-Anglicans?"

"Appalling!" said Mr. Nicholls.

"What earthly good would a university be to a Dissenter?" cried Mr. Grant. "Without a thorough knowledge of Greek and Latin, he wouldn't survive two days!"

Every one laughed except me. All at once my appetite was gone. The chit-chat continued for an hour or more. Mr. and Mrs. Grant made no move to leave the room, and as it was still raining hard, there was no opportunity for Mr. Nicholls and me to walk outside, or to have a single moment in which to converse in private. At length I said my good-byes, no less conflicted in mind with regard to my feelings for Mr. Nicholls than I had been when I arrived. In my concern that our meeting should remain undiscovered, I allowed Mr. Nicholls to walk me only as far as the gate which led to the flagged field path heading back to Haworth.

"I fear I shall not have the opportunity to return for some months, as I just started in my new position," explained Mr. Nicholls regretfully, his voice nearly drowned out by the loud drumming of the rain on our umbrellas.

"I am sorry, sir."

"May I have the honour of continuing to write to you, Miss Brontë?"

"You may, sir." (My shoes were now very wet indeed.) "It was good to see you, sir."

"And you, Miss Brontë. Good-bye."

On the 19th of September, Mrs. Gaskell came to visit me: her first visit to Haworth. For four days, I poured out my heart to that good and wise lady, confiding everything that had happened, and all the confusion of my thoughts and feelings.

"How hard-hearted your father is!" cried Mrs. Gaskell on our second afternoon, as we rambled on the heath, which had faded to the natural green and brown of early autumn. "How can he object to Mr. Nicholls's occupation, when he is a clergyman himself? And as you say, Mr. Nicholls has proved his worth; he was your father's right-hand man for eight years."

"Papa is entirely unreasonable on this point. He wants me to marry a great man—a man of wealth and standing—or none at all."

Mrs. Gaskell shook her head. A woman of medium build, she was half a head taller than I, with a pale complexion and pleasant features; her soft, dark brown hair was swept up under a bonnet that matched the deep violet hue of her fine silk dress. "If money is the primary issue, could not Mr. Nicholls find a house and a more lucrative appointment, as the pastor of his own parish?"

"He should have, Mrs. Gaskell, many years since; but if he did, he would be required to move away, and then we certainly could not be together."

"Why not?"

I sighed. "You may think me wrong, or foolish—but papa, for all his faults, is an old man, and we are each other's last relation in the world. He will never give up his parish until the day he dies. I gave papa my word that as long as he lives, I would not abandon him to a solitary existence; and I never will."

"Well, I must say—after all your father has said and done, for you to stand by him so loyally—I respect you for it, Miss Brontë; but I do not know that I should be capable of it."

"He has stood by *me* loyally all my life, Mrs. Gaskell; I owe him something for that. I admit: at times I am so angry with papa now, I cannot bear to be in the same room with him. He has treated Mr. Nicholls very cruelly and unjustly; yet in truth, I have behaved no better. I witnessed Mr. Nicholls's suffering for months, and did nothing about it. With one word from me, he never would have left Haworth; yet in spite of everything, Mr. Nicholls remains persistent in his aim, and unwavering in his affections."

"That speaks well of him. Tell me, Miss Brontë: do you like Mr. Nicholls? Do you respect him?"

"Very much. Yet, he is a man of many contradictions." I voiced my concerns about Mr. Nicholls's Puseyite prejudices, and my fears that they would stand in the way of my association with her (for Mrs. Gaskell was a Unitarian, and her husband a Unitarian minister) and some of my other friends. "Should not a husband and wife be in accord in *this*, the most important of all subjects: their basic religious tenets?"

"Not necessarily. If a foundation of love and respect exists, I believe a couple can survive in harmony despite disparate religious beliefs."

"Perhaps so," I replied, still unconvinced, "but this is not my only concern. We are different in other ways. Mr. Nicholls is actively concerned with the needs of the community—an excellent clerical virtue, and worthy of one's highest regard—while I am more reclusive, a devotee of the writer's life. And when it comes to my work, while Mr. Nicholls admires it with a sincere enthusiasm—" I broke off with a blush.

"Do you mean that Mr. Nicholls presents more of a layman's view when it comes to critiquing your writing and such? That you fear there are places where he cannot follow you intellectually?"

"Sometimes."

"Do not be embarrassed to admit this to *me*, Charlotte," said Mrs. Gaskell, as she took my arm. "You are a very intelligent woman, and not many men *could* keep pace with you. At the risk of self-aggrandisement, I shall make a confession: I have had the same concerns with my own dear husband at times, these many years."

"Have you?"

"William is a very devoted clergyman, just like your Mr. Nicholls. For all his success and intelligence, however, and all his support of my work—it was at *his* suggestion that I turned to writing, to distract me from my grief when our first two sons died in infancy—my fiction is not something which my husband can discuss at any length, nor with much depth and insight; but that is what friends and fellow writers are for. One man cannot be everything to a woman, nor should he be expected to be. This disparity in your aptitudes can be a good thing, Charlotte. Mr. Nicholls can ground you a bit more in the real world, and you can introduce him to goodness in sects where he thought it could not be."

I considered that. "Mr. Nicholls *does* have a most sincere love of goodness wherever he sees it." We were heading back through the fields now, and when we reached a stile, I paused and said, "How do you manage it all, Mrs. Gaskell? How do you find time to write, when you have a husband, a house, and children to care for?"

"It is not easy, but a clever woman can find time to do the things that matter to her." She looked at me with great seriousness. "If it were not for your father's opposition, would you wish to marry Mr. Nicholls? Could you love him?"

"I wish I knew."

"If Mr. Nicholls truly loves *you* as much as you say he does, I think you owe it to yourself, and to him, to find out."

Something was holding me back. Although Mr. Nicholls and I continued to exchange secret letters, in which he expressed his regard for me in the most passionate possible language, I still, inexplicably, could not bring myself to take the next crucial step: to defy papa, and insist on my right to openly pursue a relationship with my prospective suitor.

Then one night in mid-December—when rain pounded against the rooftop and spattered against the casements, and the east wind wailed through the eaves like a Banshee—I had a dream.

In my dream, there was no storm; it was a bright and cloudless summer day. I was walking across the moors, and had just begun my descent towards a familiar wooded hollow, when I spied two distant figures hiking along the river-bank in my direction. It was Emily and Anne! My heart pounded in a frenzy of shock and joy as I half ran, half flew down the incline and along the stony path to meet them.

"Emily! Anne! Is it really you?"

I longed to take them in my arms; but the sisters in my dream stood aloof, their faces sullen and clouded with disapproval. "We cannot stay long," said Emily. "We have only come to bring you a message."

"What message?"

"We have been watching you, and we are very disappointed," said Anne.

"Charlotte: you are alive," said Emily. "You have all of life's gifts at your disposal. Yet you ignore them, and act as if you are as dead and buried as we are."

"What do you mean? How do I act dead and buried?"

"You are buried in the past, just as Branwell was," answered Anne.

"That is untrue," I countered defensively.

"Do you think we do not know your secret?" said Emily. "Do you think we cannot see?"

"What secret? What do you see?"

"Charlotte: we know what happened that night in the garden in Brussels," said Anne.

"You know?" I whispered, mortified.

"We know," repeated Emily, "and we know about the letters. We know you still read them."

My cheeks flamed. "It has been years since I last looked at those letters."

"Yet you still think of him," accused Emily. "All the heroes in your books, save one, are professors, or Belgian, or both! Even your Mr. Rochester is modelled after him. Why do you think that is?"

I could not answer.

"Monsieur Héger's memory has created such a fixed idea in

your mind, that it keeps you blind and ignorant of what is right in front of your nose," declared Emily.

"You have let it hold you back far too long," added Anne.

"It is time," said Emily, "to move on."

"Move on," repeated Anne, "and leave Belgium behind."

I awoke with a gasp to the inky darkness of the stormy night, my heart racing.

Belgium, again.

As the first dim rays of a cold December dawn filtered in through the shutters, I reflected upon my dream. It had been ten years since my return from Belgium. I thought I had long since moved on from my ill-fated relationship with Monsieur Héger; but were my sisters right? Had I truly been buried in the past all this time, worshipping, against will and reason, at the altar of a man who had not loved me? Was that obsession holding me back even now, preventing me from opening my heart to the love of another man?

Oh! Oh! Why, oh why, I wondered suddenly, had I wasted so much time, aching with regret for something that could not be? A paroxysm of sadness overcame me, and I wept. How long I remained thus, lying in bed, sobbing from the depths of my soul, I cannot say; but I poured out all the grief I had denied myself over the past decade. I wept for my sisters and brother, who had been taken from this life far too soon; I wept for my broken spirit, engendered by their loss; and I wept at my own folly, for allowing a secret infatuation to consume and blind me for so many years.

At last, my tears were spent. My head ached; my throat was raw; my eyes burned; at the same time, something nagged at the corners of my mind: there was something important, I realised, that remained undone.

I rose and quickly dressed. From my dresser drawer, I un-tombed the rosewood box, and unwrapped the slim, beribboned packet of letters within. I glanced at the hearth: it was stone cold; it was too early, as well, for a fire in the kitchen; but burning was not a proper fate for these documents in any case, I decided.

The sun had nearly risen now. Ignoring the pain which yet thudded within my skull, I trod silently downstairs to the larder. I found a thick glass jar residing therein, containing the last dregs of a marmalade I had made the previous summer. I transferred the jar's meager contents to a plate, and thoroughly washed both jar and lid. I then took Monsieur Héger's letters, made a little roll of them, placed them in the jar and sealed it. Wrapping myself up against the cold, I took the jar and set off across the fog-enshrouded moors, to that same distant hollow where I had encountered my sisters in my dream.

No snow had yet fallen, but the ground was hard and covered with a frost; I knew that digging would be impossible, but I had something else in mind. The object of my journey was an ancient, gnarled tree which grew beside the river-bed, beneath whose shady bower my sisters and I had passed many a pleasant summer hour with a book. Although very old, the tree was of sound timber still; and I knew of a rather large hollow near its root, which was partly hidden by a thick carpet of overgrowth and creepers.

I went directly to the tree; like all its counterparts, it was now a winter skeleton; the river just beyond it was a noisy, raging torrent, its dark waters seeming to tear asunder the wood as they fumed white mist. I bent to my knees on the hard, damp ground; I cleared away the frozen moss and vines and found the hole, which was as deep as my arm.

"Are you aware," an inner voice intoned, "of what you do? This is a case of art inspiring life, rather than the other way round." I paused in surprise; in some ways, I realised, that was true. In *Villette,* Lucy Snowe buried her precious letters from Dr. John Graham, when she surmised that their relationship was over; but that scene, I now understood, came from my own ignored, subconscious desire to perform this act myself.

I thrust the jar within. *"Au revoir, Monsieur Héger,"* I said firmly, and without regret.

I replaced the covering of moss and vines. This done, I stood and wrapped my arms about me, shivering in the early-morning air. I had not, I thought with satisfaction, just hidden a treasure; I had buried a grief—a grief that should have been interred ten long years ago.

All at once, I felt an almost magical sense of release, as if a fairy had touched me with her wand, and in so doing, had lifted an enormous weight from my soul. With a smile, I noticed that my headache was gone.

When I returned to the house, I found papa reading the morning paper in his study. I took a seat before the glowing hearth beside him.

"Papa, I have something to confess to you."

He set down his paper and magnifying glass. "Yes, my dear, what is it?"

"These past six months, I have been writing to Mr. Nicholls."

"What? Writing to him? What do you mean, letters?"

"Yes, papa: letters, and he has been writing letters to me. I also saw him in September, at the Grants'. I know you expressly forbade such contact, and I feel guilty for having deceived you in this way."

After a short, frowning silence, he said, "I'm glad you told me. I hope you got it out of your system, and have seen the error of your ways. Deceitfulness and dishonesty are the Devil's own work. Promise me that you'll never see or write to that man again, and I'll forgive you."

"I am not seeking your forgiveness papa, nor shall I make any such promise. In fact, I am here to state the opposite: I have every intention of writing to Mr. Nicholls again, and of seeing him again, for a sizeable period of time, I hope—that is, if he is still interested in seeing me."

"You'll see him over my dead body!"

"I hope that will not be necessary, papa; but see him I will. I am not saying that I intend to marry Mr. Nicholls; but I am determined to become better acquainted with him, to give us both an opportunity to discover if we are truly suited to one another or not—and it will be far easier to do so *with* your knowledge and approval, than without."

"I shall never give you that approval! I tell you, he's not right for you, Charlotte!"

"Papa: listen to me. I am not a young girl, nor even a young woman any more. At your death, I shall have £300, besides the money I have earned myself, and nowhere to live. Perhaps, if I can still write, I can earn more; but there is no guarantee my next work will sell. I can live modestly on the income from the money I have, but I will be alone—*all alone*—an old maid, lonely, bitter, and no doubt pitied by every one. Is that the fate you wish for me? Would you not rather have me marry, if I find a man with whom I can be happy?"

"Confound it, woman! Can't you understand? You are my last surviving daughter. You are all I have!" Tears started in his eyes, and his voice faltered. "All your life you have been subject to ill health. You are, I fear, not strong enough to marry."

I felt my cheeks redden; his unspoken meaning was clear. "Women marry and have children every day, papa. I may surprise you. I am stronger than you think."

He shook his head, and wiped his eyes. "I've said it before, and I'll say it again: if you must marry, choose some one higher up—a man more accomplished and successful, a man from a great family—a man worthy of your standing as one of the most celebrated women authors of the day. A man like Mr. George Smith!"

"Mr. Smith is engaged to be married, papa."

"What? Is he?"

"I just learned of it a few days past. Mr. Smith has fallen in love with a young society beauty, just as I always predicted."

"Oh dear. How disappointing. I had high hopes for you in that quarter."

"I never did—and you must not delude yourself on that point any longer, papa. Men of Mr. Smith's ilk would never be interested in a woman like me. I have never been pretty, and now I am old. How many more chances will I have of matrimony?

Mr. Nicholls may be poor, but he loves me! Moreover, he loves me for who I am, not for the 'celebrated author' that I have become. Do you think there are many men who would have served eight long years waiting for me?"

"Mr. Nicholls is nothing but a curate! Worse yet, *he comes from nothing*—a penniless family of illiterate, Irish farmers! Can you truly imagine yourself the wife of such a man? He crosses the Irish Sea every autumn to see *his people*, as he calls them, and you can bet he'll expect you to accompany him. I know what *his people* are like, my girl! I came from such a family myself, and I have not returned to Ireland once since I left it, for good reason! The poor Irish are nothing like the English. They lack manners and good breeding; they are lazy, slipshod, and negligent in matters of housekeeping and hygiene; their daily habits and customs would mystify and appall you; and as to intellectual interests and pursuits, they are perfectly indifferent. Is that the kind of family you want for yourself?"

My cheeks again grew warm. Diary, I am mortified to admit it, but this consideration *did* bother me a little. I was not worldly enough to know if papa's assertions were true or merely a reflection of his own experience, but I had heard such assertions about Irish negligence from others. When I had, as a young woman, allowed myself to dream of marriage, I had imagined myself being welcomed into a new, extended family who were not only loving, but well-read, cultured, and refined: intelligent people whose minds were similar to my own, and who lived in conditions at least equal to my own, however modest. I knew, though, that this was only senseless vanity and pride, and of no true importance; and I shoved the thought aside.

"One cannot and should not judge a man by his family," said I vehemently. "Mr. Nicholls has none of the faults you just described—if faults they be—and that is all that matters to me."

"I do not understand it. How can you even *contemplate* marrying a poor curate?"

"I think I must marry a curate, papa, *if* I marry at all; not merely a curate, but *your* curate—and if I *do* choose him, he must live in this house with us, for I will not leave you."

Papa stood up, his eyes flashing with fury. "Never. I will never have another man in this house. Do you understand me? *Never!*" With that, he stalked from the room.

For a full week, papa did not speak a word to me. The air in the house was so thick with tension, that at times I thought I could not breathe. One morning, as I sat taking breakfast alone, I heard Tabby hobble into papa's study and berate him loudly.

"This idiocy has like t' gone on long enought," cried the old woman. "Ye pass our poor Miss i' th' hall wi'out so mich as a kind look or word; ye stalk abaat th' house like a mad tyrant! What gives ye th' right, sir, t' tell a woman nearly forty year o' age, what she can an' cannae do? Do ye wish t' kill yer only daughter, sir? This may well be her ony chance for true happiness. Let her take it, ye foolish owd man!"

That afternoon, papa gave his begrudging permission for me to "see that gentleman," with no promises beyond that. It was all I needed. That same day I wrote to Mr. Nicholls, informing him of my intention: that I should like to renew our acquaintance in person, with the idea of reconsidering his proposal, to discover if we could come to a better understanding.

Mr. Nicholls wrote back like lightning, and fixed our meeting for the earliest opportunity that he could get away. He came in the third week of January for a ten-day visit, again staying with the Grants at Oxenhope. This time, he was able to present himself openly and above-board at the parsonage. On the day Mr. Nicholls arrived, however, to my great embarrassment, papa received him in such an unpleasant and hostile manner, that we were obliged to leave the house at once to seek privacy and peace of mind.

I donned my warmest cloak, hat, gloves, muff, and boots, and the two of us set off on a walk. The day was very cold with an iron sky, but thankfully there was little wind. Heavy snowfalls in the new year had transformed the surrounding hills and dales into a billowy white ocean, filling the depressions in the moors to meet the rises in a level, and disguising familiar landmarks. Many an inexperienced visitor who dared to cross those frozen hill backs had been known to lose their way, or to sink up to their necks in the snow. We embarked instead on a safer route: the well-tramped path across the snowy fields between Haworth and Oxenhope.

As Mr. Nicholls and I ambled along, our cheeks rosy and our breath forming clouds in the air, our feet made soft crunching sounds against the densely-packed snow. The path was just wide enough for two, requiring us to walk in close proximity, side by side; in our exertion we often bumped up against each other, prompting him to say "Excuse me" so many times in the first ten minutes that I told him to please refrain from further apology: he might bump into me as often as he liked.

Despite this somewhat awkward beginning, I noticed that Mr. Nicholls did not seem quite as nervous at this meeting as he had been the previous September; in fact, when I glanced up at him, I caught him gazing down at me with affectionate eyes and a smile upon his face.

I smiled in return and said, "Mr. Nicholls, now that we—at last—have this opportunity to speak alone and in person, I wish to begin by thanking you for your unwavering constancy over the past year, in the face of every obstacle. Furthermore, I wish to apologise for my father's unconscionable behaviour during that time, and for my own prolonged confusion and indecision."

"I appreciate that, Miss Brontë; but I've always felt your father was perfectly justified in his objections to a union between you and myself, and I understand your own reluctance."

I looked up at him again, expecting to detect some trace of sarcasm in his countenance, but there was none at all: his expression and tone conveyed the utmost in sincerity and humility. I shook my head in wonder and renewed respect. "Had I been treated by my parson as you were, Mr. Nicholls, during your last six months in Haworth, I do not believe that I could be as gracious or forgiving."

"How else should I be? You're the world to your father, and he to you. He had higher aims for you than to marry his curate. I cannot blame you for feeling similarly, and for not wishing to disappoint him."

"His pride and ambition for me must be exorcised, sir; there is no need or place for it. You have proved your worth with years of selfless commitment to this community. Indeed, in the months since your departure, the negligence and incompetence of your successor has reminded every one in Haworth of what they lost in saying good-bye to you."

He frowned in surprise. "What has Mr. de Renzy done—or not done—that's so appalling?"

"Oh, the list of his deficiencies is far too long to bear repeating, sir. Rest assured that no permanent damage has been done, however; and perhaps, when papa overcomes his prejudices and sees reason, these discrepancies will even do some good." Our eyes met; we shared a laugh. As we strolled on in the silence of early afternoon, I took a deep breath of the wintry air and added: "Mr. Nicholls: I believe I mentioned in my letter that I hoped, on this visit, we might become better acquainted."

"You did say that, Miss Brontë; although in truth, I'm at a loss as to what you meant by it. We've been acquainted now for nearly nine years already."

"True; but it occurs to me that—as a result of living here, where I grew up, and your many conversations with my father—you know a great deal more about me, than I know about you."

"Is that so?"

"It is. I know almost nothing about your life in Ireland before you came to Haworth, Mr. Nicholls. Will you enlighten me? Will you tell me something about yourself?"

"If you wish. How far back would you like me to go?"

"I think birth would be a good place to start."

He laughed. "All right then: my birth. I was born thirty-six years ago, on the 6th of January, on a day so cold, it's said that my father chipped a tooth on his soup, the dogs were wearing cats, and when the midwife announced, 'it's a boy,' her words froze up solid right in the air."

Now it was my turn to laugh.

"Like all my brothers and sisters before me, I was born at Tully Farm in Killead, in County Antrim, Northern Ireland. My father William came from Scotland originally; he was a hard-scrabble farmer, living off the land. My mother Margaret came from nearby Glenavy. She was also of Scottish descent, but her family were members of the Established church."

"Ah! I have long thought I detected a slight hint of Scottish in your speech."

"Have you? And here I thought I'd rid myself of it. Well, my mam was a good woman, but she worked so hard to help keep the farm going, all the while giving birth to ten children one after the other, that she had little time or energy to be affection-ate. I was the sixth child in line. Killead wasn't a bad place; as I recall, all the houses were small but neat and well-kept, with gardens. Although I left that house when I was young, it'll always be fixed in my memory: one big room with lime-washed walls and a thatched roof, and it stood one and a half storeys high."

"One and a half storeys? What do you mean?"

"The ground floor was just a large, flagged kitchen. Our sleeping loft was upstairs under the rafters, but we had no stairs. We used notches in the wall to get up there."

"Notches in the wall? And a one-room house, for twelve people?"

"Yes. We had a stable at one end and a byre[66] at the other, with a circular horse-walk at the back for churning butter. 'Twas a hard life, although I didn't know it at the time. We often had nothing but milk and potatoes to eat for weeks on end, with only the odd piece of meat from the pigs and chickens, but we didn't starve. I thought it perfectly natural to sleep three or four to a

---

[66] A cow shed.

bed. Sheets were in such short supply, Miss Brontë, that my mam cut them into little strips, and gave us each a scrap to use as a shield between our faces and the coarse woolen blanket."

"Oh, Mr. Nicholls! I cannot imagine such a thing. Even at the Clergy Daughters' School, we were not so impoverished as that."

"I didn't know I was impoverished. When you are very young, you don't question what you don't have. It was just my life. I would've been a farmer, no different from my father and my two eldest brothers, with no education other than a few years at the local schoolhouse, had it not been for the grace of God and my Aunt and Uncle Bell."

"Your Aunt and Uncle Bell?"

"Uncle Bell was my mam's brother. He was a clergyman and a teacher, and a bit better off than my father. One day when he came to visit, he saw our house bursting at the seams and my parents overwhelmed at having so many mouths to feed. I overheard the grown-ups talking. My father was worried. He said my two eldest brothers were to inherit the farm, and my sisters, he figured, would marry or go into some kind of service; but what was to become of his two younger sons? Uncle Bell—even though he had two small children of his own at the time—offered to take me and my brother Alan back home with him to Banagher, to raise as his own, and my parents agreed."

I looked at him, shocked. "Just like that—your parents gave you away?"

"They did." There was a flicker of pain in Mr. Nicholls's eyes.

"How old were you?"

"Seven. Alan had just turned ten."

"Oh! That is very young indeed to leave your mother and father!"

"It was—and a heart-rending decision for my parents to make, I'm sure—but a kind and selfless act on the part of my uncle. I'll never forget the sight of my mother and father sobbing in the doorway of the house as we drove away. I never saw them or my brothers and sisters again."

"Never? Why not?"

"My parents insisted it would be too hard on all of us; that if Alan and I were to have a fresh start in life with a new family, we must not look back."

"Oh!" This revelation pained me so much, I could barely speak. My heart went out to Mr. Nicholls; all at once, I felt I understood him better than I ever had. No wonder he kept his emotions so bottled up inside; no wonder, when he did allow himself to feel and commit himself to some one, he formed such a deep and permanent attachment.

"It proved, however, to be the beginning of a new life for me, Miss Brontë. My aunt and uncle took us into their home and their hearts, and treated us as part of their own growing family. Their children—eventually there were nine of them—"

"Nine!"

He nodded, with a sudden smile. "My first cousins became as younger brothers and sisters to Alan and me. Aunt and Uncle Bell were loving and generous, and shared whatever they had. Because my uncle had a school, we got an excellent education into the bargain, and when we'd grown, he managed it so Alan and I could attend Trinity College. He passed on nearly fifteen years ago. I miss him dearly—as does all the family."

"I am sorry."

"Thank you. I owe everything I am to-day to my Uncle and Aunt Bell. She's a wonderful woman. I'd love for you to meet her one day."

"It would be an honour. How interesting to think that we were both raised by a maternal aunt."

"We do have that in common."

"What was your aunt and uncle's house like?"

"Their house?" He hesitated. "It was filled with loving hearts, and I was made very welcome there. In the end, that's all that matters, don't you think?"

"I could not agree more."

"My aunt and most of my cousins still live in Banagher; that's who I visit every autumn, when I take my holiday."

"Oh! All this time, I assumed you went back to see your mother and father."

"No. My mother died when I was twelve. My father passed away five years ago, at the age of eighty—or so I'm told. For years, I felt guilty that I wasn't there when they died."

I shook my head sadly. "I know what it means to lose a mother so young. I was just five years old when my own mother passed away."

"It leaves a great, empty space inside you, that can never be filled, don't you find?" At my solemn nod he added, "I imagine that's why all the major characters in your books are orphans, is it not, Miss Brontë?"

I admitted that it was. We walked on, talking in this companionable manner until we reached Oxenhope village, at which point we turned around and retraced our steps. When we returned to the parsonage, we had tea in the dining-room (papa feigned an illness, and did not join us.) Mr. Nicholls's visit continued for nine more days, and every day, as we walked back and forth along the same snowy path, we spoke frankly about our lives, both past and present, carefully (so far) avoiding the future.

Mr. Nicholls shared amusing tales of his days at Trinity College, and talked with affection and good humour about his brother Alan, and of the scrapes and mischief they had got into as children—stories about pranks they had pulled on their younger cousins, and times they had skipped school to take long walks in the country-side with the family dogs, to go boating on the Shannon River, or fishing in the nearby streams.

"It was there that I learned to catch a trout by hand; I never used a rod or reel. What fun we used to have, tickling the slippery little devils, and sometimes flipping them out of the water at each other's faces, just for fun."

His stories made me laugh, and created a very different picture in my mind of the young Arthur Bell Nicholls, than that which had been there formerly. "I always imagined you as this stern, serious little boy, who followed all the rules and did everything right."

"In truth I suppose I was. I was always the voice of dissension in these little escapades—I dearly loved my aunt and uncle, and didn't wish to upset them—but that didn't stop me from aiding and abetting my brother every now and again."

I told him, in turn, of my own childish adventures with my brother and sisters. "In addition to endless reading and scribbling, one of our favourite pastimes was to act out our little stories. We would ramble across the moors, and pretend it was the Country of the Genii. The moors became our Arabia." I nodded towards the frozen landscape beside us. "All that you see before you—to us it was a vast desert, endless plains of undulating sand under a burning sun and cloudless sky. The fog, we envisioned as a refreshing desert mist; and we always discovered an immense palace surrounded by palm trees, entirely encrusted with diamonds, rubies, and emeralds, and illuminated with lamps too bright to look upon."

"Straight out of *The Arabian Nights* and *Tales of the Genii,* eh?"

"Have you read them?"

"Of course. Hasn't every child in Christendom? Why do you sound so surprised?"

"I don't know," I replied, suddenly pleased to discover that he had grown up with the same works. "I suppose I thought the *Tales* too frivolous for a future Church of England clergyman, and particularly for such a staunch devotee of Dr. Pusey's *Tracts for the Times.*"

Catching the irony in my tone, Mr. Nicholls went quiet for a moment, then looked at me and said in a serious voice, "Perhaps it's just as well that this topic came up now."

"Perhaps it is. I *have* been meaning to speak to you about it."

"I'm well aware that you don't share all my religious preferences, Miss Brontë—that you hold a more liberal view."

"I do not wish to criticise you over matters so deep-rooted and delicate of conscience and principle, Mr. Nicholls, but—if we were to consider a future together—would you be able to accept my own views as important to me?"

"I can and I do, Miss Brontë."

"Would you be equally as able to welcome, with an open heart, certain friends of mine who share my beliefs?"

"Your friends' beliefs are their own affair. I'll honour and respect them, just as I hope they—and you—will honour and respect mine."

"Would I be allowed to give free vent to my own opinions, however different from yours, without fear of censure?"

"Of course."

"Would you agree to at least *listen* on occasion, and consider my view-point?"

He laughed. "I will. I promise."

On our last day together, when we returned from the same snowy walk and were saying good-bye at the parsonage gate, Mr. Nicholls made yet another promise which brought us even closer to an understanding.

"I know, Miss Brontë, how much you love your father, and how deeply concerned you are for his welfare. I know as well that you would never leave him, and I want to set your mind at ease on that point. I've only taken a temporary curacy at present. I've not sought a living elsewhere, and I've refused those that have been offered to me, because I feared that you would not follow me there. Am I correct in this assumption?"

"You are, sir," I replied softly, both surprised and greatly moved.

"I want to assure you that *if* we were to marry, Miss Brontë, I'd return to Haworth permanently, and I vow to do everything in my power to faithfully care for your father until the end of his days."

I felt a rush of affection for him then. "Thank you, Mr. Nicholls. I realise that such a declaration cannot be easy, considering the unjust manner in which papa has treated you. It is a credit to your integrity and forbearance. I am also aware that a promise from you is not mere words: you will follow through, and this lifts a great weight from my mind."

He frowned. "For all this to work, however—for me to return

to Haworth—your father must be willing to accept me not only as his possible, prospective son-in-law, but as his curate again."

I nodded. "He is, as you know, a very stubborn old man. Once he makes up his mind, it is hard work to bring him round to another point of view." I looked up at him then, with a wondering smile. "Mr. Nicholls, have you truly turned down a more lucrative living on my account?"

"Several, Miss Brontë; and I'll continue to do so, if you'll but give me any hope that you might reconsider my proposal."

"I *am* reconsidering it, sir, and I assure you, it is with a very different outlook than I formerly possessed."

A hint of optimism darted through the cautious expression on his countenance. "I will hope for the best, then."

I removed my gloved hand from my muff and held it out to him; he took it and held it fast between his own two hands.

"Thank you for coming, sir. I shall write again very soon."

"And I'll come back as soon as ever I can." We stood thus for some moments, our eyes fixed upon each other. He let go of my hand with apparent reluctance, and we said good-bye.

Twenty

iary, when I first began to write these pages a year ago, my life had been thrown into a maelstrom of turmoil and confusion, occasioned by Mr. Nicholls's unexpected proposal of marriage. Over the past twelve months, I have sought the comfort of memory and pen to help me understand the past, in the hopes that it might help guide me into the future.

Now, I find that I can put off my decision no longer. My inner voice will not keep still. It cries: "*Can* I be a wife?" More importantly: "Can I be *his* wife—for all eternity?"

My cheeks grow warm as I pen these words; I am ashamed to admit it, diary, but I am a little disappointed that I do not feel the kind of passion for Mr. Nicholls that I have always imagined a heroine should feel for a hero. Where is the tense anticipation of the next treasured meeting, the bated breath, the flying into one another's arms at first sight, the wildly beating heart and frantic meeting of lips? When Mr. Nicholls looks at me, when he touches my hand, I do not feel the thrill that I believe a lover's look and touch ought to instill.

Yet, at the same time, I *have* come to feel a true esteem and affection for Mr. Nicholls. He is a dear man. With all that I have learned during his recent ten-day visit, many of my doubts regarding our incompatibility have been assuaged. It means a great deal to me that he knew my brother and loved my sisters, and has promised to help care for my aging father. Is it not better to secure the fidelity of such a man, and to relieve a suffering and faithful heart, than to unfeelingly abandon one so truly attached, to pursue some vain, empty shadow?

I am grateful for Mr. Nicholls's tender love to me. I believe it possible that I can learn to love him in time.

Providence in His goodness and wisdom have offered me this destiny; it must, then, be the best for me.

Twenty-one

❧

iary: it has been many months since I last wrote herein. Forgive me for the delay, but so much has occurred in the interval, that I have scarcely had a moment to breathe.

As it turns out, having *decided* to accept Mr. Nicholls's proposal was only half the battle—or should I say, the journey—which lay ahead of me. For although my mind was made up, no lasting happiness could be achieved until my heart and soul had also been won; and that—well, *that* is the rest of the story. My tale would not be complete unless I were to go on and reveal everything that followed—even though certain parts of the story are of such a highly personal and intimate nature, that even now I blush to recall them.

For two months after Mr. Nicholls and I took that last snowy walk and I determined to accept his offer, I put all my efforts into convincing papa of my suitor's many merits. I reminded him of the faithful service Mr. Nicholls had rendered him during his eight years in office, and compared his efforts to those of his successor, the despised Mr. de Renzy. I informed him that

Mr. Nicholls's uncle had been a school-teacher; surely that meant that *some* members of his family were educated, and not worthy of his scorn. I told papa that if he took Mr. Nicholls back as his curate, approved of our marriage, and allowed us to live at the parsonage, he would be gaining a son-in-law whose added income could only prove beneficial to us all.

Perhaps it was this pecuniary stratagem which produced the required effect; perhaps it was the fact that Mr. de Renzy had so exacerbated papa's nerves, that he now welcomed almost any substitute; perhaps it was from sheer exhaustion after listening to my arguments day in and day out; but for whatever reason, a miracle occurred: papa gave his consent to the marriage.

When Mr. Nicholls returned to Haworth on the 4th of April, papa's former antipathy towards him had vanished as surely and completely as the newly-melted snow. On the second day of his visit, Mr. Nicholls, reacting to this new-found civility with nervous excitement, insisted that we walk back across the moors to the same river-bank where we had sat and talked together so congenially for the first time, nearly six years before.

Although early spring, it was yet very cold, and pockets of snow still clung in the hollows and dales along the mossy river-bank. There were no flowers yet, but the stream rushed with its usual force and fume, and the trees were studded with the promise of fresh, new leaves. When we reached the familiar spot which we had once inhabited, within the privacy of the surrounding hills, we stopped side by side to admire the spectacle.

"I love this place," said Mr. Nicholls. "I discovered it not long after I came to Haworth. It is one of my favourite spots for contemplation."

"It is one of mine, as well. I used to come here frequently with my brother and sisters when we were children."

We fell silent. I knew why he had taken me here; I guessed what was coming; my heart pounded warily at the thought of it, but I was ready. He turned to face me, his gloved hands clasped before him as he gazed down at me, affection in his eyes, and nervous anticipation in his tone.

"Miss Brontë: forgive me for speaking plainly, but more than a year has passed since I first spoke to you on this matter, and I don't wish to waste another minute. You know my feelings: they remain unchanged. I love you. I always have, and I always will. May I renew the offer that I made to you so long ago, with the hope of a different response? Will you have me, Miss Brontë? Will you marry me?"

"I will."

Joy lit up his countenance. "You will?"

"I will." My pulse throbbed at the momentousness of the promise I had just made. He seemed equally overcome. We both stood frozen in the shock of the moment; now he stepped forward, closing the gap between us, and put his hand at the small of my back. Bending his head to mine, he kissed me: a brief, hesitant first kiss that necessitated the navigation around our noses and the avoidance of my spectacles; but it was also a gentle kiss, tender and true. "I love you, Charlotte," said he softly. It was the first time he had ever called me by my Christian name.

I gazed up at him in fond silence, hoping my eyes would convey my sincere affection; I sensed his disappointment that I had not repeated his sentiment, but I could not say what my heart did not yet feel.

He took off his gloves then, and withdrew from his coat pocket a small box, which he opened and held out before me: it contained a delicate gold band enhanced by a spray of five pearls. "I bought this ring for you. I had to guess at the size. Will you wear it?"

"I would be honoured." I removed the glove from my left hand, and he slipped the ring upon my tiny finger. Another miracle occurred—or perhaps my future husband was simply a more astute judge of such things than I could have guessed— but the ring was a perfect fit. "It is beautiful, Mr. Nicholls. Thank you."

Bringing my bare hand up to his lips, he kissed it and said with quiet confidence, "No more *Mr. Nicholls*. I would have you call me *Arthur,* now."

I could not help but smile. My two childhood heroes—the Duke of Wellington, and my imaginary Duke of Zamorna—had also both been Arthurs.

Miss Wooler had acted as a peacemaker between Ellen and myself, and my friend and I had ended our estrangement with a renewal of correspondence the previous month. When I wrote to Ellen now, informing her of my engagement, she replied with congratulations which I could only hope were heart-felt and sincere.

Considering how long and strenuously papa had fought against the idea of my marriage, I was astonished by how quickly he came round to a very different view, once his consent was given and the engagement became a *fait accompli.* Aside from an occasional disappointed sigh about Mr. Nicholls's "humble beginnings," papa's illusions of ambition on my behalf seemed at last to have dissipated into disgruntled acceptance.

Now, both papa and Mr. Nicholls—or Arthur, as I tried to remind myself to call him—seemed anxious to have the matter settled, and pressed for an early wedding date. Papa gave Mr. de Renzy his notice; Arthur wrote to announce that he could leave his curacy at Kirk Smeaton on 11 June; and a date was fixed for the 29th of June.

The date seemed very soon; there was so much to accomplish before the wedding, and little more than two months in which to accomplish it. I went about my preparations calmly, with moderate expectations of happiness. At the beginning of May, I went to Brookroyd, where any lingering traces of awkwardness between Ellen and myself were swept away, as she helped me to choose my trousseau in two days of shopping at Leeds and Halifax.

I was determined to purchase nothing too expensive or extensive, and that my new bonnets and dresses should all be capable of being put to good use after my wedding day. In the end, we selected fabric for two new gowns: one, a splendid mauve silk, and the other a plain barège[67] with a little green spot in it. As to my wedding dress, nothing would satisfy Ellen but white, which I had been determined that I would not wear.

"White is the colour of night-shirts and chemises, and the frocks of dewy-eyed young girls," said I. "I am far too old to be married in white."

"You cannot be married in anything *but* white," insisted Ellen, as we surveyed the fabrics displayed on the counter before us, "and you must have it made up in one of those lovely new French styles that I have seen in the fashion magazines, with beading at the bodice and clouds of white tulle." Holding up a bolt of white silk against my chest, she said with a satisfied smile, "Oh! Charlotte! No colour has ever suited you so well."

In my secret soul, I had to admit that I had always dreamt—if I ever married—of being attired in full, traditional bridal regalia. "I suppose I *could* wear white—but I will have none of your fancy new French styles." After glancing at the price of the fabric, I quickly added, "And I would not think of silk; it is too expensive for a gown which will, in all probability, never be worn again. I will stick to muslin—plain book muslin, with only a tuck or two in front."

Ellen frowned as she set down the bolt of silk. "You are very stubborn, Charlotte—but this is your wedding, so I shall not argue. Oh! Look at this lace! It will make an exquisite veil."

"My veil shall be a simple square of tulle, and it shall cost no more than five shillings. If I must make a fool of myself, it shall be on an economical plan."

I did indulge in one extravagance: for the chemises, night-shirt, and undergarments that I was to make myself, I purchased—for the first time in my life—several yards of white satin ribbon and lace for trimmings. "After all" (as Ellen insisted, with the

---

[67] A gauzelike, silky dress fabric.

most serious of expressions), "these garments will be *seen* by your husband."

I left the fabric with the dressmaker at Halifax. A week after I returned to Haworth, Arthur came again to visit. For the first few days he was a bundle of nerves—worried, I think, that I might change my mind. When I reassured him that I would do no such thing—and I would be proud to be his wife—he became calmer, and offered to help make the arrangements for the wedding itself, kindly acquiescing to my wishes for a quiet ceremony.

"I fear I have become a sort of curiosity in the neighbourhood: the Brontë spinster who is marrying at long last. I dread the idea of arriving at the church to find a throng of gawking on-lookers."

"I will do my best to ensure that does not happen," promised Arthur. "Not a soul in Haworth outside ourselves, the rector, and the parish clerk will be aware of the day, if I can help it."

We agreed that Ellen should be my bridesmaid, and that our only guests would be Miss Wooler and Mr. and Mrs. Grant. (Mrs. Gaskell, aware of Mr. Nicholls's antipathy to Dissenters, chose not to attend.) As papa did not wish to conduct the service, Arthur arranged with his friend the young Reverend Sutcliffe Sowden—who had also been a good friend of Branwell's—to officiate. In lieu of wedding invitations, we sent out announcements. My list was small, comprising only eighteen names; to my amusement, however, there was no end to the string of parson friends to whom Mr. Nicholls wished to send cards. I was required to double my order at the printers', and to request sixty envelopes.

In the final month before the wedding, I sewed madly against time, and undertook the remodelling of the little storage room behind the dining-room, to convert it into a study for Mr. Nicholls. The workers closed up an outside doorway, laid a new floor, added a fire-place and refinished the walls; I made up a set of new green and white curtains that exactly suited the new wall-paper.

Before I knew it, June had slipped past, the study was finished, and my trousseau was complete. The strain occasioned by the alterations to the house and my own sleepless apprehension in the weeks preceding the event, conspired to weaken my constitution; just before the wedding, I came down with the first symptoms of a cold. My excitement, however, served to banish any thought of threatening illness from my mind. It was with the greatest joy that I received Ellen and Miss Wooler, who (according to the thoughtful and considerate arrangements which Mr. Nicholls had made for them) arrived at the parsonage the day before the wedding by the same train and cab.

The last day passed in a flurry of final arrangements. With my friends' help, I finished packing my trunk, and nailed on the card with the direction of the first stop on our honeymoon tour: an inn in northern Wales. After a brief visit there, we planned to take a steamship to Arthur's native Ireland for a month-long tour, where I was to meet his family.

Mr. Nicholls joined us for supper, pale-faced and in a state of nervous anxiety equal to my own. In order to call as little attention to the morrow's nuptials as possible, and because we were to depart on the first leg of our honeymoon that same day, he had arranged for the wedding to take place at the earliest allowable hour: 8:00 a.m.

Everything seemed to be going according to plan. When we concluded evening prayers, however, papa was beset by a sudden coughing fit, which left him weak and tired. To my dismay, he said: "I feel unwell. I fear I have caught your cold, Charlotte. I think it best if I do not attend the ceremony tomorrow."

Mr. Nicholls blanched and said in consternation, "Surely, Mr. Brontë, you cannot mean to miss your daughter's wedding?"

Papa coloured a little and averted his gaze. "I'm sorry, but it cannot be helped."

"If you do not attend, papa," said I, greatly disappointed, "who will give me away?"

"I'm certain you can find a way to manage without me."

Despite the coughing fit, I did not believe papa was truly ill; such a complaint had not, in the past, prevented him from conducting business as usual in the parish. In viewing the expression on his face (a sort of panic, which he struggled in vain to hide), I ascertained what his pride could not bring him to say: that agitation over this formal separation from his last surviving child, was still more than he could bear to see—or sanction—first-hand.

I heaved a sigh, but I knew better than to try to argue with my father in such a mood. Martha, Tabby, Ellen, and Miss Wooler all looked as discomfited as I.

"Let us consult the prayer book," suggested Arthur. "Perhaps there is a provision for such a situation, and a substitute would be allowed."

We applied to the book in question; Mr. Nicholls found the requisite page; with a triumphant nod, he cried, "Aha! We are in luck. It states that, in the event that a parent or guardian is not available, it is perfectly acceptable for a bride to be given away by a friend."

The room fell briefly silent. Ellen said: "I would be glad to perform the service—but it does not seem right, Charlotte. I am younger than you. A bride should be given away by some one closer to her parent's age, do not you think?"

I nodded in some distress. Miss Wooler rose to the occasion.

"I would be honoured to give you away," offered that good lady, "if it would be amenable to you."

"Oh!" I cried, delighted, as I wrapped my arms around her. "The honour is *mine*. Thank you so much, my dear, dear friend."

Mr. Nicholls kissed me good-bye at the front door, expressing his concern about my cold. I assured him that I felt well, on the whole. The household retired for the night. Miss Wooler slept in the room that had once been Branwell's; Ellen, as always, shared my chamber.

"Do you realise," said Ellen, as we lay back upon our pillows, "that this is the last time we shall ever share a bed together?"

"Yes," I replied, a little sadly.

"I shall never forget the first time I saw you all those years ago, hovering in tears by the schoolroom window at Roe Head."

"You gave me comfort and friendship when I had none. I can never thank you enough for that, Nell."

Ellen turned and gazed at me fondly. "We were good for each other, I think."

"We still are."

Sudden tears welled in her eyes. "I cannot believe it is all over—that you are truly getting married to-morrow."

"Do not look so sad, Nell. I am not going anywhere. I shall be a man's wife, yes; but I shall still live here, in this very same house, just as always."

"With this marriage, Charlotte, your life will alter in ways that you and I cannot even begin to imagine."

"That may be true; but whatever happens, I promise I will always make time for you in my life. You are my dearest and closest friend, Nell, and I cannot think how I would get on without you."

"I feel the same, my dearest Charlotte." Ellen wiped away her tears and closed her eyes. After a small silence, in which I thought she might have fallen asleep, she said in a quiet voice, "Are you very afraid?"

"Afraid? Of what?"

"Of—" In the dim light of late evening, I could discern the blush which spread across her cheeks. "Of your wedding night."

It was my turn to blush. Here was a subject we had not broached in many years; and at the mention of it, my heart began to pound. "I am not afraid," I replied truthfully, "but I suppose I am very—well, curious—and perhaps a little apprehensive. I do so want to please my husband, or at the very least, not to disappoint."

"Has any one advised you about the—the proceedings?"

"No! Whom should I apply to for advice? I have no married friends with whom I could speak on such a topic, unless you count Tabby, who is so old and has been widowed so long, I daresay she has forgotten, and Mrs. Gaskell—but somehow it never seemed appropriate to ask her."

"I can see how it would not."

"I admit, I know very little about what to expect, or what will be expected of me. It is a bit mortifying to think that, at age thirty-eight, I know less about this matter than some girls know at eighteen."

"Mama says it is a rite of passage that every married woman must experience for herself. My married sisters *still* tell me nothing."

"It does seem unfair that information on this subject is not more readily available—but I am not a complete ignoramus. I am acquainted with the physiology of the male anatomy, and I *have* read a great many novels."

"Novels are always so enigmatic on the subject. I once read about a woman being *ravished*. What does that mean, exactly?"

"To be violated; to be seized and carried away by force."

"Oh!" cried Ellen in dismay.

"Yet it also can mean something very different: to be overwhelmed by emotion; to be enraptured."

"Well, *that* could be very nice."

"Indeed it could."

"Do you think," said Ellen with a giggle, "that Mr. Nicholls will ravish you?"

"I do not know. I hope so." At this, we were both overcome by school-girlish laughter for a full minute.

When we had recovered our composure, Ellen said: "Oh! I just remembered something else my mother once told me. She said: a wife must trust to her husband, and follow his lead; and above all, she must not be shy with him."

"Shy?" Our eyes met, followed by another outburst of confused laughter. "Well, since that is the only piece of advice I have received on the matter, I will take it to heart."

Twenty-two

⁕

Diary, I married him.

The 29th of June, 1854, began as quietly as any other Yorkshire morning. The birds did not sing any louder than usual; the sun did not rise with a glorious burst; the sky at dawn was dim and grey, shrouding the country-side in a muted haze; there was, in short, nothing to set it apart from any other misty morning in early summer. Except that it was *very* different: it was my wedding day.

I had spent a restless night, too filled with nervous apprehension to sleep. The moment the sun crept over the horizon, I rose, and Ellen soon followed. I attempted to help arrange Ellen's hair, but my hands so trembled that she seized the brush from my grasp and finished the job herself. She then sat me down and insisted on plaiting up my tresses in a fashion she deemed "appropriate to the occasion." So long was she in accomplishing her task, that I grew impatient; at last she was satisfied. Ellen donned the new dress she had commissioned for the event: a pretty brown frock with patterned stripes and fringe around the shoulders and bodice.

My wedding dress suited me: it was plainly fashioned of

white muslin with delicate green embroidery. My white wedding bonnet—the dressmaker's design—was a more elaborate confection than I had anticipated, but very sweet: it was trimmed all over with white lace and white flowerets, and adorned with cascading ribbons and a pale band of small white flowers and green ivy leaves.

When I was thus attired in gown, bonnet, and gloves, Ellen let out a gasp. "Charlotte! You are so lovely. Look at yourself in the mirror. You have not yet taken a single peep!"

I moved to the looking-glass. At first, all my attention was drawn to my nose, and to the pronounced shade of pink that had overtaken it as a result of my slight cold. When my view widened, however, I found myself astonished. The figure reflected therein—adorned from head to toe in snowy white, brown hair elegantly swept up beneath a beribboned cap of flowers and lace—was so unlike my usual self, that it seemed to me the image of a stranger.

There was something remarkable, I thought as I gazed in wonder, in the traditional garb of a bride; it could turn even the plainest woman into something of a beauty.

"I am ready," I announced softly, "for my veil."

At five minutes to eight, Ellen and I emerged from my bedroom, with my mantle of transparent, lace-edged tulle draped over my head and face. Papa was standing just adjacent, in the doorway to his bedroom; his eyes widened, as if both startled and pleased by what he saw.

"God be with you, child."

"Thank you, papa."

Tabby and Miss Wooler were waiting below, all smiles.

"Ah! Lord, child!" cried Tabby, wiping away tears from her wrinkled cheeks. "Ye be a sight for sore eyes."

Miss Wooler, voluminously attired in pale grey silk, her equally pale ringlets splendidly arranged beneath a tasteful hat, proclaimed me "very lovely indeed." Martha joined us in the hallway with a bashful smile and handed me a bouquet of white flowers, all tied up with white ribbons, whispering, "For ye, ma'am. I know ye said not t' go t' ony fuss, but I couldn'a help mysel'. They be from my mum's garden, ma'am. Oh! Don't ye look jist like a snowdrop!"

So unaccustomed was I to such praise, that I could not help but blush. "Thank you, Martha."

"I'm t' tell ye 'at Mr. Nicholls stopped by, jist a few minutes past. Th' parson an' clerk have arrived, an' all be ready an' waitin' at th' church, whenever ye be ready."

Martha and Tabby had insisted on staying behind, to complete the preparations for the wedding breakfast. My attendants and I issued out the door, my mind in such a whirl of excited apprehension, that I scarcely knew whether the morning was warm or cold, or if the sky had yet turned from grey to blue. I crossed the lawn in a sort of daze; I had passed this way thousands of times before, but suddenly everything felt strange and unfamiliar. Was this really me, tensely gripping this bouquet of white flowers, on my way to church to become a bride?

Miss Wooler opened the garden gate. As I slipped through into the churchyard, past the first row of gravestones, a sudden, unaccountable chill came over me. I faltered for an instant and took a little breath, all the blood seemingly draining from my face.

"Charlotte? Are you all right?" asked Miss Wooler in concern.

I glanced up at the grey old house of God rising tall and serene before me, and saw a rook circling around the steeple. The sight of the wild creature winging through the sky with such free abandon seemed to me a good omen, and filled me with a new-found sense of calm. I took a deep breath and smiled. "I am fine."

At that moment Mr. Nicholls exited the church, very handsomely dressed in his best black suit. When he caught sight of me across the yard, he froze; the expression that overtook his visage was one of such pure delight and admiration that it made my heart sing. I hurried to his side.

He took my gloved hand in his; I felt his own hand trembling. "You look—you *are*—beautiful, Charlotte."

My heart began to pound; I wanted to tell him how wonderful he looked, but I was too choked up to speak; I could only return his smile as, hand in hand, we rushed inside the temple together.

As I had hoped, the church was nearly empty, the sole occupants of the seats in front being Mr. and Mrs. Grant. Reverend Sowden was waiting at the altar in his white surplice. Three other men stood nearby: the sexton, John Brown; a young pupil named John Robinson (whom, Arthur whispered, he had prevailed upon at the last moment to fetch the old parish clerk); and the clerk himself, Joseph Redman. The only person of importance not present was my father, I noted with regret; but I had little time to consider the matter, for Arthur squeezed my hand and said, in a low voice, "Are you ready?"

I nodded.

"Then here we go." He left my side and held out his arm to Ellen; she took it; he promptly escorted her down the aisle. I waited, my heart thudding so loudly in my ears that I felt certain Miss Wooler must be able to hear it as she moved into position beside me; we then traversed the length of the church together. As we approached the altar, Arthur gazed at me with a fixed and beaming countenance.

Mr. Sowden asked, "Who gives this bride away?"—Miss Wooler answered, "I do"—I took Arthur's arm, and we moved into position at the communion rails.

The ceremony, by design, was brief. Reverend Sowden opened with the customary explanation of the intent of matrimony; I tried to listen, but in my excitement, my mind would not focus. The whole proceeding was unreal to me, as if I were wrapped in the middle of a dream. It seemed I had barely drawn three breaths when Mr. Sowden began uttering that all-too-familiar speech:

"I require and charge you both, as ye will answer at the dreadful Day of Judgment when the secrets of all hearts shall be disclosed, that if either of you know any impediment why ye may not be lawfully joined together in matrimony, ye do now confess it . . ."

Upon hearing these words, I could not help but think of my own Jane Eyre, and the dire circumstances which had succeeded that proclamation at her wedding to Mr. Rochester. A side glance at Mr. Nicholls—whose twinkling eyes caught mine—insinuated that he was possessed by the same thought, and we shared a silent smile.

Thankfully, there was no meddling Mr. Mason present on that occasion to declare an impediment. All at once, I was required to slip off my glove and receive the thin gold wedding band which Mr. Nicholls slipped on my finger, to join my ring of pearls; then Mr. Sowden decried, "I now pronounce you man and wife. You may kiss the bride."

Mr. Nicholls lifted back my veil, bent his head to mine and gently placed a kiss upon my lips. I heard our friends burst into applause. My new husband grabbed my hand and rushed me out into the vestry, where we signed the church register (how strange to inscribe my name as Charlotte Nicholls!), witnessed by Ellen and Miss Wooler. Mr. Grant then opened the door and remarked, with a little laugh: "Prepare yourself: it seems your secret is out."

Indeed, as our little party issued into Church Lane, we encountered a sizeable gathering of old and humble friends and neighbours lining the passageway, who smiled, bowed, and curtseyed as we swept past. Ellen hurried ahead, mysteriously insisting that she had some service to perform. Arthur heartily shook hands with several of the well-wishers; I nodded and smiled, still enwrapped in a daze of disbelief. After all the worrying and thinking and planning—add one white dress and a few words spoken by a parson in the church—and I was married!

Papa met us at the front door of the parsonage, dressed in his Sunday best. He was so sufficiently recovered in health and spirits that he smiled as he shook every one's hands, and warmly ushered us into the dining-room for the well-laid wedding breakfast: a delicious assortment of fresh breads and cakes, cheeses, eggs, cold ham, butter, summer fruit, and a variety of jams. To my surprise, the mantelpiece was also decorated with a beautiful bouquet, and brightly-coloured flowers were scattered across the table.

"Thank you, Martha," I said. "Everything looks wonderful, and the flowers are beautiful."

"It were Miss Nussey who decorated th' table jist a few minutes past," replied Martha confidentially, "but I picked them flowers mysel'. I were up afore dawn, I was, an' raided every garden i' th' village."

Martha served the tea and coffee as we all took seats at the table. Papa became the life and soul of the party, telling such a profusion of jokes concerning the state of matrimony, that the group was kept laughing into stitches for the better part of an hour.

When we had finished our repast, Mr. Grant rose and said, "I'd like to propose a toast to my good friend Arthur and his new bride." Every one lifted their glasses. "We all know how long you have been hoping for and anticipating this day, Arthur. You deserve only the best—and the best is what you have found in Charlotte Brontë—or should I say: Charlotte Nicholls. This woman was not an easy catch—but now you have got her, I hope you'll be sensible enough not to ever let her go."

Laughter rippled through the room; then Mr. Grant continued: "Arthur is very proud of his homeland across the sea, and in his honour, I have learned an Irish blessing for the occasion, which I would now like to share. Arthur and Charlotte: May you enjoy a long life together, good health, and prosperity; and in all your comings and goings, may you ever have a kindly greeting from them you meet along the road."

"Hear, hear!" cried all assembled.

Ellen stood, and after wishing us much happiness, said: "I wish to offer an Irish toast of my own: May you both learn to love and appreciate each other for your strengths, and to forgive your weaknesses; and may you live as long as you want, and never want as long as you live."

Applause followed. Miss Wooler then stood and raised her glass. "To continue the theme, in the words of the Irish: May the joys of to-day be those of to-morrow; and may your anger set with the sun and not rise with it again."

Mr. Sowden was next: "May your troubles be less, and your blessings be more, and nothing but happiness come through your door."

I thought the toasting had surely reached its conclusion, when papa rose to his feet with a twinkle in his eyes and said: "When it comes to Irish blessings, I can outdo you grand people any day of the week. I will, however, restrict myself to my favourite passage only: To my dearest daughter and her bride-groom, my friend and esteemed colleague, Arthur Bell Nicholls, I would like to say:

May your mornings bring joy, and your evenings
  bring peace.
May your troubles grow few, and your blessings
  increase.
Your lives are very special; God has touched you in
  many ways.
May his blessings rest upon you, and fill all your
  coming days."

A hearty cheer erupted amidst much clapping of hands. Arthur now stood. "Thank you one and all for your lovely sentiments, which do my countrymen proud." His eyes beamed with affection as he looked down at me, and said with raised glass, "To my own dear Charlotte: you have made me the happiest man on earth. I vow to devote my life to making you as happy as you have made me to-day."

I stood and admitted how glad I was to be his wife, and how blessed we were to have such good and devoted friends. After the drinking and applause that followed, Arthur announced that we were obliged to be on our way, as we had a train to catch. Ellen and I hurried upstairs, where she helped me change into my new going-away dress: a long-sleeved misty mauve silk with a thin stripe, which had been simply tailored with a tucked bodice and full skirt according to my own design.

Our trunks were then loaded into the waiting cab; amidst a great clamour of hugs and kisses and good wishes, we said good-bye to our wedding guests and climbed aboard; and the vehicle rushed us off towards Keighley station.

As I settled back into our seat in the carriage en route to Keighley, my new husband's hand sought and found mine. When I looked up at him, I saw tears in his eyes.

"Arthur, what is it? What is wrong?"

His breath caught in his throat; he wiped his eyes and said, after a struggle, "Nothing. I am only happy: happy because you are sitting here beside me; happy because God has seen fit to answer my prayers; happy because we are, at long last, united as man and wife." He squeezed my hand affectionately, his eyes brimming with emotion. "I love you."

I wanted to respond in kind—to say those same three words that I knew he so wanted to hear—but somehow the words would not yet come. "Arthur," I began, but he put a finger to my lips.

"Hush. I know very well how things stand between us, Charlotte; but I know, too, that this is only the first day of the rest of our lives. It is enough that you are here."

We travelled all day by train to Wales, a location entirely new to me. Arthur, with boyish excitement, pointed out from the train window many interesting landmarks along the route, which he had traversed so many times before on his way to and from Ireland. The day was chiefly fair, with some gleams of sunshine; by the time we arrived in Conway, however, the weather had turned wet and wild. We were soon sheltered at a comfortable inn, where—fearing that Ellen might be feeling a little bereft on the occasion—I immediately scribbled a brief note to apprise her of our safe arrival.

The hotel clerk, on receiving it, said, "Very good, Mrs. Nicholls. I'll see to it that it gets posted, ma'am."

It was the first time that I had been addressed by a stranger as "Mrs. Nicholls," and the appellation came as a little shock to the senses. At supper, Arthur, concerned that my cold should not become worse, made sure that we were positioned at the table closest to the hearth. As we listened to the howl of the wind and the hammering of the rain on the roof-top and window-panes, we laughingly remarked that the sounds were pleasantly reminiscent of home.

"To-morrow, weather permitting, we'll head along the coast to Bangor," said Arthur. "I've never stayed long enough in the region to see the scenery, and I've heard it's magnificent."

"I look forward to seeing it together."

He smiled, highly pleased. Our meal of roast fowl was promptly served. The food was of high quality, the fire cheerful, the staff attentive, and our conversation amiable. I could not help but notice, however, a small change in my husband, which had begun with our arrival at the inn. Despite his attempts to disguise it, there was a return of the slight awkwardness of manner which had so marked his behaviour in the months preceding his proposal, and in the early days of our courtship.

As to the *cause* of his change in demeanour, I could not be certain—but I sensed it might be occasioned by the same fluttering of stomach and nervous apprehension which had begun to infiltrate my own sense of well-being at the very same time—brought on by thoughts of the night which lay before us: *our wedding night.*

Arthur and I had chastely kissed several times in the past three months; we had held hands; but that was all. And *that,* I knew, was about to change. I assumed that Arthur knew more about these things than I. He was a *man,* after all, and *Irish.* I was not afraid; but as I had admitted to Ellen, I was anxious, expectant, a little shy (which Ellen's mother had sternly warned against!), and more than a little excited.

We ascended the stairs after supper in silence. When we reached the door to our chamber, my heart began to pound in anticipation. What would happen next? Would Arthur lift me in his arms, and carry me across the threshold? Would he hurry me inside, slam the door, and draw me immediately into his fervent embrace?

No.

Quietly, Arthur unlocked the door. He paused. In a gentle voice, with averted gaze, he murmured: "Shall I come in with you? Or—perhaps you would prefer to prepare for bed alone?"

I hesitated, speechless with shock and disappointment. I had not anticipated this eventuality. What was the proper reply?

My husband—apparently perceiving my dismay—quickly added: "Do not distress yourself. I'll go downstairs for a few minutes, and I'll knock when I return."

No! I wanted to cry. *Do not go!* But in my shyness, I could not produce the syllables.

"Be sure to lock the door," said he, as he handed me the key; and he was gone.

With a pang of confused regret, I entered our chamber and locked the door as bidden. Mortified tears sprang into my eyes. I had been nervous, yes; I had been devoid of appetite at supper; but all that had sprung from excited anticipation. Being left to undress alone was certainly *not* the manner in which I had expected to begin my wedding night.

If I was honest with myself, I had hoped (a little) that my new husband, however gentlemanly he had been to date, would turn into something of a rake after the nuptials had been performed and privacy achieved. In my imagination, I had seen him overcome with passion as he impatiently took off—or ripped off—my clothes; or at the very least, *he would be present to* help remove said garments himself, one article at a time. Surely that is how the passionate Mr. Rochester—a man so very experienced in

unhooking bodices and unlacing corsets—would have deflow-
ered his Jane!

Clearly, however—I realised with a sigh—that was not to be
my lot. Arthur Bell Nicholls was too polite and too proper a
man to succumb to—as Ellen had put it—any ravishing.

I glanced about the room, truly taking it in for the first time.
It was simple, but clean and tasteful: a comfortable-looking
four-poster bed stood against one wall; a mahogany wardrobe
rested against the other; there was a single chair and two small
tables: one which held a ewer and a basin, the other a candle and
a small mirror. The drapes were drawn. A fire burned brightly
in the hearth, illuminating the room with its flickering glow.

From somewhere down the hall, I heard a clock strike nine. I
lit the candle, then began to undress with haste, so as not to be
caught in a state of deshabille when my husband returned. I
hung my dress in the wardrobe, stowed my undergarments in
my trunk, washed quickly, and slipped into my long-sleeved
white cotton night-shirt, which I had modestly fashioned with a
ribbon tie at the neck, and a thin strip of lace adorning both collar and cuffs.

No sooner had I tied the ribbon at my throat than I heard
approaching footsteps in the hall, and a gentle rap at the door.
Trembling, and with racing heart, I went to the door and
opened it.

Arthur glanced at me as he entered; the colour rose to his
cheeks and he nodded in greeting, averting his eyes. Quickly
and silently he removed his coat, emptied the contents of his
pockets on a table, and then sat down on the bed to remove his
shoes. Oh! I thought, irritation spiralling through me as I
watched him. Was this the most that I could expect? Was there
not an ounce of romance in this man's body? I was his wife! I
was standing before him, entirely naked beneath my night-shirt!
Yet he was halfway across the room, unlacing his shoes! Could
he not see that I was waiting, wondering, hoping—that I longed
for a touch—a kiss—an embrace—or at the very least, some
small token of *verbal* affection?

The silence was unendurable. I felt compelled to break it.

"It is—a nice room," I blurted. The moment the words left my lips, I felt the blood rush to my cheeks and I winced inwardly. Was that the best I could do? At this moment, of all moments, did I really wish to discuss the merits of our accommodations?

"It is," replied he, as he removed his socks. "I particularly requested one of the larger chambers. I wanted it to be nice for you."

"It *is* nice. Thank you," I replied, realising with renewed embarrassment that we had now, for the third time in the space of a minute, called the room "nice."

Grabbing my brush (with annoyance), I sat myself down at the little table before the looking-glass, where I methodically began to remove the pins from my hair. I had known from the start that my husband was not a poetical man; I suppose, I thought grimly, I had been naive to expect romance of any sort.

When I had unfastened the last pin, and the full weight of my long hair cascaded about my shoulders, I heard Arthur's footsteps approach. In the small mirror before me, I saw his reflection: he now stood immediately behind me, bare-chested to the waist, revealing his well-built and masculine chest, which caused a sudden and unexpected fluttering within my own.

His voice, when he spoke, was softer and deeper than I had heard in a long while. "May I have the honour of brushing your hair?"

The question took me by complete surprise. Arthur could not have known it, but the brushing of my hair had always been one of my fondest pleasures, a cherished nightly ritual that I had greatly missed in the five years since my sister Anne had passed away. "Do you—know how?" I asked in my confusion—a ridiculous question.

"I do."

I handed him the brush.

"Will you come to the bed?" said he. "It will be easier if we both can sit."

I rose; I removed my spectacles and took his offered hand;

I allowed him to lead me to the bed, where I sat down beside him, my back turned to him. He began, with measured, steady strokes, to brush my long locks. Anne, in years past, had been sweetly attentive when she rendered this service; Ellen ditto; but their ministrations—as I soon discovered—had been merely perfunctory, when compared to the tenderness and dexterity of the man who now performed it.

My head tingled as the brush bristles grazed against my scalp; again and again, I felt my husband's finger-tips gently caress the nape of my neck, as he lifted up my tresses from therein and pulled the instrument through my hair with long, luxurious strokes. Every touch of his fingers against my skin sent an unexpected, electric throb coursing through my body.

"I take it," I said breathlessly, "that you have brushed hair before?"

"When I was a boy, my mother and then my aunt used to allow me to perform this duty. I admit, I had only the most innocent and dutiful of motives then." In a low and husky tone, he added at my ear, "I cannot tell you how many hundreds of times I've played out this moment in my mind with you, Charlotte, since the day we met."

My pulse was, of a sudden, pounding so loudly in my ears that I could no longer speak. It was as if, in the smooth and rhythmic motions of finger-tips and brush, he were intimately touching every single inch of my body. My eyes fell closed; my head fell slightly back; all my tension seeped away, like a delicious, liquid glow pouring through a sieve. *This,* I remember thinking (when I could think at all) *must be what an opiate feels like.*

I felt him sweep my hair up above my neck once more; a pause; and then the welcome pressure of his lips, warm and caressing, against the side of my neck. A jolt of pleasure shivered through me; now his lips planted another kiss, and another, working their way forward towards the base of my throat.

I gasped aloud. He now reached around, untied the ribbon at my collar, and pulled open my night-shirt at my throat. His finger-tips softly caressed my exposed skin along the length of my collar-bone, first one side, then the other; now he ventured a few inches lower, beneath the fabric, to caress the upper reaches of my breasts, and the cleft that divided them. I gasped again.

Taking me by the shoulders, he turned me to face him on the bed. Now he bent his head, gently applying his lips to every spot that had been formerly touched by fingers. With each kiss against my bare flesh, I heard myself utter a little moan. My pulse pounded; my body was on fire. I had never known a sensation such as this; I had never, even in my wildest dreams, *envisioned* such a touch, or such a feeling. All at once I craved, more than anything I had ever craved in my life, the pressure of his mouth against my own; and suddenly it was there: his lips were on my lips, seeking, sharing, communing, in a long and loving kiss.

When the kiss ended, I opened my eyes to find his just an inch away, gazing at me with burning intensity and a desire that matched my own.

"Oh!" I cried, as I wrapped my arms around my husband and pulled his lips to mine once more.

I awoke with the first rays of dawn, to find myself in my sleeping lover's embrace, my cheek warmly nestled against his chest. Memory stirred; as I recalled the events of the night before, a flush of pleasure overcame me, and I could not help but smile.

"Good morning," a deep voice intoned against my hair, as strong arms wrapped around me.

"Good morning," was my whispered reply.

"Did you sleep well?"

"I did. When I slept at all."

I heard and felt his rumbling laugh. He shifted; we resettled to face each other, smiling into each other's eyes, heads cradled by the same pillow. His finger-tips traced the length of my cheek. "What are you thinking?" he inquired softly.

"I was thinking that the world seems to me a very different place this morning, than it did yesterday."

He kissed me, and smiled.

"Arthur," I said shyly.

"Yes, my love?"

"Last night, was I—did I—?" I could not bring myself to finish the thought.

He blushed. "You were lovely. You *are* lovely. In any case, I believe there is no right or wrong in this kind of thing."

"You believe—?"

He studied me across the pillow. "I can see there's something you wish to ask me. Go ahead, wife. Out with it."

I felt the blood rush to my cheeks now. "Well, I suppose I was wondering—did you ever—was there ever—"

"There has only been one other woman in my life, in the way that you mean—or for that matter, in any way at all. It was a long time ago, and of course, things never progressed anywhere near this far. Is that what you wished to know?"

I nodded. A little thrill ran through me. I was gratified to think that I had been Arthur's first, just as he had been mine. "May I inquire as to who she was?"

He kissed me, a bemused twinkle in his eyes. "Do you really wish to discuss *that*—now?"

"I am only curious."

His hand ran up and down the length of my arm, causing my flesh to tingle. "She was a school-teacher's daughter. I was seventeen years old. For six months, I lost my head and my heart—until she summarily broke it, by running off with a peddler."

"A peddler?"

"He sold household supplies, as I recall, off the back of a cart. Whether it was the pots and pans that attracted her, or the promise of travel and adventure, I never knew; but one day I looked up and she was gone."

There was such good humour in his eyes as he spoke, that I could not hold back a smile. "Did you love her?"

"I thought I did at the time. But what does any one know at seventeen? It certainly made me more cautious, from that day forward, about to whom I was willing to give my heart." He caught my hand in his, brought it up to his lips, and kissed it. "When I look back at the episode now, I can only cringe, realising how unsuited we were to one another. I thank my lucky stars that she broke it off; otherwise I never would have left Banagher, or gone to university, or on to England."

"I am grateful, too," said I, adding in wonder: "Was she really the only one, Arthur, in all these years?"

"She was."

"And since you came to Haworth—"

He pulled me to him, and as our bodies locked together in his warm embrace, I realised that he wanted me again. "Since the day we met," said he, his tone deep and husky as his gaze bore into mine, "I've had eyes for no other woman but you, my love." Then his mouth closed on mine, and all conversation ceased.

Later that morning, we travelled along the coast of northern Wales to Bangor, where we stayed four nights. Although the weather was not entirely favourable, we were determined to make the most of the opportunity; and, hiring a gig and driver, we contrived to see some magnificent scenery. One drive indeed from Llanberis to Beddgelert, which followed a steep-sided river valley and passed lakes and dramatic waterfalls, surpassed anything I remember of the English lakes. I bemoaned the fact that, owing to the chill air and constant drizzle (or threat of it), Arthur would not consider driving out in an open carriage.

"You're still fighting off a cold," said he, "and I'll not take the chance of making it worse, by exposing you to inclement weather."

After the first two hours trapped in the carriage, however, we were both so beset by the urge to clamber off on foot along the glorious mountain sides and dales, that we frequently implored the driver to stop and let us out. So it was that, as the days unfolded, we took brief, exhilarating rambles in the countryside, alternating with periods of awed observation through the windows of the coach. Admittedly, even these quiet moments held their own charms, for it was very pleasant indeed to sit beside my new husband, whose hand always eagerly sought my own.

Every evening we would return to the inn chilled but invigorated, where we would warm ourselves by the fire over a quiet supper, and recapitulate with enthusiasm all that we had seen and experienced. At night, when we adjourned to our chamber, and I succumbed readily and willingly to my husband's embrace, I found myself enveloped in a cocoon of happiness and pleasure such as I had never known. Each night drew us closer; we came to laugh about that first night, when Arthur had vanished at the top of the stairs and left me to undress alone. Now, he insisted on performing the most intimate of those ministrations himself.

Modesty prevents me from writing more; I can only say that, my husband proved to be more nimble and expedient at unlacing a corset than any one could rightfully expect from a man of God; and no husband could ever have been more tender, more sensitive, or more devoted to his wife than mine.

Alas! On the heels of all this happiness, an event occurred which wreaked havoc in the tender bond built during that first week of growing intimacy, and which threatened to tear a permanent rent in the very fabric of my marriage itself.

Twenty-three

W̲e went to Ireland.

Our sojourn in Wales had been but an hors d'oeuvre preceding the primary objective of the honeymoon trip. Arthur was eager to take me to his native country: to share with me his favourite haunts, to introduce me to his family, and to the home where he was raised. He had as yet ventured very little information on these subjects, however. When I had inquired again about his family and their residence, he had shrugged and looked away, replying quietly, "They're good Irish country-folk, well-meaning and kind of heart. Aunt Bell and my unmarried cousins still live in the same house where I grew up. I love them all dearly; but I'd rather you meet them and judge for yourself."

I had determined, at that moment, that no matter how poor his relations' accommodations might be—or how rough of character they were—I would admire and love them all for his sake.

On Tuesday 4 July, we crossed Anglesey by rail to Holyhead, where (thankfully) the weather was calm, and the passage good. I had, however, never possessed a sea-farer's stomach. Arthur tried to distract me during the first part of the voyage with a long stroll about the deck. As we inhaled the bracing sea-air, we made whispered observations about the various passengers on board.

"They look very happy," observed I of a young couple walking hand in hand, and engaged tête-à-tête in a quiet conversation.

"Perhaps they're also newly-weds," said Arthur, smiling as he took my hand.

"Who is that gentleman?" I whispered, nodding towards a fat man seated on a campstool, sheltered from the breeze.

"A barrister, no doubt. I do hope, for his sake, that the stool's of a sturdy make."

We shared a quiet laugh. I spotted another twosome strolling towards us: a bearded gentleman in his early forties, whose well-cut coat and hat declared him to be a man of wealth and status, and a sad-eyed, pretty young woman half his age (his daughter, I presumed), wearing a velvet pelisse over an exquisite dress of rose-coloured silk; she carried a matching parasol and wore a truly fabulous hat, beneath which spilled a profusion of light brown curls.

"If not for her elegant attire, does she not—in face and figure—remind you of my sister Anne?" I said.

"She does, a bit."

The girl, on catching my eye, smiled briefly and then averted her gaze. "I wonder why she looks so sad?" I mused. Before my husband could reply, the bell rang announcing luncheon. I knew Arthur must be hungry, and he did not suffer from the same malaise as I. "Arthur: I am in no mood to eat, but please go on without me."

"Are you sure? I hate to leave you alone. What'll you do?"

"I shall take another turn about the deck. If I feel very unwell, I shall go down into the cabin and lie down. If not, you will find me at the rail—just there."

"Well; if you're certain you don't mind," responded Arthur, and, making sure that I was well wrapped up and in no danger of taking a chill, he left to seek his mid-day meal.

I spent the interval as promised, continuing my tour of the ship's deck. Eventually, I made my way back to my chosen spot at the rail to wait for Arthur's return. For some minutes I stood quite still, delighting in the feel of the cool sea-breeze against my cheeks, and drinking in the view of the sparkling, deep blue waves, the sea-birds on their crests, and the pale, beclouded sky overhanging all. As I stared at the horizon, I thought I glimpsed a far-off coast beginning to emerge through the dense white haze.

"Is that Ireland?" asked a feminine voice behind me.

I broke from my reverie, as the young, richly-dressed woman in rose-coloured silk, who I had earlier observed, took her place at the rail beside me. I smiled at her question; based on the ship's itinerary and course, what other expanse of land could that be in the distance before us? "Yes, it is Ireland. Is this your first crossing, too?"

She nodded. "How I wish the ship would turn around, and I could return home!" A look of such pervasive sadness crossed her pretty face, that my heart went out to her.

"Why are you going to Ireland?"

"To visit family I have never seen. Oh! My heart is breaking as I speak." Tears sprang into her eyes. "I am in love, you see. My young man is the first son of a baronet and very wealthy— but not wealthy *enough* for my father. Papa says I *must* marry a duke or earl—he will accept nothing less—and to keep us apart, he is taking me to Ireland for six months, where he hopes I will 'come to my senses.' Six months! That is half a year! How papa can imagine that such a separation will dull my love for Edward, I cannot imagine!"

"Perhaps things may yet turn out all right, if you are patient."

"What good will patience do? I shall die if I cannot marry Edward—but papa has forbidden me from ever seeing him again."

"If you and your lover prove as steadfast in your affections six months from now as you are to-day, and if your young man has an opportunity to prove himself worthy, perhaps your father will have a change of heart."

"He will never change his mind."

"You cannot be certain of that. I have some experience in this. I once found myself in a situation similar to yours."

"Did you?"

"Yes. My father violently disapproved of my suitor, and forbade the match for more than a year. In time, however, he came to see that he was wrong—and we are now married."

"Are you truly?" The young lady dabbed at her eyes with her handkerchief. "The tall gentleman I saw you with before—is he your husband?"

"Yes."

"He looked very nice."

"He is indeed."

"I suppose you have been married for many years, now?"

"Less than a week, in fact. We are on our honeymoon."

"Your *honeymoon*? What? At your age? Well, who would have thought! Are you madly, deeply in love?"

The question caught me off guard; I blushed. What business was it of hers, I thought, to ask such a personal question? At the same time, I could not help but ask myself: what *did* I feel for my new husband? Mentally, I answered: I felt an overwhelming affection, admiration, and gratitude, that had blossomed with our new-found intimacy, and had grown with each passing day into something very sweet and deeply felt. Was that love? Oh! I realised with a sudden rush of joy—yes, yes it was! This tender feeling was far more solid, more sincere and true than the all-consuming, restless passion I had once equated with the emotion. This was indeed *love*! I *did* love my husband! I loved him!

Before I could reply, the young woman said, "How long you are in answering! I did not mean to make you so uncomfortable. Your husband—from his dress, I suppose he is a vicar?"

"He is a curate."

"Only a curate? He looks far too old to be a curate."

I bristled. "He is not so very old."

"I cannot even *imagine* marrying a curate. He must be very poor." She touched my arm with a sympathetic look. "I understand now. No wonder you did not eagerly proclaim your love for him. You must have felt rather desperate at your age to marry *any* man—but to have no choice but to marry a *poor curate*—I am *so sorry*. That would be a big step down in the world for any one."

I stared at her, shocked by her remark, struggling to remind myself that the young, beautiful, and rich were rarely tactful. "Certainly my future with him will not be brilliant," I replied steadily, "but I trust that—"

The young lady's eyes suddenly widened in dismay as she looked up, her attention caught by something over my right shoulder.

I whirled around—only to find Arthur standing just a few feet behind us. From the look of deep hurt and mortification on his countenance, I realised that he had overheard, at the very least, the last part of our conversation. "Arthur!" I began; but without a word, he turned and strode deliberately away.

I felt the colour drain from my face, as first a chill, and then the heat of shame spread through me. "Excuse me," I said to the young lady, and I rushed after my husband. His stride far exceeded mine, however, and it was some minutes before I caught up with him, on the opposite side of the ship, where he stood at the rail gazing sadly out to sea. "Arthur, I am so sorry. Whatever you heard—"

"Charlotte. I am no fool. I have known you too long and too well to retain any illusions. I know you do not love me."

"Arthur!"

"I read *Villette*. I remember what your brother and sister said. I know to whom your heart belongs—and always will belong."

I gasped, alarmed and pained to think that my husband harboured this misconception. "No—wait—"

"I understand the kind of man you dreamt of marrying, Charlotte, and how ill that dream compares with the reality.

That girl was right: you married beneath you. I suppose you did feel desperate. God knows you took long enough to make up your mind. There is little I can say or do about any of that now, except to hope that one day you might come to feel differently; but what hurts—what really rankles—is that you'd see fit to discuss those complaints with a complete stranger."

My cheeks burned crimson. "I was not complaining, Arthur. I have no complaints. That young lady was upset about her own situation, and I only said—"

"You *said* your 'future with me will not be brilliant'—and right you are about that."

"It was wrong of me! I should not have said it, or thought it. I am so sorry. I never meant to hurt you. But Arthur—"

He held up a hand to silence me. "Enough. Let us not spoil the voyage. We need say no more about it." The joyous tone which had formerly marked all his speech was gone; the warm, affectionate spark had fled from his eyes, leaving behind a hollow, resigned expression, that tore into my heart like a knife. "I'll take a walk now on my own, if you don't mind." He turned and strode away.

Oh! What had I done? When that young woman said those awful things, why had I not firmly and immediately rushed to my husband's defence? With a few, ill-chosen words, I had just destroyed every ounce of goodwill and affection that my husband and I had built together over the previous weeks and months. How could I ever repair the damage that I had inflicted?

I spent the last part of the crossing in our berth below, feeling increasingly ill—whether sea-sickness or anxiety was the greater cause, I could not tell. Arthur did not join me. The ship docked at Kingstown just before midnight. As we gathered on deck, the cold, damp air and black scowl of the night only served to compound my misery. The lights of the foreign harbour appeared not as sparkling jewels, but like unnumbered threatening eyes. A stiff formality now existed between Arthur and me—and I had no one to blame but myself.

* * *

We disembarked to find Arthur's brother Alan awaiting us. The two men shouted out with joy at the sight of each other and embraced warmly. Alan Nicholls was nearly three years older than Arthur and greatly resembled him, with the same dark hair, the same fine twinkling eyes, and the same strong build.

"Alan: may I present my wife, Charlotte," said Arthur, nudging me forward gently, his hand at my back. His features were a perfect mask, giving no outward sign of the inner turmoil from which I knew he suffered. Indeed, no one observing the ensuing dialogue could have an inkling that a disagreement of major proportions had occurred between us only a few hours before.

"Well, well! So this is your dear Charlotte! At last we meet," cried Alan, as he turned to look me over with a warm, appraising smile. His deep voice and lively Irish accent so closely resembled my husband's, that had I closed my eyes, I might not have been able to discern the identity of the speaker. "Arthur's been raving about you so long and so loudly for so many years, we were beginning to wonder if you could be quite real. I'm relieved to see that you are." With that he took my hand in his and kissed it, then boldly leaned forward and planted a firm kiss on my cheek. "Welcome to the family, sister."

"Thank you," said I, returning his warm smile.

After our luggage was located and loaded into a cab, we rumbled off across the cobble stones, on our way into Dublin.

"I've taken the next two weeks as a holiday," said Alan. I knew that he had left Trinity College early without matriculating, and was now a shipping agent who managed the Grand Canal from Dublin to Banagher. To my delight, I found him to be a sagacious, well-informed, and courteous man. "There's a league of family members waiting to meet you at Banagher, Charlotte—eager to make the acquaintance of the woman who stole our Arthur's heart."

"I look forward to meeting them."

"That's a few days off still," interjected Arthur. "I'm hoping to show Charlotte around Dublin first."

"Of course," said Alan. "Our home is your home, and I'll be happy to escort you any place you like."

Alan's small, two-storey house exceeded my expectations; although modest, it was comfortable and on a very nice street. As the hour was so late, his family was all asleep, and we retired the moment we arrived. When I crawled into bed beside Arthur, I apologised again for what had happened on the ship and made another attempt to explain—and to express my feelings—but he only turned his back to me and went to sleep. I was so heart-sick that I slept fitfully. Whether it was due to the stress and excitement of the previous few days, the chill air of the sea voyage, or my depression of spirits, I could not say—perhaps it was a combination of all these things—but I awoke the next morning to find my cold much worse, and myself possessed of a deep cough. Worse yet, the bed beside me was cold and empty.

I issued downstairs to find Arthur engrossed in happy conversation with his brother in the parlour, before breakfast. I put a smile on my face, determined not to let our personal troubles infect our visit. I was immediately introduced to Alan's family. His wife, an attractive and gracious woman, bade me welcome, and voiced her regret that she could not join us on our sightseeing excursion; she thought it best that she stay home with their two lively children. Every one expressed concern about my health, but I assured them that I would be equal to their plans for the day.

"I just learned that two of my cousins will be joining us," said Arthur.

He had no sooner spoken when the first of said cousins—Joseph Bell, handsome, dark-haired, and twenty-three years old—bounded in the front door and presented himself with a beguiling smile and a thick Irish brogue. "Top of the mornin' to you, one and all. Arthur! How are you, old man?"

The cousins warmly embraced; it was a unique pleasure for me to witness such a display of physical affection between men. "Charlotte," said Arthur, as both men turned to me, "may I present my cousin Joseph."

"Welcome, cousin Charlotte," said Joseph, bowing low before me with a grand flourish. "It is both an honour and a pleasure to meet you."

"And you, sir," I replied, impressed by his refined English manners.

"Your reputation precedes you," continued Joseph with enthusiasm. "I loved *Jane Eyre*. A truly remarkable book."

"Thank you," returned I, with a little blush, "but it is really just a simple tale."

"A simple tale?" said he to Arthur, with a laugh. "I see your wife is modest as well as brilliant. You have got yourself quite a catch, cousin." (Back to me now, *sotto voce*:) "And *you*, Mrs. Nicholls, have done very well for yourself, besides. You'll never find a better man than my cousin Arthur—even if he is a bit too stern and crotchety at times."

"Joseph is the most brilliant student at Trinity College," explained Arthur proudly. "Alan tells me he just gained three premiums as prizes."[68]

"That should tell you something about the quality of the competition," added Joseph with another laugh.

Having been led by papa and Ellen to believe that Arthur's family were illiterate, uneducated, wild Irish barbarians who lived in squalor, and by Arthur himself to expect only "country-folk," I had never expected to find a Trinity student among them—much less one so charming and highly honoured. I barely had time to assimilate this astonishing new personage, when another equally disarming cousin appeared at the foot of the stairs and entered the room. She was twenty-four years old, and just as handsome and well-mannered as her younger brother; a true Celt in appearance, with her dark curly hair simply but fashionably arranged.

"You must be Charlotte," exclaimed she in a sweet but lively voice, as she stopped before me and curtseyed. "I'm Mary

---

[68] Prestigious undergraduate awards given annually to select scholars of superior merit.

Anna." She walked with a slight limp, which, I learned, was the result of a riding accident as a child; but as she and every one else seemed completely unconscious of it—and it in no way hampered her energy or her ability to get around—I soon forgot all about it.

Mary Anna darted an adoring look at Arthur, then sat beside me on the sofa and took one of my hands in hers. "Arthur has been my favourite cousin ever since I was a little girl. When he wrote to say he was getting married and bringing over his bride, I said, 'I can't wait two entire days for them to reach Banagher! I must go to Dublin myself!' I wanted a chance to know you before the rest of the clan, for there are so many Bells, I fear you'll become sick to death of us in no time and long to escape."

"I am certain that will not happen," said I with a smile, "but I am very glad you came, Mary Anna, and grateful for some female company. From what I see, there are entirely too many men on this honeymoon tour."

Every one laughed at that. This feeling of goodwill continued for the rest of the day—indeed, for the next two days—during which time our little party of five rode over a great part of the city, visiting many of the main sites. Arthur's brother and cousins, on further acquaintance, proved themselves to be so kind, courteous, well learned, and intelligent, that I felt immediately welcome and at home.

Arthur continued to be as thoughtful and solicitous of my needs as always, insisting that we not see too much lest I become overtired and further aggravate my cold; yet, there was an unspoken distance between us—an aloofness on his part of which, I believe, only I was aware—and a complete withdrawal from physical intimacy of any kind, which occasioned me much pain. Outwardly, he kept up an enthusiastic appearance, and seemed keen to share with me his old haunts at the university he'd attended.

I was particularly impressed by the ornate Venetian Gothic Museum, and the Trinity College library—a noble building in the classical style. As we left, I said wistfully, "If only these hallowed halls of learning could be opened to womankind. There is so much to learn. How thrilling it would be, to attend such a university!"

"Had you been allowed to go to university, Charlotte," said Arthur, as he held out his arm to me, "I believe you could have succeeded in any profession you liked. You are more literate, talented, and clever in your sleep than most men are in their best waking hour, and you have already achieved more than most men achieve in a lifetime."

There was a hint of his old sparkle and admiration as he spoke, and for a moment my heart leapt with hope. Perhaps, I thought, his wounded pride was recovering, and we could regain the closeness and warm affection we had shared before that terrible moment on board ship. But as I thanked him with quiet gratitude, he glanced away, his smile vanished, and his hard-edged mask fell back in place.

On Friday, the 7th of July, we said good-bye to Mrs. Alan Nicholls and the children, and Alan escorted the rest of our party by rail to the Bell family home at Banagher. Fatigue, excitement, and my cold had by this time taken their toll; I was not feeling at all well, and my cough had become very bad.

At Birr Station (I found Birr to be a charming old market town and former garrison, dating, I was told, to the 1620s) we were met by a coach, which I assumed had been hired for the occasion. This notion was dispelled when Arthur proudly introduced me to the driver, an elderly man who had been in the employ of the Bell family for more than thirty years, and as such had known Arthur since he was a boy. The old man (for whom Arthur held an undisguised and mutual respect and affection) graciously bowed and doffed his hat, his crinkly face lighting up with a smile. "Welcome, ma'am. 'Tis a great honour to meet our dear Arthur's wife."

I was surprised indeed to discover that the Bells had kept a carriage and driver for more than thirty years—a luxury my family had never been able to afford—but perhaps, I thought, such things were less expensive in Ireland than they were in England. We drove seven miles through idyllic, verdant countryside, arriving in late afternoon at Banagher, King's County's most westerly town, beautifully situated on the Shannon River.

"My goodness!" I exclaimed, as our carriage rumbled up the single, inclined street from the Shannon Bridge to the church, passing closely packed, eighteenth-century stone houses on either side. "This village is very much like Haworth."

"Indeed," replied Arthur. "I have often made the comparison. Perhaps that is why I felt so instantly at home at Haworth when I first moved there."

We had proceeded a quarter mile up the high road past the church, through a lovely wooded area, when Mary Anna said, "A few minutes more, and you will be able to see Cuba House."

"Cuba House?" said I. "What is that?"

"Why—our family home," responded Mary Anna.

"What an unusual name. How did it come to be called Cuba House?"

"A local man, George Fraser, was governor of Cuba more than a hundred years ago," explained Alan, "and made his fortune on that island, growing sugar. He came back and built the house. Now the Avenue and the Royal School are also called Cuba, in his honour."

"The Royal School?" I repeated. "What is that?"

"The school was founded by Royal Charter in 1638 by Charles I," replied Joseph. "Our father was headmaster for many years, and since he died my brother James has been filling his shoes. Of course it will be nice and quiet now, with all the students gone on holiday." On seeing my startled expression, he added, "But surely Arthur has told you all this?"

I glanced at Arthur, who was looking out the window, a gentle blush crossing his countenance. "No. Arthur told me your father was a clergyman and a school-teacher. I assumed he had taught at a small local school, not a prestigious one founded by Royal decree—and I had no idea he had been headmaster."

Joseph laughed, and punched Arthur playfully in the arm. "Holding out on your own wife, were you, cousin? Or were you just being modest?"

"Uncle Bell *was* a clergyman and a teacher, as well as a head-master," insisted Arthur quietly.

"He also held a Doctor of Laws from Glasgow University," added Alan. "He was quite a brilliant man."

"Here we are now," announced Mary Anna.

The carriage halted before a pair of imposing iron gates; the gates were opened; we drove in; with astonishment, I gained my first glimpse of the Bells' home.

I had expected a humble cottage or "country house," as Arthur had so casually referred to it. Instead, the edifice before me—set back from the high road by a wide, grassy field, surrounded by finely wooded grounds, and approached by a grand avenue of lime trees—was the epitome of a gentleman's country-seat. The house itself was immense and built of brick and stone, with a mansard roof, pedimented portals, and a balustrade terrace. A row of lower, brick-and-stone school buildings fanned out from behind it and to the right side.

"Oh!" I cried, unable to contain my amazement and delight. "It is so large, and so beautiful! Arthur: is this truly your home?"

"It is not *mine*," replied Arthur, but I could see that he was beaming with pride. "It is only where I grew up."

"It is not really any of ours," admitted Joseph. "The house is the headmaster's lodgings. We have been fortunate enough to live here for many decades, first because of my father's tenure, and now because of our brother James."

"My family occupies Haworth parsonage under similar circumstances," said I, "so I fully understand; but oh! It is nothing like this. What a magnificent home!"

"The Bells also own other, smaller houses," interjected Alan. "My uncle bought up a great deal of land in the surrounding area, which they still let and farm."

"Papa was twelve years older than mama," added Mary Anna. "People used to tease her that she married an old man for his money, but it was love—true love. She worshipped him until the day he died."

As we pulled up before the entrance and descended from the coach, a great many people—family and servants alike, as well as four highly spirited dogs of various shapes and sizes—spilled out from the front door of the great house into the drive. Arthur and I were welcomed and introductions were made amidst much exclaiming, hugging, and kissing.

Alan Bell, the eldest son at thirty, was a clergyman; James Bell, twenty-eight, was headmaster of the school; and Arthur Bell, twenty-six, hoped to become a surgeon; all were obviously college-educated, and appeared to be true gentlemen by nature and cultivation. Even the youngest son, William, who was just fifteen, was a charming lad who would surely follow in his brothers' footsteps. The two married daughters, I was given to understand, could not join us; but Harriette Lucinda Bell, aged twenty, was present—a very pretty girl with manners as amiable and pleasing as those of her sister Mary Anna. So many new people were presented to me at the same time that I was quite overwhelmed, but I sensed at once that Arthur's cousins were all intelligent, kind, and highly-cultured people, and that I was going to like them very much.

Reigning over this happy, vivacious brood was Mrs. Harriette Bell, Dr. Bell's widow, and the aunt and "adoptive mother" of Arthur and Alan Nicholls.

"You cannot imagine how much I have looked forward to this moment," said Mrs. Bell, as she graciously held out her hands to me. A strikingly handsome woman with stylishly coiffed dark hair, and attired in a deep blue silk dress in the latest fashion, she carried herself with the ease and grace of an English matron: all kindness and good-natured refinement. Her accent, surprisingly, also sounded more English than Irish. "I have been worrying the servants for days, hoping to arrange everything just so for your arrival. We have put you in the green room, Arthur, on the ground floor—it has a very fine fire-place, and I think the best view. I hope you will find it to your liking."

"It will suit us perfectly. Thank you, aunt," said Arthur, kissing her, as we issued inside. The large, high-ceilinged entry way was paved in marble; I could see into the adjoining dining-room, which was lofty and spacious. In short order, an elegant English tea was served in the grand drawing-room, which was panelled in oak, and handsomely and commodiously furnished. Every one sat down on the assortment of chairs and sofas and began eating, drinking, and chatting gaily.

As I sipped my tea, gazing at the splendid house and all the new faces about me, everything—and every one—so exceeded even my wildest imaginations, that it was almost too much to take in. I had heard so much about Irish negligence, yet I had seen none of it since I arrived in that country; and all I saw before me was the highest order of English refinement and repose.

As I listened, I learned bits and pieces of information about the Bells: that Mrs. Bell and her daughters all played the piano and were avid needlewomen and keen gardeners; that every one in the family read widely; and that all passionately loved animals.

"We must have had at least thirty dogs in this household over the years," said Mrs. Bell as she set down her tea-cup, "but far and away, the best was my dear little Fairy." I saw every one's eyes roll as Mrs. Bell continued wistfully, "Just a wee ball of fluff he was, entirely devoted to me—and so happy to see me when I returned from my honeymoon, that—"

"—the poor little thing died of absolute joy," finished the entire assembly *en masse*, followed by a collective laugh.

"If you had known my little Fairy," insisted Mrs. Bell with dignity, "you would not laugh."

A round of dialogue ensued in which every one, with affection and enthusiasm, described the attributes of their favourite pet. When it was my turn, I talked about our own dear Flossy. Arthur maintained that he had been most fond of a large brown dog of uncertain breed that he had found when he was ten years old, and had been allowed to keep as his very own. All of this was fascinating to me, and illuminated the animal-loving side to my husband that I had always admired.

"How you did love that ugly hound, Arthur," observed James with a laugh, "but in truth, you were equally as fond of the wild animals that roamed through our fields." Turning to me, James added, "Once, when Arthur was about twelve or thirteen, father gave orders to have a grove of trees lopped at the side of the house. Arthur put up such a fuss, insisting that the trees afforded shelter to the squirrels, that father abandoned his plan."

A spate of good-natured teasing followed, as Arthur's cousins derided his devotion to the protection of large, furry rodents. I smiled in awe and wonder as I looked across the room at Arthur, who appeared more relaxed and happy than I had ever seen him. A rush of affection overwhelmed me; how little, I suddenly realised, had I known about my husband when I married him! How much better did I understand him now—now that I was able to see him interact with those he loved, and those who loved him, in the home where he was raised. He appeared to me in a new light here in his own country. He was clearly a great favourite with his family, and truly in his element in this grand place.

I realised, too, with a stab of sudden shame, how wrong papa—and I, by extension—had been about Arthur. Papa had, for so long, flatly denounced the very idea of a union with Mr. Nicholls, insisting that it would be a degradation, that he was nothing but a poor curate from a "lowly family." How quickly papa would change his tune, could he but see the splendid home and family from which that worthy curate sprang! The Brontës, by comparison—and the Bruntys before them—were of so much humbler stock than the Bells, that it was ludicrous even to compare them.

Arthur had known all this, I realised; yet he had said nothing. Even on board ship, when he had overheard that young woman's cruel statement that I was marrying beneath me, and my own inadequate and poorly worded reply, he had not attempted to acquaint me with the truth. Joseph had called him modest; but I saw now that it was more than that. Arthur had hoped to be judged for himself, not based on where he came from, or what his relatives possessed.

Oh! How desperately I wished that I could be alone with my husband, to tell him how I felt: how thankful I was to God, for blessing me with the affectionate devotion of such an honourable, unboastful man; how much I truly loved him; and that I only hoped I could endeavour to deserve him.

As I stood and was about to go to him, however, I suddenly felt faint; I dropped back into my chair; it was all I could do not to topple to the floor, and I was then seized by a long, wracking cough.

"Dear me, you are not at all well, Charlotte!" cried Mrs. Bell. "I have been concerned about that cough ever since you arrived. Arthur! Do not tell me you have been dragging this poor woman all over Wales and Dublin in this condition?"

"My cold only took hold in the past day or two," I said quickly. "Arthur has been watching over me very diligently, and insisted that I rest many times when I would have preferred to push on myself."

"Well! You look all in," declared Mrs. Bell, crossing to me and offering her arm. "We must get you right to bed without delay, and get some nice hot soup in you. Maureen!"

A rosy-cheeked servant appeared. "Yes, ma'am?"

"Tell cook to heat up some of that broth she made, and bring it to our guest in the green room. And tell Agnes she is wanted."

"Yes, ma'am," replied the servant as she dashed off.

Before I knew it, I had been undressed by the aforementioned Agnes, a capable-looking servant of about fifty years of age, and I was soon ensconced in a large, soft bed, in a room three times the size of our parlour at the parsonage. A turf-fire burned brightly in the wide old chimney, adding a measure of cheer to the otherwise ancient but comfortable surroundings. The rosy-cheeked servant brought me hot soup on a tray, and withdrew.

I had taken three spoonfuls when Arthur entered and crossed

to my bed uncertainly, asking in a worried tone if there was anything he might do.

I gazed up at him, my pounding heart full of all that I wished to say; but just as I opened my mouth to speak, Mrs. Bell strode in and said deliberately: "Arthur, you may leave your bride to me." Sitting down on a tapestry-covered chair at the side of the bed, she proceeded to pour something from a medicine bottle onto a spoon. "I have tended hundreds of colds in this household, and I've never lost a patient yet. A sickbed is no place for a new husband. Go visit with your cousins."

Arthur said reluctantly, "If you insist, aunt." He bent over me, planting a gentle kiss on my forehead. "I am so sorry you are ill, Charlotte, but I promise you are in good hands. There's no finer nurse in King's County, and that's a fact."

"Arthur," I began, reaching out to take his hand, but I was stopped by another cough.

"Hush now. Get some rest, my dear, and feel better," said he, as he moved to the door.

I know not what medicine Mrs. Bell gave me, but after I finished my broth, I fell instantly asleep, slept straight through dinner, and remained insensible until the next morning.

Twenty-four

I awoke to find sunshine peeking around the edge of the curtains. The sunken pillow and tousled sheets and counterpane beside me gave evidence that my husband had indeed shared my bed, and then left it again without disturbing me. Presently, there came a gentle knock at the door.

"Come in," said I, hoping it was Arthur; but it was Agnes, the grizzled servant who had helped me to bed the night before.

"Ah! Good. Ye're up," said Agnes, entering with a tray. She was short and stout, with grey hair tucked up neatly under her cap, a pleasant, lined face, and a thick local accent. "Th' mistress bade me bring ye breakfast." She set down the tray and flung open the curtains. Sunlight streamed in through the tall windows, which offered a lovely view of the lush green grounds. "I hope ye slept well, Mrs. Nicholls?"

"I did, thank you, Agnes."

"An' how are ye feelin' this mornin'?"

"A bit better," I replied, but then a deep cough overtook me.

"Well, ye've got a wee bit more colour i' yer cheeks this mornin', I see, from what ye had when ye first arrived. That's a good sign, it is. Me mistress allus says, there be nothin' like a nice long sleep an' a day o' rest in bed t' cure what ails ye, an' I couldna agree more. I've brought ye some porridge an' tea, an' a bit of toast. Do ye feel up t' eatin' a little somethin'?"

"I will have a few bites, thank you. Agnes: have you seen my husband?"

"Our Arthur? Aye, that I have!" said Agnes in a fond tone, as she rearranged the pillows about me and helped me to sit up in bed. "He was up early, he was, an' hoverin' about, worried t' death about ye. Yer husband is a good man, if I do say so myself, Mrs. Nicholls. I've known him since th' first day he come here—such a sweet little lad he was—allus lookin' for ways t' be of help t' others, allus wantin' t' be and do good. From that day t' this, I've never heard him speak a complaint, nor a word against anybody, nor a word that wasn't th' God's honest truth, an' ye don't often find that i' a boy—or a man. I tell ye, ma'am, ye're a most fortunate person, for that ye've got one o' th' best gentlemen i' th' country."

Agnes spoke these praises with such deep affection and respect, that my heart swelled and tears sprang into my eyes. Before I could utter a comment, however, the good servant positioned my tray on my lap, and went on:

"Ah! But ye asked about Arthur's whereabouts, didn't ye? An' me, prattlin' on! Well, ma'am, he was hoverin' about, as I said, an' gettin' on th' mistress's nerves, so she said t' him, she says, 'Arthur, there's no way on God's green earth that that dear wife of your'n is leavin' her sickbed to-day. A full day's rest is what she needs, an' some proper nursin'. Ye go on,' she says. After much grumblin' and complainin', she finally convinced him t' go out for a picnic on th' river wi' his cousins an' their friends."

"Oh! He is gone? Will he be away long, do you think?"

"Well, ma'am, these young folk be so fond o' goin' out on th' Shannon—every one has got a boat, or can hire or borrow one now—an' th' weather bein' so fine this time of year—I shouldna think they'd be back afore supper."

I thanked her, greatly disappointed. Agnes added more turf to the fire, and left the room.

I ate my breakfast in silence, with little appetite. Not long after the tray was removed, Mrs. Bell came in to see me. All day long, that dear lady nursed me with kindness and skill, interspersed with periods of rest so that I might recoup my strength. Later, when I awoke from my nap, she drew up a chair to my bedside with her needlework, and settled in for a chat.

"I promised Arthur I would keep an eye on you and make sure you got well. You are dear to me already, you know, because you are our Arthur's wife; and of course, I have a soft spot in my heart for any one English. I may have been born in Dublin, but I went to school in London."

"So that explains it: you do seem—and sound—very English to me."

"I did not stay in your country long, truth be told, and I was a very little girl at the time; but it made a lasting impression on me. My father, you see, decided it would be an advantage for me to be educated at an English school like a true lady; so he took me there with a view to leaving me. After only three weeks, he returned to bring me home, having found life quite insupportable without me. In those three weeks, however, I learned high English, I saw London illuminated after Wellington's victory at the Battle of Waterloo—"

"After Wellington's victory? How thrilling!"

"And I met the Queen."

"The Queen?"

"She called at the school to see a child in whom she was interested, and was told, 'We have a little Irish girl here.' Evidently I was considered something of a curiosity, and was brought downstairs to be presented. She was a little old thing—funny, is it not—her name was also Charlotte."

I laughed in delight, and wondered wistfully: is this what it would have been like to have a mother? I could not remember the last time some one tended at my sickbed. It was a strange and wonderful feeling, as if I were a little child again.

Mrs. Bell and I talked amiably all afternoon. She asked me about my own childhood, and then told me about Arthur's. "He and his brother fit right in with the family, and Arthur took to school like a duck takes to water: a fine student, always vying for top honours in his classes, and the same when he went to university. He was a teacher for a while, you know, and a more caring and dedicated teacher the world has never seen. I could not have been prouder than when he announced his intention of entering the clergy. Alan Nicholls is a good man, too. I love all my children, Charlotte, and I know your Arthur and Alan are not really mine; but a mother could not wish for finer sons, and I thank God every day that he gave my husband the wisdom to bring them into our lives."

How wonderful it was, to hear Arthur so highly praised by the woman who had raised him! At the same time it filled me with shame, for it served to remind me how gravely I had misjudged and undervalued him, for so many long years.

That evening, I heard the boating party return in high spirits, proclaiming their hearty appetites. I rose and quickly dressed, determined to join them for supper. I was received with great fanfare in the dining-room, where every one pronounced me looking much improved.

"You must come with us next time, Charlotte," insisted Mary Anna. "There is nothing so relaxing as a quiet float down the Shannon this time of year."

"I'm glad to see you up and feeling better," said Arthur as he sat down beside me at the table. "I felt badly about leaving you."

I was treated to a brief glimpse of the affection to which I had earlier become accustomed; but then, as if reminding himself to veil his emotions, his smile fled and he glanced away. Oh! How maddening it was to be in a roomful of people, with no opportunity to speak! I was about to lean over and whisper in Arthur's ear a request to withdraw privately for a brief word, when Mrs. Bell suddenly exclaimed, "My goodness! Charlotte has been here two days already, and I think we have all quite forgotten—we are in the presence of a celebrated authoress!"

To my chagrin, all and sundry pounced on this topic as if it were a subject of the greatest fascination, forcing me to relinquish any thought of leaving the table. As the first course was promptly served, Mary Anna said excitedly, "We remember, mama, but we have all tried *very hard* to remain mum on the subject—not wanting Charlotte to think we loved her only for her literary genius."

"I adored *Jane Eyre*," proclaimed her sister Harriette, beaming. "It is truly the best book I have ever read."

"The three volumes each appeared separately here in Ireland," said Mrs. Bell. "We were so electrified by the novel, we could hardly endure the suspense between one part and another! We drove to Birr especially to get each new edition at the earliest possible moment. Of course we had no idea, at the time, who the author was."

"Do not think your admirers are limited to the women in the family," added Alan Bell. "We've all read *Jane Eyre* and *Villette,* and loved them. I enjoyed *Shirley* as well, particularly your bevy of curates. I can't remember when I've had such a good laugh. Is it true—as our Arthur has so proudly stated—that he was the basis for that little bit at the end, about Mr. Macarthey?"

I smiled, glancing at Arthur with affection—(willing him to *see* in my eyes, what I had not yet had the opportunity to say aloud)—but he was not looking at me. "It is true, sir. Of course, that was several years ago, before I came to know Arthur as well as I do now."

"I think he came off rather decently," said Joseph. "As I recall, you described him as decorous, hard-working, and charitable—if a little too easily upset by Quakers and Dissenters."

Every one laughed. Mrs. Bell urged, "Tell us, Charlotte. We have all been dying to know: who were your models for Mr. Rochester and Monsieur Paul Emanuel?"

I noticed Arthur stiffen beside me and his face hardened. A chorus went up from the others: "Yes! Yes!" "Who were they?" "Were they based on any one real?"

Quickly, I replied: "They were an amalgam of qualities I

have either loathed or admired in men I have met—and men I have imagined—ever since I was old enough to hold a pen."

"Well, I think Mr. Rochester quite the most romantic man ever portrayed in fiction," admitted Mary Anna with a sigh.

A lively argument then ensued, as to whether Mr. Rochester was a deplorable character, or a good man trapped by unfortunate circumstances; and a discussion about Jane herself, whom every one seemed to think the most excellent of heroines. Eventually Mrs. Bell asked about my *nom de plume*.

"As you can imagine, we are all *most* interested in the origin of the name 'Currer Bell.' Such a fine surname!" (Laughter.) "Is the 'Bell' a coincidence?"

"Not exactly," I replied. I acquainted them with the particulars regarding the derivation of that name, which prompted another burst of hilarity from the group.

The clock was just striking nine when Alan Nicholls suggested that we remove to the drawing-room and engage in a game of charades, an idea met with great enthusiasm by the entire party. I begged to be excused on account of my cold; I said my good-nights; and as every one filtered away in the other direction, I retired in a state of confused exhilaration and exhaustion, saddened that my husband had not, at the very least, offered to accompany me back to our room.

The drapes in our chamber were open; it was a mild summer evening, and the sun would not set for a while yet. Something drew me to the window. To my surprise, I saw Arthur exit the house and cross the great lawn, accompanied by two of the dogs; he seemed to be heading for the woods at the side of the property.

I grabbed my shawl and hurried outside, my heart pounding.

"Arthur!" I shouted, but he was too far ahead of me to hear. I pressed on, across the expanse of grass and into the trees, fruitlessly calling his name. I followed the sound of the barking dogs through the woods, until at last I came upon a small clearing, where I found Arthur throwing a pair of sticks to his happy, bounding companions.

"Arthur!" I called again, as I made my approach.

He turned and strode back to meet me, surprise mingled with his reserve. "I thought you went to bed," said he, stopping a few feet away. "You shouldn't be out in the night air."

"It is a mild night, but I would have braved a snowstorm! Oh, Arthur, Arthur! I have wanted so desperately to speak to you. We have not had a moment alone in such a long time."

"Charlotte—" he began, frowning.

"Please Arthur, just listen to me. I must speak! First: regarding *Villette*—I did write, in that book, about a man I once knew; but it is just a story."

His eyes met mine. "Did you love him?"

"I did—a long time ago; but I do no longer, any more than you still have feelings for the girl who caught your fancy at seventeen."

He fell silent, taking that in. The dogs came bounding back; Arthur grabbed the sticks from their mouths and hurled them into the distance. As the dogs raced off again, I went on:

"The day of our crossing, I was only trying to comfort a young lady whose father did not approve her choice of husband. I used *us* as an example of how things could turn out *right*, if she could only wait, and her beloved could prove himself. But she was spoiled, rich, and prejudiced; she turned everything on its head by criticising you, knowing nothing about you, and I—to my everlasting shame—did not rise to your defence as I should have. I see now that I was just as blind and prejudiced as she was. I had no idea that you had such a cultured family, or lived in such a fine place as this! But even if you had come from the poorest of families, Arthur, it should not have mattered. All that matters is *you*: the man you are to-day—and you are far more than my equal in every way. I am proud to be married to you, Arthur. I love you! I did not realise how much I love you until that moment on the ship, when she asked me how I felt; that is why I took so long to reply. I love you, Arthur, and I am so sorry I said and did anything to cause you pain. Can you ever forgive me?"

Tears sprang into his eyes. He stepped forward and took my hands in his. "You cannot imagine how long I have hoped and dreamt of hearing you say those words. Do you mean it, Charlotte? Do you truly love me?"

"I do, with all my heart."

As the dogs raced up and circled at our feet, my husband pulled me into his embrace and kissed me, over and over again.

We stayed at Cuba House a week—one of the most delightful weeks of my life. We took leisurely boat rides on the Shannon and long walks into the country-side; we enjoyed delicious picnics and evenings filled with merriment, music, and dancing. During that time, I fully regained my health; at all times, I felt comfortable and completely accepted; and it was with great regret, and heart-felt promises to return the next year, that we took our leave of the Bells.

We spent the remaining two weeks of our honeymoon making a tour of western Ireland, including a stop in Kilkee, a most picturesque sea-side town set above a deeply curving bay. It was the first time since our arrival in Ireland that my new husband and I had been alone. We relished this time together, and the opportunity it afforded to renew our intimacy, and to increase our knowledge of each other. Our first morning in Kilkee, when we went out to the top of the cliffs and saw the Atlantic coming in below, all white with foam along the spectacular shore-line, I was so overwhelmed at the glorious sight that I longed to sit and look and be silent, rather than to walk and talk. Arthur not only graciously acceded to my wish, but admitted that he had had the same thought.

As we visited all the famous beauty spots of Ireland, taking in the magnificent scenery along the way, I enjoyed the kind and ceaseless care and protection of my husband, which made travelling a different and far more enjoyable matter from what it had heretofore been. Most pleasurable of all, however, was the deep contentment which enveloped me in the pure delight of Arthur's company. Many was the time he would pull me into his arms for an unexpected caress, and pronounce with deep sincerity: "Thank you for marrying me. You make me very happy." With certainty and joy, I returned the sentiment.

On our honeymoon, I was indebted to my husband not only for this newfound happiness, but for saving my life.

As we were making a guided trek on horseback through the narrow, winding mountain gorge at the top of the Gap of Dunloe near Killarney, my mare slipped and became unruly. Arthur quickly dismounted from his pony and grabbed the bridle of mine, to lead her. Suddenly, my mare reared; I was thrown off and landed on the stones beneath her. I felt her kick and plunge around me; I thought the end had come, and that I should be crushed underfoot. Arthur, in consternation, let the creature loose, and she sprang over me.

"Charlotte!" cried Arthur in terror, as he lifted me up in his arms. "Are you hurt?"

I was stunned by my misadventure, but assured him that the mare's hoofs never touched me. As the guide retrieved our horses, Arthur set me down and held me tightly to his chest; I felt the pounding of his heart against my cheek. "For a moment, I thought I'd lost you," he murmured against my hair.

I lifted my face to my husband's, and standing on tiptoe, I planted a kiss on his lips. "You will never lose me. I love you too much to let you go."

When we returned home on 11 August after more than a month's absence, my husband and I were inundated with visitors from every part of the parish, some coming from quite a distance. Wishing to show our appreciation for the hearty welcome and general goodwill shown by the parishioners, Arthur and I decided to hold a small village entertainment. We invited all the students and teachers at the Day and Sunday schools, as well as the church bellringers and singers, to a tea and supper in the schoolroom.

Preparing for the event took some doing. When the appointed hour arrived—when, on that warm August evening, the tables

were all laid out in the schoolroom and across the yard, surrounded with benches, covered with white cloths and decorated
with flowers, and the food (prepared by many hands) was at last
in readiness—to our amazement, nearly five hundred people
walked up! Arthur, beaming with delight, welcomed our guests
with a brief but gracious speech, and the parishioners took turns
making toasts to Arthur's return to the parish, and to our wed-
ded happiness.

"To Arthur an' Charlotte," proclaimed one man—an amiable farmer—with a raised glass and a ready smile, "two o' th'
finest people i' th' parish, who finally had th' good sense t' get
married. May yer lives together be long an' prosperous, an' yer
home blessed wi' mony childer." The hearty applause which followed brought a deep blush to my cheeks.

Mr. Ainley, to my mind, gave the most affecting toast of
all—all the more effective in light of its brevity. In a clear and
booming voice, he simply said, "T' Arthur Bell Nicholls: a consistent Christian, an' a kind gentleman. T' yer health, sir."

As the congregation shouted their approval, I took Arthur's
hand and squeezed it, gazing up at him with shining eyes. I
thought: to merit and win such a character as that—a consistent
Christian, and a kind gentleman—was far better than to earn
either wealth or fame or power. How fortunate I was, to have the
love of such a man!

I discovered, in short order, that my life was greatly changed.
Time—an article of which I had once had a large stock on
hand—now seemed to be in very short supply; as a wife, I had
scarcely an unemployed moment. The French newspapers I
used to read now stacked up in a neglected pile; I was wanted
continually by my husband, constantly called for, constantly occupied. It was a strange thing at first, yet I found it a marvel-
ously good thing.

The mere fact of being wanted was, to me, a blessing after
the total solitude of recent years. Arthur seemed to find such

pleasure in my company as he performed his many duties, that I could hardly refuse; and I, too, found great pleasure in the going and the doing. Entertaining visiting clergy and visiting the poor, organizing parish tea-drinkings and teaching at the Sunday school—the very same duties I had been obliged to perform as the parson's daughter—took on a whole new aspect of interest and importance, now that I was the curate's wife. Marriage, I discovered, was drawing me out of myself, in the best possible way.

At the same time, although I was very happy, I admit I sometimes missed my creative life. There was little opportunity for writing of any kind. I was obliged to scribble these diary pages in fits and starts, whenever a spare moment presented itself, or more often late at night, when Arthur was asleep.

Arthur began the practice of trying out his sermons on me, to seek my opinion before presenting them to the congregation. In his new, benevolent mood, his sermons were often sweet and uplifting, touching the better springs of man's nature. When he menaced me, however, with something to a lesser standard, I did not hesitate to express my agreeable disappointment—and improvements were often just as agreeably made.

As I settled into the routine of my new life, summer turned to autumn, and autumn strode relentlessly towards winter. Arthur and I went into Bradford and had our pictures recorded by the new process called photography. It was so strange and wonderful to see the completed images. I was not too fond of mine, but Arthur liked it, and I thought Arthur looked particularly handsome in his, gazing off to the side with a gleam in his eyes and that contented half smile on his countenance.

My father, God bless him, continued in good health; he would, I hoped, be with us for many years yet. The reconciliation between Arthur and papa—once so unimaginable—remained untroubled. It became an hourly happiness to me to see how well the two men got on; never was there a misunderstanding or wrong word between them. Every time I saw Arthur put on his gown or surplice and conduct a service or perform a sacred rite, I felt great comfort, knowing that my marriage would, as I had hoped, secure papa good aid in his old age.

Arthur and I grew closer with each passing day. There was always some new quirk or eccentricity on both our parts to discover, to laugh about, to adjust to. Faultless my husband was not; neither is any human being, and I am certainly no exception; but we neither of us expected perfection. We learned to tolerate those aspects of our habits and personalities that did not precisely meet our expectations, to treasure those that did, and to view with good humour everything that fell in between. There was no harassing restraint between us; together, we were at perfect ease, because we suited each other.

I was thumbing through *Jane Eyre* one day, and found this passage. Tears stung my eyes as I read it; for at the time of its composition, these words were but an expression of an idealised state of marital bliss which—until now—had existed only in my imagination:

> I know what it is to live entirely for and with what I love best on earth. I hold myself supremely blest—blest beyond what language can express; because I am my husband's life as fully as he is mine. No woman was ever nearer to her mate than I am: ever more absolutely bone of his bone and flesh of his flesh. I know no weariness of my Edward's society: he knows none of mine, any more than we each do of the pulsation of the heart that beats in our separate bosoms; consequently, we are ever together. To be together is for us to be at once as free as in solitude, as gay as in company. We talk, I believe, all day long: to talk to each other is but a more animated and an audible thinking. All my confidence is bestowed on him; all his confidence is devoted to me; we are precisely suited in character—perfect concord is the result.

Those words which I had penned so many years ago, from the depths of a lonely and longing heart, were now a perfect reflection of the wonderful new life I was living with my Arthur. My husband was so good, so tender, so loving and true; my heart was knit to his.[69]

One night in late November, as Arthur and I sat cosily before the dining-room fire, listening to the howling of the wind around the house, my thoughts began to drift to a similar November evening, a year previously. As I paused in my knitting, I realised that there was only one thing missing from my life to make it thoroughly complete: something which had once been as vital and central to my being as breathing.

I glanced at my husband, whose handsome dark head was bent attentively over his newspaper. "Arthur, what were you doing at this same time, a year ago?"

"A year ago? I was sitting in a lonely, rented room in Kirk Smeaton, dreaming of a life with you." He put down his paper, reached out and took my hand. "What were you doing?"

"I was sitting in this very same room, alone. To stave off loneliness, I started a new book."

"A new book? What became of it?"

"I think I wrote about twenty pages, and then set them aside to write a letter. A certain correspondent, as I recall, was being very persistent at the time, with regard to a marriage proposal."

"Did the gentleman's persistence pay off?"

"It did. He waged a long and relentless battle, so completely convincing his quarry of the validity of his enterprise, that in the end, she felt *she* had been the true victor, in being won."

Arthur laughed and squeezed my hand. Then, growing serious, he said, "If you were alone at this moment, Charlotte—if I were not here with you—would you be writing?"

"I suppose I would."

"Do you wish to write now?"

---

[69] Colossians 2:2, "That their hearts might be comforted, being knit together in love."

I went quiet for a moment. "Would you mind if I did? Would you feel that I was ignoring you?"

"Of course not. Haven't you been writing something anyway, in the months since we've been married? A diary, I think it is?"

My pulse began to quicken. "Yes, I have. I did not think you knew. Do you object?"

"Why would I object? Charlotte: you are a writer. I knew that long before I asked you to marry me. It's what you love, and a part of who you are. I'll love you whether you write or not. If you've had your fill of it, then stop. If you enjoy keeping a diary, then keep it. If you have a story you burn to tell, then get your paper and your ink or pencil, and go tell it."

With rapidly beating heart, I dropped my knitting and ran upstairs, retrieved the pencilled pages I had abandoned the year before, and brought them down with me. As I resumed my seat by the fire, I said, "My sisters and I used to read our works aloud and critique them. Would you like to hear what I've written so far?"

"Fire away."

I read the twenty-page fragment aloud. It was the story of a motherless young girl who attends an English boarding school, who discovers that her father has lied about his title and estate, and does not intend to pay his daughter's fees. She then finds a new and unexpected benefactor. Arthur listened with interest and attention. We then entered into an interesting discussion in which Arthur shared his opinions and concerns. He worried that I might be criticised for writing again about a school, but I explained that this was only the beginning, and I intended to take the story in an entirely new direction. He admitted that he liked it very much, and thought it promising.

"Do you?" A little thrill ran through me. "It has been so many years since I had any one with whom to discuss my work—but—how would I find the time to write a book? Our days are so full already."

"We can set aside a few hours every day for the occupation,

if you wish—and I promise," he added with teasing eyes, "to offer my *invaluable* advice whenever requested, and otherwise to
stay out of your way."

"Thank you, dearest." I kissed him, aware that I was doubly
blest: not only was I married to one of the best of men—a loving
partner with whom I could share all the joys and concerns of
everyday life—but I knew now that I would never again be alone
where my writing was concerned.

Diary, it is now Christmas Eve, 1854. Nearly two years have
passed since I first began to write these pages. I feel now that I
can end my tale, having brought it at last to as satisfactory a
conclusion as all my books—yet even better, because this story
is true.

In preparation for the holiday, Martha and I have devoted two
days to the baking of cakes and mince-pies and other assorted
culinary rites, required for our Christmas dinner tomorrow—
after which, in my sisters' and brother's honour, we intend to read
aloud passages from *Wuthering Heights, Agnes Grey,* and two of
Branwell's favourite published poems. We have cleaned down the
house, and rubbed it with beeswax, oil, and innumerable cloths
until it shines in every quarter. I have arranged every table, chair,
bureau, and carpet with mathematical precision, and had enough
coal and peat brought in to ensure that good fires are kept up to
warm and brighten every room.

As I sit at the dining-room table now, surveying the glittering
results of our efforts, I hear papa and Arthur conversing genially
in the study across the hall. The sound of their deep Irish voices
engaged in friendly banter never ceases to make me smile.

My mind wanders; I cannot help but smile at another memory: a conversation which ensued between Arthur and myself
last night, as we prepared for bed.

I had just pulled the pins from my hair, when Arthur stepped
up behind me. With a dark gleam in his eyes, and a deep timbre
to his voice, he said: "May I brush your hair?"

In the six months that we have been married, I have been

the fortunate recipient of my husband's hair-brushing ministrations on occasions too numerous to count—sessions which always led to such a delectable conclusion, that I have often mischievously left my hairbrush lying out on the bed, waiting with great anticipation for the moment that it would be discovered and put to good use. At his request now, my heart began to pound. Without a word, I sat down on the bed beside him and relinquished the brush to his care.

He pulled the brush through my long tresses with sure, deft strokes, his fingers gently sweeping my hair back from my neck, a touch which always made me tingle. As I relaxed into his luxurious attentions, he said in a low tone, "Mrs. Nicholls: now that you are an old married woman, may I ask a question that I have long wished to put to you?"

"You may ask me anything, my dear boy."

"All those years ago, when I first came here to tea—what was it that you *thought* I said, which gave you such offence?"

"Do you really wish to know?"

"I do."

"You will think it all vanity and nonsense."

"Even so."

I sighed, and blushed at the memory. "I thought you called me an ugly old maid."

"What?" (All hair-brushing ceased) *"Ugly?* No! I never said that! I said *angry.* And angry you were, like a hell-cat, breathing fire and brimstone—but ugly? I would never even think such a thing."

"Would you not? *Did* you not, even then, dearest?"

"Never." Arthur put down the hairbrush and turned me to face him on the bed. "Don't you know me well enough by now, my darling, to know my feelings for you? I thought you beautiful on that grey, miserable, drenching April day nearly ten years past, when I first set eyes upon you—when you answered the door with your dress and face and hair all covered in flour. Your beauty has grown with each passing day, as I've come to know and understand the woman you are inside. You're the most beautiful woman on earth to me, Charlotte Nicholls, and you always will be. I love you."

My heart soared. In the reflected glow of my husband's adoring gaze, I truly did feel beautiful for the first time in my life.

"And I you," I whispered in return, as I melted into his embrace.

Author's Afterword

At the close of 1854, as Charlotte Brontë finished writing these diaries, she appeared to be the happiest and healthiest she had ever been in her life. In her letters, she spoke tenderly of her husband, admitting that "every day makes my own attachment to him stronger." Visiting friends commented on how well Charlotte looked, and on the complete contentment of the newly married couple. Ellen confessed that "after her marriage—a halo of happiness seemed to surround her—a holy calm pervaded her, even in moments of excitement."

These blissful months of health and domestic joy, however, were tragically very short-lived.

At the end of January 1855, Charlotte became ill. Arthur, wishing to have better medical advice than Haworth could offer, sent for a doctor from Bradford, reputedly the best doctor in the region. He confirmed that Charlotte was pregnant and suffering from morning sickness, and—not alarmed by her condition—he recommended bed rest.

Charlotte's health continued to deteriorate. To her husband and father's intense dismay, over the next six weeks, Charlotte became so severely weakened with nausea, fever, and vomiting that she could not eat, and eventually she could barely speak. Her servant Martha Brown said that a bird could not survive on what little Charlotte ate. In the few brief, weakly penciled notes that Charlotte wrote to her friends from her bed during this time, she praised her husband lovingly in every one. On 17 February she made her will, overturning the cautious settlement she'd made before her marriage, now leaving her entire estate to her beloved Arthur, instead of her father.

In March, Charlotte's condition briefly improved; the sickness suddenly stopped, and she craved food and ate eagerly; but it was too late. She fell into a wandering delirium as her life slipped away. Toward the end of the month, when she awoke from this stupor for an instant, and saw her husband's woe-worn face and heard his murmured prayers to spare her, she whispered, "Oh! I am not going to die, am I? He will not separate us, we have been so happy."

Early on Saturday morning, March 31, 1855—just three weeks short of her thirty-ninth birthday—Charlotte Brontë died. Arthur held her in his arms in a convulsion of grief. Charlotte's death certificate made no mention of her pregnancy, stating that she died from "phthisis," the same progressive wasting disease from which her brother and sisters had perished. Modern medical opinion, however, cites *hyperemesis gravidarum* (excessive sickness in a pregnant woman) as the cause, or at least a contributory cause. Whether the poor quality of the water in Haworth (which carried the typhus that killed the family's faithful servant, Tabby, only a month earlier) was another contributing cause of her death, will never be known.

Patrick Brontë, distraught over his daughter's death, and particularly upset by the many charges and questions raised by the public over the identity of the reclusive but celebrated Currer Bell, asked Mrs. Gaskell to write a story of Charlotte's life, which that lady painstakingly researched and famously executed. Arthur—although strongly opposed to the idea of the biography, and especially to the idea of publishing Charlotte's letters, which would render public what was to him very personal and sacred—reluctantly yielded to Patrick Brontë's wish and assisted Mrs. Gaskell in any way he could.

When *The Life of Charlotte Brontë* was published by Smith, Elder & Co. two years after Charlotte's death, it became a sensation comparable to the first publication of *Jane Eyre*. In the same year, Charlotte's first novel *The Professor* was published, although it was overshadowed by the enthralling story of her own life.

Arthur Bell Nicholls fulfilled his promise to his wife, and remained a faithful caregiver to Patrick Brontë for the six years which remained of the old man's life. When Patrick died, he left everything to his "beloved and esteemed son-in-law, the Reverend Arthur Bell Nicholls." If Arthur expected, after quietly and conscientiously carrying out the duties of curate for sixteen long years, to be rewarded by inheriting the living of Haworth on Patrick's death, he was to be bitterly disappointed. The position depended on the nomination of the Church Trustees, now a new and younger generation who owed no allegiance to Patrick Brontë, and some of whom Arthur may have offended by his formal and unbending ways. By a vote of five to four, Arthur was callously rejected.

Arthur packed up his belongings, including various Brontë mementos and many of Charlotte's personal and literary possessions, and returned to Banagher, Ireland, taking Plato, Patrick's last dog. The Royal School was still being run by his cousin James Bell. Arthur's Aunt Harriette was living in a small, pretty house at the top of the hill, which stood on twenty acres of land. Arthur joined her and her daughter Mary Anna there and lived a quiet life, becoming a farmer and giving up the church altogether. Martha Brown, the Brontë servant who had once so disliked him, became a good friend and made long and regular visits.

Mary Anna had always loved her cousin; nine and a half years after Charlotte's death, she and Arthur quietly married. By every account this second marriage, although childless, was a happy one, based on companionship and mutual understanding rather than passion. Arthur was open with Mary Anna about his feelings, admitting that "he had buried his heart with his first wife." To her credit, Mary Anna understood. The Richmond portrait of Charlotte hung in their drawing-room for more than forty years, until the day Arthur died in 1906, at age eighty-eight. When pressed, Arthur wrote and talked with great pride about his celebrated first wife, but he shunned publicity for the rest of his life.

During Arthur's last years, he shared some of Charlotte's juvenilia, pictures, and other keepsakes with one of her biographers. If Arthur had indeed been the keeper of Charlotte's diaries, it would have been entirely consistent with his nature—and his intense desire for privacy—to keep the precious volumes hidden from the public: buried yet carefully and lovingly preserved, by the man who had always adored her, in the cellar of that house on the hill in Banagher, Ireland.

FROM

**SYRIE
JAMES**

AND

AVON A

Q & A WITH AUTHOR SYRIE JAMES

What inspired you to write *The Secret Diaries of Charlotte Brontë*?

I have always adored the novel *Jane Eyre*. I wanted to know and understand the woman who wrote it. As I delved into my research, I was captivated not only by the engrossing saga of Charlotte Brontë's relationship with her family and her emergence as a novelist, but by what I saw as the missing link: the untold story of her relationship with Arthur Bell Nicholls. To think that this tall, dark, and handsome man carried a silent torch for Charlotte for seven and a half years, and that her feelings for him went from intense dislike to deep and abiding love—I knew that would make a fabulous story!

How much do we actually know about Charlotte Brontë's life?

We are privileged to know a great deal, thanks in large part to the wealth of correspondence which William Smith Williams preserved after Charlotte became published, and to the unguarded letters—nearly five hundred in all—which Charlotte wrote to Ellen Nussey over a twenty-four-year period. Arthur was so concerned about what might happen if Charlotte's correspondence fell into the wrong hands, that he insisted Ellen burn all her letters upon receipt; fortunately, Ellen did not comply. Charlotte's letters are a wealth of information regarding her intimate thoughts, beliefs, daily struggles, and personal relationships. Many of the settings and incidents in her novels, by her own admission, were inspired by situations in her own life. She gave us valuable insight into her feelings about her sisters, and the evolution of their writing, in her introduction to the second edition of *Wuthering Heights* and *Agnes Grey*.

We are also indebted to Ellen Nussey for the variety of insightful biographical notes and reminiscences she wrote about the Brontës, and to Mrs. Gaskell, for the in-depth biography she wrote shortly after Charlotte's death. Mrs. Gaskell visited every school Charlotte had attended, and interviewed or corresponded with all the important people who had touched her life; she even sailed to Belgium to meet Monsieur Héger (Madame Héger refused to see her). Although Mrs. Gaskell whitewashed Charlotte's "affair" with Monsieur Héger to preserve her reputation, her well-researched work provided the basis for every subsequent Brontë biography ever written.

Which parts of *The Secret Diaries of Charlotte Brontë* are true? Which parts did you "conjecture"?

The novel is based almost entirely on fact. All the details of Charlotte's family life, her experiences at school, her friendship with Ellen, her feelings for Monsieur Héger, the evolution of her writing career, and her relationship with her publisher, George Smith, are all true and based on information from her letters and biographies. The letters on pages 90–91 and 154 are real, as are the critical notices the sisters read about their poetry and novels. According to Ellen Nussey, Charlotte really did tell a story about a "somnambulist walking on shaking turrets" to her fellow pupils at Roe Head School, which reduced one girl to shivering terror . . . "all told in a voice that conveyed more than words alone can express."

The details about Mr. Nicholls's childhood are factual. I faithfully recounted Charlotte's experiences on her honeymoon in Ireland with the Bell family. The only fictitious characters in the novel are the Malones, the Ainleys, and the young lady on board the ship—people and situations I invented to add local color or dramatic conflict. All the other characters in the book—even the girls at Roe Head School—are based on real people.

The details of Mr. Nicholls's passionate and agonized proposal of marriage, as well as its stormy aftermath and Patrick Brontë's vehement opposition, are all based on fact, and were meticulously recorded in Charlotte's correspondence. Charlotte and Mr. Nicholls's strolls from Haworth to Oxenhope during those bitingly cold days in January 1854 are so well-known, that the path came to be called "Charlotte's Lane." Although Charlotte's letters reflect a subdued expectation before her marriage, her respect and affection for her husband blossomed on their honeymoon, and grew into a love so strong, that she later wrote of Arthur, "my heart is knit to him." I was obliged to conjecture some of the events during the earlier years of Charlotte and Mr. Nicholls's acquaintance, to flesh out their love story—and I imagined Monsieur Héger's kiss in the garden (much of his romantic dialogue about "meeting again in thought" comes straight from a letter he wrote to another student)—but based on what we *do* know, I feel this telling is very close to the truth. And the "conjecturing" was a great part of the fun of writing the novel!

How did you do your research?

I pored over countless Brontë biographies. I read all their poetry, their published novels, the juvenilia, and Charlotte's voluminous personal correspondence. I studied the art of the Brontës (quite remarkable!). I read everything I could find about the life of Arthur Bell Nicholls. I went to Haworth, and made an extended visit to the Brontë Parsonage Museum, which has been preserved to reflect the way it looked when the Brontës lived there, and is furnished with many of their possessions. What a thrill it was to "haunt" the rooms and lanes where Charlotte and Emily and Anne actually lived and walked, and to stroll through that gloomy graveyard in the pouring rain! Even more thrilling was my precious ninety-minute visit to the Brontë library, where I was allowed to don protective gloves and read a selection of original letters and manuscripts penned by Charlotte and other members of the Brontë family.

While in Yorkshire, I was also granted a private tour of the former Roe Head School, which still actively functions as a private school. The main building, inside and out, looks much the same as it did in Charlotte Brontë's day—and the legend of that mysterious attic dweller, the Ghost of Roe Head, still abides!

EXCERPTS FROM SELECTED CORRESPONDENCE OF CHARLOTTE BRONTË

ON READING AND WRITING

From Poet Laureate Robert Southey

(to whom twenty-year-old Charlotte had sent a selection of her poems)

12 March 1837

Madam— . . . It is not my advice that you have asked as to the direction of your talents, but my opinion of them; and yet the opinion may be worth little, and the advice much. You evidently possess, and in no inconsiderable degree, what Wordsworth calls the "faculty of verse." I am not deprecating it when I say that in these times it is not rare . . . Whoever . . . is ambitious of distinction in this way ought to be prepared for disappointment. But it is not with a view to distinction that you should cultivate this talent, if you consult your own happiness . . .

The day dreams in which you habitually indulge are likely to induce a distempered state of mind; and, in proportion as all the ordinary uses of the world seem to you flat and unprofitable, you will be unfitted for them without becoming fitted for anything else. Literature cannot be the business of a woman's life, and it ought not to be. The more she is engaged in her proper duties, the less leisure will she have for it, even as an accomplishment and a recreation. To those duties you have not yet been called, and when you are you will be less eager for celebrity. You will not seek in imagination for excitement . . .

But do not suppose that I disparage the gift which you possess, nor that I would discourage you from exercising it. I only exhort you so to think of it, and so to use it, as to render it conducive to your own perma-

nent good. *Write poetry for its own sake . . . and not with a view to celebrity; the less you aim at that the more likely you will be to deserve and finally to obtain it. So written, it is wholesome both for the heart and soul; it may be made the surest means, next to religion, of soothing the mind, and elevating it. You may embody in it your best thoughts and your wisest feelings, and in so doing discipline and strengthen them.*

From Charlotte's reply to Robert Southey

16 March 1837

Sir— . . . *At the first perusal of your letter I felt only shame and regret that I had ever ventured to trouble you with my crude rhapsody; I felt a painful heat rise to my face when I thought of the quires of paper I had covered with what once gave me so much delight, but which now was only a source of confusion; but after I had thought a little, and read it again and again, the prospect seemed to clear. You do not forbid me to write. You only warn me against the folly of neglecting real duties for the sake of imaginative pleasures; of writing for the love of fame . . . You kindly allow me to write poetry for its own sake, provided I leave undone nothing which I ought to do, in order to pursue that single, absorbing, exquisite gratification . . .*

Following my father's advice—who from my childhood has counselled me, just in the wise and friendly tone of your letter—I have endeavoured not only attentively to observe all the duties a woman ought to fulfill, but to feel deeply interested in them. I don't always succeed, for sometimes when I'm teaching or sewing I would rather be reading or writing; but I try to deny myself; and my father's approbation amply rewarded me for the privation. Once more allow me to thank you with sincere gratitude. I trust I shall never more feel ambitious to see my name in print; if the wish should rise, I'll look at Southey's letter, and suppress it.

To a number of celebrated writers

(including Wordsworth, Tennyson, Hartley Coleridge, and Thomas De Quincey; accompanied by a copy of their "unwanted" book, *Poems*)

16 June 1847

Sir—My relatives, Ellis & Acton Bell and myself, heedless of the repeated warnings of various respectable publishers, have committed the rash act of printing a volume of poems.

The consequences predicted have, of course, overtaken us; our book is found to be a drug; no man needs it or heeds it; in the space of a year our publisher has disposed but of two copies and by what painful efforts he succeeded in getting rid of those two—himself only knows.

Before transferring the edition to the trunk-makers,[1] we have decided on distributing as presents a few copies of what we cannot sell. We beg to offer you one in acknowledgement of the pleasure and profit we have often and long derived from your works.

I am sir, yours very respectfully,
Currer Bell

From C. Bell to Messrs. Smith, Elder & Co.

19 October 1847

Gentlemen: The six copies of "Jane Eyre" reached me this morning. You have given the work every advantage which good paper, clear type and a seemly outside can supply—if it fails—the fault will lie with the author—you are exempt. I now await the judgment of the press and the public.

---

[1] For use as a lining in leather traveling trunks.

To journalist, novelist, and dramatist George Henry Lewes

12 January 1848

When authors write best, or at least, when they write most fluently, an influence seems to waken in them which becomes their master, which will have its own way, putting out of view all behests but its own, dictating certain words, and insisting on their being used, whether vehement or measured in their nature; new moulding characters, giving unthought-of turns to incidents, rejecting carefully elaborated old ideas, and suddenly creating and adopting new ones. Is it not so? And should we try to counteract this influence? Can we indeed counteract it?

To Ellen Nussey

3 May 1848

I have given <u>no one</u> a right either to affirm, or hint, in the most distant manner, that I am "publishing"—(humbug!) . . . Though twenty books were ascribed to me, I should own none. I scout the idea utterly.

To William S. Williams

14 August 1848

The first duty of an Author is—I conceive—a faithful allegiance to Truth and Nature.

To William S. Williams

2 October 1848

My unhappy brother never knew what his sisters had done in literature—he was not aware that they had ever published a line; we could not tell him of our efforts for fear of causing him too deep a pang of remorse for his own time misspent, and talents misapplied— Now he will <u>never</u> know. I cannot dwell longer on the subject at present; it is too painful.

To William S. Williams

21 September 1849

    The two human beings who understood me and whom I understood are gone. . . . The loss of what we possess nearest and dearest to us in this world, produces an effect upon the character: we search out what we have yet left that can support, and when found, we cling to it with a hold of new-strung tenacity.

    The faculty of imagination lifted me when I was sinking three months ago, its active exercise has kept my head above water since—its results cheer me now—for I feel they have enabled me to give pleasure to others— I am thankful to God who gave me the faculty.

To William S. Williams
(*Upon reading Jane Austen's* Emma)

12 April 1850

    I read it with interest and with just the degree of admiration which Miss Austen herself would have thought sensible and suitable—anything like warmth or enthusiasm; anything energetic, poignant, heart-felt, is utterly out of place in commending these works: all such demonstration the authoress would have met with a well-bred sneer, would have calmly scorned as outré and extravagant. She does her business of delineating the surface of the lives of genteel English people curiously well; there is a Chinese fidelity, a miniature delicacy in the painting: she ruffles her reader by nothing vehement, disturbs him by nothing profound: the Passions are perfectly unknown to her . . . even to the Feelings she vouchsafes no more than an occasional graceful but distant recognition; too frequent converse with them would ruffle the smooth elegance of her progress . . . what sees keenly, speaks aptly, moves flexibly, it suits her to study, but what throbs fast and full, though hidden, what the blood rushes through . . . <u>this</u> Miss Austen ignores . . . if this is heresy—I cannot help it.

ON LOVE AND MARRIAGE

To Ellen Nussey

1 April 1843

It is an imbecility, which I reject with contempt, for women, who have neither fortune nor beauty, to make marriage the principal object of their wishes and hopes, and the aim of all their actions.

To Ellen Nussey

2 April 1845

I know that if women wish to escape the stigma of husband-seeking they must act and look like marble or clay—cold, expressionless, bloodless; for every appearance of feeling, of joy, sorrow, friendliness, antipathy, admiration, disgust are alike construed by the world into an attempt to hook a husband. Never mind! Well-meaning women have their own consciences to comfort them after all. Do not, therefore, be too much afraid of showing yourself as you are, affectionate and good-hearted; do not too harshly repress sentiments and feelings excellent in themselves, because you fear that some puppy may fancy that you are letting them come out to fascinate him.

To Monsieur Constantin Héger

18 November 1845 (Translated from the original French)

Monsieur— . . . The summer and autumn have seemed very long to me . . . I will tell you candidly that during this time of waiting I have tried to forget you, for the memory of a person one believes one is never to see again, and whom one nevertheless greatly respects, torments the mind exceedingly and when one has suffered this kind of anxiety for one or two years, one is ready to do anything to regain peace of mind. I have done everything, I have sought occupations, I have forbidden myself the pleasure of speaking about you—even to Emily, but I have not been able to overcome either my regrets or my impatience—and that is truly humiliating—not to know how to get the mastery over one's own thoughts, to be the slave of a regret, a memory, the slave of a dominant and fixed idea which has become a tyrant over one's mind. Why cannot I have for you exactly as much friendship as you have for me—neither more nor less? Then I would be so tranquil, so free—I could keep silence for ten years without effort . . .

To forbid me to write to you, to refuse to reply to me—that will be to tear from me the only joy I have on earth—to deprive me of my last re-maining privilege . . . when a dreary and prolonged silence seems to warn me that my master is becoming estranged from me—when day after day I await a letter and day after day disappointment flings me down again into overwhelming misery, when the sweet delight of seeing your writing and reading your counsel flees from me like an empty vision—then I am in a fever—I lose my appetite and my sleep—I pine away.

To Ellen Nussey

10 July 1846

Who gravely asked you whether Miss Brontë was not going to be married to her papa's curate? I scarcely need say that never was ru-mour more unfounded—it puzzles me to think how it could possibly have originated. A cold, far-away sort of civility are the only terms on which I have ever been with Mr. Nicholls. I could by no means think of mentioning such a rumour to him even as a joke—it would make me the laughing-stock of himself and his fellow-curates for half a year to come. They regard me as an old maid, and I regard them, one and all, as highly uninteresting, narrow and unattractive specimens of the coarser sex.

To Ellen Nussey

14 September 1850

What is the "twaddle about my marrying, etc.," which you hear? . . . Whom am I to marry? I think I have scarcely seen a single man with whom such a union would be possible since I left London. Doubtless there are men whom if I chose to encourage I might marry, but no matrimonial lot is even remotely offered me which seems to me truly desirable: and even if that were the case, there would be many obstacles; the least allusion to such a thing is most offensive to papa.

To Ellen Nussey

15 December 1852

He entered, he stood before me. What his words were you can guess; his manner, you can hardly realise, nor can I forget it . . . He spoke of sufferings he had borne for months—of sufferings he could endure no longer—and craved leave for some hope . . .

That he cared something for me—and wanted me to care for him—I have long suspected—but I did not know the degree or strength of his feelings.

To Ellen Nussey

11 April 1854

In fact, dear Ellen, I am engaged . . . What seemed at one time impossible is now arranged . . . I trust to love my husband. I am grateful for his tender love to me. I believe him to be an affectionate, a conscientious, a high-principled man.

To Margaret Wooler

12 April 1854

The destiny which Providence in His goodness and wisdom seems to offer me will not, I am aware, be generally regarded as brilliant, but I trust I see in it some germs of real happiness.

To Margaret Wooler

10 July 1854 (Banagher, Ireland)

I must say I like my new relations. My dear husband too appears in a new light here in his own country. More than once I have had deep pleasure in hearing his praises on all sides. Some of the old servants and followers of the family tell me I am a most fortunate person for that I have got one of the best gentlemen in the country. His Aunt too speaks of him with a mixture of affection and respect most gratifying to hear.

To Ellen Nussey

26 December 1854

Arthur joins me in sincere good wishes for a happy Christmas & many of them to you and yours. He is well—thank God—and so am I—and he is "my dear boy" certainly—dearer to me now than he was six months ago—in three days we shall actually have been married that length of time!

To Ellen Nussey

21 February 1855

My dear Ellen—I must write one line out of my weary bed . . . I am not going to talk about my sufferings, it would be useless and painful—I want to give you an assurance which I know will comfort you—and that is that I find in my husband the tenderest nurse, the kindest support—the best earthly comfort that ever woman had.

To Amelia Taylor (wife of Joseph Taylor—Mary Taylor's brother)

Late February 1855

As to my husband—my heart is knit to him.

SELECTED POETRY BY THE BRONTËS

There are nearly five hundred known poems by the Brontës. Here are excerpts from a few of my favorites. The first seven are from "Poems: by Currer, Ellis and Acton Bell."

"Life"
by Currer Bell (Charlotte Brontë)
Life, believe, is not a dream
So dark as sages say;
Oft a little morning rain
Foretells a pleasant day.
Sometimes there are clouds of gloom,
But these are transient all;
If the shower will make the roses bloom,
O why lament its fall?

"Parting"
by Currer Bell (Charlotte Brontë)
There's no use in weeping,
Though we are condemned to part:
There's such a thing as keeping
A remembrance in one's heart:
There's such a thing as dwelling
On the thought ourselves have nurs'd,
And with scorn and courage telling
The world to do its worst . . .

When we've left each friend and brother,
When we're parted wide and far,

We will think of one another,
As even better than we are.

"Gilbert, Part I: The Garden"

*by Currer Bell (Charlotte Brontë; a reflection on her
Brussels experience)*

Above the city hung the moon,
Right o'er a plot of ground
Where flowers and orchard-trees were fenced
With lofty walls around:
'Twas Gilbert's garden—there to-night
Awhile he walked alone;
And, tired with sedentary toil,
Mused where the moonlight shone . . .

Gilbert has paced the single walk
An hour, yet is not weary;
And, though it be a winter night
He feels nor cold nor dreary.
The prime of life is in his veins,
And sends his blood fast flowing,
And Fancy's fervour warms the thoughts
Now in his bosom glowing.

Those thoughts recur to early love,
Or what he love would name,
Though haply Gilbert's secret deeds
Might other title claim.
Such theme not oft his mind absorbs,
He to the world clings fast,
And too much for the present lives,
To linger o'er the past.

But now the evening's deep repose
Has glided to his soul;

That moonlight falls on Memory,
And shows her fading scroll.
One name appears in every line
The gentle rays shine o'er,
And still he smiles and still repeats
That one name—Elinor.

There is no sorrow in his smile,
No kindness in his tone;
The triumph of a selfish heart
Speaks coldly there alone;
He says: "She loved me more than life;
And truly it was sweet
To see so fair a woman kneel,
In bondage, at my feet.

"There was a sort of quiet bliss
To be so deeply loved,
To gaze on trembling eagerness
And sit myself unmoved.
And when it pleased my pride to grant
At last some rare caress,
To feel the fever of that hand
My fingers deigned to press.

"'Twas sweet to see her strive to hide
What every glance revealed;
Endowed, the while, with despot-might
Her destiny to wield.
I knew myself no perfect man,
Nor, as she deemed, divine;
I knew that I was glorious—but
By her reflected shine;

"Her youth, her native energy,
Her powers new-born and fresh,

'Twas these with Godhead sanctified
My sensual frame of flesh.
Yet, like a God did I descend
At last, to meet her love;
And, like a god, I then withdrew
To my own heaven above.

"And never more could she invoke
My presence to her sphere;
No prayer, no plaint, no cry of hers
Could win my awful ear.
I knew her blinded constancy
Would ne'er my deeds betray,
And, calm in conscience, whole in heart,
I went my tranquil way.

"Yet, sometimes, I still feel a wish,
The fond and flattering pain
Of passion's anguish to create
In her young breast again.
Bright was the lustre of her eyes,
When they caught fire from mine;
If I had power—this very hour,
Again I'd light their shine."

"Remembrance"
By Ellis Bell (Emily Brontë)
Cold in the earth—and the deep snow piled above
    thee,
Far, far removed, cold in the dreary grave!
Have I forgot, my Only Love, to love thee,
Severed at last by Time's all-severing wave?

Now, when alone, do my thoughts no longer hover
Over the mountains on that northern shore;

Resting their wings where heath and fern-leaves
    cover
That noble heart for ever, ever more?

Cold in the earth—and fifteen wild Decembers,
From those brown hills have melted into spring:
Faithful, indeed, is the spirit that remembers
After such years of change and suffering!

Sweet Love of youth, forgive, if I forget thee
While the world's tide is bearing me along;
Sterner desires and darker hopes beset me;
Hopes which obscure but cannot do thee
    wrong!

No later light has lightened up my heaven;
No second morn has ever shone for me;
All my life's bliss from thy dear life was given,
All my life's bliss is in the grave with thee.

But, when the days of golden dreams had perished,
And even Despair was powerless to destroy;
Then did I learn how existence could be cherished,
Strengthened, and fed without the aid of joy.

Then did I check the tears of useless passion—
Weaned my young soul from yearning after thine;
Sternly denied its burning wish to hasten
Down to that tomb already more than mine.

And, even yet, I dare not let it languish,
Dare not indulge in memory's rapturous pain;
Once drinking deep of that divinest anguish,
How could I seek the empty world again?

"A Day Dream"

By Ellis Bell (Emily Brontë)

On a sunny brae alone I lay
One summer afternoon;
It was the marriage-time of May,
With her young lover, June . . .

The trees did wave their plumy crests,
The glad birds carolled clear;
And I, of all the wedding guests,
Was only sullen there! . . .

There was not one, but wished to shun
My aspect void of cheer;
The very gray rocks, looking on,
Asked, "What do you here?"

And I could utter no reply;
In sooth, I did not know
Why I had brought a clouded eye
To greet the general glow.

So, resting on a heathy bank
I took my heart to me;
And we together sadly sank
Into a reverie.

We thought, "When winter comes again,
Where will these bright things be?
All vanished, like a vision vain,
An unreal mockery!

"The birds that now so blithely sing,
Through deserts, frozen dry,
Poor spectres of the perished spring,
In famished troops will fly.

"And why should we be glad at all?
The leaf is hardly green,
Before a token of its fall
Is on the surface seen!"

Now, whether it were really so,
I never could be sure;
But as in fit of peevish woe,
I stretched me on the moor,

A thousand thousand gleaming fires
Seemed kindling in the air;
A thousand thousand silvery lyres
Resounded far and near;

Methought, the very breath I breathed
Was full of sparks divine,
And all my heather-couch was wreathed
By that celestial shine!

And, while the wide earth echoing rung
To that strange minstrelsy
The little glittering spirits sung,
Or seemed to sing, to me:

"O mortal! mortal! let them die;
Let time and tears destroy,
That we may overflow the sky
With universal joy!

"Let grief distract the sufferer's breast,
And night obscure his way;
They hasten him to endless rest,
And everlasting day.

"To thee the world is like a tomb,
A desert's naked shore;
To us, in unimagined bloom,
It brightens more and more!

"And, could we lift the veil, and give
One brief glimpse to thine eye,
Thou wouldst rejoice for those that live,
BECAUSE they live to die."

"Lines Composed in a Wood on a Windy Day"
By Acton Bell (Anne Brontë)
My soul is awakened, my spirit is soaring
And carried aloft on the wings of the breeze;
For above and around me the wild wind is roaring,
Arousing to rapture the earth and the seas.

The long withered grass in the sunshine is glancing,
The bare trees are tossing their branches on high;
The dead leaves beneath them are merrily dancing,
The white clouds are scudding across the blue sky.

I wish I could see how the ocean is lashing
The foam of its billows to whirlwinds of spray;
I wish I could see how its proud waves are dashing,
And hear the wild roar of their thunder to-day!

"Home"
By Acton Bell (Anne Brontë; Composed at Thorp Green)
How brightly glistening in the sun,
The woodland ivy plays!
While yonder beeches from their barks
Reflect his silver rays.

That sun surveys a lovely scene
From softly smiling skies;
And wildly through unnumbered trees
The wind of winter sighs:

Now loud, it thunders o'er my head,
And now in distance dies.
But give me back my barren hills
Where colder breezes rise;

Where scarce the scattered, stunted trees
Can yield an answering swell,
But where a wilderness of heath
Returns the sound as well . . .

Restore me to that little spot,
With gray walls compassed round,
Where knotted grass neglected lies,
And weeds usurp the ground.

Though all around this mansion high
Invites the foot to roam,
And though its halls are fair within—
Oh, give me back my HOME!

"Celebrating Mr. Nicholls's Victory Over the Washerwomen of Haworth"

By Patrick Brontë, November 1847 (Composed with teasing affection for his curate)

In Haworth, a parish of ancient renown,
Some preach in their surplice, and others their gown . . .
The Parson, an old man, but hotter than cold,
Of late in reforming, has grown very bold,
And in his fierce zeal, as report loudly tells,

Through legal resort, has reformed the bells.
His curate, who follows—with all due regard,
Though foild by the Church, has reformed the
    Churchyard.

The females all routed have fled with their clothes
To stackyards, and backyards, and where no one knows,
And loudly have sworn by the suds which they swim in,
They'll wring off his head, for his warring with women.
Whilst their husbands combine and roar out in their
    fury,
They'll lynch him at once, without trial by jury.
But saddest of all, the fair maiden declare,
Of marriage or love, he must ever despair.

"I Saw A Picture, Yesterday"
*By Branwell Brontë (Unpublished, in draft form; c. 1843,
1844; Written at Thorp Green, after Mrs. Robinson showed
Branwell her self-portrait.)*
Her effort shews a picture made
    To contradict its meaning
Where should be sunshine painting shade,
    And smile with sadness screening;
Where God has given a cheerful view
    A gloomy vista showing
Where heart and face, are fair and true
    A shade of doubt bestowing

Ah Lady if to me you give
    The power your sketch to adorn
How little of it shall I leave
    Save smiles that shine like morn.
Ide keep the hue of happy light
    That shines from summer skies

Ide drive the shades from smiles so bright
    And dry such shining eyes

Ide give a calm to one whose heart
    Has banished calm from mine
Ide brighten up Gods work of art
    Where thou hast dimmed its shine
And all the wages I should ask
    For such a happy toil
I'll name them—far beyond my task—
THY PRESENCE AND THY SMILE.

"Lydia Gisborne"
By Branwell Brontë (Unpublished; composed in July or
August 1845, after his dismissal from Thorp Green. Lydia
Gisborne was Mrs. Robinson's maiden name.)
Cannot my soul depart where it will fly?
Asks my tormented heart, willing to die.
When will this restlessness tossing in sleeplessness—
Stranger to happiness—slumbering lie.

Cannot I chase away life in my tomb
Rather than pass away lifetime in gloom,
With sorrows employing their arts in destroying
The power of enjoying the comforts of home?

Home it is not with me bright as of yore
Joys are forgot with me, taught to deplore
My home has ta'en its rest in an afflicted breast
That I have often pressed but—may *no more.*

THE WORKS OF CHARLOTTE BRONTË

Novels

Jane Eyre, 1847
Shirley, 1849
Villette, 1853
The Professor, published posthumously, 1857

Published Poetry

Poems by Currer, Ellis and Acton Bell, 1846

Early Writings

Listed chronologically; novelettes in italics. Most are tiny manuscripts composed in miniscule script, attributed to Charlotte's pseudonym "Lord Charles Wellesley."

There was once a little girl, c. 1826–8
The History of the Year, 1829
Two Romantic Tales: includes "A Romantic Tale"
    (The Twelve Adventurers) and "An Adventure in
    Ireland," 1829
The Search After Happiness, 1829
The Adventures of Mon. Edouard de Crack, 1830
The Adventures of Ernest Alembert, 1830
An Interesting Passage in the Lives of Some Eminent Men
    of the Present Time, 1830
The Poetaster: A Drama in Two Volumes, 1830
Tales of the Islanders, 1829–1830
Young Men's Magazine (including Blackwood's Young
    Men's Magazine), 1829–1830
Albion and Marina: A Tale, 1830
The African Queen's Lament, 1830?

Something About Arthur, 1833

The Foundling: A Tale of our own Times, 1833

The Green Dwarf: A Tale of the Perfect Tense, 1833

The Secret and Lily Hart: Two Tales, 1833

A Leaf from an Unopened Volume, Or The Manuscript of An Unfortunate Author, 1834

High Life in Verdopolis, Or The Difficulties of Annexing a Suitable Title to a Work Practically Illustrated in Six Chapters, 1834

Corner Dishes, 1834

The Spell, An Extravaganza, 1834

My Angria and the Angrians, 1834

The Scrap Book: A Mingling of Many Things, 1835

Passing Events, 1836

Roe Head Journal (Fragments), 1836–1837

Julia, 1837

Mina Laury, 1838

Stancliffe's Hotel, 1838

Henry Hastings, 1839

Caroline Vernon, 1839

Farewell to Angria, 1839

Unfinished Novels

Ashworth, 1841

Willie Ellin, 1853

Emma, 1853 (twenty-page fragment. The book was later finished by author Clare Boylan and released in 2003 under the title *Emma Brown*.)

NOVELS BY ANNE AND EMILY BRONTË

Wuthering Heights, by Emily Brontë, 1847
Agnes Grey, by Anne Brontë, 1847
The Tenant of Wildfell Hall, by Anne Brontë, 1848

BOOK CLUB/READING GROUP STUDY GUIDE

The Secret Diaries of Charlotte Brontë

DISCUSSION POINTS

1. Discuss the Brontë family dynamics. Describe Charlotte's relationship with her sisters, Emily and Anne. Why was Charlotte so devoted to her father? How did her relationship with her brother Branwell evolve and change over the years, and what influence did he have on her life?

2. What secrets did Charlotte and her siblings each keep, and why? Whose secret had the most devastating impact on the family? How did Charlotte's secret affect her life and her work?

3. Who are your favorite characters in the novel, and why? Who is your least favorite character?

4. What are your favorite scenes in the novel? What was the saddest scene? The happiest? The most uplifting? Did any scene make you laugh or cry?

5. Discuss Charlotte's relationship with Mr. Nicholls. When does he begin to care for Charlotte? How does he quietly go about pursuing her? How does the author maintain romantic tension between the two? Do you think Mr. Nicholls changes and grows over the course of the story?

6. In Chapter Five, Charlotte tells Ellen Nussey, "I am convinced I could never be a *clergyman's* wife." She lists the qualities she requires in a husband. How does Mr. Nicholls measure up to these expectations? What are his best and worst qualities? Why is Charlotte reluctant to accept Mr. Nicholls's proposal? What does Charlotte learn about herself—and her husband—after she marries? Do you think he turns out to be the ideal match for her?

7. What impact did Charlotte's experience at the Clergy Daughters' School have on her life and her work? How different was her experience at Roe Head School? In what ways did it change her life?

8. What was it about Monsieur Héger that endeared him to Charlotte, and made such a life-long impression on her? Why do you think he cut off all communication with her? Discuss the ways in which Charlotte's experience in Brussels changed her, and influenced every one of her novels.

9. Did hearing the story of Charlotte's life in the first person enhance the reading experience for you? What are the benefits of telling this story from the main character's perspective, rather than the third person? What are the limitations?

10. How does Charlotte's dream imagery serve the story?

11. Discuss the ways in which the Brontës' financial circumstances, unique childhood, education (or lack of it), and environment—living as the only educated family in a remote village, surrounded by the moors—affected their lives, their personalities, and their writing.

12. Why were Emily, Charlotte, and Anne all so insistent on keeping their writing ambitions a secret? Why did they

choose an androgynous pseudonym? Once published, how did the reality compare to the dream for each of them? How did Charlotte's life change when she was no longer able to "walk invisible"?

13. How did Charlotte feel about a woman's role in Victorian England, when domesticity and motherhood were considered to be a sufficient emotional fulfillment for females? Would you consider Charlotte a feminist in today's terms? Do you think Charlotte's views affected her feelings about marriage?

14. Strict laws at the time gave a husband ownership of his wife's body, her property and wages, and custody of their children. Discuss other conditions in Victorian England, with regard to women—i.e., health, sanitation, food, travel, career opportunities, courtship, sex, and conventions of feminine beauty. How did they differ from our lives today? In what ways are things still the same? Given the choice, would you wish to live in Charlotte's era?

15. Branwell was initially considered the brightest artistic hope in the Brontë family. What personal, educational, and societal factors contributed to his demise? How did Charlotte's feelings for Monsieur Héger affect her opinion of the way Branwell handled his affair with Mrs. Robinson?

16. What examples of irony can you find in the story? For example, why is it ironic that Emily's novel, *Wuthering Heights,* was so poorly received during her lifetime? Discuss the fates of Mr. Nicholls, Patrick Brontë, Charlotte, and her siblings; in what ways are they all ultimately both tragic and ironic?

17. **Has *The Secret Diaries of Charlotte Brontë*** changed your perception of Charlotte or the other people in her life? Did you learn anything that surprised you?

18. Examine the many ways in which Charlotte dramatized her own life experiences in her novels. How many people, places, and events from her real life can you identify in *Jane Eyre*? In *Shirley*? *Villette*?

19. Compare and contrast Charlotte Brontë and her fictional creation, Jane Eyre, in terms of physical appearance, personality, romantic sensibilities, and psychological desires. How successful is each woman in rising above the societal limitations placed upon her? Do they each ultimately remain true to themselves?

20. How successfully does the author capture Charlotte Brontë's voice? Did the novel inspire you to read or reread Charlotte's works, or the works of her sisters?

Syrie James

SYRIE JAMES is the author of the best-selling novel *The Lost Memoirs of Jane Austen*, which was named a Best First Novel of 2008 by *Library Journal*. A member of the Writers Guild of America, Syrie is also a screenwriter and lecturer. Syrie received a B.A. in English and Communications from the University of California, where she was awarded a departmental citation for outstanding accomplishment in English. Syrie lives with her husband and their two sons in Los Angeles. She welcomes visitors and messages at her website www.syriejames.com.